Ferocious

LESLIE MCADAM

About this book

When a scrawny, pink-haired ragamuffin tries to rob me at knifepoint, I respond the way any sensible person would and invite him to dinner—where he proceeds to threaten my entire ten-year plan simply by being his effervescent self. Much to my annoyance.

There's no room in my life for a gorgeous criminal named Rowan. I need to check off the next item on my list: Find the right, respectable husband. I can't be an accessory to a life of crime.

And yet, my perfect plan's been a bust. Yes, I have millions of social media followers, a prestigious job, and an expensive car, but I'm realizing I want more from life. My casual hookups aren't making me happy. I'm … lonely.

While Rowan's a tattooed menace, he does something to my heart, and I can't seem to stay away from him. Let's not get started on how I like seeing my marks on him. Everywhere.

Rowan isn't who I'm looking for, but it seems he's not who we think he is, either. Which creates an entirely different set of problems with much, much higher stakes.

I'm in way too deep to get out. If I even want to.

Ferocious *is a stand-alone contemporary M/M romance about Rowan, a rideshare-driving twink with a penchant for violence, and Charlie, a grumpy lawyer. It features first times, primal play, kidnapping and other crimes, and a philodendron that likes to ride in the car. HEA? Definitely.*

Playlist

"Beat the Devil's Tattoo"—Black Rebel Motorcycle Club
"Ultraviolence"—Lana Del Rey
"Livin' La Vida Loca"—Ricky Martin
"Casual"—Chappell Roan
"Soul of a Man"—Beck
"Heart of a Dog"—The Kills
"The Wild Boys"—Duran Duran
"Goodbye To All That"—Sufjan Stevens
"The One"—Wild Child
"everything i wanted"—Billie Eilish
"Think I'm In Love"—Beck
"My Blood"—twenty one pilots
https://music.apple.com/us/playlist/ferocious-charlie-and-rowan/
pl.u-zPyLA5gFq9VoV

Preface

I began writing Ferocious in November 2023 and turned it in to my editor a year later. (I'm not a fast writer.) On January 4, 2025, I went to the Getty Villa in Pacific Palisades. We drove along Pacific Coast Highway, and I even ground-truthed the distance Rowan travels in chapter one. (I'd overestimated it, by the way.)

Three days later, most of the Palisades burned to the ground.

I have family members who lost their home in the Eaton Fire in Altadena. All of California was affected by the devastation. We hurt.

I look at this book as a love letter to Los Angeles. May she rise from the ashes.

I will be donating a portion of the proceeds from this book to fire relief efforts in Los Angeles.

I've come to embrace a quote I saw by Helen Hoang, along the lines that a romance novel is a place where readers can safely experience a wider range of emotions, because we know there will be a happy ending. My author's notes are a way of framing for you what that range of emotions may be and doing my best to highlight particularly sensitive issues, so that you'll be aware of the kind of experience I intend. (Of course, I could intend all kinds of things ... but you, as reader, bring your own experiences, which may be in total conflict with mine. Indeed, you bringing your own experiences into the author's world is one of the main joys of reading. It's possible for someone to be very sensitive to content I don't even think to bring up. We're all doing our best.)

So, for starters ...

In the author's note in *Notorious*, I wrote that the *IOU* series is intended to feature generally nice people getting their HEAs in an atmosphere of relatively low homophobia. My editor highlighted the phrase "generally nice people" and commented something along the lines of, ahem, what about Rowan?

Okay. Yeah. Him.

Here's the thing: While he's feisty—fine, he's violent and

hostile—I truly believe that Rowan is as "generally nice" as Cam or Noah or Jules. He's just not nice in a socially acceptable way. It's an *I will seek revenge on anyone who hurts you or me* way. So, does that mean he's not generally nice? Up to you. I think he is, but you're free to reach a different conclusion.

If you agree with my editor, though, then I amend my statement in the *Notorious* notes: The *IOU* series is intended to feature generally nice people (except Rowan) getting their HEAs (including Rowan) in an atmosphere of relatively low homophobia. My statement holds true for Charlie, by the way, since he's plenty nice; he's just grumpy.

Moving on. Rowan (23) calls Charlie (29) "Daddy." Charlie "hates" it but calls him "baby boy." That dynamic is consistent from the time they meet and pretty much *does not change*; neither one truly gives in. In other words, I fear they're going to annoy everyone, because those who want them to have a "real" daddy-boy relationship will be disappointed (there's no age play), as will those who dislike daddy-boy (because the terms are used throughout). Rather than apologize for doing what the characters wanted to do, I figured I'd warn people, and readers who hate everything having to do with that dynamic can put the book down now. Sorry to see you go, but it's better for all of us this way. Or, if you decide to read anyway and you're particularly irritated, at least you were warned.

While I'm at it, do I need to mention that a certain suspension of disbelief is required? It is, throughout. For example, while I reference real places, they're used fictionally. So if I say there are no houses from the north end of Malibu to what would be Sycamore Canyon, there aren't any. Google Maps may tell you differently, but it didn't write this book. Also, I was having fun with *Ferocious*. You're welcome to take the book however you like; my intent was entertainment, not a documentary.

Moving along again ...

Charlie is in an open relationship at the beginning of the story, though there are no on-page sex scenes with any other partners.

Charlie and Rowan make the bare minimum effort at safe sex. I'm back to "Are they nice people?" Maybe. Would they follow all rules and be conscientious about their own health as well as the health of others? Kinda. But also kinda not, and it didn't feel true to these characters for them to be perfect.

I'm usually not specific in my author's notes about the kind of sex that's in my books, but in addition to the usual blow jobs and whatnot, *Ferocious* has CNC/primal play with minimal prep. Skip chapters thirty-three and thirty-four, as well as the bonus chapter for newsletter subscribers, if you're okay with everything but that. Or go to them directly, if that's your thing.

Of course, in real life, I believe in safe sex. As I believe in peace and nonviolence. But unlike what I support IRL, a lot of crimes are committed or attempted in this book. Listing them all is a spoiler, but for those of you who want to know, there's car theft, mugging, assault, battery, child abuse, kidnapping, murder, extortion, and cybercrime, either referenced or on page. Probably some other things, too—I'm not a prosecutor. If you read *Notorious*, you knew Rowan was going to be violent. But not too violent, because this is still a low-angst romance. (No guarantees about how Rowan is going to act in future books, though.)

Also, there's recreational drug (cannabis) and alcohol use, illness and death of a parent, homophobia, depictions of poverty and unsheltered/unhoused individuals, and references to infidelity and suicide. If I missed something I should add, please let me know at info@lesliemcadamauthor.com.

Thanks for going on Rowan and Charlie's saga with them.

Love,

Leslie

Charlie Cooper's Ten-Year Plan

(DATED NINE YEARS AGO)

By my thirtieth birthday, I will:

1. Graduate in the top 10 percent from a top ten law school.

2. Secure a high-paying job at a superior law firm.

3. Buy a home in a good neighborhood on the Westside.

4. Own a Land Rover.

5. Have ten million social media followers.

6. Have a perfect wardrobe hanging in my closet.

7. Get my hair cut every ten days and be well-groomed at all times.

8. Call or visit Mom and Dad once a week.

9. Marry a man who is handsome, well-dressed, and earns more money than me. He will be at least five years older. Taller and built. Hot ass. Can cook. I propose with a Cartier Love ring.

10. Adopt a cat.

Part One

CHAPTER 1

Rowan

Drumming my fingers on the steering wheel in time with the heavy metal song blaring from my speakers, I squint and scan the empty road ahead, then huff out a breath. All right. Where are you?

It's just after sunset, and I'm speeding north on a twisty, four-lane section of PCH, well past the county line from Malibu. The Pacific Ocean surges to my left, churning from a recent storm, and green-gray scrubby hills rise on my right. The setting is so majestic that they routinely film car commercials here, with the landmark Mugu Rock as backdrop. Beyond that, there's nothing but strawberry fields for miles. A few cars zoom past me going south, then I'm alone on a vacant road again. Well, just me and Wilbur.

Biting my lip, I turn the music volume down to better hear the app's robotic instructions. "In 1,000 feet, your rider will be on the right."

I scoff. Wanna bet? There's no one around. I still slow down.

Up ahead is a campground entrance. It's November—Thanksgiving was yesterday—so I can't imagine it's a popular time for camping. But who knows, maybe my passenger, "Pierce," (brand-new account, no ratings) went on a long one-way hike and is now catching a ShareARide home.

Or maybe he's an axe murderer.

Equally likely? Or do I have too much imagination? My money's on my imagination getting away from me, although I guess there's a possibility that he's a criminal. Takes one to know one, after all.

Do I care either way? Nope. As I've been telling myself since I accepted the gig: *Surge pricing. Worth it. You don't want to drive the hundred miles home without making enough to pay for the gas.*

So, yeah, I'm taking a calculated risk. Deliver newbie Pierce where he wants to go, then hunt down some dinner. Food's now a more pressing need, since I forgot to eat lunch, and my stomach's starting to gnaw on itself like an ouroboros.

A flash of a phone light up ahead. I scan the app. The movement matches the dot on my screen. *There he is.*

I yawn. Today's been a long damn day that's part of a long damn *life*. I'll never understand why Black Friday shoppers want to go to Walmart at two a.m. (and I have no idea how they were planning to get back home with their big-screen TV or whatever, not my problem). It's been nonstop since then. I navigate toward my passenger—er, now I see I'm going to have *passengers*—and brake when I get close.

Two men are standing in the dirt next to a speed limit sign. At their side is a box big enough to hold a very small coffin—or me. Or me in that coffin.

Sheesh, Rowan. Don't be so morbid.

Fine. It's the size of a petite coffee table. That's what normal people would think. Although why the hell are they out by a campground with a box? Is their camping gear in it?

The guys are larger than me, but that's nothing new. At 5'4" in shoes and a hundred and mumble-mumble pounds, I'm no one's definition of a big, buff man.

But if you call me a twink, I'll cut you.

Something's off about these guys. A weighty sensation hits my gut, and my pulse quickens. My fingers find the familiar hard shape of the switchblade in my back pocket. Maybe I should drive on by ...

Calm down. They're regular ShareARide customers. You need the money. And you can handle yourself.

I steady my breath. These dudes aren't that big. They're just ... normal. I'm the one who's below average.

Stop thinking everyone's going to beat you up. You're not twelve.

One of the hoodie-clad men wiggles his lit-up phone screen at me in the universal signal for "Are you my ShareARide driver?" Though it's hard to tell, he seems to match the description of the thumbnail photo of the rider: medium brown hair and a beard. His companion is built like a bulldog, squat and powerful. Neither of them is particularly handsome, which is shallow of me to notice, but hey, I window-shop.

I pull to a stop at the side of the road near them, pushing the button on my door to roll down the front passenger window. The bulldog-shaped dude stands so I can see him in my headlights, while the other one—taller—approaches the car.

"Rowan?" he asks in a reedy voice, peeking around Wilbur, who's dangling from his spot up front. He reacts the way people usually do when they first see my hair and tattoos, as well as when they catch sight of Wilbur. It's a restrained double take. Like they want to be cool, but I still surprise them.

I nod. "Pierce?"

"Yep." Pierce lifts the handle to the front passenger door and opens it partway, then stops, a hand rubbing his throat. "Um. Can I ..." He trails off and gestures at the large box sitting on the ground as if he's trying to figure out how to fit it in my car.

My car's an older, pre-owned Corolla. (I lied to ShareARide about how old my car is. X's hacking skills are legendary—the VIN matches the plates and everything. I also fudged how old I am, which is easy to do in my weird-ass birth certificate situation.) But my car's not what's stopping him.

Wilbur, my heartleaf philodendron, is suspended from a macramé hanger tacked to the ceiling over the seat next to me. Wherever I go, Wilbur goes, just as he has for the past fifteen years. #PlantDad. Wilbur's been my faithful companion ever since my nomadic childhood. He's seen a lot. But with him in the front seat, there's no space for anyone to sit, let alone to store a large box.

Which is precisely why he's there: No one can get too close unless I want them to.

"Will it fit between you two in the back seat?" I ask, already knowing the answer.

Pierce shakes his head. "I don't think so. Do you want to move the plant?"

Now it's my turn to shake my head, trailing a finger over Wilbur's wide leaves. "Just put the box in the trunk."

"Okay."

I pop the trunk, then decide I'd better earn my tip. I put the car in park and get out to help Pierce maneuver the box. My bare arms prickle from the brisk ocean air. Should've grabbed my hoodie from its spot under Wilbur. Meh, this'll only take thirty seconds.

I walk to the back and go to yank up the trunk lid, but before I can, Pierce opens the rear passenger door and dives headfirst into the back seat, his buddy already at the wheel. The doors slam shut as my car peels out, kicking up dust and rocks, charging up the road toward Mugu Rock as fast as an old Toyota can go. I watch as it bounces over a pothole, nearly losing the duct-taped bumper.

Wait. That didn't … That couldn't happen. They didn't …

Then my heartbeat thunders. My eyes bulge, and my muscles tense.

My car!
Shit!

Adrenaline shoots through my body, and I see red. Literal red from the taillights *of my fucking car*.

"Fuckers!" I let out a primal scream, kicking at the dirt, then race after them. My body is shaking. My vision is cloudy, and my ears are pounding. "I'll kill you!"

But it's no use. I'm not that fast. My car takes off on a joyride up the coast and around a bend, while I'm left panting on the side of the road, thighs burning, anger boiling over.

It's gone. I have no car, no hoodie. I pat my jeans pockets. *Goddammit, they have my phone.*

The only things on my person are my wallet—fat lot of good that will do, with the overdrawn bank card—and my knife.

And those assholes have Wilbur.

Tears sting my eyes, but I've learned not to cry when bad shit happens. I haven't cried in eight years. I'm not going to now. Instead, I picture walls going up inside my brain. I retreat behind them, and no one can find me.

A calming breath. Through my nose. Like a bull.

What the fuck am I going to do?

I let out another scream, then pace and yell until I'm hoarse. Returning to the box, I kick at it, and it goes flying.

It's empty.

Fucking scammers! I can't believe I got conned. I can't believe I lost Wilbur. I want to shred the box to ribbons, but that could dull my knife.

I sit down on the shoulder of the road with my head in my hands, the ocean crashing on the rocks across the way.

I will do violence upon the thieves. I'm adding them to my vengeance list.

Right now, though, I have to solve a problem.

* * *

It's pitch black by the time I've made my way down the beach to civilization. I don't know how far I've walked. I haven't passed any houses, and counting speed limit signs doesn't tell me distance. All I know is that it's cold and I have no hoodie. Also, I'm hungry, angry, lonely, and tired, as my nice foster mom with twenty-seven years' sobriety taught me to assess when everything was wrong with life. Not that knowing that makes it possible for me to change anything. I'm raging at the world. Pretty sure my feet have blisters. My throat's dry, but there's no water—no potable water. The air is sticky with salt and the cold beach humidity, and it stinks like seaweed.

At first, I considered flagging down someone and hitchhiking, but it'd be just my luck to come across creepers worse than Pierce —if that even is his name. So I keep trudging along the road, or down in the sand, depending on how wide the shoulder is, trying to keep my sneakers dry. I'm shivering uncontrollably.

Am I going to have to walk the whole hundred miles home to Lancaster? How long would that take? Will I collapse from hunger before I make it?

What's going to happen to Wilbur?

Down the coast a ways, flames from a beach bonfire flicker.

As I keep walking, I reach a few cars parked along the highway, the first ones I've seen the entire time I've been on this march.

I must be into the northernmost part of Malibu, which is a long, twenty-plus-mile strip of coastline wedged up against hills. I'll probably see the first mansion soon.

Must be nice to have no cares in the world. All the money to do all the things.

I pause in the inky night, watching the party of shadowed figures eating and drinking: some sitting in chairs, others standing and talking.

They're playing some kind of loud metal music. When I get closer, I realize I recognize the band—it's one of my favorites.

I park my ass in the cold sand and sit, watching them.

A plan hatches.

I'm going to observe for a while. See if an opportunity presents itself. At a minimum, I can rest after walking for miles and miles.

One man is sitting near the fire but off to the side, away from most of the others. Something about him calls to me.

He seems ... lonely.

Easy prey?

I can stay where I am and watch. I'll keep my distance until the right moment. Then I'll make my move.

CHAPTER 2

Charlie

Is someone watching us?

The hair stands up on the back of my neck and all along my arms, an uneasy sensation washing over me. I look over my shoulder, but I can't see anything. The light from the bonfire makes the darkness surrounding us feel even more impenetrable than it really is. With all my friends laughing and snuggling and mesmerized by the flames, who knows what evil's lurking out there ready to pounce?

Whatever, Charlie, it's just the offshore breeze. You're making shit up.

I bury my bare feet deeper into the cold sand—I want my sneakers to stay nice, so I took them off as soon as I set foot on the beach—feed the fire another piece of driftwood, and watch it burn.

There's no bogeyman waiting to get us. Why would there be? It's the happiest time of the year.

I guess.

"As you all know, we're gathered here today to protest the capitalistic economy," Jules says in his melodic British accent.

He's a pop star who's dating Sam, one of my colleagues and

friends, and we're outside their home north of Malibu. Home, beachfront mansion, whatever. The irony of this as a location for our anticapitalism protest isn't lost on me.

Or maybe it's the *perfect* location.

Normal people call today Black Friday. Jules is calling it *Blackest* Friday and wants us to go through some kind of group bonding rite where, instead of shopping and supporting the economy, we all burn mementos of past trauma, accompanied by a screaming death metal soundtrack. I could not be less into this if I tried, but better to be here than at home while all my friends have fun without me.

Sam's sprawled on a blanket in the vee of Jules's long legs, back plastered to Jules's front. I grind my teeth. At least Sam's comfy. I'm definitely not.

I shiver. Again, I glance behind me. Nothing's out there. I've seen too many movies.

The flames dance higher, and my face roasts while my back freezes. I don't have a cozy, solid person to block the cold gusts from the ocean that slither down my neck. Tristan wouldn't have come if I'd invited him, not even as a friend. He's, well, not *happy* in the closet … it's just where he stays.

How do I feel about that? It's fine. Kinda.

I zip up my jacket, wrap my arms around my stomach, and huddle closer to the fire.

The chatter continues over the blaring metal music. Out of the twenty or thirty of us, no one except Sam and me seems to hear Jules's attempt to get our attention. In addition to the music, the constant, unseen waves hitting the shore sound louder in the dark. There are forces that we can't—and never will be able to—control.

Damn, I'm being poetic. I've only had two drinks, so I'm not sure where all this <<mood>> is coming from. Oh, that's right. It's because I'm perpetually bitter and feeling pretty useless.

I attempt to loosen my clenched jaw, but I'm not successful. I could try to pretend all the disgustingly sweet couples don't make me sick to my stomach, but why bother? I don't need to deny how their out-and-proud bliss is affecting me. I grimace at my self-pity and sullenly glance around at my contented friends, coworkers, and family members, many of whom are being openly affectionate.

My best friend, Danny, and his partner, Alden, sit across from me, their hands all over each other—somewhat discreetly, at least. Danny turned in his man-whore card for Alden, leaving me to fend for myself at the bars without my wingman. Don't get me wrong, I pull just fine, and I still see Danny at work. But I do miss spending both quantity and quality time with my best friend.

Noah and August, the founding partners of Weston & Ramirez, are next to Aldanny, holding hands. Nogust finally admitted that they've been in love with each other their whole lives. I lost the office pool on when that would happen. (My vote was never. I'm not an optimist.)

Scattered around in beach chairs and on blankets are other attorneys from our office, including my sister, Reyna, plus some office staff members and my brother.

And then there's me. Sitting on my own. Like a loser. Because I don't have a real boyfriend, partner, or husband. I just have Tristan, who might as well be someone I met in band camp. Not that I was ever in a band.

Dear thoughts, shut the hell up.

Off to my left, my brother, Camden, is snuggling with his husband, Shelby, who's also our receptionist. We've all—including Cam—recently learned that Cam isn't straight. Cam wraps a protective arm around Shelby and draws him close, whispering something into his ear. Shelby melts against Cam. My chest gets tight.

Am I happy for Camby? Yes.

Jealous of their happiness? Oh my god, yes.

Hey, at least I'm honest enough to admit it. So, like, props to me.

It's not like I can't get laid—and regularly, by a decent guy.

Tristan checks all my boxes. He's rich, tall, older, handsome, established. Fantastic cook. He's got his shit together. We're not exclusive, which is the way I like it.

I've never put pressure on him to come out. That's up to every individual, and his family's super conservative, so I understand why he's not comfortable doing it … but maybe I should at least talk about it with him. Because it's been five years now, and we're still doing the *me on my back every other Friday at his house* thing. And that's a little lonely the other twenty-eight or twenty-nine days of the month.

No wonder I'm a jealous bastard. Maybe I want to be arguing with my own special boyfriend—whoever that is—over how toasty to make a marshmallow.

At least, when I *am* with Tristan, the sex is good.

I toss another twig into the fire.

Okay, the sex isn't amazing, either. It's just nice. Like everything with Tristan. No drama. Easy. Scheduled. Kind of boring. Safe.

Well, I do have one complaint: Sometimes I want to top, and that's never going to happen with Tris. I'm vers, he's not. It's a minor issue.

Quit whining, Charlie. Grow up. Stop wallowing.

Maybe I'm wishing for something that doesn't exist. Maybe I'll never have the feelings I think I should have. Tristan's the perfect man. If I ever introduced him to my mother, she'd start planning the wedding before we had time to say hello. That's not going to happen, though, until he's out. So unless I invite someone else, I'm always going to be alone at events like this.

With a few taps on his phone, Jules turns down the music, and now the conversations quiet, people looking to him expectantly. He grins and spreads his hands. "Is everyone ready to burn cursed objects?"

"I can't wait," Sam says. "Did everyone bring something from their past that they want to get rid of?" A few nods. "Who's going first?" There's some shuffling around as people prepare to share.

Danny hops up to tell a story about a ring and his tool of a high school boyfriend and a disastrous prom date that turned him off love for a decade. He finishes his speech, tosses the promise ring into the fire, and goes back to cuddling with Alden.

One by one, my friends stand up and talk before burning a meaningful symbol from their past. Something that they want to move beyond or forget: bad relationships (I don't have those; Tristan and I aren't in a relationship, period), bad family issues (I don't have those, either), bad choices (I also don't have those). (Except one.)

"Charlie! Bro! It's your turn," Danny calls.

I stand up, move so close to the fire I feel its flames lick the stubble on my cheeks, and pull a folded-up piece of paper from the inside pocket of my jacket. "This is the ruling on the last motion for summary judgment I lost," I begin.

Danny throws a marshmallow at me. "Boo!"

"Hey, I was bummed about losing," I protest, even though it sounds hollow. I just want to make videos and not practice law at all. But I can't tell my entire firm that.

"Fair enough," Danny says.

"And ... it sucked. The end." My comments are met with a few laughs and whistles. I crumple the paper up and throw it in. The flames grab it instantly, and it turns to ash. Danny and Cam both give me looks, like they're aware there's something I'm not saying. But they know me well enough not to press in front of a group.

We keep going around the circle. I learn a few things about my friends that make me feel like I know them better. When we're done and it's a socially acceptable time for me to leave, I put my socks and shoes back on, give my brother and my friends bro hugs and my sister a kiss on the forehead, and wave goodbye to everyone else.

"See you tomorrow, Charlie!" Shelby calls, wrapped around Cam like a blanket burrito.

"Yeah, see you." We're all going skiing tomorrow. I nod toward my brother's hurt ankle, the reason why he and Shelby got married in the first place. "You gonna be okay?"

He winces. "Yeah. I'll take it easy, but I'm cleared."

A pained look passes over Shelby's face. Not sure what that's about, but given what he said about his past trauma he was burning, I suspect he's got some shit to work through. Cam's a good listener. I'm sure he'll help.

"Where are you parked?" Cam asks.

"Up the road a bit." I gesture north. I'm on the side of PCH away from the party. Jules and Sam have a gated compound with some parking, but space isn't infinite. Well, technically, it is, but that's not what I'm talking about.

Cam peers over my shoulder, but with our eyes used to looking at the bright bonfire, it's hard to adjust to the dark, and I'm not sure he sees anything. "Want us to walk you to your car?"

"Nah," I scoff. "It's fine. You can quit being the overprotective older brother."

"Like that's gonna happen," Cam says. But he and Shelby wave at me and start walking south toward Sam and Jules's house. Other people stay behind, enjoying the fire.

My hands shoved in my pockets and my shoulders hunched, I head toward my car, watching my step in the sand, which is full of driftwood and other debris. The moon provides just enough light that I can avoid stumbling.

I should text Tristan, although I'm not sure what I want to say. There are the hookups who you want to introduce to your family, and there are the hookups you don't want your friends to know about. Tristan's neither of those.

But, as I keep reminding myself, he's perfect. If I were to describe my ideal man, it's him, at least physically. Plus he's elegant and sophisticated and easy to be with.

When I get to the car, I'll text him ... something. Like whether there's any chance of us doing something outside of his house that's still sort of private. Possibly a hike? Less chance of him being seen by someone he knows out on the trail, and het guys go hiking together, I'm sure. Maybe he'd go for that.

Away from the fire, the wind off the water is freezing. A lone sports car speeds down the highway blaring hip-hop, though the sound of the surf overshadows everything. I go to open my car door.

Out of the corner of my eye, I see someone lunging at me from behind my car. He tackles me to the ground.

What the fuck?

I land with my hands under my chest to brace my fall, but my chin still scrapes the asphalt. My breath's knocked out of me.

Oh my god.

Shit.

Dammit.

The cool, biting edge of a ... knife? Yes, *fuck*, a *knife*, a fucking knife, presses into my throat.

CHAPTER 3

Charlie

Hyperventilating, I try to buck the attacker off, but they're straddling my back, knees holding my arms to my torso so I'm squashed to the ground, knife blade still threatening my vulnerable skin.

It happens so fast, I don't react except for a yelp, a grunt, and a "What the fuck?"

I'd have thought that my childhood martial arts training would've made my reflexes faster, but nope. He caught me off guard.

I assume it's a man, at any rate.

Fear floods my body. Because what the actual hell? Am I going to get my throat slit right here on the side of the highway?

Breathe, Charlie.

Think.

I stop moving. I might be able to get up on my knees and throw the guy, but I'm not willing to risk it when, if I move wrong, he'll slice my jugular.

While the person who is … mugging me? … smells like he needs a shower, there's also a sweeter, muskier, woody scent about him. Like he's been living in the sage.

His hot breath fans over my ear, and my skin prickles.

The blade touches my skin. I don't think he's drawing blood yet, but the knife feels *really* sharp. My muscles are contracting so hard in my effort to freeze that I'm shaking. Which is counterproductive, but I can't control my reaction. My heart rate's spiked, and my adrenaline's redlining.

"Fucking give me your keys and wallet, man." His cool drawl sounds young and, surprisingly, not as wound up as I'd expect. He seems bored.

Is this unexciting to him? Dick.

If he's young, and—I wiggle my back slightly—doesn't weigh too much, I may be able to get the upper hand if I just keep my wits about me. Which is hard to do when my body's in fight, flight, or freeze mode.

"My wallet? I don't have any cash," I rasp, feeling the burn on my chin from it kissing the asphalt. Damn. I scraped it hard. My palms might also be torn up. And my knees.

"I don't believe you," he snarls.

"Come on," I mutter. "Who carries cash anymore? If you really want my Costco card, it's yours. The rotisserie chicken isn't *that* good."

I've always wondered if my snark would disappear in moments of crisis. That question is now answered. Not that I spent hours of every day on the topic or anything, but—

"I mean it." The guy shifts his weight to, I don't know, hold me down more, but it gives me an opening.

"Yeah, sure. And no, I'm not giving you my car. Do you know how much it cost?" It's now or never. I press into a pushup, then throw an arm up and twist my hips to flip the guy off me and onto his back, where he lands with an "oof." His knife nicks my skin as we move, but I can tell the cut is shallow. I'm not gushing blood—none even trickles down my neck. Positioning my knee across his hips, I focus on his knife hand. He's fighting me, kicking and wriggling, but I push his pinky back until he yelps, then wrench the knife from him and throw it as far as I can before grabbing both his wrists and pressing them to the ground.

Now I'm straddling him, staring into his face. Our eyes lock, and some force crackles between us.

What the actual fuck?

He's just a kid. Well, maybe early to midtwenties, so at least five years younger than me, from what I can tell in the light from the streetlamp a distance away. He's got unruly pink hair and tattoos scattered along his bare arms and neck.

And he's damn pretty.

Not just pretty. His face has an unearthly beauty. Ridiculously big eyes. Straight nose. Pouty mouth. Clear, pale skin. A mole on his cheek. Multiple piercings in his ears and a nose ring.

He's also really small. His black T-shirt's painted on, showing off his super slim arms. He's short, too, and just … tiny. He seems feral—a guttersnipe. His hands are like ice cubes. Where's his jacket?

What the hell was he thinking? I'm a *lot* bigger than him. Twice his weight.

His nostrils flare, and his eyes widen, though I'm not sure how well he can see me. My face is probably in shadow. On the other hand, I imagine he was watching me as I walked to my car, so he already knows what I look like.

"I got jumped by a twink," I blurt.

"Fuck you," he growls. "Don't call me that." He bites his lower lip, and before he can sneer again, a lost expression flashes across his face. One that makes me pause.

What the hell am I doing? He's young and scared.

Now I feel like a bully, which is ironic as hell—he had a *knife* to my *throat*. But someone needs to be the adult in the room. Might as well be me.

He's clearly desperate. It doesn't seem like he's on drugs—he doesn't smell like weed or anything chemical.

He grunts and tries to shove me off him, but I stay put, even though his feet are scrabbling at the pavement and he's doing his damnedest to knee my balls. The angle won't work for him, though.

"Why are you trying to rob someone twice as big as you? Do you have a death wish?" I hiss.

"Maybe." The kid spits in my face.

I tsk, letting it drip back down onto him. "Someone should teach you some manners."

"They tried. They failed." He's breathing hard.

"Yeah, I can tell." I'm very aware of my own heartbeat.

The guy's eyes are blazing, although I can't quite tell their color in the low light. They're very dark. Navy blue, maybe?

A car whizzes by. I'm not surprised they don't stop, even if they saw us. Right now it looks like, what? I'm making out with him?

I glance down. He wouldn't be so bad to make out with. If he weren't trying to kill me. And maybe had a shower.

Tristan wouldn't care. We're not jealous of each other's hookups. Hell, maybe he'd want to watch. Not that either of us would say we're into voyeurism, but you don't know some things are your kink until you try them.

And I don't know why I'm feeling defensive. Nonmonogamy is valid.

"If I get up, are you gonna run away?" I ask.

He shrugs.

That's a yes, I decide.

"What do you care?" the pint-sized terror sneers.

My response comes from a well of sincerity deep inside me that I don't usually let out. "That's a really good question that I don't know the answer to." I tilt my head and get in his face. "Why do you need the money?"

"No reason."

Brat. "Bull. Shit. If you're going to rob me, at least tell me why."

"I don't have to tell you shit." He again attempts to throw me off him, but he's just not strong enough.

Part of me wants him to keep fighting, because I love getting physical. That part of me should probably be locked up. The rest of me is responsible ... most of the time.

"True," I say airily. "But you attacked the king of the assholes, and I have ways of making you talk."

The kid presses his lips tighter together.

"Is it drugs?"

"No." His eyes dart from side to side, but I've got him trapped.

Is it sick and wrong that I'm enjoying having him pinned under me? That I liked being scraped up by him and that I want to dish it right back? Mess up his angelic face—especially since he's obviously a tiny devil?

Maybe it's something more basic. "Do you need money to pay someone off?"

He snorts a laugh. "No."

"To pay rent?"

He doesn't answer. Okay, that's something. Is he living on the street?

"When's the last time you ate?"

He narrows his eyes and again tries to knee me. This time it hurts a bit, but I stay put. "Fuck you."

"That's not what I asked, baby boy."

Where the hell did that come from?

But he is a baby.

He shivers, and I see the moment he decides to change his tactics from dickhead to flirt. His eyes go extra big. He swallows a few times. Then he coos, "Oh, we've met?" Setting a trap to get me to let him go so he can escape, I'm sure.

"Not that I know of," I say before I can stop myself. Because I think I'd have remembered this kid. He's not my usual type.

"Never mind. I'll show you." He continues struggling under

me, but now he's smiling. And that smile sets off some kind of fireworks under my skin. "Let me up."

Is he …

He's getting hard under me.

Damn, that's making my dick react, too. There's something seriously wrong with me.

"No. Way. Get off of you so you can stab me? Yeah, that's smart." I roll my eyes.

"Fine," he huffs.

I go back to my earlier line of questioning. "Are you hungry?"

The guy bites his lip and looks away. That's enough of an answer for me. I scan my mental inventory for late-night eateries around here and come up with a couple of options.

Charlie, what the goddamned hell are you thinking? This kid's dangerous and clearly out to hurt you.

Sounds like fun.

Still holding his wrists pinned above his head, I do a quick assessment. I have a black belt in tae kwon do, although I'm way out of practice. I'm not sure where the kid's knife landed. My error was not being aware of my surroundings, but I'm good now. I can take him easily.

I eye him. He still looks desperate, but also somewhat defeated.

"I'm gonna let you go," I say slowly, "and we're gonna have a talk. If you want, I'll drive you to get some food."

"Why the hell would you do that?"

I shake my head. "I've got no clue. Maybe the Christmas spirit's entering my body early."

The kid grins, and it makes my insides go squishy and my dick get harder. "You've got something that can enter my body early."

He doesn't want me, he just wants to be free. I let the comment pass by. "So, you hungry?"

He swallows. "Aren't you scared I'm going to take you out on the way to the restaurant?"

I scoff. "I can disarm you in two seconds flat. I did it once, and I can do it again. So, no." I eye him. "I *will* pat you down before you get in the car."

"Okay, Daddy," the urchin says.

My dick plumps even more. "Don't call me that," I snap.

Very slowly, I release one of his wrists, then move off him, and he scrambles to sit up.

I expect him to go racing down the street, but he doesn't.

I take a seat on the cold, rough asphalt next to him and wipe the gravel out of my palms. I didn't tear my jeans, so that's a plus. "I'm Charlie," I say. "What's your name?"

"Rowan." He's rubbing at his wrists.

I'm a little surprised that he doesn't hesitate to tell me. But then maybe he just gave me a fake name. Who knows?

He reaches out to my neck and pulls his hand back with a drop of blood on his finger. "It's not a bad cut. You don't need stitches or anything. I'm ... I'm—"

"Yeah, whatever," I mutter. "You're a doctor?"

Rowan scoffs. "Nope. But I've seen ... things."

"I'll bet. Tell me about it at dinner. There's a Thai restaurant in Malibu that's open really late. Want to go there? Best thing available right now."

I don't imagine the hunger in his eyes. "Yeah, okay," he says, trying to play it cool. He dusts off his own hands, and I see him looking around for the knife. I calculate the amount of damage he can do to me or my car, but while I don't want to underestimate him, I don't think it's that much. I'm sure I can hold my own. Like, 95 percent sure.

I gesture to my car. "Come on. And don't try anything."

Rowan holds up his hands like the little criminal he is. "Okay, fine."

"How did you know this was my car?"

"I was following you."

"Hmm."

We get to my vehicle, but before I open the door, I order, "Put your hands on the side, and spread your legs."

"Oooh, kinky. I like it," Rowan coos, doing as I say and sticking out his pert ass.

"Whatever." I move closer to him, and in the dim light, I can just make out that he has "baby boy" inked at his nape in a calligraphic script.

Holy shit, that's sexy.

I glance down at his ass, which nicely fills out those tight jeans.

What would it be like to mark his skin, focus on that tattoo while I was …

Never mind.

I need to get this kid some food, and then I can go back to my normal life, Tristan and all.

Since his arms are bare and his T-shirt's thin, it's clear he's not hiding anything on his torso. But I pat down his waistband, pockets, and legs—especially his ankles.

He's got nothing but a wallet. I open it up, and his license says his name is Rowan Jones. Not a liar—or, at least, not about his name. His address is somewhere in LA. There's a bank card, and that's it.

I shrug off my jacket and drape it over his shoulders.

Rowan whips his head around. "What the hell?"

"Just wear it," I say gruffly, pushing the button to unlock the car. "Get in."

He stares at me, tugging the dark brown suede bomber jacket closer to his body. I shoo him toward the passenger seat, questioning my life choices. After a beat, he climbs inside.

I close his door and scan the area where we were wrestling. I spot the hilt of his knife shining in the moonlight, maybe fifteen feet away. I sprint to pick it up, then get in the car.

"Retrieved your knife," I say. I close up the switchblade and stick it under my seat near the door, out of his reach. Then I put my seat belt on and gesture at him to do the same. "Buckle up."

He smirks at me, but he gets a funny look on his face as he snuggles into the jacket, sliding his arms through the armholes. Then he puts on his seat belt.

I'm sure I've just made the biggest mistake of my life.

CHAPTER 4

Rowan

My eyes roam both sides of the highway as Charlie drives south in his pristine black Land Rover. I have no reason to believe he's going to take me where he says he is, so I'm paying close attention to our route. My fingers twitch on my thighs, and my heartbeat ratchets up, while my adrenaline is crashing hard. I'm tired and hungry and strung out. My feet are sore. How far did I walk? Five miles? Ten?

I'm not sure why I trusted a total stranger enough to get in the car with him, especially without my beloved switchblade in my pocket, but my other plan failed spectacularly. I thought I'd just, you know, *relieve* the first viable prospect I came across of their spare cash and go on my merry way home, either taking their car or figuring out a way to call a cab. Hey, I've never had to mug anyone before, and I'm usually pretty good with a knife. It seemed like a brilliant idea at the time—and the part of me that loves danger was getting off on it.

Except I overestimated my potential for success via violence and underestimated Charlie's ability to defend himself.

Here's the new plan: I leap from the car at the first stoplight and get the hell away if something—*anything*—goes wrong. Or I could throw myself across his lap and try to grab my knife, but that might cause an accident, and I'd prefer to avoid that.

Or I can do what I usually do, and wing it.

I drag my fingers down my cheeks and throw my head back against the tall seat. Ugh, this is a clusterfuck.

The farther we go, the less I think Charlie's taking me somewhere to dismember me and the more I think he's actually going to buy me dinner.

I fidget even more. Who is this guy? Not knowing is … unnerving.

I chew on my bottom lip, glance over at Charlie daddy, and shiver. Every streetlight we pass that shines on the planes of his face makes me want to look at him more. He's an absolutely welcome distraction from the shit show of my life.

Enjoying looking at Charlie is just me having good taste. Charlie's the tall, dark, and model-handsome type, with shortish dark brown hair, eyes that might be brown or might be hazel, and a surprisingly powerful body that's a thing of beauty. High cheekbones, strong jaw.

Total daddy.

And don't get me started on this soft, thick suede jacket that's warming me up better than his car heater, which has finally kicked in. It's the yummiest thing I've ever put on my body. It smells like maybe cedar. I like.

I'm grimy from walking for however long, on top of getting up early and all that adrenaline. I want to get cleaned up, because I feel gross, but for now I'll let Charlie's fragrance distract me.

I glance at him. The small trickle of blood down his neck looks black in the dark. His chin's busted up, too.

Dammit. My fault.

He seems like someone who's very precise, judging by his perfectly trimmed hair. His clothes fit him well, and other than what I've done to him, he's completely unblemished. It seems like he puts a lot of effort into his appearance, although I suppose I do, too. But Charlie sparkles. Not literally; he just has that polish. Something about his overly careful looks is making me want to mess him up. Am I a sick puppy?

Hell, I *know* I am.

My eyes are gritty from dehydration, and there's a lump in my throat. Maybe I shouldn't have hurt him. I wish he'd yell at me or something. Then I'd have an excuse to get out of his car—and this predicament.

But do you want to?

I kind of want to stay and see what happens. I'm so damned tired and hungry, and maybe Charlie actually wants to help me.

Plus, I don't have that many options. Nobody's got my back. And I don't even have a phone at the moment.

So the only person I have is Charlie—who may require some minor first aid. I lean forward in my seat and open the glove compartment.

Charlie snaps his head toward me. "What are you doing?" he asks, his tone sharp.

I hold my hands up. "You need something for the scrapes on your chin and neck. Don't you have napkins or baby wipes or something?"

A muscle moves along his hard jaw. "I'll clean up when I get to the restaurant."

"I don't mind looking—"

"There's nothing in the car I can use."

And ... he's right. This car's entirely void of personality. No crumpled receipts, not even for gas. No lip balm or pens. No dancing hula girls, air freshener trees, or other talismans. The only clue the fancy SUV gives me as to who Charlie is, is the radio, which is on a station playing major alt hits—an oxymoron. He could use a plant or two to liven the space up.

A pang hits my chest at that last thought, so I sit back and watch the clock on the dash, paying attention to where we are and how far we've gone and trying to ignore the angry, hollow feeling in my stomach.

About twenty minutes after I pulled a knife on him, this hot man who should be modeling tweed and cashmere sweaters for traditional British clothiers pulls us into a total dive of a Thai place. A hand-painted sign reads "Jasmine Gardens." LED signs from the Signs-R-Us store (or wherever you get them) flash in every window, advertising boba tea and fresh smoothies and letting us know they're open until midnight. Faded fake ivy hangs around the weather-beaten white door. We're on the mountain side of PCH, wedged in next to a trailer park that must have fifty-million-dollar-views in the daytime.

But it's past nine p.m., if Charlie's car clock is accurate, and I'm so hungry they could serve us cardboard and I'd consider eating it.

Charlie reverses into a space in the gravel parking lot behind the restaurant and turns off the engine. We're not the only ones here, which makes me feel less uneasy. He hops out, and I follow him, holding his jacket close to my body.

He waits for me at the front of his car like he thinks I'm going to run away, but where would I go? That's the whole reason why I'm in this predicament.

On the way to the entrance, we pass by a man huddled in a dark alcove with a dirty blue sleeping bag wrapped around him. Charlie pulls out his wallet and places a twenty in the cardboard box that reads "Anything helps," anchoring it with a rock clearly kept there for that purpose.

"Thanks, man," the guy mutters.

"Uh-huh," Charlie says.

He didn't glance over to see if I was watching. He didn't make a big deal about it. He didn't try to tell the guy what to do with the money. He just … bought the man a meal, maybe.

Like he's getting me a meal.

That makes something warm expand inside my chest. I know

the guy might use the money for drugs, but whatever. I still like Charlie's compassion—which is also evident around my shoulders. The chilly ocean air's much easier to handle with a jacket. Charlie's hangs well below my ass, but I'm never taking it off, even if it's huge on me. I'm also going to buy whatever this scent is if and when I get money again.

We step up to the restaurant's front door, and I get a look at him in better light. His biceps stretch the waffle weave fabric of a dark gray Henley. Yum. Also, now that we're standing next to each other, it's dawning on me what a terrible idea it was to pick him as my victim. I hadn't accounted for how big he was when I saw him coming from the beach. Or that this jacket hid a very nice body.

A perfect one, in fact. I'm getting the impression that Charlie has high standards. Eating dinner with me will bring down his average.

Wait a minute. I tug on Charlie's sleeve. "I thought you said you didn't have any cash," I whisper.

Charlie opens the door for me and shows me inside. He lifts an eyebrow. The hair on my arms and nape rises, despite the warmth of his jacket. "I lied."

My hands go to my hips. "Lying isn't the best way to start a relationship."

Charlie huffs a laugh, then bends down to speak in my ear, his lips tickling my skin. "Neither is assault and battery."

I'm breathless and lightheaded, and I don't know if it's from him or from hunger. *Nrgh*. Probably both. "I'll be sure to tell our kids."

A teenage girl walks up to the front, grabbing menus without slowing her stride. "Two?"

"Yes," Charlie says, and we follow her. "We're not having kids," he mutters over his shoulder to me. "Or starting a relationship."

"That's what you think." I'm teasing, but as the words come out of my mouth, I'm picturing being with Charlie and not hating it. "You'll see."

Charlie rubs at one of his brows as he slides into the booth we're shown to. I take the seat across from him, exhausted but enjoying the view. He's got that classic leading man look to him, with a bit of an attitude. Like RBF. He doesn't have a sneer, and it's not like he's smelled something awful. He's not looking down on people. He just seems kind of pissed. Or maybe it's that he's brooding.

Ohhh, he's *my* brooding hero. I love it.

Also: hazel. His eyes are hazel.

While I'm joking about the "my hero" thing, I'm also kind of … not. Every minute we're together is making me want two more. It's like compounding interest: One minute turns into two, two turn into four, four turn into eight. Soon I'll be wanting to spend the rest of my life with him.

That doesn't seem like a hardship.

CHAPTER 5

Rowan

"You should go clean your cut," I say, pointing at the drops of dried blood on Charlie's neck. And cringing, since I caused them. Also the scrape on his chin. Oops. I do have a conscience inside me somewhere, even if my moral compass is set to "reserved spot waiting for me in hell."

Also, I'm so hungry I may start eating sugar packets, so it's no wonder my thought-to-mouth filter isn't working.

"I'll do it after we order. What do you want?"

I pick at the chipped pink polish on my fingernails. "Whatever you get is fine. I can't think properly."

Charlie's brow wrinkles, and he bites his lip, then nods.

A server comes by with two glasses of water. Charlie slides both of them closer to me. I down half of one in a few gulps, then wipe the water dribbling down my chin with the back of my hand. I'm a damn mess.

Plus, now that I'm safely inside a building for the first time in hours, my body's sinking into the seat, and my thighs are quivering. I may not ever get up again.

After I finish my water, I start on his. Then I look up at him. "When I get money, I can pay you back."

Charlie waves me off. "Don't worry about it."

"Then I can treat you for our second date."

"This isn't a first date."

"Yes, it is," I insist. I'm smiling, but inside, something sorts itself out. Yeah, I'm counting this as a date. And if I have anything to say about it, there'll be more of them. "Where should we go for our next date?"

"We're not going on any goddamned date."

"You invited me to dinner. It's a date. You agreed."

"I did not agree." He glares at me. I must be one sick motherfucker, because I love his glares. I love how they make me feel seen.

"Let's go bowling. That sounds fun, right?" Plus I'm good at it.

"I'm not going fucking bowling with you," Charlie says.

I don't know him yet, and I don't care. Because I'm going to know everything about him as soon as I can. My dick likes this plan a lot.

How did I end up in a situation like this?

Because you have impulse issues and make thoughtless decisions, my high school guidance counselor's voice says in my head. *And you get hostile when threatened.*

Fuck you, Mrs. Cheez Whiz. Or whatever the hell her real name was. It's not like she helped me in any way. It's not like she believed me when I told her about the kids in my group home—

Charlie signals the server, not in an asshole way but in a "Hey, could you help us out" way, and orders what seems like far too much food for two people: chicken satay, fresh rolls, pad thai, two curries, and two Thai iced teas.

"Thanks," I mutter.

As Charlie's ordering, I notice his phone, which is face up on the table. There are a bajillion notifications from Ad/VICE, the social media service. Squinting, I can see that they're all for a CoopBros account. I'll have to look him up when I get a phone. A few texts come in—from a Danny and a Cam and a Tristan. My savior's popular with the men.

"Are you gonna run away if I go wash up?" Charlie asks after the server departs.

I shake my head.

He studies me for a moment, then nods, seemingly satisfied with something he saw. Maybe the exhaustion written across my face. I'm too tired to move, much less run. He takes his phone with him when he gets up.

When he returns, I'm busy shoving an entire fresh roll into my mouth.

"Hey. Don't eat too fast, or you'll get sick."

I nod and try to chew, but I end up swallowing half the roll in one bite. Our waters are refilled, and after I take a sip, I ask, "What's CoopBros?"

"How old are you?" Charlie shoots back.

"I asked first."

Charlie stares at me, then exhales slowly. "It's my and my brother's Ad/VICE account." He opens the app and holds his phone out for me to see.

Twelve million followers. That's impressive. "Charlie Cooper and Cam Cooper. DIY tutorials on home improvement projects," I read out loud. A few videos have quick previews I can see, which seem to be time-lapse videos of Charlie and some other dude, presumably his brother, building shit together.

My victim—hero?—is a social media star. I wouldn't have thought it to look at him. I mean, yeah, he's one of the hottest guys I've ever met, but he's kind of sullen. Maybe there's more to him, though. Maybe he turns on when he gets in front of a camera. I'm about to click on a video that looks like it'll teach me how to build a bookshelf, but he signals me to give him the phone. I hand it back reluctantly. Nosy me wants to dig in and find out more about him.

"And I'm twenty-nine," Charlie offers. Interesting. Younger than I expected.

He can still be a daddy.

"I'm twenty-three," I say. As far as I know.

He nods, then tilts his head and studies me. "I don't understand why you pulled a knife on me."

Because I was desperate. I play it off, grinning. "I'm ferocious."

Charlie bursts out laughing. Then he pauses and blinks, like what he just did surprises him. I get the feeling he doesn't laugh much.

I narrow my eyes and tap my fingers on the tabletop.

"No offense"—he gestures generally at me—"but I'm pretty sure there are birds bigger than you."

"You wouldn't want to get pecked in the eye by one of them, either."

Charlie chuckles again, and it's a warm, rumbling sound. "That's true. I'm not into that—the pluck-out-your-eyeballs thing."

"I'm totally into it," I say, not entirely lying.

"Yeah, right."

"No, really."

Charlie goggles at me. "Why?"

I raise an eyebrow. "When you stop growing at age twelve, while everyone around you gets bigger and bigger, you develop some coping strategies to deal with bullies." Ugly images flash through my mind, and I put them in the drawer I usually stuff them in.

"Fucking hate bullies," Charlie growls.

The vehemence in his voice distracts me from what I was going to say. "Did you have to deal with them?"

"Yeah. My big brother tried to defend me, but I got sick of him getting into fights on my behalf. So I started martial arts training. Tae kwon do."

I snort. "Just my luck to go after you."

Except ... it really was good luck. I sip my iced tea, starting to feel human. I'm not panicking over all the shit that's happened today. And I like sitting here across from Charlie.

Charlie seems to read my thoughts. "It seems like some kind of luck, yeah." He studies me intently. "So you got picked on growing up. What about recently? Is that what happened?"

"No. Well, yes. I'm a ShareARide driver, and my passengers this evening stole my car."

Charlie's hands clench and unclench on the table, and a vein pops in his neck. "Holy hell. We should call the police." Charlie makes a move to get up, like he's going to go storm the station. Or start his own one-man hunt for my car.

I feel happy. Weightless. He doesn't know me, and yet he's willing—eager—to fight my battles. No one else ever has.

"Like the police will do anything." I wave a hand. "They've never once helped me. Your privilege is showing."

He's almost unnaturally silent. Then he grits out, "That's unacceptable. They can't let those assholes get away with stealing from you. It's not right. They're supposed to protect you. It's right there on the sides of the cars."

Seeing Charlie be so pissed on my behalf is making me weirdly happy. He's got an intensity that I'm very much digging.

"First priority after you eat. You call," he orders.

Sheesh, Daddy. "Can't. My phone was in my car." Along with my plant.

He waves his cell at me. "After you eat, we're calling them. They need to know the car has been stolen so they'll keep an eye out for it and so you're not responsible for anything the thieves do with it."

I slump in my seat and nod.

"Does ShareARide track your car?"

"If the app is on. If they were smart, they threw my phone out the window."

"Well, we should check the app. See if it has any data. In any case, your aversion to the police doesn't explain why you thought it was a good idea to tackle me *with a knife* instead of, you know, telling me what had happened and asking if you could have a ride."

"I'm used to people seeing that I can fit inside a matchbox, so they think they can walk all over me. So I usually teach them a lesson or two about how they can't. I've learned a lot since I was a kid—I figured out self-defense and learned a few moves."

Did any of that make sense? I don't want to tell him my entire life story in a Thai restaurant.

"What you did to me was offense, not defense," Charlie points out.

"True. I also learned some boxing. Weapons. Knives are my weapon of choice. Bad things in little packages."

Charlie's eyes trace me up and down, and it's the sexiest look I've ever been on the receiving end of. "Is that you? A bad thing in a little package?"

Fuck yes. "Yup."

The chicken skewers come, and I stuff them in my mouth so fast I almost poke myself with the wooden stick in my hurry to try to get to the meat.

"Again, Rowan, don't eat too much too fast," he says, taking a bite of chicken. I mowed through the fresh rolls, not leaving him any. "Slow down, or you'll get sick."

"Yeah, yeah," I mumble around a huge mouthful of food. He's such a goddamned daddy. I may make it my mission in life to get him to admit that.

"Do you *want* to get sick?"

I swallow. After another bite that I chew more slowly, I shake my head.

"How are we going to get you home? I could call someone for you."

"There's no one."

"No one?"

"Yep. Well, maybe one friend, but he's just a kid. I usually take care of him. No one else is trustworthy." Except maybe Chet and Fabian, but I haven't seen them in ages.

"You know you sound totally paranoid," Charlie says matter-of-factly.

"Just because you're paranoid doesn't mean they aren't after you. That's a line from something."

"*Catch-22*, I think."

"I'm impressed." I down some more water. I'm finally starting to feel like my blood sugar is stabilizing.

"I went to high school," Charlie notes.

"Good for you. Me, too. That was one of the few things I remember from English class."

Charlie looks like he's trying to figure out just how deep he's gotten himself and whether there's a snowball's chance of getting out. I'd laugh, but I'm still eating chicken. It could use more spice, but I'm too hungry to bother asking for chili sauce. Finally, he says, "Yeah. Okay."

"Hey," I say quietly. "Thanks for feeding me. And for not pressing charges."

"Yet," he says. But there's humor in his eyes.

"Fine, yet."

"And you're welcome. Anyone would do the same thing."

"Um, no. Anyone would *not* do this. Most people would have had the police come and put me in handcuffs. Why didn't you?"

Charlie sighs and rubs his face. "I have no clue." He gestures at me. "You're just a fucking kid—"

"Not a kid—"

"Right, plus you were actively trying to harm me. But I guess I see more in you. Maybe I'm"—he raises an eyebrow—"confused."

"If you are, then I am, too. Getting in a car with a strange man. Pretty sure I saw an after-school special about that premise." I pause. "Or it's my normal job."

I'm definitely feeling better. Food and hydration work

wonders. By the time the main courses arrive, I'm practically stuffed just from the appetizers.

And a reflexive voice inside me says I should probably ditch Charlie. I look around. Where would I go, though? Or rather, how would I get home? Guess that's a problem for post-dinner Rowan. Besides, I like Charlie, so I don't know why my brain is trying to get me to go away from the man who is so definitely made for me.

"Where are you going to go tonight?" Charlie asks, picking up on my thoughts.

"I dunno."

"Where's home?"

"Lancaster."

Charlie jerks his head back. "Holy shit, that's a serious drive."

While Lancaster is in LA County, it's way the hell in the boonies. "I do it all the time. I usually take someone from Lancaster where they need to go in LA, drive around all day, then try to pick up someone going back. I'll figure something out. Maybe there's a bus."

"Do you want me to take you to Lancaster?"

I shake my head. "You don't need to do that. It's like two hours. Each way."

"Isn't anyone going to be worried about you?"

"Nope." Floyd probably wouldn't notice if I didn't ever return. At least, not until the rent was due.

The server stops by and refills my two water glasses. An instrumental version of a Julian Hill song is playing quietly on the sound system. I fidget.

"Come home with me," Charlie says, out of nowhere.

I wrinkle my nose. "That's a terrible idea. Why would you trust me in your space? What if I murder you in your sleep?"

"Are you going to?"

"No," I admit.

"That's why."

"I only hurt"—kill—"people who deserve it. And you're being kind."

"Did I deserve to be mugged?"

"That was different. It was an emergency."

Charlie raises a dark eyebrow. "Look, you don't have to. But if you don't have any other good options ..." He toys with a bite of curry. "My place isn't very fancy, because I just moved in, and I don't have a lot of shit for you to steal and hawk."

"Not that I was planning to," I mutter. Also ... "Are *you* going to murder *me*?"

"Hell no." Charlie punctuates his emphatic delivery with a forkful of rice.

I bite my lip, thinking about it. I could just say screw him and figure something out.

He keeps talking. "I've got a couch. And I can take you to your place in the morning. I have to get up early, because I'm meeting some friends for a ski weekend. I can drop you off on the way."

This is a terrible idea.

I'm in.

It can be safely said that I have no idea what I'm doing right now. All I know is that I don't want to say goodbye to my victim. If this is the last time I see Charlie—if he drops me off somewhere —I think I'll end up moping around for the rest of my life. Not that I'm prone to exaggeration.

So, finally, I nod.

Charlie presses his lips together in satisfaction.

Pretty quickly, I'm stuffed. "You done?" he asks. He's poked a little bit at the food, but he basically got it just for me. That makes something shift inside me.

"Yeah. Thank you." I gaze at him, and he's looking back at me just as intently.

"You're welcome."

Before we leave, Charlie makes me call the police on his phone, right from the table. After seeing Charlie's car, I'm embarrassed to say what I drive. I do it anyway.

They tell me to come in to do a full report, and with Charlie mouthing at me that he'll give me a ride, I agree to stop in tomorrow.

I don't want to go into a police station, but I'm not sure it's a good idea to avoid it.

Charlie pays the bill and gets what we didn't eat packaged up in boxes, and we pile back into his Land Rover.

As Charlie drives to his house—which appears to be somewhere on the Westside—I chew on my fingernail. The combination of a full stomach and the past few hours is getting to me, and I'm crashing. I rest my head on the window and close my eyes, feeling very drowsy. I don't remember anything else about the drive.

CHAPTER 6

Charlie

With Rowan fast asleep in my passenger seat, I drive down to Venice. We arrive at my narrow, tree-shaded street full of funky old homes and remodeled monstrosities, and as I pull into my garage, I see my tiny two-bedroom bungalow with different eyes.

I told him the place wasn't much, but if he's renting a room somewhere, this might seem like the height of luxury to him. I've been lucky with contingency fees on a few cases, and Cam and I make some extra money from our videos on Ad/VICE, so even though I had student loans and all, I was able to buy this place recently. And I like it. It's home. That said, I wasn't faking modesty when I said it isn't fancy. It's not complete yet.

Nerves tighten my stomach, and I blow out a noisy breath. Maybe I'm feeling a little defensive. I'm taking a risk, having this guy in my house. But what's he going to do? Steal my laptop? Fine. Everything's in the cloud. I'll get another one. Take my television? I don't care. It's all replaceable. And I'm pretty sure I could over-power him easily should I need to do so.

Still, Rowan's dangerous, and I'm letting him stay here while I sleep. *Wrong move, Charlie.* This could be disastrous. I can't help myself, though. I'm feeling protective of this bird in my cage. I discovered him. I'm the human taking his mermaid tail. He's the selkie I found who's lost his skin. So I'm going to take care of him until he can get home again. That's all there is to it.

I sit in the garage for a moment, looking at Rowan. In sleep, he looks utterly innocent, his tan lashes fanned out and his lips slightly parted. I find myself smiling. He might be drooling. He's certainly drowning in my jacket. I want to just pick him up and carry him inside, but I'm pretty sure he'd bite my neck the second I leaned into him.

Wonder if I'd like that?

I stiffen. No. I like my men established. Older. Wiser.

Not like Rowan.

I push the button on my visor and close the garage door, then turn the engine off.

Rowan startles and looks at me, blinking rapidly. There's fear in his eyes at first, which I don't like, but then he focuses on my face and smiles.

That smile.

"Hey," I say, my pulse in my throat.

His tongue darts out to touch his upper lip, and I track the movement. "Hey."

"We're at my house. Do you want to use my phone to text someone the location?"

Rowan raises an eyebrow and tilts his head. "I don't have anyone's number."

"You can borrow my laptop and see if you can find a friend on social media."

He nods. "Yeah, maybe. It's okay."

I unbuckle my seat belt and get out, leaving his knife under my seat but grabbing the leftovers.

He follows me into the house and looks around, stopping in the entrance to the small living room to take his shoes off, which I do, too. "This place is, um—"

"A work in progress?" I ask, setting my keys down and padding in stocking feet to the kitchen to put the food in the fridge. "My room's the only one with a bed, so you'll have to take the couch unless you want to sleep on the floor in the other bedroom. I've been too busy to do what I want with this place. It was built in the twenties, remodeled in the seventies, and then gutted in the nineties. It's a design nightmare that I'm hopefully going to make into a dream home, with Cam's help."

"That's cool."

"At least I have drywall, so it's better than the way his place used to be. He lived with studs for a while."

Rowan's eyes shine, and he gives me a saucy grin. "Oh? Sounds fun."

"Not that kind of studs," I say, chuckling. "Anyhow, these bare white walls are ... potential."

"Potential. Okay." Rowan nods, wrapping my jacket even tighter around himself.

I open my mouth to say something at the same time he does. "You go first," I say.

"You sure?"

"Yeah, what were you going to say?"

"It's nothing."

"Do you want to take a shower?" I nod toward the bathroom.

"Yes, Daddy. Oh, man, that would be amazing," he purrs.

"Not your fucking daddy."

"Uh-huh, whatever you say."

He's such a brat. Why do I like it?

Rowan follows me into my bathroom. I find him a spare toothbrush from the dentist and hand him a towel, then step out. "Want me to wash your clothes?"

"That would be cool, yeah. They're pretty gross."

"Okay, I'll get you something to change into. Hang on."

Before I can move, Rowan pulls off his shirt. He's got ink scattered across his torso, but it's not like he's entirely tatted up.

Then, his blue eyes locked with mine, he throws his wallet on the counter, drops his jeans and underwear, tugs off his socks, and hands the whole lot to me.

Even though I try not to, I get a good look at his body. His body that, even though he's small, is very much a man's, with some definition in his abs and a happy trail down from his belly button to an uncut cock. He smirks and turns, and as I catch a glimpse of some cartoon tattoo on his ass, he closes the door.

For a moment, I stand in the hallway holding his dirty clothes.

What the hell? Who is this guy?

Once I come to my senses, I throw his clothes into the washer in the garage, along with a few things of mine. I grab him a thick white T-shirt and black sweats from my room and set them outside the bathroom door. They'll be too big on him, but they'll have to do. Then I open the hall cabinet and pull out a sheet, blanket, and pillow for him and put them on the couch.

Over the noise of the shower, he's singing "Livin' La Vida Loca." His voice isn't half bad. He's not Jules Hill, but he can hold a tune.

I don't want to hang out in the hallway like a creep, so I busy myself putting away a few things and changing into my own sweats. Thankfully, I already packed for tomorrow. I'm going to be dead tired, but I can rest after skiing. Or something.

The bathroom door opens, and steam billows out. Rowan's got a towel wrapped around his waist, and his pink hair is darker when wet. It's going every which way like a cartoon character's.

I gesture at the clothes on the floor. "Those should do to sleep in."

He smiles. "Thanks." He puts on my T-shirt, which barely covers the tops of his thighs. It's positively indecent. "This works." He follows me out to the living room.

Too late, I realize I watched his every move, and I'm still staring at this pink-haired menace.

"Couch okay?" I'm too much of an asshole to give him my bed. "Or did you want the floor?"

"Couch is great, yeah. Thanks." He pulls the towel off and goes to hang it up in the bathroom.

"There's sweatpants there." I point.

"This is good."

I don't want to be thinking about him naked from the waist down. "So you're just gonna Donald Duck it?" I ask.

Rowan's brows knit together, and then he bursts out laughing. "What, because I have no pants on?"

I spread my hands. "Or any number of other cartoon characters who don't bother with pants. Winnie the Pooh ..."

Rowan gives me a little finger wave. "Unlike a cartoon animal —or a Ken doll—I'm anatomically correct." He wiggles his hips, and his junk swings under my shirt.

Crap.

It's mesmerizing.

I don't think I'm going to be able to handle this much longer if he walks around tempting me. It's not like I don't want to fuck him. He's old enough, even if he's not what I think of as my ideal. He's into guys, clearly. Is there some moral reason why I shouldn't just bend him over my couch and take his ass?

I'm not going to see him after tonight, of course. He's not partner material. Not on my plan.

I hear a cough, and Rowan's wearing an evil grin, perfectly aware of what he was doing. "My eyes are up here."

"You sure you don't want me to take you somewhere tonight? I don't mean to be keeping you here. You're free to go. You're not kidnapped." Although if he wants to leave, it'll be awkward, since he'd be either taking my clothes or wearing his wet.

"That's good." He opens his mouth to say something more and then stops.

I tilt my head. "What were you going to say?"

"Just ... you don't seem like the kind of man who invites strangers home with him out of charity."

"Nope. But I can be like Han Solo rescuing Leia from the Death Star. Maybe there's a reward for your safe return."

He looks up at me with that lost expression. The one that flashes over his face before he replaces it with a cocky grin or fierce determination. It pops up for just a moment, then it's gone. Like I imagined it.

But I didn't. Rowan's lost.

I want to tell him that he can stay more than one night, even if I'm out of town. I may be buying myself a problem here, but whatever. I guess I'm ... intrigued.

Who is this lost boy? He's so damn beautiful and interesting. I'm not sure what is going on with him, but it's more than he's telling me.

He has no reason to trust me. Like I have no reason to trust him.

And maybe that's what's going on. That thrill of the unknown. The potential for danger. The fact that he's made me feel more in a few hours than I have in years.

The fact that when I'm with him, I feel a spark I've never felt before.

I want to stay up and talk with him, but in only my T-shirt, he's a little too tempting. Also, it's getting pretty damn late, and he seems worn out. Rowan's got a courageous face, but anyone can tell that it's just bravado. There's no way he isn't scared shitless underneath it all.

"In the morning, we'll go to the police, get you a phone, and take you back to your home," I say.

"You don't have to—"

"I insist."

He bites his lip and nods. "Thanks."

"Cool. Night."

"Good night, Daddy," Rowan coos, back to being a flirt, and

blows me a kiss. I redden as I walk into the bathroom. What is it with this guy?

I inspect my face in the mirror. My chin's got a red scrape, and there'll probably be a scab, but it's not that bad. The cut on my neck is tiny, but I put ointment on it and my chin anyway. My palms aren't that chewed up, thankfully, but I clean them up a little better than I managed in the restaurant.

After brushing my teeth, I crawl into bed in my underwear, then lie in the dark, wondering what the fuck I'm doing. I've clearly lost all sense of self-preservation. Normal people don't invite the dude who tried to mug them into their house. I could be dead by morning.

Except Rowan doesn't want to kill me, I don't think. He may want to strangle my dick, but that's a different story.

I stew for a while, knowing that I'm not doing this correctly. That I should've gotten Rowan a hotel or something. Or otherwise let him fend for himself with less assistance than inviting him to stay with me.

I don't have the heart for that, I guess. Some people would say I don't have a heart, period. But I do. I'd text Tristan, but it's late, and he's probably asleep. So instead, I text Danny.

CHARLIE

In case I die, I'm with a really random dude. His name is Rowan Jones.

DANNY

In case you die? WTF?

CHARLIE

I'm being a drama king. Ignore me. But I guess it's like how if one person knows where you are, then nothing goes wrong.

DANNY

Pretty sure that's not how that works. Also you didn't tell me where you are.

CHARLIE

At home. So if I'm stabbed then he did it.

DANNY

That's not reassuring.

Are you sure you're okay?

No. No, I'm not sure I'm okay. I went from feeling sorry for myself to being blasted by a dude with a personality the size of the sun.

CHARLIE

I'm fine. I'm just messing with you. Good night.

DANNY

Night, asshole

Love you, bro

CHARLIE

I hate you.

I hear the couch squeak a little bit as Rowan gets settled. I'm tempted to go out and check on him, but that's nuts. I need to just let him be.

At the same time, part of me wonders if I should sleep with a knife under my pillow tonight.

I flop around for what feels like hours, thinking about Rowan.

Who is he? What the hell is up with his living situation? Why doesn't he have any friends or family to turn to?

And why does my dick get hard when I think about his face? Or that ass in those painted-on jeans. Or when he's still damp from the shower and wearing nothing but my T-shirt.

I shake my head. Tristan. I should be thinking about how he has two inches on me (height, not dick size). Five years. How he's got an investment account. He wears real clothing like button-down shirts instead of tees and loafers instead of Vans. He's a good top.

But damn if I don't want to be the one in charge sometimes. I get the idea that Rowan would let me do anything to him. And that sends a surge of electricity through me like I've never felt before.

I reach into my boxer briefs and fondle my dick, stroking it idly a few times. That feels better. But it aches more the moment I stop.

I might as well indulge.

I push my underwear all the way off, then slick myself up with a little lube from the bedside table. Oh yeah, that's *much* better.

As I play with my balls with one hand and my cock with the other, I think about how Rowan would look on his knees with his mouth stuffed full of me. How those big blue eyes would water. How he'd gag and retch and both beg me to stop and beg me not to stop.

My imagination is pretty damn good. And it's going to have to do tonight, since it's all the action I'm getting.

I can usually make a jack-off session last as long as I want, but tonight the orgasm is ripped out of me faster than usual. I come, gasping, hot spunk landing on my stomach. I bite back any louder noise, and then I lie there, my dick spent, wondering what the hell I just did.

I needed to come, clearly. We'll ignore the fact that I was thinking about Rowan.

I clean myself off with tissues and put my underwear back on. Then I get up and wash my hands, hoping not to wake my guest.

To reiterate: What the actual fuck have I done?

I've objectified my guest without his consent and creeped even myself out.

When I fantasize, I don't think about anyone I know. Not Tristan or any of the guys I pick up at the club.

In any case, Tristan, not Rowan, is my type. I should take Tristan home to my mom when he's ready to come out. Jerking off to the little menace is the closest I'll ever come to touching Rowan.

53

CHAPTER 7

Rowan

With my heart revving like a street bike engine, I gasp and sit up straight, my brain in the middle of a nightmare. I apparently fell asleep on some couch somewhere. I throw off a sweltering blanket.

Wait. I'm not wearing pants. I tug the covers back over me and try to blink the sleep out of my eyes.

Shit. Where am I?

Nothing greets me but unfamiliar white walls and the early dawn. And a bone-deep tiredness.

Then yesterday comes rushing back. Having my car stolen, Wilbur stolen, my phone stolen, and then walking forever until I met—okay, tried to stab—sexy Charlie. And then he fed me and took me home with him. I'm not sure who's the weirder one here, him or me?

Him, definitely. I'm the picture of mainstream tradition. It's possible I'm also the picture of a disheveled mess.

I yawn and pad to the bathroom on sore, blistered feet. After taking care of business, I look at myself in the mirror. I have wicked bedhead, but the pink is holding up, and I look cute.

That'll do. I poke around a bit in Charlie's cabinets, because who doesn't snoop when they're at someone else's house?

He has PrEP, a shaver, deodorant, some kind of hinoki lotion—that must be what smells so nice—hair care products, face cleanser and moisturizer, and some other grooming supplies, all neatly arranged. A few over-the-counter meds, and under the sink there's a douche bulb in a box, but not much else. He's very organized.

As I splash water on my face, I think about the way Charlie looked sitting across from me last night at the restaurant, all handsome and worried about me. He doesn't say much, but he has a way about him. It's obvious he cares about people, even though if I were to ask him, I'd wager he'd say he doesn't.

A thrill goes through me. I get to see him again. Is he still in bed? I should join him.

I open the bathroom door to Charlie's face.

My hand flies to my chest like I'm a maiden from the Victorian age. "Gracious. You frightened me."

He raises an eyebrow. "That feels like an accomplishment, since I don't think you get frightened very easily, you little menace."

Charlie is standing here, shirtless, in sweatpants. Light gray sweatpants hang low on his hips—so low that I can read the waistband of his boxer briefs. I may need to take a photo so it will last longer, but it wouldn't be as good as the real thing. He's tanner than I am, and he's got more muscles. What does he do for a living? Something related to his videos? Is it construction work?

He's watching me look him over, and his eyes heat.

"You know, between the two of us, we're wearing a complete outfit," I note.

Some sort of miracle occurs, and Charlie Cooper smiles.

It causes a chain reaction in my body. My chest expands, and then nerves zing through me, energy pulsing across my skin.

"Yeah, I guess that's true," he says. "Want coffee?"

I nod and follow him to the basic, clean kitchen, acutely aware that my morning chub is hanging a little below the hem of the shirt I'm wearing—and it's getting thicker the more I take him in.

Charlie goes to the coffee maker and dumps grounds into the filter, his ass looking so sexy in those sweats. As he fills the carafe with water, I walk over to the cabinet that I guess holds coffee mugs, but I'm wrong.

"Mugs are the next cabinet over," he says, without looking at me. He pours the water into the machine.

I deliberately go in the opposite direction from where I think he means. How long will it take him to notice me?

"The other side." I hear a button click, and now I think he's turned toward me. I wiggle a bit, then stretch to reach the cabinet, and as my shirt rides up, I hear a muffled groan from behind me.

God, it's fun to tease him. Only I don't want to be just a tease. I'd be happy to follow through.

"These ones?" I ask, glancing over my shoulder.

Charlie said he was Han Solo before, and now he's Han frozen in kryptonite. Carbonite? Jell-O? Whatever the hell it was. I glance down at the front of his sweatpants.

I think he's noticed me.

Then he clears his throat and seems to come to his senses. He grabs two mugs from the cabinet he'd pointed me to. They're cool —chunky, handmade pottery, each one different.

"Those are awesome."

"Thanks." Charlie pours both of us coffee and hands me one of the mugs.

Does that mean thanks for complimenting his taste? Or did he maybe make them?

I don't know him well enough to ask. Not that that's stopped me before.

"Did you sleep okay?" Charlie asks.

Yawning, I nod. "Yeah. Thanks."

I turn to Charlie and stretch to put more of my assets on display.

He rolls his eyes, but they don't go far from looking at my junk.

"Cream?" I ask.

"Are you asking for it?" he mutters.

"Yes, I'd like to get creamed." I use my most chipper voice.

He goes to the refrigerator to pull out some half-and-half. Our fingers brush as he passes it over, and another shiver rushes through me.

Once our coffees are doctored up, I lean with my forearms on the counter, my ass sticking out, while he has his back to the refrigerator.

C'mon Charlie, look at me.

"How long is your drive today?" I ask over my shoulder.

Charlie spins.

I wiggle my booty.

Charlie wants me. He just needs to admit it.

He clears his throat. "It'd be around six hours if I were leaving from here. From Lancaster, I'm not sure. Anyhow, I need to get a move on. We've got a lot to do, with the police report and all."

"Don't let me mess up your plans. I can fend for myself."

He sips his coffee. "It's fine." His voice is deeper than usual. Success? "We just can't dawdle too much. Do you want to take another shower before we leave?"

So I can jerk off to thoughts of him? Or maybe he could join me. I shrug. "I could." I stand up straight to face him and look down at my bare legs.

"I put your clothes in the dryer when I got up, so they should be done soon."

"I can just be naked in the meantime." The idea of Charlie watching me walk around naked makes my dick twitch. Or more than twitch. I've never paraded around like that in front of a stranger (or anyone) before, but there's a first time for everything.

He groans. "Shit, you really are going to kill me. And it's not going to be with that switchblade of yours. It's going to be with your ass."

That wasn't a no, so I take it as a yes. I strip right there, shrugging off his T-shirt and putting it neatly on the counter.

He doesn't stop me. And his eyes are like a fiery anime wolf's. "Menace," he mutters.

I half expect him to pounce, but he doesn't. He just watches me, although his hands are clenching and there's a bulge in his pants. I feel slightly foolish standing there with my dick partly hard. So I give it a stroke, because I might as well make myself feel better if I'm going to be parading around. I stroll down the hall to the bathroom to brush my teeth.

Charlie doesn't follow me, but from his choked noise, I know he can see me sashay.

I smile. I use the toothbrush Charlie gave me and set it in the little cup by the sink, deciding that I'm just going to make myself comfortable here.

I jut my butt out and finish rinsing my mouth, then spit louder than necessary.

Charlie appears in the doorway of the bathroom.

"Like what you see?" The mirror gives me a clear view of the erection tenting his sweats. I wiggle my hips.

"Yeah." His voice cracks.

That's enough. I'm taking over.

With two long strides, I get to Charlie and throw my arms around his neck. I tug his face to mine, close my eyes, and kiss him, breathing in his cedar scent. I've startled him, obviously, because he stays stock-still for a moment.

But then he clutches me to him, palming my bare ass, and kisses me back like I've never been kissed before.

Charlie's hot tongue clashes with mine. It's not sweet—he's murdering me with his lips. He tastes like coffee, and I taste like mint. His stubble scrapes my jaw.

And both of us are getting fully hard fast.

I scratch his chest, clawing at him, needing him to be closer.

The fabric of his sweats feels amazing against my naked dick, and I'm sure I'm getting it damp with my precome. My hands slip into his waistband, so I'm touching his warm skin, and the kiss gets deeper. We're grabbing at each other. A savage pleasure runs through me as I make him chase my tongue, and then I battle back so hard our teeth clang together.

Charlie's hands spread my ass, and he thrusts against my dick as I do the same to him. Lust sweeps through me. I can't get enough of him.

He takes a step forward and slams me into the bathroom wall next to the recessed shower. The painted surface is cool on my bare skin, and I gasp. I open my eyes and can see the mirror behind him. Watch him kissing me. Watch his big frame overpowering me. Those broad shoulders. Those rounded biceps. That tight ass. I try to climb him, scrabbling against him, my nails raking his back. Needing more, more, more.

He reaches down and starts stroking my dick, and my moan echoes in the small space.

This. This is what I've been needing. I'm leaking so bad. I didn't jack off yesterday.

"Didn't mean to do this," he mutters against the delicate skin behind my ear. "I was gonna leave you alone. But I want you."

"I want you, too, sexy," I pant. "I've been trying to get your attention since I met you."

He chuckles. "Is that what we're calling assault with a deadly weapon these days?"

"Yep," I gasp.

"Were you watching me at the bonfire?"

I nod. "I think I picked you because I wanted you."

"Weird way of showing it."

I go to lick his neck, but he turns and his tongue slides against mine, swallowing down any more words.

I slide my hands down his back and shove at his pants and underwear. Between the two of us, we get them down and he steps out of them, and I get a quick glimpse of the goodness he's got going on under his clothes. Damn. I want. But before I can stare too much, he draws me closer so our hard dicks are rubbing directly against each other. He's bigger than me. Then again, he's bigger than me everywhere.

Charlie has some moves. The way his hips are undulating—gah. So good. Our height difference doesn't even matter with how he's got his legs bent. His strong hands grip me to him, and he's clutching my ass. I'm clawing at him.

"Dammit, I can't get enough of you," I whisper. This time I do manage to lick his neck, up the strong column from his collarbone to his chin. "You can do anything you want to me. Anything."

He groans and fumbles behind me to turn on the shower. I take a short step to the side, panting, and tilt my head. "What are you thinking?"

"I want lube, and body wash will do."

I nod like a bobblehead doll, because yes, he is full of good ideas. "Plus we'll get clean."

"Yeah, sure. We'll go with 'showering with you to get off is an efficient use of time.'" He kisses me harshly. "Damn, you're sexy."

That makes me glow inside. His hand on my dick feels perfect. With his other hand, he gently cradles my balls. "You'd better stop that, or I'm going to come too soon," I warn, grabbing for his dick and loving how it's a steel pole. A steel pole I want to worship with my mouth. One I want to split me open.

He shoots me a wicked grin that I like very much. Then he sucks on my throat. "Will anyone be pissed if I leave a mark?"

"Fucking do it," I demand. With good, hard suction, he licks and bites my skin. I keep rutting against his hip and his dick, marking up his skin with my nails.

He manhandles me into the shower once it's warm, and now

we're kissing under the spray, which he adjusts so it's not in our faces.

I want to live in this shower. I want to live naked with Charlie.

"Turn around," he orders, and I do, the spray hitting my belly button and erection. He stills, his hands on my waist, his hard dick poking my ass.

"What?" I ask.

"This goddamned tattoo." His lips trace the ink on my nape, and he licks it, then sucks on it. "Whose baby boy are you?"

"Yours, Daddy."

"I'm not your fucking daddy. But … you're definitely a baby boy." He murmurs something else I don't catch, then bites the back of my neck—not that gently. It makes my cock twitch harder. The rougher he is, the better, and he seems to know it.

Charlie pumps some body wash onto his hands and coats his hard cock. Then he reaches around and starts stroking me with one slippery hand. As he bites my neck again, he slots his cock between my ass cheeks and thrusts down my crack while he jacks me in time with his movements.

"Oh, god." I'm in heaven.

Then he shifts, squirting out more body wash and bending his knees so he can fuck into the space between my thighs.

Over and over and over again. His rhythm's brutal, and his hand is still wrapped around me, strong, warm strokes sending me flying. I hang on as long as I can, letting him pound against me and under my balls, wishing he were inside me but loving how he's totally lost control. The spray washes away the suds on his hand, but he adds more, focusing on the tip of my cock, the best part. He changes the angle by pulling my hips back, and I let myself come.

Fast. Hard and fast.

"Charlie," I whine, my brain zapping out as my come hits the tiles.

He ruts into me again, and then he groans and shudders behind me, still licking and sucking my neck.

After a moment, he spins me around and we're kissing again, less frantic than before. Our spent cocks brush against each other as he pulls me close. I'm panting into his mouth, my entire body feeling *alive*.

"Fuck, Charlie," I whisper, and kiss him even harder.

"Yeah. I know, baby."

Our kisses slow, so we're now taking long draws from each other, not wanting to separate. His hazel eyes are still heated. Still wanting me. But slightly sated.

After we calm down, we soap up each other's hair. We don't do that great of a job of either shampooing or keeping it out of our eyes, but I don't care. The slight sting is worth it to be this close to him.

We've been rubbing together so much I'm half hard again, and so is he, but he has things to do. I, on the other hand, would rather avoid returning to my normal life.

Charlie is the sexiest man I've ever met. I'm nowhere near ready to say goodbye to him.

We rinse, and he turns the water off. After one last soul-searing kiss, he gets out of the shower and hands me a fluffy towel.

My eyes are stinging again, and it's not from the shampoo.

He catches my expression, and a wrinkle forms on his forehead. He tilts up my chin with his finger. "What's that look for? We didn't do anything you didn't want to, did we?"

I bite my lip. "No, I just don't want this to be over yet."

His brows shoot up. "Oh. Yeah. Okay." He leans down and kisses me again, long and deep. "You're really something else, Rowan."

"So are you."

"We'd better get going. I'll grab your clothes out of the dryer."

I watch him walk away, a towel around his hips and marks all over his torso from where I scratched him.

I want to do that again.

Please?

Being around me is hazardous to his health. And yet I don't want to let him go.

63

CHAPTER 8

Rowan

Oonce the Land Rover is packed up with Charlie's skis on top and a duffel and more ski equipment in the back, I figure we're heading to the police station, but instead he pulls up in front of a mobile phone store.

I shift uneasily in my seat. "I don't have money for a phone."

Charlie waves a hand. "You need a phone," he says in what I'm starting to think of as his command voice.

The command voice may be my favorite Charlie voice. I want him to command me to get down on my knees. I'd do it right here if he used that voice.

"But..."

Charlie's eyes soften. "Let me do this, Rowan."

I swallow past a lump in my throat and nod. A prepaid burner phone might not be that expensive.

He gets out of the car. I follow him inside and go to the display with the cheapest phone options.

He shakes his head and selects a more expensive phone. "Get the good one," he says. "I'll pay for it."

It's clear Charlie has some money, what with the home on the

Westside, the fancy car, and the twelve million Ad/VICE followers. I still don't like taking advantage of him.

I open my mouth to protest, but he won't let me argue and ends up buying me a phone with a six-month prepaid plan.

I've never had anything good that lasted six months.

Once the phone is activated, he takes it and texts himself before we even leave the store. Then I grab his hand as we go out to his car. Charlie glances down at our joined hands and squeezes gently.

"If there's anything else you need, get in touch with me. No more trying to mug people in parking lots," he orders.

"Yes, Daddy," I whisper, and he turns his head sharply but doesn't say anything.

Might as well double down. While he's looking, I let go of his hand and change his name in the contacts from Charlie to "Daddy," being sure to hold the screen so he can see it. He rolls his eyes.

Then I text him.

ROWAN

What color tuxedos should we wear at our wedding?

His phone pings, and he snorts when he looks at it. While he's standing right next to me outside his car, I still like watching the three little dots dance as he composes his reply. Finally the message, shorter than it should be for how long it took him, hits my phone.

DADDY

No weddings

ROWAN

Okay, we can discuss it on our second date.

Silence. I grin at him. He shakes his head, smiling that elusive smile.

But I'm not going to take no for an answer. And I think Charlie doesn't want me to.

We get back in the car, and he puts the address of the police station into his map application.

"I may not have mentioned this last night," he says, "but they'll want to get your fingerprints so they can tell which ones are yours and which are the criminals'." He reconsiders. "The criminals *other than you.*"

My instincts are screaming *fuck the police,* but I need my car back. And my plant. So I nod.

I still don't like it.

"Don't you have to be somewhere today?" I remind him as I buckle up.

"We're not planning on skiing much today anyway, given the drive. Mostly tomorrow, and then I'm taking Monday off from work so we can get a morning session in before we head down the mountain."

"Okay," I say warily. I'm still wondering why he's willing to spend half his day driving me around, but it beats hitchhiking to Lancaster, so I'm not going to complain.

At the station, after I show the cops "Pierce's" ShareARide profile from the app on my new phone and give them as much information as I can remember, they do indeed fingerprint me. Even though Charlie warned me to expect it, I must make a face, because he raises an eyebrow.

"They already have my fingerprints," I whisper, even though I don't care that the officer can hear me. At Charlie's questioning look, I say, "Juvenile adventures with the law. But it still feels like they're taking something away from me."

Charlie's face morphs from his usual broody self to something softer. "I get it."

"It's funny," I say, thinking about it. "I balk at fingerprints, and yet I sent in my DNA to one of those online services."

"There's a difference between the cops and a private company, I suppose."

"Yeah. True."

"Did you find any long-lost relatives?"

"Nope. I have no matches. Zero relatives. Period."

"You mean in the database, right? Not, like, your parents and siblings." Charlie leans in closer, and I want to pull him closer still. I want him to wrap his arms around me and hold me tight. I want to dig my nails into his back and claw through his shirt until we're locked together so tightly nothing can pry us apart ...

Hmm, that's maybe a little creepy. But I'm okay with that.

"I don't know who my birth parents are. Either of them." So now I'm spilling my guts to distract myself from the discomfort of being here. Great.

"Oh, wow. I had no idea. So you were ... were you adopted?"

A lump forms in my throat. "No. Just a lot of foster homes and group homes."

"That sounds really hard."

I shrug, used to feeling rootless. "I just think it's odd that I don't even have a third cousin twice removed or whatever. Nothing. *No one* shows up with my DNA."

Charlie's expression is dubious. "Maybe your relatives don't feel comfortable putting their information in databases like that. Like you with the fingerprints."

"Could be."

It feels like he doesn't believe me. I pull up the website on my brand-new phone, log in—I thankfully remember my password— and show Charlie the whole lot of nothing that pops up connected to me.

"See? It's so weird. You'd think I'd have *someone*."

"Yeah, that's pretty weird. I haven't used the site, but I've heard of people using it to find out about secret infidelity. A friend learned she had a cousin when he showed up with the right percentage of DNA matching. I suppose it's possible that there's no one living who is a blood relative."

"I guess. But it seems far-fetched, don't you think?"

I review and sign the police report when they hand it to me, not liking that they have so much of my information: my brand-new phone number, my address, and my fingerprints. But I suppose this is what I have to do if I want any hope of getting my car back.

"Do you think the tools who took my car just went for a joyride until they ran out of gas?" I doubt it. That's not the kind of luck I have. But I might as well try to be optimistic while I can.

"It's possible. I think you'll get it back."

It's nice to have someone by my side. More than nice.

* * *

A couple of hours later, Charlie's pulling up in front of my crappy apartment in Lancaster. Built in the eighties, remodeled never. The stucco siding is falling off in places, and everything is faded from the harsh desert sun.

"Um. This is me," I say, trying to grow a backbone.

Charlie looks over at me, his face tough to read. He opens his mouth and closes it.

I swallow hard. "Thanks. For everything."

He nods. "Take care. And like I said, text me if you need something."

"Oh, I'm gonna be texting you even if I don't."

Charlie chuckles at that. Then he reaches down, fumbles under his seat, and hands me my knife. "Use this carefully." He tilts his head. "Or don't."

I unbuckle my seat belt and crawl across the center console into his lap. "If you think this is the last you're seeing of me, you're very, very wrong, Charlie Cooper." Then I kiss him hard. He leans in, kissing me back just as fiercely. His hands steady me, but what I want to do is topple over with him on top.

That's not all I want. I want to cut his clothes off with the knife he's just returned to me. I want to draw his blood and suck his cock and make him scream. I'm probably better off not telling him those parts. Yet.

I settle for "We are very, very right together."

"How can you be right for me?" he whispers. "You're not in my plan."

A knife blade bigger than the one I carry around lances through my stomach, and I scoot back, accidentally hitting the horn. We both flinch. "What plan?"

His cheeks redden. "When I was twenty, I came up with a ten-year plan for myself. It had stuff on it like going to school, buying a house. It was ambitious at the time, but I've gotten most of it done. The only things I haven't checked off are to get a husband and a cat."

I try not to laugh. I got "baby boy" tattooed on my neck as an attempt to manifest my future, so who am I to judge anyone else? At the same time, is he rejecting me? "What kind of man did you imagine you'd marry?"

He clears his throat. "Taller than me."

Not what I was expecting as the first criterion. "Shut up."

"It's true." He squirms under me. "I wanted him to be rich and well-dressed and to be at least five years older than me."

I wince, and he sees. "Well, your plan is wrong, because I'm none of those things, and yet I'm the one you want in your bed. And your life. You'll see."

His eyes flick to the heavens. "Uh-huh. You're great, Rowan, but this was just a one-night thing." Then he bites his lower lip. "There's a guy I've been seeing. He's ... I guess you'd call him a long-term hookup. We're not exclusive or anything. But he's every-thing on my list ..."

And I'm not. He doesn't have to finish his sentence. I know

what he's thinking. My chest hitches, and my arms fall to my sides, heavy and tired. A cold sweat breaks out along my hairline, and my nose starts to run.

I tighten my fists and press my lips together. Because even though Charlie's saying he doesn't want me long term, his body doesn't lie. He wanted me this morning, and he wants me now. He can deny it all he wants, but I know the truth.

Sensing my inner turmoil, Charlie says, "Look, I'm just being honest with you. Isn't that for the best?"

"Sure," I say, biting my lip. "Who's this guy you're seeing? And any other hookups. I need a list of the ones I can meet." And kill.

Charlie chuckles. "You don't need to know. They're not serious. That I swear."

Whoever his hookup is, he's not Charlie's husband, partner, or boyfriend. So he's no threat to me.

But getting Charlie to realize we should explore this thing between us is going to take time. Time we don't have right now.

I know how to get out of a situation where I'm not welcome. I'm just unsure of whether this is one of those situations. With a flourish, I open my knife and hold it under his chin. "For old time's sake."

He stares at me with eyes like fire. Then, with a smile, he says, "Get the hell out."

Closing the knife again, I kiss him long and deep with lots of tongue, until we're panting. We break apart, and he squeezes my ass one more time. I get out of the car with just my phone and knife. Oh, and an erection.

I slam the door shut, but he rolls down the window. "Take the leftovers." I grab the small Styrofoam cooler. Charlie's suede bomber jacket is lying next to it, and I help myself to that, too.

He gives me an up nod and puts the car in gear. He drives slowly back down the street, and I watch him until he turns at the corner. I go up the steps and knock on my own door, hoping my roommate will let me inside.

I need my fucking keys.

I need my goddamn car.

I need Wilbur.

I *really* need Charlie. But he doesn't need me.

My neck bends forward, and my shoulders curl over my chest. I tug at my T-shirt hem. My body feels broken, my skin too tight.

Fuck. Why did I ever meet Charlie?

After a few excruciating minutes, Floyd lets me in. The house is skunky with the familiar scent of weed. Floyd's in his late twenties. He does cleanup on construction job sites when he can get the work and gets hauled back into prison when he can't.

At least that's the snapshot of his life I've gotten from him. I try not to talk with him too much. I give him rent every week—I'd never have enough to pay the whole thing at the beginning of the month—and otherwise leave him alone.

Floyd is lanky and badly dressed, with permanent red eyes from all the drugs. I have no idea how he gets jobs on construction sites. They must not test. I always ask him for the addresses where he's working so I know not to ever go inside those buildings.

Floyd doesn't ask me where I've been or whether I'm okay. He doesn't ask me why I don't have a house key anymore.

No one worries about me.

"Hey, Floyd, can I borrow your key? I need to get another one made. Someone stole my keys. And my phone. And my car."

"I'll do it. Just give me the money," he says. "Oh, and that sucks."

Wow. Such empathy. "Do it, and I'll Venmo you. It can't be more than my last ride paid, right?" Ugh. Having no money sucks.

"Yep."

I walk into my room. There's an empty spot where I usually put Wilbur. I bite my lip and press my fist to my chest. I miss him.

Something inside me drops out, and I feel ... empty. I slide to the floor and draw my knees up to my chest.

I'm not sure how long I stay there, but eventually I figure I'd better get to sorting out my life.

I finish setting up my new phone and look more carefully on the ShareARide app to see if there's a place for it to record my car's location. There is, but the last entry is not far from Pierce's pickup location on PCH. Guess he was smart enough to ditch the phone right away. I cash out the pitiful amount in my driver account, then find my friend Xavier on Ad/VICE. I had his number in my old phone, of course, but that does me exactly zero good.

X and I have known each other since he was thirteen and I was seventeen. We were both in the same group home for a while. He's the only person I've really stayed in touch with, in part because I always want to protect him, and in part because he's a computer genius who's helped me with my eternal search for my birth parents.

ROWAN (ON AD/VICE)

Hey, I have a new phone number. Tell me yours, and I'll text you.

XAVIER

Here you go:

ROWAN (VIA TEXT)

It meee.

XAVIER

What happened?

ROWAN

Long story. Short version is, my car got stolen, and I manifested the daddy of my dreams.

My phone rings, and I answer with a chuckle. "Hey."

"What the actual fuck?" X says.

I summarize the past day, leaving out the sex. And Charlie's beau.

Beau, fuck buddy, whatever. Charlie's dude who's perfect for him. Who's not me.

I can't keep the sigh out of my voice. "Daddy's six foot two inches of tall, dark, and handsome perfection."

"When are you going to see him next?"

"That's a problem without my car." I rub my neck.

"What are you going to do?" X asks.

"I guess wait until the police find my car? If they do. I did have insurance, thankfully. Crappy insurance, but still. Maybe I can get a different crappy car."

"Send me the profile of this Pierce dude. Let me see what I can find."

"I will."

"Would you still want to drive for ShareARide, after something like that?"

"Hell no. But what I want to do won't pay the bills."

He snorts. "How many times do I have to tell you that being the main character in your own life is only a good gig if you're famous?"

I grimace. "Yeah. I know."

I just wish I had a second main character in my life to love.

Could that be Charlie? Part of me thinks so, but if what he said in the car is true, he doesn't want me for more than what we did. He's got Mr. Perfect already.

But I'm not going to stay away. Charlie's going to be mine.

He won't know what hit him.

CHAPTER 9

Charlie

"**D**ude, watch out for the tree branch!" Danny yells.

I duck and swerve, but the pine needles brush the top of my head.

Shit, that was close.

I need to pay attention to the slope and not to the pink-haired menace occupying all of my thoughts and blowing up my phone. I can't wait to get down to the bottom to see what else he's texted me.

Rowan's this huge enigma that I can't stop thinking about.

Since I left him at his apartment yesterday, he's sent me more than a dozen texts, starting late last night after I was settled into my cabin in Mammoth.

MENACE

Hey, Daddy.

I took the longest nap on the planet, and now I'm wide awake and thinking about you.

My roommate says hi

I probably shouldn't try to sext you with my roommate nearby but I don't think he'll actually care since he's vaped too much weed tonight

I wish I could see you again

Am I coming on too strong?

I am, aren't I? Are you going to block me?

Well, I'll keep sending you texts until you tell me not to

CHARLIE

Hey

MENACE

OMG you're alive. What's going on? How's skiing? Tell me everything.

CHARLIE

I just settled in the cabin

MENACE

Do you miss me?

CHARLIE

Sure

MENACE

That wasn't convincing

CHARLIE

Who do I need to convince?

MENACE

Me, obviously

CHARLIE

Menace.

MENACE

I don't think I've properly thanked you for not pressing charges

CHARLIE

Yet

MENACE

Yes, yes. Yet.

Thank you. For more than that.

CHARLIE

Yep.

MENACE

So back to the sexting …

CHARLIE

Despite myself, I'm interested.

Rowan then sent me a selfie of himself wearing my leather jacket, which he stole, and nothing else. It's a tease of a picture, taken with him looking over his shoulder. He's biting his finger and grinning at the phone, with the jacket hiked up so one ass cheek shows.

Jesus.

CHARLIE

Fuck me. You're hot. Give me a few minutes alone with that photo.

MENACE

[Heart eyes emoji]

My hand found my dick very fast. It was convenient that I was all alone in a small cabin with no one to disturb.

This morning's text was:

MENACE

So on our second date, shall we go to the movies? Or is that too normal? Do I need to take you, like, to Rocky Horror?

We're not going on a second date

I can't just give in. It's not in my nature.

Everyone accuses me of being an asshole, and maybe that's in large part because I'm so focused on achieving the goals in my plan that I end up ignoring any side quests.

And maybe sometimes those side quests could be things I actually want.

MENACE

Yet.

The cold air whips against my skin. It feels good to be out and skiing, but as usual when I'm with my friends, I'm jealous of them being paired off while I'm lonely in my own cabin. Tristan would never attend something like this. Too public.

Tristan isn't the reason I'm so distracted, though. How can one chance meeting change everything? Rowan feels like a tropical storm. A force of nature. He may have a gravitational pull, for all I know.

"Where's your brain at, dude?" Danny calls.

I don't answer him immediately. In part because we've hit a steeper slope where we have to pay attention or we'll go off into the trees. But once the terrain is less dangerous, he skis right up next to me.

"Um, Charlie. Dude. Don't make me ask again. What's up with you?"

"I got together with that guy I thought was going to murder me," I start, smiling as I think about Rowan prancing around my house wearing my T-shirt and nothing else. Or wearing nothing.

Danny stops right there in the middle of the slope. I nearly run into him, but I stop, too, facing him, our skis pointed perpendicular to the mountain. "Charlie Cooper. What happened?"

I'm pretty sure my cheeks redden, and I'm glad he can't see

them under my sunglasses and scarf—although if he asked, I could attribute the color to exercise or sun or wind exposure. I'm also *very* glad he can't see the scrape on my chin or the cut on my neck. My scarf is useful for more than one reason today. "I hooked up with him after the bonfire."

Even though that's technically true, it feels like the biggest lie I've ever told. Not just because of everything I'm leaving out, but because it felt like more than a hookup. I get this excited flutter in my stomach every time I think about Rowan.

"Okay," Danny says slowly, watching a kid snowplow down the slope. "What's the problem? I thought Santa Barbara closeted dude wouldn't care."

"He wouldn't."

He turns to me. "Then, again, what's up? You're thinking way too much about murder guy."

"He's not a murderer." I gesture, demonstrating that I am indeed alive and well. "The problem is, he doesn't fit into my ten-year plan."

"You're still doing that shit? Fuck your plan. Explore shit with the murder boy."

"He's just a hookup."

Danny's still staring. "Right. You don't get hung up on hookups."

"Why do you think I'm hung up on him?"

"Because you're distracted."

Tugging at my collar, I wince. "Am not."

"Are too."

"See?" I say. "This is the problem with knowing someone for seven years or so. When I act childish, you act the same way back."

"Only because you deserve it. What's his name? I forgot."

I relent. "His name's Rowan. He's younger, smaller, not my type."

Danny shoots me a skeptical look. "Yeah, yeah, I've seen who you take home from the club. You think you're all into being bossed around, but I know the truth."

"What are you talking about?"

"You secretly want to be in charge."

"Well, maybe ..."

Maybe I do want to overpower Rowan. I can't stop thinking about what he looked like naked. I'm drawn to the hunger in his eyes when he watches me—like I'm the only thing that's ever existed in the history of ever. He intrigues me, with the glimpses he's given me of his sad background and the fact that he's down on his luck and yet has so much energy.

"And this Rowan got under your skin?"

The sun is bright in my eyes, even with sunglasses, as I glance up. "Kinda. Maybe. Yeah."

I want to ditch this ski weekend and drive back home so I can see him—room deposit, friends, and even my plan be damned.

Several more skiers whiz by us. "Fine. When you're ready to talk about him more, let me know. I'll be here," Danny says.

* * *

When we break for lunch, I take a few minutes to sneak in a quick call to my mom. I always call about this time. She picks up on the first ring.

"Charlie!"

"Hey, Mom. I'm calling you from the ski slopes in Mammoth. We're going to go get some lunch, but I figured I'd call you first. What are you doing today?"

She tells me about the hiking she's been doing with her friends and a new recipe she tried and how she and Dad are starting to decorate for Christmas, but they want all the kids to come back home to put ornaments on the tree. I listen dutifully, and then she asks, "What about you? Skiing, huh? Are you having fun?"

"Yes, I am."

"Who are you with?"

"Reyna, Cam and Shelby, Danny and Alden, and a bunch of other people from the office."

"No friend for you?"

"I have a cabin to myself."

She clucks her tongue. "Charlie, I worry about you."

I won't roll my eyes, since I'm an adult. "I'm fine."

"I just wish you had someone special in your life."

"That's you, Mom."

Her voice is warm. "Charmer."

We talk a few minutes more, and she lets me go. Since the signal is good in the lodge, I also post a video I edited a while back and had ready to go. It's a compilation of Cam and me fixing up his pool house. It's been a while since I posted, and it gets views fast—likely because Cam's wearing a backward baseball cap and no shirt for most of it. I remind myself not to take views for granted. I respond to a few comments to keep the algorithm happy, then put my phone away.

With those tasks checked off, I clomp into the restaurant, which is basically a cafeteria. But it's the best kind of cafeteria, with an entire wall of windows looking out at the snowy mountainside. The decor is rustic and kind of midcentury functional. I like it. It's also industrial strength to handle getting beat up by all the ski boots, but it's cozy, except for the areas closest to the doors.

Shelby and Alden sit down at a large table to hold it for our group while the rest of us get food. We all start shedding outer layers, hanging them up on the convenient hooks nearby.

When I take off my scarf, Danny stares. "What happened to your chin?"

Camden scrunches his nose. "Yeah. Where'd you get that scrape?"

Why are my cheeks burning? I rub my chin, thinking less about the scrape than about what Rowan and I did the rest of

Friday night and yesterday morning. "Would you believe me if I said I cut myself shaving?"

"Nope," Cam says, hanging up his ski jacket.

Danny grins. "Did you finally get someone to agree to your fantasy of chasing him down in the woods and—"

Cam holds up his hands. "Whoa, TMI. Not shit I want to know about my brother. I'm getting in line for food. Any requests, baby?" Shelby asks for a chicken sandwich, and Cam drops a kiss on the top of his head before striding over to the counter. Shelby's eyes follow his every move.

Crossing my arms over my chest, I tell Danny, "We never should've played drunken truth or dare."

Shelby perks up, sitting straight and clasping his hands together. "Oh, you absolutely should have. If not for a slightly drunk dare, Noah and August would never have gotten together."

"True." I sigh. "Don't worry about the cut. It's nothing."

Danny opens his mouth, then shuts it and nods, and he and I join Cam in the lunch line.

To my relief, when we get back to the table and everyone digs into their lunch, the topic of conversation has shifted away from me. But I don't escape entirely. Cam corners me when Shelby and Alden are chatting and Danny's refilling his drink.

"Charlie," he starts, leaning over, his voice low.

I take the last bite of my burger. "What's up?" I ask, my mouth full.

Cam peers at me in his big brother way. He's always had some kind of intuition when things were happening to me that weren't good. "That's what I wanted to ask you. Everything okay?"

I swallow. "Yeah, of course. Why?"

His voice is low and steady. "At the bonfire, you seemed ... more of a loner than you usually are."

"I'm fine." I wave a hand.

Cam presses his lips together, his jaw set. "That means you're not. Everything okay at work?"

I shift in my seat. "The office is great. You know everyone who works there is amazing."

"Uh-huh. But it still seems like something's bothering you."

Shit. Cam's making eye contact like it's an Olympic sport. He's not going to let this go. And bottling up this part of me has made me even more bitter than usual.

If I can't tell my secrets to my brother—the one I first came out to, and who recently came out to me—then who can I confide in?

Glancing around, I can see that everyone's in their own conversations, and I don't think I'll be overheard. "I guess I'd just rather be doing our videos than practicing law."

Saying the words out loud makes my throat thick, and my gaze flits around the room again before settling on my brother.

"You mean ... doing them more seriously? Instead of working at the firm?"

I nod.

Cam raises an eyebrow. "Is that all that's bothering you?"

I huff. "Here I go telling you my deepest, darkest secret, and you act like it's nothing. It's not nothing to me. I'd be throwing away my education."

"Charlie. Your happiness is more important than anything else. I know you put a lot of work into studying and getting to where you are, but that doesn't mean you have to stay there. Sometimes it takes a while to figure out who you really are. Look at me." He smiles. "I thought I was straight."

Despite myself, I chuckle. "Yeah, that was a big one for me to get used to."

"But you did. Fast."

I shrug.

"Tell you what. Let's ramp things up, do as many videos and projects as we reasonably can. See if we can get more sponsors. Maybe something will take off and you can quit or figure out a way to get a film job instead of toiling at something you don't enjoy.

There's nothing that says you have to stick with a decision you made when you were, what, twenty?"

It sounds like a pipe dream to me. My stomach gets all floaty.

But it can't be that easy. I'd be letting too many people down if I quit the firm.

And I wouldn't be finishing what I started. I don't like unfinished things. My career can't be one of them.

Still, though, Cam is making me think that it's possible for me to someday not be a lawyer.

And maybe, someday, to be happy.

CHAPTER 10

Charlie

After some more skiing in the afternoon, we clean up, have dinner, and then head to the main room of the lodge that services all the cabins. It's full of rustic wooden furniture, thick leather sofas, and rugs with colorful patterns. A large fire roars in the fireplace, and the room smells of a combination of dust and pine—both fresh and well-used.

I'm sipping my third whiskey and, frankly, wishing Rowan would show up. But that's not going to happen, especially since he doesn't have a car. I'm tempted to leave and pick him up from his shitty apartment. I know I'm being judgy, but Rowan deserves better.

Except I shouldn't drive, with how tired I am and how tipsy I'm getting, so I stay to the side as usual. I'm just … numb. Empty. I prop my head on my fist, elbow on my knee, and feel apathetic about life. I swallow down the whiskey, the burn warming my cheeks more than the fire and the heated room.

Reyna excuses herself from the date she brought with her and joins me on the plaid couch, a glass of white wine in hand. "So, what happened to your chin?"

"Everyone keeps asking me that. Cut myself shaving."

She gives me that little sister accusatory stare. "Cam said you had a sex accident."

I throw up my hands. "Then why did you ask? And no, it wasn't a sex accident. Sheesh." I glare at her.

She grins at me. "Okay, let's start over. How's it going, big brother? Have fun skiing?"

Be a human, Charlie. "Yeah, it was gorgeous today." My voice sounds completely lacking in any emotion.

"You seem a little down," she points out.

I cross my arms, then uncross them. *This is your sister. You can talk to her.* And maybe the booze is getting to my brain, loosening my tongue more than usual.

"Everyone's all finding their someone," I say. "And here I am, all alone. Even you brought someone with you this time. I'm ... a sad sack of jealousy."

"Oh, CharlieBoo. It won't always be like that."

I stare into the fire. Pour another drink from the bottle on the coffee table. Swallow it. Feel the burn. Look around at everyone around me. See Reyna waiting patiently for me to say something. Check my phone for the tenth time in the past two minutes, seeing if Rowan's texted. Pour another drink. Finally, I say, "I guess I'm lonely. Even surrounded by people."

I should want Tristan. He checks all the boxes. But I don't. I want Rowan. I barely know him, and I can't get enough.

My emotions must be written all over my face, because Danny glances at me, and then he and Alden get up and move to sit on the love seat facing me.

"Charlie's a moody bastard tonight," Reyna says.

"So that guy you're hung up on isn't the right one?" Danny asks.

"What guy is this?" Reyna asks, both eyebrows raised.

Which in turn raises my hackles, because the last thing I want is Reyna telling our mother I'm seeing someone. Mom was crushed when Cam's ex-girlfriend left him at the altar—though now that Cam's with Shelby, that's kind of water under the bridge. There's no way I'm bringing someone to meet the family unless it's serious, though.

"I met him Friday. I barely know him. Don't plan a goddamned wedding for me," I mutter. Then I down yet another shot.

Danny looks at Alden with a radiant smile. "Sometimes it just takes meeting one person to make your entire world fall into place."

"You're getting soooo far ahead of me," I say. "I. Just. Met. The. Guy."

"Sounds like you might have a crush, though," Danny says.

Reyna perks up. "Aww, CharlieBoo, that's so cute! Who is he?"

I roll my eyes. "His name'shrowan, and he'shh a total menace."

"But you like him," she continues.

"Yeah." I huff and stare at my empty glass. Okay, I'm drunk. "There's sumfin about him I can't get out of my system."

"So what's the hang-up?"

"If you met him, you'd know he isshn't on my plan."

"Oh, he sounds better and better," Reyna says.

"Whatever. I'ma ... I'mmm going to bed." I've had enough. I don't need to see their happy faces.

Maybe I need a new ten-year plan. I can get to work on that after I turn thirty.

* * *

I stomp through the dark night back to my cabin. I open the door, take off my boots and jacket, and stand swaying in the entryway, my vision blurry. It's not horribly late, I don't think. I manage to pull out my phone and text Tristan. He's the one I'm supposed to want.

CHARLIE

How come your not out

*Youre

You're

TRISTAN

Hi, stranger. Haven't seen you in a while.

And wtf? You know why.

CHARLIE

I'm in Mammoth. Thinking about you.

He doesn't reply for a long time. Did he fall asleep?

TRISTAN

I didn't know you were going there. If you'd told
me, I would've lent you my family's cabin.

Fuck. Of course Tristan has a cabin up here. His family has everything.

CHARLIE

Sorry, it wasn't that well planned.

Lies.
And I apparently have nothing else to say to Tristan tonight.

TRISTAN

It's okay. I'll see you on Friday. Going to bed.
Night.

CHARLIE

Night.

I still want to hear someone's voice.
Before I know what I'm doing, I dial. "Rowan?" I start to pace around the cabin.
"Charlie. Hey." Rowan sounds hesitant, but not sleepy.

My pulse jumps in my throat, and I feel breathless listening to his voice. "I misss you," I blurt.

Silence. A long, drawn-out silence where my heart pounds and my palms start to sweat. Then, "I miss you, too."

I rock back and forth on my feet. "Isss ridiculousss that I misss you. I barely know you."

"Have you been drinking?" There's a smile in his voice.

"Kinda yesh." I lick my lips.

"That's so cute. Tell me more about why you miss me."

Why does his voice make my dick hard?

"I dunno. You're kind of ruining me." I'm also dizzy. Whether it's from the altitude or the whiskey or talking to him, I don't know.

"Excellent. That's my grand plan," he tells me. "When can I take you on that date? What do you think of axe throwing?"

I yawn. "No dates," I say reflexively.

Why are you like this?

"Why are you so stubborn?" Rowan asks, echoing my thought, but there's amusement in his voice. I think he sees me as a challenge.

I stop pacing, because the room's spinning. I open a bottle of water and take a drink, which helps some. Finally, I blurt, "Because if I'm not stubborn, I'm scared you're going to chew me up annnnd spit me out annnnd wreck me."

A long pause. Then Rowan whispers, "I'm never going to do that. *Never.*"

And somehow the fierceness of his answer helps me believe him. "Forrrrrr the record, I'ma never gonna do that to you, either."

"Good." Rowan sighs. "Look, Charlie. I know we don't know each other well, but I want to get to know you. I like you."

"Yeah, I likeyoutoo." Now we're talking like we're in elementary school. "Tell me one thing about you. One thing no one knows."

Without hesitating, Rowan says, "In school I carried around

Frank's RedHot sauce in my backpack. Instead of a laptop or pens and paper."

I burst out laughing. The room's still spinning slightly. "Why?"

"Well, what if I was hungry and I wanted chicken, but I wanted it to be spicy?" Now he's laughing, too.

"I guess I see your point. I jusss dunno anyone who carries around Frank's. Lube and condoms, yes. Extra sauce, no." I pause. "I used to carry around Uno cards."

He snorts. "Why?"

"What if I wanted to play cards but didn't have any?"

"I see your point," Rowan says, echoing my words since I echoed his, I think. I down the rest of the bottle of water, needing to sober up.

"Tell me something else," I say, loving just talking to him. Loving how much I want to get inside his brain and see how it works.

And again, Rowan doesn't wait even a second. "I've spent way too much time trying to figure out if there were more doors or wheels in the world."

I blink at the phone. "I've … never thought about that."

"My mind works in mysterious ways."

"It's cool," I say. "I like the way your mind works."

I hear him yawn.

"Are you tired?" I ask.

"Kinda, yeah."

"Then go get some sleep," I say. I want to call him baby, but then he'll call me Daddy, and enough of that shit.

I also want to talk with him all night long, but that's a bad idea, too. I think I need to go to bed.

"Night, Charlie," Rowan says softly.

"Night."

CHAPTER 11

Charlie

Tuesday morning, I drag my thankfully no-longer-hungover ass to the office. I look at all the happy people around me and feel the same jealous pangs I've been feeling lately—except they don't seem to hurt as much as they did last week.

I focus on getting my work done. I yell an appropriate amount at opposing counsel. I get my hair cut during lunch. Same as every week.

Lather, rinse, repeat.

It's not all bad. Wednesday evening, I edit some footage Cam and I never posted about a fountain he built in his backyard and post it. And there's something new: Rowan's texts are the high-light of my week. Things escalate unexpectedly Thursday afternoon.

MENACE

I went to the free clinic today. Here's my STD screening.

He sends me a half-assed photo of a panel of common tests, all negative.

I'm overcome by a vision of licking his tattoos. I'm amazed that he's so responsible—that's usually my thing.

So, of course, I give him crap.

> CHARLIE
>
> And you're sending me that because …

MENACE

[Winky face emoji]

I'm thinking of your dick

Specifically, I'm thinking of your fat, hard, long dick in my mouth. I'm drooling. I want you.

Join me

Rub your dick

Make yourself come

Think about me blowing you

I did not intend to get hard at the office, but … it happens. Nogust has surely fucked here, and I wouldn't put it past Aldanny, either.

MENACE

Are you hard yet?

> CHARLIE
>
> You're going to be the death of me

MENACE

Or I'll make you come alive

Do it

Close your door, daddy

Let me take care of you

I shut my door and lock it, then reach inside my suit pants to grip my aching cock, my back to the door.

> MENACE
>
> Now that I think about it, maybe I'd just ride you.

"Goddammit," I whisper as Rowan's texts keep coming. I hastily undo my belt and slide my pants down.

> MENACE
>
> You'd like that, wouldn't you? Stretch me and lube up my hole so you slide right in. I'll take your cock to the hilt. I'd be stroking my cock, and you'd be holding on to my hips, slamming me down on you hard.

I'm shuttling my hand up and down my cock. If I'm doing this in the office, I gotta be quick.

Now I get a voice message. I awkwardly click on it, and Rowan's voice comes through my phone speaker. "I'm doing this hands-free, because now I'm jerking off to the idea of you, Daddy. I want your dick in my ass, and I want it now. Oh, god," he moans loudly, "that gets me so hard." There's a gasp, and I hear Rowan coming.

"Shit," I say under my breath, and then I listen to the message again.

My phone buzzes, and it's a photo of Rowan's chest with his come on it, glistening white.

I beat off even faster, desperate to reach that high. My pants slide lower down my thighs. I hear footsteps in the hallway, and Shelby buzzes someone over the PA system. Fuck, I need to come.

> MENACE
>
> Either way, I want you all over me
>
> I want you to make it so I don't walk for a week

Gasping, I come into my hand, my balls drawn up tight, my release only taking the edge off the need I've felt the past few days.

I slump against the door.

What the hell did I just do? I've never done anything like this in the office. I'm always a professional, to the point where I sometimes show no emotion, no matter what.

Shit, I'd better put my dick away. I grab some Kleenex and wipe myself up as best as I can, tucking myself into my pants and tucking my shirt back in. Then, hoping my cheeks aren't burning too much, I slip to the bathroom to wash my hands and clean up better.

When I return to my office, I have more texts from Rowan.

MENACE

Daddy? You there?

Charlie?

Did I scare you away? You probably had to take a work call, huh?

It takes me a moment to look up my medical records, but I find them.

CHARLIE

I'm back. I needed a minute.

Here's a screenshot of my STI results from my physical earlier this month. All neg. Have only been with one guy since then, and we always use protection.

MENACE

Their loss.

CHARLIE

And you made me come just now.

MENACE

My evil plan is working.

I wanna do it again many, many times.

The next morning, Rowan greets me with:

MENACE

Where do you think we should go on our fifth date?

CHARLIE

Shouldn't we have a first date first? And one that doesn't involve a crime?

MENACE

Are you asking me out? That's so cute! I accept.

Texting with him is fun—and sometimes alarmingly hot—but I'm frustrated by its limitations. This isn't the medium to find out what he loves and hates, and why. I want to know his history. I want to know everything.

Then I shake my head. No, this menace isn't the one for me.

He's cute and fun and wild, but I have a plan. How am I going to achieve my goals if I let myself get derailed by the first guy who comes along who's out of the ordinary? I should tell him to cool it, but I can't seem to get myself to.

So I leave him on read for the rest of the day. I need to get my work done.

I have a standing date tonight.

* * *

I park in front of Tristan's 1920s California Mission–style home in the Santa Barbara hills on Friday evening. The house is classic. Elegant. Perfect. Like him.

While I like my house—or rather, its potential—this one's a dream home. White stucco walls, red tile roof, heavy wrought iron accents. Magenta bougainvillea climbing up the side, and a view down to the ocean. The ideal place to have friends over for brunch, if we could entertain friends together. But because Tristan's in the closet, so am I, when I'm with him—even though I told my parents I was gay when I was thirteen.

I've been here a hundred times. Maybe more. Tonight feels weird, though. I'm sitting in my car with the radio turned off, willing myself to walk inside. My heart's beating faster than usual, and my stomach feels queasy. What's wrong with me?

Get out of the car, Charlie.

Tristan opens the door just a moment or two after I knock.

He's a few inches taller than me, and as usual, he's dressed nicely. Tonight he's wearing flat-front dark gray pants and a pale blue shirt with a subtle white stripe. His dark hair is longer than mine but not long, and artful stubble shades his chiseled jaw.

Every other time I've been here, he's ushered me inside immediately, since he's nervous about his neighbors seeing us, but tonight he greets me with a big kiss at the door, both hands clasping me behind the neck.

What the hell?

"Hey," I say when we separate, resisting the urge to wipe my lips.

"Come on in, babe." Tristan glances behind me and gasps. "Oh my god, what happened to your car?"

I whip my head around, but I don't see anything amiss. "What's wrong with it?"

"It's dirty."

"Ha. I haven't gotten it cleaned since I went to Mammoth. Too busy."

Tristan raises an eyebrow. "That's not like you. But I guess we all change and grow." He takes a step back and lets me inside, one arm going around my waist to tug me to him.

For once, I'm not liking the feeling of being smaller than my partner. I close my eyes, trying to get my head in the game. Me coming here is our routine. Something delicious is in the oven.

Tristan's always been a good cook. And he usually feeds me before we fuck.

"What's up with the ..." I wave my hand at the door. "You don't care about old Miss Sadie across the street anymore?"

He lets me go and walks over to his bar cart full of crystal stemware. "I don't. Champagne? Or wine? Your usual red?"

"Sure." Why is my chest tight? I sit down in my regular spot on the couch.

Tristan pours me a glass of pinot noir—Fitzpatrick, a local winery run by a friend of his—and hands it to me, then pours a glass for himself. He settles into the leather armchair next to me. As usual.

We do this. We hang out, eat, and bang, and then I leave.

"How was Mammoth?" he asks, and I'm grateful to him for interrupting my thoughts.

"Good." I'm super chatty tonight. But there's a weird pain in the back of my throat.

"That's great," he says. "It's tough to get away this time of year. Finals are going to start soon, and I'll have grades to turn in." He smiles. "But winter break is a compensation."

"Must be nice to have so much time off."

Tristan nods. "I do enjoy it." He sips his wine, then sets the glass down on a coaster on the coffee table. "I made lasagna. It's a new recipe, but it sounded good. I've been feeling really optimistic lately. Wanting to try new things."

"It smells delicious."

I look around at the modern art on the walls. The kitchen table where he's bent me over and fucked me. The hallway to his bedroom that I know all too well.

We chat a little more, and he offers to refill my glass. I accept, although I shouldn't. We move to his dining room table, and he serves the lasagna, which is delicious, and the longer I stay here, the wronger it feels.

Rowan has no claim on me.

I'm not dating him, no matter what he says in his texts. I told him about Tristan. And it's normal for me to pick guys up at One, my usual club, a few times a month.

But I feel like I'm betraying Rowan.

I shove the thought to the side. I'm allowed to fuck whoever.

Tristan's been silent for a few minutes, eating, but now he looks up at me. "I've decided to come out," he says in a rush. "Times are changing. It's been long enough. And I'm not sure who I've been kidding, anyway."

It's not like Tristan to blurt, and I almost choke on my wine. "Wow, that's great," I say sincerely. "I'm happy for you. How can I support you?"

He gives me an uncharacteristically tentative smile. "If you … if you wanted to go on a date with me sometime, I'd like that. A real date. Out in public. Actually, there's this faculty event at work coming up. I'd like you to come."

I should be happy. This is what I've wanted for five years. Instead, my stomach feels like it's weighed down with lead, and I'm tempted to turn and run.

A step toward another one of my dreams coming true … but it's all wrong. Now that he's willing to … Why couldn't he have decided this two weeks ago?

Shit.

"Thanks," I say. I open my mouth to continue, but nothing comes out.

"What?" Tristan asks. "I thought you'd be proud of me."

"I *am* proud of you." I pinch the bridge of my nose. "It's just … god, we need to talk."

He tilts his head and blinks, then lets out a breath. "Okay." He draws out the syllables.

"I met someone."

"*Met* someone, or met *someone*?"

"The latter. He's …"

Tristan takes a careful sip of his wine. "Okay," he repeats. "What does that have to do with my coming-out party?"

"You and I have always been free to get together with other people, but ... but I can't ... He's not ..." I take a deep breath and try again. "This guy is all wrong for me."

He smirks. "All wrong for you?"

My lips pinch together in a tight smile. "So wrong. You're ... perfect." I throw up my hands. "He's ... not."

"And yet you want him and not me." It's not a question. I can't read his expression, either. Is he pissed? I've sometimes thought, perhaps arrogantly, that Tris was more into me than I was into him. But he doesn't seem upset. He's reacting like a rational adult.

Something about that strikes me as wrong—but it's likely just my ego talking.

"I don't know what the hell I want," I say. "All I know is that he's completely messed up my life, and I can't seem to get him out of my system." I take a deep breath. "We aren't like that, you and I, but I felt like I needed to tell you about him. And I ... I should go."

I still can't read Tristan.

"I'm sorry," I whisper. I stand, and he does, too, coming around next to me.

Tristan leans forward to kiss me, and I take a step back. He frowns. "No goodbye kiss?"

I shake my head.

He pokes his tongue into his cheek. "You do have it bad."

My cheeks burn. "Maybe so. What's really bad is that I barely know him."

Tristan's a good, honest guy. He's perfect on paper, and he's perfect in real life.

He's just not the one for me.

Tristan huffs and looks at the ceiling. "Yeah. I tell you I'm ready to come out and take you somewhere in public, and you tell me you're not interested anymore. Figures my timing would be this off."

"I'm sorry. I don't know what else to say." My brain cycles through things like *we can still be friends* or *I'll call you when this doesn't work out*, but I'm not that flavor of asshole.

"There's not much more *to* say." Now he sounds bitter and deflated. Shit. Tristan is a nice guy. I didn't mean to hurt him.

But I'm making the right choice, for reasons I'm starting to unpack. I've been pretending for five years that I wanted Tristan to come out. *If only he was available*, I'd tell myself—*that's what's stopping us from taking our relationship further.*

And it was never true. In some ways, Tristan's closet was my closet, too. I've been able to live in it, knowing I didn't have to give myself to anyone as long as Tris wasn't out.

This is the first time in my life I've wanted to consider exploring things with just one man. And it figures that he's a barely solvent, college-age criminal with daddy issues.

His ass is great, though. So, one thing on my list?

His ass is the least of the reasons I'm fascinated by him.

"Would you go to the party anyway?" Tristan asks. "As a colleague? I could use a wingman. It's on a weeknight, a Monday, so I know I'm asking a lot of you, but ... I guess I consider you a friend, still, even if we're not, you know, fucking anymore."

I look into Tristan's gentle brown eyes. Here he is being all brave and vulnerable, and I just ruined his party. "Sure, Tris. I'll go with you. Text me the details."

"I will. Bye, Charlie."

I drive the hour and a half home and don't even realize I never turned the radio back on until I pull into my own garage.

CHAPTER 12

Rowan

On Saturday morning, I'm roused from a really nice dream about Charlie Cooper in which we were wearing little clothing and being very active by a few strong, sharp knocks on the front door.

Charlie. He could be surprising me—

I race down the hall in nothing but my hot pink briefs and swing open the door. A woman, probably midfifties, is standing there holding a stack of papers. "Are you Floyd Bordner?"

So much for getting my hopes up. As usual. I shake my head.

"Does he live here?"

My hand goes to my hip, and I shiver as the cold desert air hits my bare chest. "Who wants to know?"

"What's your name?" she asks.

I raise an eyebrow. "Again, who wants to know?"

She thrusts the papers into my hands, and I take them involuntarily. "Here is a copy of the summons and complaint in the matter Lancaster Apartments versus Bordner and Jones."

"What?" Squinting at the small type, I rub my eyelid.

"You're being sued. Or, rather, Floyd and everyone else who lives here are being sued."

I gape at her. "What do you mean?"

She takes a photo of the front door with her phone and fiddles with it, likely sending an email. "I can't answer any questions about the lawsuit. I'm just a process server." Turning on her heel, she heads down the rickety staircase.

The papers she gave me feel like they're giving off an electrical charge. I close the door and stand in the hallway reading them. I don't understand a lot of the words, like "unlawful detainer," but I get the gist of it. We're being evicted for nonpayment of rent.

Which is bullshit, because I've paid the rent. I've paid the rent instead of eating.

My nostrils flare.

While I want to stomp, I'm barefoot, so it wouldn't have the desired effect. Instead, I pad down the hall to Floyd's room and fling his door open so hard it hits the wall behind it, likely leaving a hole. He sits bolt upright in bed. His room has slightly more furniture than mine. Which is to say he has a real mattress, as well as a chest of drawers that's littered with bongs, beer cans, and trash.

"Wha?" Floyd rubs his eyes.

"Is there something you want to tell me?" My fingers are itching. I should've brought my knife with me, but no, I'm just standing here in my underwear.

I'm sure I could get creative if need be.

He squints at me. "What are you talking about?"

Sweeping my arm out, I throw the papers at him. Some of them land on the mattress. Others fall to the dirty carpet. "We're being evicted."

Floyd's jaw drops. "Oh, shit."

"Yeah. Oh, shit. Why are we being evicted? I've been paying you rent." Heat flushes through my body.

His open mouth turns into a yawn, which turns into a shrug. "I must've forgotten to send it in."

My voice is dangerously quiet. "What do you mean you 'forgot'?"

"Um, I haven't paid the landlord."

"How long?" I ask. "How long has it been since you've paid them?"

He scratches his chin. "Maybe two or three months."

"Two or three months!" I screech. "What the fuck?" I'm so tempted to hurt him right now. But I hold myself back. Floyd is skinny, but he's also tall, and I learned my lesson about tackling guys bigger than me with Charlie—at least, doing so without backup and a good plan.

I may add him to my vengeance list, though.

His palms are up in a "Who cares?" gesture. "Relax, I'll talk to him. We'll get it taken care of."

"With what money? I don't have any income right now."

"I could sell some weed."

I scowl. "You don't have any you haven't smoked."

"Just relax," Floyd repeats. "Let me sleep. We don't have to move out today. There isn't a hearing date listed."

"You've gone through this before?"

"Yeah. Don't worry about it, man. I'll figure this out in the morning."

I'm *definitely* adding Floyd to my vengeance list. "It *is* morning!"

"Close the door on your way out."

Huffing, I leave, slamming his door shut, and start pacing in the hallway.

What am I going to do for money? For transportation? For housing?

Because it's pretty hard to be a ShareARide driver if I don't have a car, and it's pretty hard to rent a room if I don't have any money coming in. And I can't stay here if we're getting evicted.

My hands are trembling. I've survived this week on Charlie's leftovers plus the ramen and soup I had in the pantry, but that's all out.

I don't know what I can do.

Back in my room, I look around at my meager belongings. Some clothes. Deodorant and shampoo I keep in here so Floyd won't use them. A couple BL mangas. (*Dick Fight Island* is the greatest story ever told, and I will fight anyone—with my dick, if need be—who says otherwise. Unless they say it's *Dick Fight Island*, volume 2. I also had to own *Ore Miko* and *Birds of Shangri-La*, but I've never had enough money to buy all the other manga I want for my shelves. If I had shelves. And don't get me started on *Secret XXX*, which sounds pornier than it is. Although it's plenty porny.) A vape I barely use. A sleeping bag on an air mattress, both from Walmart. My new phone and charger.

My phone. *Charlie.*

Before I know what I'm doing, I pick up my cell to call Charlie, but at that exact moment, there's an incoming call from a number that's not in my phone—which isn't surprising, since the only numbers in there are Charlie's and Xavier's.

I'm about to decline the call—because who answers calls from numbers they don't recognize?—but then I remember that almost no one knows this number. So I answer.

"This is Officer Ramirez from the Los Angeles Police Department. May I please speak to Rowan Jones?"

I scratch my bare belly and hunt around for a hoodie. "Um, this is Rowan."

"Good news, Mr. Jones. I believe we have recovered your vehicle. We will need you to come in and identify it."

My heart leaps. "Really?"

She lists off the make and model, and it's my license plate.

"Oh my god, that's great news! Where is it? Is it impounded?"

"No, we don't impound stolen vehicles."

"Okay. Where do I have to go?"

She lists the address, and my stomach sinks. It's at least a two-hour drive away, and that's if I had a car. The public transportation system in California sucks, and I don't have the money for a ShareARide. Ironic.

Also ... is Wilbur okay? I know I should be more concerned about my car, but in reality, I want my plant, too.

"Okay," I say, after I've scribbled down the information on the back of a Taco Bell receipt. "Thanks."

I'm going to need help getting to the police station. I hit the button for Charlie, hoping I'm not asking him for too much. He left me on read yesterday, which I don't love. On the other hand, he said I made him come the day before, and he sent his health info, so... winning? Still, I hate to ask him for a ride. Again.

But sometimes a boy needs his daddy.

* * *

When Charlie appears at my door three hours later, his hair is more rumpled than when I saw him first thing in the morning at his house. It's like he's been running his hands through it nonstop. On the other hand, I'm clean and dressed and have had a healthy breakfast of my last off-brand Pop-Tart.

My heart leaps out of my chest at the sight of him, and I bite my lip. Charlie's wearing jeans and a flannel shirt and work boots, and he looks like some kind of mountain man. I want to climb him. He smells like that hinoki lotion he uses. (I looked it up online. Out of my price range.) "You came," I whisper.

"You called," he says.

I stand there, fidgeting. "Do you want to come inside?"

"Yeah," he says. He leans down and kisses me, and it warms up every cell in my body.

When we stop, I keep clinging to his biceps a little longer. "Thanks for coming." Finally, I take a step back and let him in.

"Of course. You need your car. And besides ..." He rubs the back of his neck. "I wanted to see you."

"I know it's not much," I say apologetically, looking at the stained futon in the living room.

"It's fine. This is where you are right now."

"Not for long," I mumble.

"What do you mean?"

I pick up the papers I was served with this morning, which Floyd left on the counter when he got up to eat cereal. "I paid my roommate rent, but he never paid our landlord. For months now."

Charlie glances at the documents and crosses his arms. "Oh. Really?" His voice is dangerously quiet.

"So I'm a short-timer here."

"Where are you going to go?"

I shrug. "I don't know. There's always someone with a room advertising online. I can find a place."

"That's not safe," he says sternly. "You could end up with some kind of weirdo who's going to hurt you in your sleep."

"I'd like to see them try."

He wraps his arms around my waist. "Rowan, I know you think you're all badass—"

I scowl.

"—and you are. But you aren't invincible." He rubs his face. "Dammit, this is a bad idea, but what if you come live with me until you get back on your feet?"

My expression morphs to one of confusion, while at the same time my heart rate speeds up. "What's your perfect man going to think about that?"

"I'm not seeing him anymore," Charlie says quietly, his hazel eyes locked on mine. He has very long eyelashes. "At least, not like that. I agreed to go to a work event with him, but only as a friend."

I blink. "What?"

Charlie tilts his head to the ceiling and lets out a heavy sigh. "Fucking him when I'm ... like this ... isn't fair to him."

"Why not?"

He sucks his cheeks in. "It just isn't."

I'm in need of some serious time to process that. Does it mean Charlie has feelings for me? Or does it mean he felt guilty about what we did? Or did he realize the guy wasn't for him, but he doesn't want me, either? I'm not sure I like him going out with the guy, even if he's not fucking him.

Shit, that's a mess.

"Come stay with me," Charlie reiterates.

I shake my head. "I can't just freeload off you."

Charlie gives me an intense stare. "You've been out of work for over a week. Where are you going to get money for another place?"

"I'll figure it out," I mutter, staring at the floor.

He puts a finger under my chin and kisses me, harder this time —until I'm breathless. "Pack your things. Let's get you the hell out of here."

Ugh, the command voice. I love that voice.

Some ingrained part of me wants to argue with him, but ... let's be honest, it's a small part. Besides, it would likely be futile. "This is just temporary," I say. "And I'll start paying you rent as soon as I get some income."

"You don't have to, but if it makes you feel better, then fine." He heads down the hall and swivels his head. "Which one's yours?"

I nod to the door on the right, and he pushes it open. My room looks even more barren when I imagine what he's thinking.

He scowls and puts his hands on his hips. "Grab your shit, and let's go."

It's the command voice again. I'm helpless against it.

It only takes us two trips to get every single thing I own shoved into the back of his Land Rover. I flip off Floyd's room when I leave. He never even came out to see what was going on.

Time for me to start over. Again.

* * *

At the police station, I show them my driver's license.

"Is this your current address?" the officer asks, pointing at the card.

Funny how they ask that every time. They must know people move around a lot. "Um. No. I'm between houses."

"Put down mine," Charlie says, and he rattles off the address.

"We'll be in touch if we find the suspects," the officer says. "We may need you to identify them."

"Okay," I say, and am heartened when the keys are back in my hand.

I'm afraid to see what kind of condition those jackasses left my car in, but I suppose it can't be that much worse than it already was. Besides, the car isn't what really matters.

"I'll show you to the lot," the officer says, and Charlie and I follow him.

There, parked in the back, is my beat-up old Corolla. I cringe. Compared to Charlie's car, it's such a piece of shit.

But ... I squint, and as I get closer, my shoulders slump. I press my lips together tight. My stomach clenches, and my heart feels like it's shrinking.

"No," I whisper, my hands flat on the passenger window.

Wilbur's gone. Those motherfucking *bastards*. How dare they take him?

"We had to tow it here, because it was out of gas," the officer says. "But we can give you a gallon or two to get you to a gas station."

I'm barely listening, and my body's started to shake.

Is it weird that I'd rather they'd found my plant than my car?

"Assholes," I mutter. "Did they just use it for a joyride?"

"It seems like it," the officer says. "If everything else is in place."

"It's not," I say. "They took my ... personal belongings."

"What personal belongings?" the officer asks.

"I had a plant in there. It has sentimental value."

More than sentimental value.

"I bet it's long gone." The officer's tone isn't unkind, but he clearly isn't going to start a search for Wilbur. He's got important things to do—which don't include finding a grown man's plant.

But at least with a trip to the gas station and maybe the car wash, I can be back in business.

The officer brings over a gas canister, and I get in the car and start it up. I try not to peel out of the parking lot, but I hate being around the police.

I follow Charlie down the street, and he pulls in at the first gas station he sees. Now is not the time to argue over the fact that there's another station down the block with a lower price.

It occurs to me that, after I fill up, I could just leave. I could sleep in my car and get some trips going and get some money and go on with my life. But before I can check my bank balance to know how much gas I can buy, Charlie slides in front of me and slips his credit card into the pump.

It's not the money. Or it's not *just* the money. It's his kindness.

Charlie may call himself an asshole, but I know the truth. He'll bend over backward to help a stranger.

In that moment, I know something else, too: He's mine.

CHAPTER 13

Charlie

Rowan's behind me, and every time I look in the rearview mirror he's still there. But I keep expecting him to take off.

I don't want him to, obviously. I don't want him living anywhere like that shithole apartment ever again.

Even so, I realize that bringing him to live with me isn't the best idea I've ever had. But he's not going anywhere without me if I have anything to say about it. At least not unless he's taken care of.

When we get to my place, I pull into the garage, and Rowan continues down the block. I tell myself he wouldn't follow me all the way here and then ditch me, but my heart rate still picks up, and I jog out to the sidewalk, sighing with relief when I see him parking in an empty space a few houses down. The spot right in front of my house is occupied by a car I don't recognize—a black Dodge Charger—with someone in it, doing something on his phone. Probably texting or looking up a location. But I don't like the look of him.

I trot over to Rowan before he gets out of his car. "You can park next to me in the garage," I call through his window.

For a second, he looks like he's getting ready to argue. It seems like that's his default setting, and given what he's told me about his life so far, I can understand why. He deserves better, though. I'm going to do everything I can to change what he expects from the world.

"Don't park your car on the street in LA if you don't have to," I say. "I'm sure you know that already."

After a moment, Rowan nods. He starts the car again and turns around, maneuvering into the space next to mine. I like seeing it there. I like the way it says two people are going to be living here. It's ... right.

"Do you want to set up your air mattress in my office?" I ask as we start hauling bags out of the back of the Land Rover.

"Is that where you want me to stay?"

Hell no. All I can think about is Rowan naked.

"I want you in my bed, god help me. I presume you don't have any objections to that?"

He smiles. "No objections."

We leave the air mattress in the garage and pile Rowan's things haphazardly in my bedroom. I like having him in my space. Do I know him? Not really. But being close to him feels right.

And let's not ignore the desire coursing through me. I keep eyeing him when I think he's not watching me. His sexy, languid movements. His wild hair and crystal-clear eyes. All those tats. That smart mouth.

I want that mouth on my cock. I keep remembering the way he sounds when he comes—both when we were in the shower and the recording on my phone, which I saved and have listened to more times than I can count. I swallow hard.

"Um," I say, looking around. "I can clear you a spot in my closet."

"I don't need it," he starts, but I glare at him.

"You do."

Rowan looks at me like he wants to argue, but he doesn't, and I feel like that's a win. He studies my face. "Really? This is okay?"

I nod. "Yep. More than." We put his clothes away, and he sets up his books in my office. That's all he has, practically.

"Want something to drink?" I ask.

He nods and follows me into the kitchen. Before I can do it, Rowan goes to the sink and starts filling two glasses with water. His ass is sticking out delectably as he leans over the counter, and I can't be certain, but I suspect he knows exactly what he's doing.

"Are you okay?" I ask.

"Yeah," he says quickly. Too quickly. He hands me one of the glasses.

"You said you were missing a plant. What plant? Why did you have it in your car?"

For a long moment, he doesn't answer me, just sips his water. Then he sets it on the counter and faces me, his hands clasped in front of him. "Like I told you, I don't know who my mom or dad were." I'm listening, even though this isn't the way I expected his answer to begin. "I grew up going from home to home. Some were foster homes and some were group homes, but I never really had a place to call mine. And that didn't change much once I was on my own. For as far back as I can remember, the only constant I ever had was Wilbur. He's a philodendron. That's a houseplant with leaves shaped like hearts. Nothing special or rare—you can probably get them at Home Depot or wherever. But he was mine, and now he's gone."

That's the saddest thing I've ever heard, I want to say, but that would be rubbing it in, and even I can refrain from being a dick some of the time. "In summary, Wilbur matters to you."

"He does." Rowan's eyes go to the floor, and he touches his throat. "I had nowhere else to turn today, even though I didn't want to admit it. Thanks for coming to my rescue. Thank you for letting me stay here. Thanks for—"

My cheeks heat. "You're welcome. I want you here."

His eyes scan me up and down, and I can't pull in a full breath when he looks at me like that. "I can't believe I'm living with the sexiest man I've ever seen," he says.

Yeah, I've had enough with keeping my hands off him.

I move forward and capture his mouth in a strong kiss. His response is immediate, opening to me and letting me plunder him.

Rowan turns and pushes me against the counter.

"Fuck," I groan. "What I want to do to you."

His hands cradle my face. Mine are behind his neck, holding him as close to me as I can.

"I really missed you the past few days," Rowan says between kisses.

"I missed you, too."

Something about Rowan makes it easy for me to be honest. Maybe because he doesn't have any preconceived notions about me. I don't have to pretend I'm something I'm not. With him, I can just ... be myself.

Rowan rubs against me, and his hand snakes down to the front of my jeans. My cock is rock hard. He grins up into my neck. "Can we fuck?"

I move my head so I can look at him. "Is that how you seduce all the guys?"

Do I want to explore his tight ass? Absolutely. Do I want to make him moan in pleasure? Also yes. I want him writhing under me.

In short, I want to fuck him, his clunky request notwithstanding. Although I suppose it was no more blunt than a lot of conversations at the club.

I assume he wants to bottom, with the way he's talked, but I need to be sure. It's been a long time since I've topped, but damn, I want to. "Do you want me inside you?"

Please say yes. Please say yes.

Rowan bites his lip and gives me doe eyes.

"I need an answer."

He shivers. "Yes."

"Do you need time to prep?"

"I should be good. I believe in manifesting—"

"Then come on, baby boy," I growl. I pick his ass up, and he wraps his arms around my shoulders and his legs around my waist. We kiss the entire way down the hall. When we get to my bedroom, I set him down carefully, then strip off my flannel and my T-shirt.

He's watching me with interest, but I notice a resolute set to his shoulders.

I cock my head. "Are you okay?"

"Yeah." His nostrils flare. "We're doing this."

I pause, my hands on my waistband. "I may be an asshole, but I'm no goddamn rapist. We don't have to have sex, today or at all. I'm not gonna force you."

"You're not. Although a secret wish of mine is that you would," he admits. "Or would pretend to. I mean, it wouldn't really be forcing me."

It seems he feels safe sharing his truths with me, too.

"What do you think?" Rowan whispers, trailing a finger up from my belly button, over my abs, between my nipples, all the way to my Adam's apple. "Do you like the idea of holding me down? Making all the decisions for me? Bending me in half? Shoving your hard cock in me while I try to get away?"

My cock could be made of titanium. "Shit, Rowan."

He smirks at me. "I like that part of you is bad."

I drop my pants and stand there in only my boxer briefs, which are tented out over my erection, letting him look for a moment. I'm so hard I'm soaking the fabric. Then I move to him and tug his T-shirt up and off. "Maybe you're right," I say.

"Be yourself with me," he orders, and I again capture his lips with mine.

Against his lips, I pant, "Same."

Rowan unbuttons his jeans and shoves them off, along with

his underwear and socks. He gives me a dazzling smile. And he's so damn erect. Without hesitation, I drop to my knees, push his foreskin back, and suck his tip into my mouth.

Rowan's knees wobble, and he whimpers. "Oh, shit. Charlie. That's ... fuck. Yes."

As I bob up and down on him, he runs his fingers through my hair, then tugs so roughly my eyes water. The bite of pain—I love that. I love how it feels to gag on his cock. It's disproportionately big, but I can still get most of it down.

My fingers go exploring between his legs, playing with his balls, pressing into his taint. Then I go back farther and circle his entrance with the tip of my finger.

He shivers. "You're gonna make me ... have anticipatory early jizz. I don't want to come yet."

I smile around his cock and pull off, chuckling. "'Anticipatory early jizz.' Only you, Rowan. Need lube, then," I say, standing up.

Rowan catches my eyes over his shoulder as he bends, his feet on the floor and his chest on the mattress, putting his perky ass on display for me. I stroke my own cock a few times before going to him.

I fall to my knees and bite each side of that peach. Then I bite the Care Bear tattoo he for some reason has on one ass cheek— Cheer Bear, if I recall correctly. The pink one with a rainbow, because of course.

"Charlie," he moans. "I need you."

"Patience." I slap his ass and watch it bounce before spreading his cheeks and licking down his crack. When I get to his hole, I stop there, focusing attention on it.

He gasps. "Oh, hell."

I keep at him, loosening his entrance. Before long, though, I can't take it anymore and grab the lube. I spill some into my hand and slide two fingers into him, but when he jumps and lets out a grunt, I scale it back to one. For all his talk, he's tight as hell.

Rowan's wriggling under me and fucking against the mattress.

I slap his ass with my other hand. "Stay still. Don't make yourself come yet."

"Ugh. Fine. It's so hard," he whines.

"I hope you're damn hard."

I watch the way his muscles move as I put that second finger back into him. The way his ass clenches around me. I'm aching to fuck him hard, but he needs prep first. I want him to howl in pain —but not too much pain.

I lick his ass cheek as I work another finger into him. I bite where I licked, then move to the other side.

Finally, I think he's ready. I get to my feet to riffle in a drawer.

"No condoms," he whimpers.

I stop and stare at him. "What? No." Except now that he's said the words, I want that so badly I can't explain it. Images of my come leaking out of him swirl around my brain.

"Why do you think I sent you my test results? I want your come in me, Charlie."

The hairs on the back of my neck stand up, and adrenaline floods my body. "I never go bare."

"I'm begging you."

Is it reckless? Not as reckless as it would've been last week, but it doesn't feel totally safe, either. I've known Tristan five years, and we always used a condom.

But. Some primal, possessive instinct is taking over, and I'm not questioning it. I want to fuck him raw.

"Okay, baby," I whisper, and I return to him, my eyes locked on the tattoo at his nape. I bite it. "*Baby boy.*" I run a finger down his spine to that ass I want to own. His chest is on the bed, our feet on the floor.

I dribble lube on my cock and push some of the liquid inside him. He's as loose as he's going to get, I think. With my breath catching, I slide my cock against his hole. He's shorter than me, but he's up far enough on the bed that we line up. I watch his shoulders, which are braced for impact.

He wants this. I want this. I'll give him what we both want.

Holding his hips, I press into him, but his body resists, and I pop out. So I try again, pushing my tip inside him, and this time I make it farther. It's hard work, especially when he's clenching up. He suppresses a yelp, but it sounds like pain, and I freeze. "Baby. You okay?"

"Ow, ow," he whimpers into the mattress.

I rub his upper arms and kiss his shoulders, then move my hands down him, trying to soothe him and ignoring how I like hearing him whine. "Want me to stop?"

"No, it's fine. I just didn't think it would hurt this much."

"Does it always hurt you?"

"I wouldn't know," he says. And my cock slides in a little more as his body gives way. His blue eyes catch on mine as he looks over his tattooed shoulder.

Shock and concern spike through me. How much am I hurting him? He didn't tell me ...

Wait, he's a virgin?

I stare down at my hard cock making its way into his body, and some primitive part of my brain takes over.

I don't know much. But I know for sure that no matter what anyone else says—and "anyone" includes my plans, my conscience, and my logic—Rowan's *mine*.

CHAPTER 14

Rowan

"This is your first time with a guy?" Charlie demands, his cock feeling so huge inside me I want to scream.

I've got tunnel vision, and my ears are ringing. I'm lightheaded from the pain, but I don't want to stop. I know it's supposed to get better.

And talking is helping. "I've been with guys," I pant. "I'm not a virgin. I just haven't been fucked before."

"Why didn't you tell me?" Charlie sounds hurt, but that's mixed with a husky desire. His voice drops to a low murmur. "I thought, what with that tattoo—among other things—you were more experienced."

I sigh. The extreme stinging pain is—thankfully—starting to ebb. Now, my skin's burning up. "That was just to piss off some foster parents. And to manifest the daddy of my dreams. You know: If you act like you already have something you want, then it comes."

My hands clench the sheets tighter and then relax as my body lets him deeper.

"I'm not your goddamned daddy," Charlie tells me for the

millionth time, his lips to my ear, his rumble warm. His muscular chest is plastered to my back.

I'm tempted to point out that he's totally my goddamned daddy.

I plant my feet solidly on the ground, ready for him. Pain won't stop my attitude. I inhale through my nose, exhale through my mouth, and say, "Fuck me like you're my daddy anyway. Take over my body. Use me. Show me what the fuss is about—"

Charlie groans so loud I think he's going to implode. His body's trembling with the effort of holding back. He's gripping my hips tight enough to leave bruises. His nails are cutting half-moons in my skin. *Hell yes.* His voice is barely more than a growl. "So this is the first time anyone's been inside this gorgeous ass." He bites my shoulder, and he's not at all gentle about it.

I moan.

Now that my body has loosened up, I'm loving the overfull feeling of Charlie being in me, around me. On top of me.

I'm overwhelmed, and I never want it to stop.

"I've used lots of toys. I've trained. Put me in, coach," I whisper.

"Okay, baby. I'll do it," and Charlie's words make my body relax even more. His tone sharpens. "But you tell me if you need me to stop."

"Just fucking move, Charlie. Please," I'm begging, and there are actual tears in my eyes that I blink away, because I don't fucking cry. They're partly from the sting, partly because this is a dream come true. Finally, *finally* a man is taking me. And it's not just any man—it's the one I particularly want.

"I will. But we need more lube." Charlie pulls out—ow—and I hear the squelch of the bottle and feel the slight motion of Charlie's body as he strokes himself. "Okay, baby. Relax and bear down." He presses inside me again, some of the cool liquid smearing on my skin, and this time I'm more ready for him.

His feet bracket mine. He takes hold of my hips and starts

thrusting into me, his cock hitting that spot that makes little bursts of light explode behind my eyes and brings my own cock to full hardness.

I loved having a dildo up my ass, but I couldn't get the right movement with one. It wasn't the same as the feeling of a big man behind me, using my hole for his pleasure. There was no warmth, no connection, no sweat dripping on my back. A toy doesn't talk.

Charlie does. He bends closer, tugs my hips off the bed, and reaches around for my cock. He starts crooning in my ear. "Do you have any idea how hot you are? How beautiful? How your ass was made for my cock? You feel so *fucking* good, baby boy. I'm going to ruin you for any other man. This ass is mine. You're fucking *mine* now."

Yes. I want to belong so badly to someone—but not just someone. I want to belong to *him*.

Scrap your plans, Charlie.

Take me.

I'm yours.

The ringing in my ears returns, but I can still hear Charlie. My breath is coming faster as he knocks it out of me. I'm clutching the bed, trying to hang on.

The constant stream of his soft words combined with his harsh fucking makes my entire body shiver.

And then everything magically gets even better. My body's loose, I'm letting him move me where he wants, and I'm meeting his strokes with my ass.

Utter euphoria takes over.

My brain and body are in harmony, and they're saying *please, yes, Charlie. Fuck me, Charlie. Let yourself go.*

Charlie's not just using my hole. The tip of his cock keeps nudging and rubbing against the part inside me that sets off fireworks. His movements are rough but somehow on the correct side of too much. It's *perfect.*

I'm basically hanging on for the ride now, and I'm not even

sure of the noises that are coming out of my mouth. I think it's something like "Oh-oh-uhhh-uhh-oh-oh, fuck, oh-uh."

Distantly, I can hear his murmured words. "Rowan, baby. I'm not coming in this tight ass until you come. I want you to come so hard you don't remember your own name. Nothing but the feeling of letting go and falling off the cliff." He tightens his grip and adjusts the angle again, and *holy fuck*. "No, you're not going to fall off it. I'm going to *throw* you off of it and then leap off with you. We're going to do it together. Ready, baby boy?"

I nod. "Hell yes, Dadd—Charlie."

He chuckles and licks from my shoulder up to my ear. From there, he sucks on the back of my neck—over the tattoo, *nrgh*—then licks down to the other shoulder. His strokes on my cock start focusing only on the tip, and the motion of him fucking into me makes me fuck his hand. Repeatedly.

Is there a world beyond this bedroom?

Pretty sure there isn't. Nothing exists but Charlie and me. Specifically, nothing exists but his cock in my ass. He's fucking me like I'm the key to the entire universe. Like I'm magic. Like I'm necessary.

"Hell. Yes. Please. I can't handle it anymore," I whimper, scrabbling on the bed. "Make me come, Charlie. Fuck, please do it. Please—"

Charlie hits some trigger inside me, and I tense up, followed by an *oh my god, fuck I'm coming, I'm coming, for the love of everything that's holy* complete release. One where I'm jetting come all over his bed, where I'm trembling. He fucks me through the orgasm, and I want him to keep doing it for eternity. I'm oversensitive, yet I want him to keep going.

He does.

I'm floating. I barely know what he's doing, and I don't care. He can have me.

I'm his.

I'm so his.

CHAPTER 15

Rowan

Finally, Charlie shoves deep and, with a low, sexy groan, starts coming inside me. His dick is pulsing, and I can tell he's lost in the ecstasy I was just in. He's rutting into me, chasing the last of his bliss.

Even after he finishes, he's still panting, holding himself over me, and making little inroads into my ass as his cock softens and he comes down from the high.

Leaning down, he reaches for my lips, and I kiss him fiercely over my shoulder. I'm sweaty all over, and my body feels as used as it did when I walked ten miles or however the hell far it was last week. Only today's exercise paid off in euphoria rather than blisters.

Charlie's hot dick slips out, and come starts running down the inside of my legs. I'm oddly fascinated by the feeling of the rivulets leaking out.

His spent dick rubs against my thigh as he kisses me again. "Stay there. I'll get something to clean you up."

"Like I could move," I complain.

But I'm not really complaining.

Because ... I get it. Why people do this. I feel so close to him. I want him inside me permanently. I want *him* permanently. I don't care if it's an impulsive decision. Something about Charlie feels very, very right.

Charlie comes back with a warm, wet washcloth, and he starts at my ankles, catching the drips. He cleans my abused hole and then produces another washcloth to take care of my sticky dick. When he's finished, he lifts me fully onto the mattress. I curl up, snuggling into his pillow, which smells deliciously like him.

"Give me a second. I'll be right back."

He goes into the bathroom and, I assume, cleans himself up. When he returns, he brings me a glass of water and some Advil. "I don't know if you're gonna be sore," he says apologetically.

I take the pills and swallow them down with the cold water. Then Charlie climbs in next to me, still naked. He holds open his arms, and I cuddle into him.

I bite my lip and put up those walls to keep from crying, even if it's the good kind of crying. The kind where I finally, *finally* got what I wanted. In so many different ways.

But no goddamned crying.

I go years without crying, but lately I've been brittle, having to fight back tears all the time. Dammit all to hell. I'm satisfied, but I also feel so alive. Yet boneless, too. Charlie smells good, like sex, and his lips are on my skin as his big, warm arms hold me. I feel very small next to him. I feel small next to most people, but even more when I'm close to him.

"I've never cuddled with any man before," I whisper.

He stiffens. "Never?"

My brain is floating away, and I start babbling, though it's the slow kind of babble where my words take a while to come out. Where all of my body is touching all of his and I'm warm and comfortable and without a filter.

The invisible guards at the entrance to my life story just wave Charlie on past. I open the door to the walls around my soul and let him in. He's allowed to know everything about me.

So here goes a small start.

"Never. I messed around with a few guys in some of the foster homes, but we couldn't get caught. It was just ... quick blow jobs behind a building or whatever."

"What about after you moved out?"

I shrug. "The things I did were still just ... get off fast."

"And you really never had anyone tap your ass?"

I guess he keeps asking because it seems like I'm lying, but I don't lie to Charlie. "Nope. Not until you. And how long until you'll do it again?"

Charlie lets that question pass. "Have *you* fucked anyone?"

"A girl, once," I admit. "We were both eighteen. It didn't go well."

"I had sex with a woman once, too," he says. "Just to figure out that part of my sexuality." He grins into my shoulder. "I'm gay."

"Yeah. Me, too."

We stay there in his bed for a while. I'm overheated with his arms around me, but I don't care. Because I love it. I love the sensation of his soft cock against my skin. His chest against my back. I want him to stay with me always.

Then my stomach growls.

He chuckles. "Are you hungry?"

I nod. "You?"

"I could eat. Want me to order something?"

"Sure."

"Do you have a preference?"

"Tacos work," I say, and he nods. "I'm good with spice."

Charlie orders Mexican food and comes back to bed, settling us into the same position we were in before.

I thread my fingers through his. "Is sex always like that?"

He holds me closer. "No."

"Hmm."

We spend the next hour kissing, and Charlie makes me come

again. We'd keep going, but the doorbell rings and Charlie answers the door wearing only his gray sweatpants.

I want to lick him all over.

At Charlie's kitchen table, wearing my briefs and one of his shirts, I crunch on chips and tacos and pepper him with questions. What's his family like? He's on good terms with his parents and his siblings. He has a sister, Reyna, in addition to his older brother, the one he does the DIY stuff with. Where did he grow up? The San Fernando Valley. He loves making movies and will spend hours editing them.

"I thought you did that for a living," I say. "Social media stuff."

He snorts a laugh. "I wish. No, I'm a lawyer."

I blink. "But your Ad/VICE account is huge." Not that I spent every waking moment while we were apart going through every single video he's made.

"That's a hobby." Charlie's voice gets an edge to it. I pass him the guac, and he dips his chip into it.

"When do you have time to do that, if you're a lawyer?"

"I'm not a lawyer twenty-four seven," he points out. I stop asking him questions long enough to eat a taco.

After I've wiped my fingers, I ask, "Do you like it?"

"My Ad/VICE? Yes. Totally."

"No, being a lawyer."

He pauses for a really long time, half a taco sagging between his fingers. "No," he finally admits. "And I think you're the only person besides my brother I've ever said that to."

Something goes all wiggly inside me, and I don't think it's from our dinner. "Why don't you do something else, then?"

"Because ... I don't know." Charlie frowns, and his eyes go sad. I hate that I made him look that way, even though I know it's a question he should have been asking himself already. That look on his face makes me want to crawl into his lap and make everything better.

"Let me guess," I say. "You don't want to let the people you work with down? Don't want to waste your education? And what that actually means is that you don't want to let them know the real you?"

Charlie stares at me. "Am I that easy to read?"

I shrug.

"Yeah." He sighs. "That's how I feel. And I don't know what to do about it."

* * *

After dinner, I help Charlie toss the trash, then stand in the kitchen, shifting my weight from foot to foot.

"Should I ... Should we ...?" I don't even know what I'm asking. I scratch the back of my neck and look at the floor while he wipes down the countertop.

I'm not used to being a freeloader. What do I do now? Go back to his bedroom? The couch? It's too early to go to sleep.

I square my shoulders. "Just ... how long can I stay?"

With two steps, Charlie is looming over me, and I love it. "There's no deadline."

Yes. Not that I want to sponge off Charlie forever. But if I can figure out a way to get past that hurdle, the "forever" part sounds pretty good.

But I need to check. "You sure? You may never get rid of me."

"Well ... I'm pretty sure at some point you're going to commit some kind of crime—"

"But you're a lawyer, so you'll get me off."

"Oh, I'll definitely get you off." Charlie leers, and it makes me laugh.

Still ... I tug at my hair. "You think I'm a criminal?" I mean, he's right, but I don't need to admit that to him just yet. Haven't I already told him enough? He knows more than anyone but Xavier.

"I *know* you're a criminal, baby. Remember how we met?"

Charlie grins and pulls me by the hand into the living room, and something swoops in my belly. "I'm good with it. Netflix?"

He turns on the television, and the next little while is the most normal experience I've had in my life: lying against this beautiful man's torso while we watch an action movie. It makes my heart go all weird.

By the time the movie reaches its climax, I'm yawning and Charlie's practically asleep. "Come to bed," he mumbles.

Where did my yawn go? Energy is surging through me. Now that I know what it's like to be with him, I want it again and again. I plant my feet on the floor and extend a hand to him. He looks at it as if to say *I don't need that*, but then he takes it anyway.

I love holding his hand.

Charlie stands, and I strip off my clothes and waltz down his hall, naked. "Night, Chaz Daddy," I sing.

Ten. Nine. Eight. Seven. Six. Five. Four—

Two big arms grab me from behind and march me forward. I shriek, giggling, as Charlie sucks on my neck, one hand snaking down to wrap around my dick.

Hell yes. This is what I wanted. I'm not sure if this is Charlie's regular personality, but it's the way he is around me. And I want to keep him that way.

I rub my ass into his groin, happy to feel a steel pole there. "Fuck me again, Daddy?" I whisper.

"Aren't you sore?" he says, licking a stripe from my shoulder to behind my ear, so slowly it aches. As he continues to stroke the tip of my cock.

Yes, I'm sore. But *yes*, goddammit, yes. "A little, but I want you inside me anyway." The soreness is nothing like how sore my feet were the day I met him. This is the good kind of ache.

"You've been teasing me. I'm not going to hold back," Charlie warns.

"Please don't."

Charlie parts his legs slightly and rubs his cloth-covered cock against my bare ass. "*Fuck*."

"Yes, please."

We've been moving toward the bed, but Charlie has apparently run out of patience, because he spins me around, lifts me up (with a chuckle at my ungentlemanly squawk), then throws me on the bed and covers me with his big, delicious body.

Attacking me with his mouth. Exploring every inch of me with his strong hands. Grinding his hips into me.

I do the same to him.

Like the first time we kissed, his sweats are rough against my skin, but the abrasion feels good. It'll probably turn into rug burn tomorrow, but right now, it's making me so damn happy.

I feel *alive*. So fully alive.

After he preps me, he positions me on my back, folded in half, his searing gaze setting me afire.

And while he isn't as savage with me as he was the first time, I still come hard.

Once we've caught our breath, he drags me into the shower to clean up, changes the sheets, and gives me more pain relief, which I probably need.

"Are you doing anything tomorrow?" I ask groggily. "Do you have to work?"

"It's Sunday, baby." Oh yeah, normal people work Monday to Friday. "I could go into the office, but it's a slow time of year, and I need a break. Normally, I'd try to fit in some shooting with Cam, but he's not ready to start on a new project quite yet."

"Then let's go bowling for our date."

"We're not going bowling," Charlie mutters.

"That's what you think." I fall asleep next to my lover. Though not before I notice that he didn't say we're not going on any dates.

CHAPTER 16

Rowan

At the newly remodeled and kinda retro-chic/intentionally kitschy bowling alley, the sweet-looking girl with the septum piercing behind the counter is asking Charlie for his shoe size. The crash of balls smashing pins interrupts the Johnny Cash song playing in the background. I've just about got my first shoe on.

I try to suppress my grin, but it won't stay hidden. Sure enough, I'm on a second date with Charlie. He grumbled about going but then insisted on paying, so I know what's up. Charlie secretly wants to be here—he's just used to hiding his true feelings. Some sense tells me he thinks if people know what he really wants, he won't get it.

Or maybe I'm projecting. Could be why the only thing that ever mattered to me was Wilbur.

I'm making it my mission to know the real Charlie. Not the one he lets others see. And I'm going to let him see me. Scars and all.

I mean, if he wants my broke ass—which is fairly obvious, given how hard he comes when he's inside me—I'm all his. I only wish I could even out the economics between us somehow. Maybe there's some other job I can get to help pay for things. Or at least take him out.

Right now, I'm not sure I could afford to take him to Taco Bell.

It's lunchtime, and this place is at about 50 percent capacity. Not a favorite with the after-church crowd, I guess. The worker hands Charlie his shoes, and he comes over to where I'm sitting in the booth by the approach area.

"It's been a while since I've done this," he says, sounding apologetic, the shoes dangling from his fingers as he shifts his weight like he's not certain where he should sit.

"That's okay. You'll have second-beginner's luck."

"I'm not sure that's how it works," he mutters. But he sits down next to me to put his shoes on, and I watch him before I slip on my second shoe.

He's a size twelve. I'm not. I love how big he is compared to me. I love that he has to lean down to kiss me. And when he bends his knees so he can fuck me, *nrgh*—yeah, I'd better not think about that here, since my jeans are pretty damn tight already.

Charlie looks simultaneously hip and ridiculous in mismatched bowling shoes with the number twelve on the back. Like he's going to a 1950s dance in red-and-blue suede saddle shoes.

He stands and walks over to select a bowling ball, and I watch every move he makes. The way the pockets of his dark wash jeans are placed perfectly on his ass cheeks. How his belt emphasizes his lean waist. How his shoulders are broader than his hips by far, and how the plaid shirt he's wearing has bulges where his biceps make it pop.

GODHE'SSOBEAUTIFUL. My heart. I want to squish him and boop his nose. And then let him have his way with me. I shiver, and Charlie looks at me quizzically. I shoot him a smile and finish tying my shoe before striding over to the rack of bowling balls. I choose one based on the fact that it matches my hair, rather than by weight or position of the finger holes—priorities, right? When I return to our lane and set my ball on the stand, I see he's taken a seat in front of the screen to type in our information.

He starts to enter "Charlie" in the scoring section, but I launch myself into his lap and take over. "Oh, no. You're not putting down your real name. I'm thinking you're gonna be 'Chaz Daddy.'"

Charlie pinches my waist like he's going to tickle me and lifts his knees up to try to tip me off. "Ugh. Fuck no. Don't call me Chaz, and I'm not your daddy."

I type as fast as I can, while he keeps trying—not that hard—to get me off of him. It's like I'm on a bucking bronco, but I keep my seat. The group at the next lane over glances at us, and I give a little wave with the hand I'm not using to type. "Too late," I say to Charlie, having hit enter. I grin, pleased.

His lips touch my nape, and his voice is husky. His strong arms wrap around me. "Then what do we put down for you?"

"'Baby Boy.' Obviously." I type it in while squirming in his lap. I hit enter again and turn to face him.

Charlie rolls his eyes, but the side of his mouth quirks up the tiniest bit. I give him a quick kiss and hop off.

Now my pants are really too tight, but thankfully it doesn't seem like anyone's paying that much attention to us. The group who looked at us earlier is cheering for one of their own.

After checking that my antics aren't going to get us kicked out or anything, I focus entirely on Charlie. I watch him exhale as he stands up, grabs his ball, and sets up at the line.

Then he bowls a motherfucking perfect strike.

"You asshole," I groan, slumping in the seat, my hand over my eyes. "You know how to bowl?"

When I peek, he shoots me a smile that blows me entirely away. A smile that makes my mouth dry and my pulse hummingbird in my throat. A smile that makes me want to tackle him, audience be damned. "Maybe," is all he says.

But two can play at that game. So I stand up with my big pink ball and pretend like I don't know how to set up or throw.

I look over my shoulder at Charlie. Then I throw the ball—perfectly—and don't bother to watch all ten pins fall.

Charlie doesn't say anything, but I do get an eyebrow raise. For him, that's like yelling. Finally, he asks, "So I guess you know what you're doing, too?"

"I had a foster family who were decent and enrolled me in a league so I'd stay out of trouble," I explain. "It was the nicest place I stayed by far. I've spent a lot of time throwing balls down a slick surface."

"My dad and I used to compete in a league when I was about twelve," Charlie says.

"Then we're evenly matched." I knew I was right to pick bowling for our second date. Next up, axe throwing. Or the shooting range. Or *Rocky Horror*—I've always wanted to see it.

We keep going, both of us getting strikes, frame after frame. I've never bowled a 300, although I've gotten close. But Charlie is bringing out my A game.

Finally, at the end, I throw a spare and Charlie gets a strike, and he does a "yusss" fist pump for his perfect score that makes me fall over laughing.

It's like he's peeled away layers of seriousness and remembered how to play. He reminds me of those dogs at the pound who need to feel safe before they can start wagging their tails.

Do I make Charlie feel safe?

Also: I think Charlie has the heart of a dog. He's loyal. He comes when I call him. He doesn't question me, even when I'm bad.

God, I want him. I want this to be real.

"Good job," I say.

"Thanks." It seems Charlie may have a shy side that I knew nothing about. No one knows, I suspect, except maybe his brother and sister.

This is very, very interesting. I nudge his arm, and it wraps automatically around me, squeezing my shoulders. Like he can't help touching me.

"Hungry?" Charlie asks.

I nod.

We walk over to the snack bar, which is one of those trendy sorts I've seen but never eaten at, with doctored-up tater tots, poke nachos, and all kinds of fruit with Tajín, along with house-brewed kombucha and beer.

Charlie orders ramen, and I get mixed kebabs with a spicy sauce, and we end up splitting both. As we sit at the Formica table, I pepper him with questions, which I think is my new favorite thing to do.

Correction: new favorite thing to do with our clothes on.

"Tell me some pet peeves," I say, licking sauce off my fingers and leaning toward him.

Charlie stares up at the black-painted ceiling, thinking for a moment. Finally, he says, "I hate bicycles built for two."

I snort out an uncouth laugh. "Who hates those?"

"Me," Charlie says. "They're annoying as fuck."

"That's ridiculous," I say, my smile making my voice sound extra fond. But I *am* extra fond of Charlie.

"You asked. Pet peeves are highly individual. What's one of yours?" Charlie sets down his chopsticks and looks at me intently, and the way he studies me—oof, I can't get enough. No one pays as much attention to me as he does. Nobody ever has.

I tap my lip with my finger. I asked. Don't I have some pet peeves? Maybe not. I blurt out the first thing that comes to mind: "I hate it when forms don't work for me. Like, I don't know my actual birthday, so I just put down what I was told it might be. I don't know the answers to a lot of the stuff that's required. I write big, so there's never enough room for me to write my name. And I hate it when there's no 'pink' option for hair color. I just don't fit into forms very well. Never have."

"You don't know your birthday?"

I shake my head. "I think it's maybe April 17."

"And that's because of your foster care situation?"

"Kinda."

He looks at me for a long time, as if he's debating whether to press me on it. But he gives me privacy. "Interesting. Forms have always been easy for me. I guess I see all forms as Kafkaesque bureaucracy. So if they want a letter, I give them a letter. If they want a number, I give them a number. Maybe I just always try to fit in."

"And I never will."

His brows furrow and release, and he tilts his head. "Do you want to?"

I shrug. "I don't think I do. Otherwise"—I gesture down my body—"I wouldn't look like this."

Charlie reaches out and tugs on a lock of my hair. God, yes, Daddy. Please. "Is your hair always pink?"

I take another bite of kebab. "It's often pink. Sometimes purple or turquoise. Or black."

"What is it naturally?"

"Kind of blond."

He nods and sips his beer. "Now that I think about it, the place where I really have pet peeves is in movies or books. I hate unlikable main characters. Or movies about movies. Movies where they have to put on a show or a play. Or when they have to go back in time to solve a problem. Or when love is the answer." Part of me wants to laugh at him for being so cynical. The rest of me feels heavy, my stomach clenched. Maybe I'm more of a romantic than I thought.

I swipe his beer when he sets it down and look at him over the rim as I raise it to my lips. "You don't think love is the answer?"

He crosses his legs and fixes me with a stare. "Shit, no. It's as bad as klieg lights."

I squint at him. "Super bright old-school movie lights?"

He nods.

"What's your problem with klieg lights, and what do they have to do with love?"

"They're a cliché," he huffs.

"Um." I chuckle at his indignation. "Most people don't pay any attention to that kind of technical shit."

"Why do you?" Charlie challenges.

"I guess because I've watched the bonus features on my favorite movies. I've picked up a few things."

"Makes sense."

Something inside me swells—a warmth, my nerve endings tingling, my pulse in my throat. I get the idea that Charlie doesn't open up to many people, and the fact that he's telling me all these things, even if they're banal ... it means something. I adore getting to know him. He's so quirky.

He slurps up some more noodles, and I don't know why I think the way he eats is adorable, but I do. "Oh, and I hate jazz," he says. "Like, free-form jazz. Regular jazz is fine. I just don't like rambling, five-minute improvisational piano solos followed by solos from every single other member of the band ... for every song. What's the point?"

I whistle. "That's a really random list."

"Most pet peeves are pretty random, aren't they?"

"True. But I love how it makes you seem all individualistic."

"I think that's the point. What are some more of yours?"

"I hate it when I can't see over someone at an event—a concert or whatever—and they won't let the shorter people go in front. I get annoyed when people think they're being all polite at a stop sign and letting someone else go first, but in reality they're being rude fuckers who are messing with the system."

"You sound irritated about all of that."

"Yep. That's why they're pet peeves."

Charlie leans across the table and kisses me. "I'll be sure to let you stand in front of me at a concert. And to take my right-of-way at stop signs."

"This is a good second date," I tell him. "Where are we going on our third? I'm thinking axe throwing."

Charlie rolls his eyes, but he doesn't protest. I take that as massive progress. I'll wear him down eventually.

Or maybe I already have.

CHAPTER 17

Charlie

I know, I know, I know. Addiction is a real medical condition with meaning and nuance requiring care and treatment, and I shouldn't be throwing the word around in this context. It's ableist. But I can't think of a better description.

I'm getting addicted to Rowan. What else do you call it when you get high from being around him? The feelings are so good, they soar. I want to know what he's doing at all times. I want him in the same room with me, at a minimum. Preferably, I want some part of my body inside him, although I'll settle for just touching him. I feel jittery when we're apart. I think about him constantly. And I don't calm down until I can see him again.

That's how people feel when they're addicted, whether to alcohol or drugs or shopping or sex or whatever, right? Without it, they can't function. If I can't have Rowan, I don't know how to be.

Yes, we've only known each other for a week. What can I say?

Unhealthy? Likely so. I don't give a damn. I just want him. All the time.

As I drive us home from the bowling alley, I get *overwhelmed*.

My heartbeat is strong in my ears and flutters in my chest. I'm fascinated by everything about him.

The way he's snarky and vulnerable at the same time. He doesn't hide anything very well, and even though, yes, we just met, I feel like I know him better than I know anyone else besides maybe my siblings and Danny.

The way he's a gives-no-fucks kind of sunshine despite having had what sounds like at best a very challenging early life. I'd never admit it, but I secretly love that he keeps telling me we're going on dates. Someday I might give in without protest. If we have a someday.

While I always assumed I was attracted to men who are older and bigger than me, I like Rowan. His anime hair. The button nose. The lines of his body and the color of his eyes. He smells like something that isn't body wash and isn't general male scent—I don't know, like someone bottled the wind and ran it through a field of dusky California sagebrush. Not in an allergy kind of way, but in a wild and free and good kind of way. And I love the way he talks. I love both his voice and the things he says. His quirky comments. "Anticipatory early jizz." Snort-laugh.

Don't get me started on that "baby boy" tattoo, although the idea that he got that intending anyone else but me makes me a little ragey. I want to make him wear collared shirts and scarves to cover it when he's not with me. I want to be the only one to see it. Because it makes my inner monster growl "MINE."

Okay, yeah. I'm having feelings for this little gremlin. I want to care for him. Make sure not only that he has food and clothing and a roof over his head, but that he's happy and healthy and intellectually stimulated. That he has whatever he needs and all the things he wants. It sounds like Rowan hasn't ever had anyone who made him their top priority, and if I have anything to say about it, I'm going to make sure that his happiness comes first from this day forward. No matter the consequences.

That doesn't at all fit into my ten-year plan, but if I'm being honest, the plan's been a massive failure. I've succeeded at everything the world says I should want—the job, the money, the looks, the prestige, the social proof—and none of it has made me happy. Maybe I need to toss the plan out the window and do something new.

We turn onto my street, and Rowan takes in the rows of cars parked along each side. "I can see why you like having a garage."

"Yeah, I'd hate to have to rely on finding street parking." I rub my chin and squint. When we left, I saw the guy sitting in that black Dodge Charger again. And he's still there now, still in front of my house. Is he watching us?

Just because you're paranoid doesn't mean they aren't after you.

This is a very clumsy attempt at surveillance, if that's what it is. Maybe I'm all wrong. "Do you get the feeling we're being watched?" I ask Rowan.

"All the time."

"No, I mean ... have you been seeing that car parked over there? It could belong to someone else on the street, I guess, but I don't remember noticing it before yesterday."

Rowan turns his head to look. "Yeah, I saw it earlier. Maybe it's someone who just moved in."

"That guy was sitting in the car yesterday, too," I say. "I don't think it's a new neighbor."

"Then I'll go talk to him," Rowan says, as I pull into the garage.

Before I can reply, he's hopped out of the car and is sashaying over to the man. He raps on the window.

The guy's in a black Adidas tracksuit with white stripes down the arms. He frowns at Rowan. "Can I help you?"

"We were just wondering why you're scoping out his place." Rowan reaches into his back pocket, pulls out his knife, and starts flipping it open and closed, his stance deceptively relaxed.

The man doesn't seem too impressed by Rowan, or by me when I take a place at Rowan's side. "Are you Rowan Jones?"

If the question surprises Rowan—and it would have to, wouldn't it?—he doesn't react. "Who wants to know?"

"That's confidential."

"Then my name's confidential, too, whether it's Rowan or Mike or Go Fuck Yourself."

Is this guy a process server? A private investigator of some kind? Is someone making an insurance claim based on something those guys did with Rowan's car?

The guy gets out of the Charger. He's not that big, but he towers over Rowan. Who, of course, steps closer. Every instinct in my body is screaming to tug Rowan back by his shirt and get in between him and the dude, but if I don't let him be his own tough self, I'll be taking away his power.

That doesn't mean I won't step in if it's needed.

I shouldn't have worried. Rowan's already got the knife pointing at the man. "It sounds like you don't belong here. So leave."

The man huffs out a laugh. "Is that how you are? Figures."

"What do you mean by that?"

"Nothin'. Just, little Chihuahuas sometimes are the loudest—"

Before Rowan slits Adidas guy's throat—or I punch the guy in the stomach—I bark, "This isn't your neighborhood. Why don't you move along?"

"Yeah, yeah," the guy says, getting back in his car. Then, under his breath, "I don't get paid enough for this shit."

While Rowan and I stand on the curb, the guy starts the car and drives away.

"What the hell was that about?" Rowan asks.

"I have no idea. Did you not want to ask him any questions? He was looking for you."

"Then he should've started off by saying what his business was. He didn't."

"Are you always this hostile?" I ask, once the Charger has disappeared around the corner. "Maybe you won a prize."

"Nah."

"Then you just like to be belligerent."

Rowan gives me the biggest smile. "It's like you know me."

I roll my eyes, and we go inside.

Stepping into my space, I note the immediate differences, sharing my home with Rowan. I've lived by myself since college, and I'm used to things being where I put them—the few things I have in this shell of a house. But now Rowan's setting his shoes in the entryway and his phone and wallet on the table by the door. His stuff is in my closet. And I like it that way. How is it that he can be so new and so established with me at the same time?

"Wanna watch Netflix?" Rowan asks.

I nod.

This feels ridiculously, uncomfortably comfortable. I don't even know what to think anymore.

* * *

I wake up Monday to Rowan under the covers sucking my dick. I groan in pleasure as his tongue massages an extra-sensitive part.

"Holy hell, baby. That's so damn hot." I run a hand through his hair, loving the way his mouth feels on me. The pressure is perfect, and between the friction and the wet, hot suction, I decide this is the best way to greet the morning.

I lift the blanket to expose his naked body, and he doubles down on sucking me. While I'm loving this, I'm not so gone that I can't tell that he's got his own hand on his cock.

"C'mere and get that cock down my throat," I order, and he slides off, his lips dark red and wet.

I tug him up to kiss him—a dirty, tongue-filled kiss—then smack his hip. "Turn around. Straddle my face."

He does so, positioning himself so his cock is dangling above me, and I tilt my head and get it between my lips. The angle's a little awkward, but we make it work, and now he's fucking my mouth while sucking on my cock.

Fuck, yes. Rowan's so hard I'm pretty sure he's going to come fast, and I let him abuse my throat, jabbing into me so I gag. He makes a move to stop when my body jerks, but I reach up and pull his ass closer, pull him deeper into me.

He comes, shuddering and salty-warm. After only a few more seconds, I'm coming, too, and then I lie back, panting.

Rowan turns around again so we're face to face, hips to hips. We kiss, and I taste us.

He pulls back. "Goddamn."

I reach out to touch him, wanting to run my hands all over his soft, tattooed skin. Rowan's eyes are glossy and bright, his pink hair a mess, and he smiles at me.

"Best way to wake up," I murmur, only a little hoarse. "Wanna do it again sometime?"

"Count on it," he whispers.

"Come on," I say. "Let's shower and get dressed."

When we're ready for the day and drinking coffee, I glance out the window and notice that the black Dodge has returned to its spot outside. I can see the white stripes of the guy's tracksuit. Shit.

Rowan must read the look on my face, and he peers out the window, too. "Oh, what's this bullshit?" Before I can stop him, he's out the door.

Dammit.

I set my coffee down and hustle out after him. Though I shouldn't condone confrontations, some part of me likes that I can't quite predict what Rowan's going to do.

Then I see him slip his knife from his back pocket. Oh, shit. I catch up with him. "What'cha doing, baby boy?" I murmur.

"My own neighborhood watch." He marches right up to the Charger. Before he can knock on the window, the guy's out of his car. In a flash, Rowan's got the knife open. "I thought I told you that you weren't welcome here. Are you some creepy Peeping Tom? You like watching us?"

"I just want to talk with you. Can you come with me?" The guy raises his hand like he's going to clock Rowan in the face or grab his hair or something, and I come up next to Rowan, hip to hip. Well, kind of.

"No. Tell me why you're here," Rowan demands.

"It's business."

"What business?"

"Personal business. I need to talk with you alone."

"Nope," Rowan says. "Leave."

"It's a public street. I can be here if I want to."

"Not if I have you arrested for stalking," I reply.

The guy chuckles, and it's a rusty sound. "Not if I have your Chihuahua arrested for assault."

"Go do your business elsewhere," I order. He looks like he wants to argue with me, but he closes his eyes and shakes his head. Then, like last time, he leaves.

So, what the fuck? Who is this guy? If he wants to talk to Rowan, why doesn't he just say what his deal is?

"I don't understand why he's hanging out," Rowan says as we walk back up to my front door. "I've already been served with that eviction lawsuit, and I've moved out. And I didn't put your address down on anything but the police report."

"Maybe he's investigating the car theft for the police. Maybe you were too impulsive when you scared him away."

"I'm pretty damn impulsive," he says. "And it usually works out for me."

"Hmm." I pick up my coffee mug, and we walk into the house.

As I'm preparing to leave for work, I say, "I feel uneasy leaving you here alone with that guy around."

"I'll be fine." Rowan grins, and it's his evilest grin. The one that makes me laugh. The one that reminds me he's fierce and fearless.

"I know. But still … call me if you need me. What are you going to do today?"

"I'll pick up some rides. I gotta get back to making money."

I don't know how much I like him working for ShareARide—especially when he got his car stolen once already—but I also don't want to be a controlling asshole. So I stay silent.

Rowan reads the look on my face. "I'll be more careful than usual. Plus, I want to see if I can find where those assholes tossed Wilbur. I may try to retrace wherever they drove my car."

"Do you even know where to start?" The chances of Rowan's Wilbur having been thrown out the window rather than taken home with the car thieves are very high.

"Yeah, it's a wild-goose chase. But I've been on one of those my entire life, trying to find my parents. So I'm good with lost causes."

"I'll help you look when I'm done for the day," I promise.

"It'll be dark. We can look together next weekend," Rowan says.

"You don't have to wait that long." I check the time. "Gotta go."

I kiss him before I get in my car, and it feels utterly domestic and utterly right.

Weird.

CHAPTER 18

Charlie

"Congrats on winning that motion to strike," Noah says, his tall form taking up most of the doorway to my office. He's got a Santa hat on, which I'm pretty sure Shelby put on him, because Noah's not that ridiculous. The rest of his outfit is a classic suit for court, sans jacket. His phone buzzes in his pocket, but he ignores it.

"Thanks," I mutter. Then I try to make an effort because one, Noah is very nice, and two, he's the cofounder of this law firm. "How's it going with you? Anything I need to know about?"

Noah starts telling me about a case he's working on, and I do my best to listen, even though my mind keeps wandering to what Rowan may be getting up to now that he's alone in the house. I wish I were there with him, instead of here in my office on the fourteenth—really thirteenth—floor of a high-rise building in Century City.

Most of the lawyers in the other firms in this building are assholes. Not so at Weston & Ramirez, which I'm grateful for even if I'd rather be doing something else. It often feels like we're this queer oasis of decency in the middle of a lagoon filled with sharks. I just happen to be our resident grump.

I've been spending the morning answering hundreds of mind-numbing questions called interrogatories. I'm not sure why I bother. No one reads this shit. At least not when it's crammed with a page of boilerplate objections.

Is it bad that I don't love my job? My parents' generation thinks I'm whining and should just put up with it and be grateful for a job that pays my bills and lets me live a comfortable life. But I don't want to put up with it. Life's too short. And yet here I stay.

Copy, paste, copy, paste. My wrist hurts with the repetitive motion.

So I guess my feelings on my job are mixed: I like the firm and the people I work with and the principles we stand for; I hate a lot of the actual work and a couple of my clients, who tend to poison the entire well.

Noah tilts his head, and the pom-pom on the end flips to the other side. "You good?"

I nod reflexively. Noah's not one I open up to. Now that I think about it, the only people I open up to besides Rowan are Cam, Reyna, and Danny. That's not a big list. But I don't want it to be a big list.

"You sure?" Noah asks.

God, he's the best. He's not technically my boss—I'm a full partner—but he still has this mother hen attitude where he wants everyone in the office to be happy. It figures he'd pick up on my thoughts when I'm wondering what the hell I'm doing here. Nothing like having a little existential crisis in the office. I feel like I shouldn't be complaining; I made my bed, and I should now sleep in it. So to speak.

Thinking of beds makes me think of Rowan in mine. And thinking of Rowan in my bed makes me think of things that are just for me. Not the things other people say I'm supposed to want. Not the things I've absorbed in my core that I think I'm supposed to do. But what I truly want, deep down inside me.

Also, hmm, when do I let people know about Rowan? I'm

hesitant to admit that I'm letting him live with me—not because I'm embarrassed about him, but because it's so early in our ... relationship. If we have a relationship. Most people don't let someone move in that they've known for only a week or so.

Although people do get roommates from the internet. They just don't usually let those roommates into their bed and sixty-nine them first thing in the morning.

Woof. That was nice.

I swallow. "I'm fine."

With another long look at me, Noah nods. "If you ever want to talk, I'm here, and you have friends at the firm, if you need to get something off your chest."

Am I really that obvious?

"Thanks," I mutter, and go back to my interrogatories. My main problem is, I don't know what I'd do for money if I left this job. I have a lot of sunk costs: My mortgage is more than a lot of people make in a month, and I don't have that much in savings. So I'm tied to my desk like I'm on a carousel and they wrapped a leather belt around my waist. Now I have to hold on for the rest of the ride.

My phone beeps, interrupting my thoughts. "Hey, Charlie," Shelby says. "Cormac Esmond is on line one. Do you want him to leave a message?"

Ugh. My least favorite client. And that's saying something.

Don't get me wrong. We have some great clients, and I've taken on some cool cases. I've done things that matter. That's just not the majority of my work. By far.

"No," I say. "Put him through." No sense in delaying the inevitable.

"Charlie," Cormac begins, "your bill is too high."

I roll my eyes. "I can assure you my timekeeping is accurate. The bottom line is, lawsuits are expensive. There isn't really any way around that."

"Well, what am I getting for this? It feels like the case is going nowhere. I'm just spending all this money, and nothing is happening."

"We are protecting your rights and being judicious about what we choose to do," I say, using the speech I've already given once today to another client. But having to justify myself and my rates gets old very fast. If people didn't get into trouble, they wouldn't need me.

"Okay, then what's going on with my case?"

"We're in the middle of the discovery phase, and I'm preparing interrogatories right now. We'll also be requesting that they send us all documents relevant to the litigation."

"Shouldn't that have been done already?" Cormac proceeds to tear me a new one, even though I've done everything I'm supposed to do.

I roll my eyes. Sure, if he were my only client—and if he actually paid my bills on time—he'd get better service. But as it is, calling me to complain that I haven't done enough when he hasn't paid for what I've done so far sits very, very wrong. "The final deadline to get it done isn't until October," I say instead. "We're actually ahead of the game."

"Hmm," he says, harrumphing. "Can't you poke at them? If I'm spending all this money, I want them to feel some pain, too. I'm the only one taking this seriously, and they're getting off scot-free."

"They aren't getting off scot-free. It's just not the time to get in front of a judge or jury yet. Lawsuits move slowly."

"Well, see if you can get them to cave. Write them a nasty letter."

My shoulders tense. I've done that already. But I suppose one way to get out my frustration with most of the human race is by drafting a cutting missive to opposing counsel. The problem is, it gets old when you do it every day. And while sometimes I care about the causes, other times—like now—I'm doing it just to do it. And that sucks.

"Of course," I say, knowing that I need to be obliging to clients. Even clients who are demanding more than they've paid for. "I'll send him something." And I make a note to increase my retainer amount so this doesn't happen again.

I type out a nasty email to the plaintiff's lawyer and send it to Cormac for approval. Merry Christmas to us all.

Then, while I wait for him to respond, I pull out a sheet of paper and title it "Charlie Cooper's [Next] Ten-Year Plan."

I stare at it. The only things on my previous list that I haven't achieved are a cat and a husband.

What do I actually want? I still want to get my hair cut regularly, and I like my clothes and house. I'm not giving up my Ad/VICE account. I'll still call my parents.

How come the only thing that I'm thinking of adding to the list is Rowan?

That seems like a very foolish thing to do. I should be writing down a number for my 401(k). I should be hiking up Mount Whitney or getting major endorsement deals or creating my own line of products related to my videos.

My fingers itch. I really do only want to write Rowan on my plan.

I crumple the paper and throw it in the trash. It's not the right time for me to figure out something I have to live with for another ten years.

CHAPTER 19

Rowan

After Charlie leaves for work, I call Xavier.

"Rowan! How's it going?" I can hear him chewing Big Red gum.

I smile. He's one of the few people who is always happy to hear from me. This is why I keep him around. "Around" meaning wherever the hell he is. Right now, I think that's San Francisco. "Hey, just wanted to let you know the address where I'm staying."

"You move again?" X's chair squeaks in the background as he likely shifts to take down the information.

"Yep."

"Shoot it to me."

I give him Charlie's address.

"Who are you living with? Another crappy roommate?" I don't blame X for being suspicious. My choices in roommates haven't been great. Even before Floyd, I lived in whatever rooms I could afford. Sometimes the people were decent, sometimes I never saw them, but sometimes it was bad—even worse than Floyd—and I needed to get out.

Feels like I've come a long way when I can tell my best friend, "No, I'm living with the hot guy I have a crush on. It's awesome.

Charlie's really grumpy, and I make him smile. He buys me food. He takes care of me. He's just … everything."

"You sound like you're in love." Xavier sounds wistful.

In love? Am I in love with Charlie? "I wish. It can't happen, though. He doesn't want someone like me. Not long term, at least." I've never had anyone want me permanently. I'm not sure I ever will.

"How do you know that?"

"He told me so." I'm still going over his words when he dropped me off that first day, although things have changed since then. He told me he broke up with the guy he was seeing—not that they were together enough to break up. But he hasn't told me he wants to be my daddy. Or, you know, date me. Yes, he's letting me stay here, but that doesn't mean anything. I've stayed in lots of places temporarily.

X interrupts my thoughts with, "Are you fucking him?"

I snort. "Sheesh. Blunt."

"Well?"

"Yeah. And it's really good."

"Must be nice," X says dreamily.

"You're still a virgin?"

"Yeah. Change the subject."

Since he and I have discussed his status ad nauseam, I oblige. "What's up with you?"

"I'm going to be going to Albrecht College next fall."

"Really? That's cool." It's a small school—and expensive. "Where'd you get the money for that?"

"Scholarship. For tuition and room and board and books and supplies. But I still need more money. I don't want to take out student loans. At some point, I hope all this hacking work is going to pay off."

"You're going to kick ass in college," I say fondly.

I can imagine his cheeks reddening. "Okay, can we change subjects again? Any new news on the DNA front?"

"Nope. It's just as much of a dead end as always. I've accepted that I'm not related to anyone in the whole world. Which is impossible, but whatever."

"I've looked for you on other DNA websites, and again, there's just nothing," he says. "Not even on the deleted sites. And I've searched for Rowan Jones—"

"That's pointless. First because Jones is such a common name, but mostly because who knows if it's even my name at all," I say. "Fat lot of good my birth certificate is. Mother: unknown. Father: unknown. Goddamn unknown."

I try to tell myself that all those unknowns mean freedom: I can be anything I want to be. But at the same time, I feel so untethered. Like there's nothing holding me to this world. I have no connections.

And it all seems like something's not adding up. Someone somewhere must want to claim me. Right?

"Maybe someday you'll get answers," X says. Unlike me, X knows who his family is. He's just better off without them.

"Or maybe my parentage is always going to be a mystery. I wonder if I'll get to meet Charlie's parents. I think they're local—he said he grew up in the Valley. Of course, he's a lawyer, so I'm sure he's super busy. Maybe he doesn't see them very often. And it's soon for meeting the family, isn't it. Or … maybe he's ashamed of me and wouldn't want them to know about me."

"Is he like that?" X's voice has gone sharp.

"No," I tell him. "I'm being whiny and needy and insecure, and that's not fair to him. Charlie seems pretty open with his feelings. I know that when he's being nice, it's because he wants to be. It's because he likes me. He's not trying to manipulate me. He just … likes me."

"That's cool. But yes, topic change, did you get your car back?"

"Yep. I'll need to start doing rides again soon. I'm a little traumatized from my car being stolen, though."

"That's understandable. I traced the account you sent me—Pierce."

I perk up. "You've found him?"

"No, it's a dead end. Let me keep researching."

"Thanks. I trust you."

"So for now are you just eating bonbons and watching TV?"

I laugh. "I haven't had time yet. I'd do some stuff around the house, except that Charlie's house is already so clean that there isn't much to do. It's also completely devoid of personality, but I don't feel right about changing things. He should decorate this place how he sees fit. Not me."

"Oh, god. Don't cook for him."

I snort-laugh. A little while after I say goodbye to X, someone knocks on the front door. I look through the peephole and see it's the guy in the Adidas jacket.

No, thank you. I don't want any.

For the rest of the day, I pace. I start snooping in Charlie's office, which is as neat and barren as the rest of his house. But I open a desk drawer, and there's a sketchbook in it.

I'd be invading his privacy if I were to open it, and I'm so damn tempted. But does Charlie have a secret, or maybe not so secret, artistic side? I suspect he made the coffee mugs we use. He likes to make videos. I wouldn't surprise me if he drew or painted, as well. I leave it alone but resolve to ask him about his artistic tendencies at some point.

Still, all day it feels like I'm being watched. What the hell? Tracksuit dude isn't here. I'm imagining things.

When Charlie gets home, it's like the world has opened up again. I throw my arms around him and jump up into his arms. He catches me easily. I want to gobble him up, and I kiss him hard, tugging on his necktie to free him from it.

"Before it gets too dark, let's go see if we can find Wilbur," he says between kisses.

"Oh my god, I can't believe I forgot to do that," I say, wriggling so he'll put me down. "I'm the worst plant dad ever."

"Nah, I'm sure you have a lot on your mind. But we shouldn't wait too long, or we'll never find him."

My heart starts beating for someone else for the first time. He's not making fun of my fixation on my plant. More than that—he's willing to drive the better part of an hour, each way, after working all day, to help me look for something seemingly unimportant that we probably won't be able to find. I bite my lower lip to keep it from trembling and square my shoulders. "I have no idea why I've become so," I wave my hands, "when I'm around you. I'm used to putting myself behind a big wall so no one can see that things get to me. Even when things were total crap in the group homes when I was a kid, I didn't cry." I look up at the ceiling. "Much. Definitely not when I got older."

"You can feel bad about missing a plant. Especially one with as much emotional significance as this one has." He wraps me up in his enveloping arms again, and it's like I'm one with him.

"Enough," I say, once I'm too hugged. "I can't feel all these feelings."

"Come on." He kisses the top of my head. "Let me change my clothes and grab some supplies, and then let's go."

He fills a backpack with snacks, water, flashlights, and jackets, and then we get in his car and retrace our route from the night we met. We go up the coast, past the Thai place he took me to.

"That's my new favorite restaurant," I blurt.

"Yeah?"

"That was the best-tasting food I've ever had." I pause. "And more importantly, the best company."

He gives me as long a look as he can without running us off the road, then turns his focus back to driving. "I liked the company, too," he says quietly. "I must be a weirdo."

"That makes two of us!"

We get to the end of the beachfront mansions in Malibu and

reach the part of the highway that's ocean on one side and mostly hills on the other.

"Aww, this is where we met!" I chirp.

He chuckles. "Fond memories of the scene of the crime?"

"Absolutely."

"Well, how far did you walk to get to here?"

I shrug. "The pickup was by the campground before Mugu Rock."

Charlie enters it into his GPS. "You walked *eleven miles.*"

"Fuck, I thought it was far." I shrug. "Marathoners would think I'm a wimp, but I'm not used to walking like that. And certainly not without a phone or jacket or anything."

He hands me a bottle of water, as if I'm dehydrated again just from being here. I don't know why Charlie takes such good care of me, but he does. And I'll be schmoopy about that, I guess.

"And they went north after they took your car?"

"Yeah." My voice is husky. "I don't like reliving it."

Charlie looks over at me. "I imagine not. Sorry. But I don't know how else to figure out where they might have gone."

We don't talk much as we drive the eleven miles, just listening to the radio station Charlie has on. "Is this the kind of music you like?" I ask after a while.

He nods. "What's wrong with it?"

"Nothing. I was just wondering."

"I get that it's kind of basic. I like it anyway. What do you like?"

"Metal and bubble gum pop." He goes to change the station, but I put a hand on his. "Leave it," I say.

"You sure?"

"Yeah, Daddy. I wanna make you happy."

He groans and keeps driving.

When we get to the entrance to the campground, I say quietly, "Pull over."

He does.

Ugh. This place. Bad vibes all around. Even in the dark, Charlie's headlights illuminate where they stole my car. "I'm not surprised the box is gone," I mutter.

"What box?"

"They tricked me into getting out of the car by having this big cardboard box. So I went to help them put it in the trunk. It was just a ruse—the box was empty. Anyway, I forgot to turn off the engine, so that was my mistake."

He shakes his head. "No one plans on bad shit happening."

"Still. I should've known better. It feels like it was my fault for being so trusting."

"I'd rather you be trusting than not," Charlie says. "Or, at least, that you trust the right people."

"I do trust you."

Charlie gives me a soft look. "Thanks."

I'm getting too much in my feels, yet again. I clear my throat. "So, from here," I say, pointing around the bend, "they took off north."

"Where in the car was your plant?"

"Over the passenger seat."

He thinks for a moment. "Okay, if the driver chucked it while he was driving, the natural thing would be to throw it out his window. Which would mean it would've ended up in the middle of the road and is likely long gone."

My heart is in my throat. Over a plant. I'm a sap. "God, that would suck."

"But you said there was a guy in the back seat, too?" He looks at me questioningly, and I nod. "He could've taken it and tossed it out the passenger side so he could sit up front." He scrubs his face. "Let's walk up the road a bit and see if we find anything." He gets the flashlights out of his backpack and hands one to me, and we get out of his car.

I note he turns it off and takes the keys. Smarter than me. Though I suppose I won't make that mistake twice.

We walk along the side of the road, flashing our lights here and there, trying to see down into any dips to where Wilbur might be lying in a ditch. After we walk a ways, we go back to the car and Charlie drives us up past where we were, then parks on the side of the road. And we repeat. We're walking in the dirt, getting blinded when cars go past us, coming across trash and debris, but no Wilbur.

Charlie's intent on helping me find my fifteen-year-old plant. He's not laughing at me or complaining. Just walking next to me, doing whatever he can to support me.

So, yeah. Just like that, in a roadside ditch, I fall in love with Charlie Cooper. Who else would take me to do something like this because he didn't want me to come alone or wait until the weekend when he'd be off work—and not even make fun of me?

Charlie's the best. I'll show him how much I care about him when we get home.

CHAPTER 20

Charlie

Reyna corners me in my office as I'm getting ready to head home. "We have to talk to Cam," she says. "He's fucking up with Shelby. He just called me asking for an intervention. If he's asking for it, you know things are bad."

Reyna's wearing an ugly Christmas sweater that lights up. She has one for every day in December, I think.

"Ugh." I groan, loosening my tie and swiveling around in my office chair. "Why does he sabotage himself? It's so easy to see the answer. He needs to get his head on straight. Just because his ex left him doesn't mean he's not lovable."

Reyna stares at me, her body entirely still, her arms crossed over her chest.

"What?" I ask, a defensive note in my voice.

"What's going on here? Who are you, and what have you done with CharlieBoo?"

I huff. "Whatever."

What's going on, Reyna, is I have my own little issues of the heart. What's going on is every night I go home to Rowan, and I want to possess him. I don't know how I went my entire life without knowing him, and now that I do, I don't like my life when he's not around. Work is intolerable. All I want to do is put on my dirtiest sneakers and go walking along ditches to see if I can find a philodendron. (If it weren't for Google, I wouldn't even know what they look like.)

Every night this week I've taken Rowan to search for Wilbur. We've slowly worked our way north from where Rowan picked up the miscreants.

We're looking for that proverbial needle in a haystack. Or Waldo. All we know is which direction they headed when they stole Rowan's car. It's just the one road for a while, and then, once it splits, they have limited choices for another while. So we go along the possible routes, checking both sides of the road to see if they tossed his pet plant out the window.

Rowan tells me he's looking during the day, too, when he's not busy. I don't like it that he's back doing rideshare work after he got his car stolen. But I bought him an interior dashcam, which I hope will cut down on the possibility of any future shenanigans. And he needs to feel useful, I think. I can let him work. That is, he doesn't need my approval or permission or anything, but I still need to remind myself not to make a fuss about it.

But ... Wilbur's still lost. It's funny how when I'm in the office doing repetitive work, I get all bored and grumpy. Looking for Rowan's plant, though, which is also repetitive and a lot more uncomfortable, is no problem at all, mostly because I want to erase that sad look from his face.

"So can you come over? We need to talk with Cam." Reyna's studying me.

"Fine. When?"

"Um, now? Follow me home. I have prosecco."

I give her a curt nod. "Give me a sec, and then yeah, I'm on my way."

"Great. Thanks." She turns on her heel, and I call Rowan.

"Hey, you okay?" I ask when he answers.

"Now that I hear your voice, I'm better," he says, sounding a little down.

"What's the matter?"

"It's just one of those days. I see all these lights going up everywhere, and I guess ... I don't know. Holidays are a weird time."

"I think I know what you mean," I say. "But I want you to tell me more. Except we can't right now. I'm going to be late coming home." It feels weird calling him to tell him this. Not since I lived with my parents have I ever felt like clueing someone in on where I was. But I don't want Rowan to worry. Not when he's been abandoned all his life.

"Okay. No problem." I can feel his ... not hurt, exactly, but his disappointment, through the phone. Like he thinks I'm going to go fuck someone else or that I don't *want* to go home to him.

"It's not like that. I want to see you. It's just ... my sister came in and told me we need to stage an intervention for my brother before he fucks up his love life. I don't think he'd want an audience for it."

I can hear Rowan relax. "Oh. That's good. That you're helping him, I mean. Is he gonna be okay?"

I make a decision to let Rowan in, at least more than is common knowledge. "It's a long story, and some of this is private stuff, but my brother married a man who works in my office—mine and Reyna's actually—so he can get health insurance. I guess they had some sort of agreement that they would split up once he healed. He's all better now, and it's like they still think they need to split up, even though they make a great couple. So my sister and I want to talk to him. I won't be long, I don't think. But go ahead and eat dinner without me."

"Okay."

"Do you need me to order you pizza or something?" Rowan's not much of a cook, I've learned.

"No, it's fine. I'll find something."

I also swear that I'm going to figure out a way to make

Rowan's holiday dreams come true. Even if neither of us know what those are. He wants a family, and it's too early to show him mine. I don't want to get my mom's hopes up. But maybe we can go do some regular holiday stuff, just the two of us. Maybe that will be enough for now.

I can't fix years of not having a support system. I can only start with me and slowly introduce him to others around me. So maybe I just take it one day at a time right now.

But the main thing I need to do tonight is save my brother from himself.

* * *

It's not far from our Century City office to my sister's house in Santa Monica, and my brother lives in the San Fernando Valley, but when I get there, Cam's already drinking beer, and Reyna's drinking prosecco. She's got a charcuterie tray out, and I reach for the crackers and brie.

Reyna decides to play innocent when she faces Cam. "So why is my big brother here, looking like he's going to burn down Los Angeles?"

Cam tells us the same thing I explained to Rowan. When Reyna asks him if it's true they need to get a divorce, Cam admits he doesn't want to, but they had a deal.

"And no one ever renegotiates contracts," I say.

Cam's eyes go to the ceiling. "Smart-ass."

After a little more sibling bickering, Reyna turns her attention back to Cam. "So you're asking us to come up with a grand gesture?"

"Yeah. I want to show Shelby I love him."

"*Love*?" I ask. Holy shit, my brother's in love. I knew they were into each other, but I guess I wasn't expecting him to just say it. Isn't love supposed to be a bigger deal than that?

"Yes, *love*. Keep up. I love him."

I try not to roll my eyes. I can't see inside his head. Or his heart. But ... fucking finally.

Good thing he can't see inside mine right now, because it's got some issues. Rowan-sized issues that I can't talk about with my siblings, at least not right now. First off, because this conversation is about Cam. It's not about me. And second off, because ... Rowan's nothing like what I planned. And yet ... he seems to be what I need.

Can I change my plans? Renegotiate my own contract?

We discuss how Cam could show Shelby his feelings. None of the three of us is good at grand gestures. Finally, we settle for Cam simply telling Shelby how he feels. Genius stuff, I know.

"At least we know he's not going to ditch you at the altar," I say, being the asshole younger brother. It's like a shirt I put on and never take off when I'm around my family.

Cam glares. "Thanks for that."

"Shelby is in love with you. You're in love with him. So I'm not seeing the big problem."

As I say those words, I get a weird prickling up and down my spine. Dammit. Am I falling in love, too? With Rowan?

"I don't know. Don't you think he deserves someone ... better?" Cam asks. And because he's being vulnerable, I decide not to poke at him.

"Who better than you? Do you trust anyone else to protect him?" I demand. I wouldn't trust anyone else to protect Rowan.

Cam stares at us.

"I think that's your answer," Reyna says to Cam. "Tell him you love him and you want to be with him."

I agree with her, but why do other people's problems feel so much simpler than mine?

Reyna gets an idea to enlist Noah's help, and soon we're just sitting around snacking on her food and talking about other things.

Cam reaches over and taps my foot, which is crossed over my

ankle. "What about you? Are you ever going to get your happily ever after?"

I snort. "Hell no. That whole concept is straight out of the 1950s—a wife, station wagon, kids, house in the suburbs. I don't want any of that shit."

"So update it to this century," Cam says. "The perfect guy?"

I shake my head. I'm so sick of being what everyone wants me to be. "I still don't want kids, a minivan, a dog, an air fryer, or more content to watch on multiple electronic devices than there are hours in my life. There will be no riding on a damn horse off into the sunset for me."

"So that means you do want a husband?" Reyna presses, as she refills her glass. "Because I noticed you didn't put that on your nope list."

I exhale. "I don't know. Do things have to be so ... hetero? For ten years, I've wanted a perfect husband. But why? I'm starting to not want to be married. Though I'll admit I kind of want a partner to argue with about whose turn it is to take out the garbage."

"Then you'd do it anyway, grouse at him, and come back in the house and show him some of that affection I think you have deep down," Cam says.

I glare at him. "Stop knowing me so well."

"Maybe you don't need a standard relationship for your happily ever after," Reyna says. "Plenty of people don't. Remember my best friend, Max, from college?"

"Yeah." I've met him a few times when he flew out here to see her.

"He's dating two firefighters in Vermont. Like, they're all in a relationship together." She fans herself. "And wow, they're hot."

I smirk, picturing it. "Good for him."

"My point is, no one outside of your relationship gets to tell you what to do or how to be. You can do exactly as you please with whoever you fall in love with."

"True," I say.

"Maybe stop comparing yourself to everyone else," Reyna says. "And start thinking about what it is you want."

"What have you been doing lately, anyway?" Cam asks.

I shrug. "Work."

Reyna narrows her eyes. "You've left work early every day this week."

"I'm kind of seeing a guy," I admit. "But it's new, and I don't know if it's serious."

"The same guy you were talking about at Mammoth?" Reyna asks.

"You had a guy in Mammoth?" Cam asks. "Why didn't I know about it?"

"Perhaps because you're all wrapped up in Shelby."

"Hmm. But you've found someone?"

"I met a guy."

"Okay." Cam's voice is tentatively happy.

"He tried to mug me."

"What the fuck?"

"So I took him to dinner?"

Silence.

"And home to my house."

More silence from my brother.

"And we've been seeing each other since just after Thanksgiving." My voice lowers. "And now I'm into him."

"Charles Jackson Cooper, what the actual fuck has gotten into you?"

I snort at my brother middle-naming me. "Him, I guess." Or vice versa. In more ways than one.

"And now you have a boyfriend." It's not a question.

Is Rowan my boyfriend? More like my new appendage. And amputating him would hurt. "Kinda. We haven't talked about that."

"When do I get to meet him?"

Something inside me is screaming that it's too soon.

But Cam? Cam will support me.

"Whenever, I guess, if you want. But it's not the kind of situation where I could take him home to Mom and Dad." They both wince. "I want to. I was just thinking about it. But you know how they get. Either Mom will start planning the wedding or she and Dad will be horrified because they think he's all wrong for me. He's got tattoos—a lot of tattoos—and pink hair. A lot of piercings in his ears and a nose ring. He's younger than me. He drives for ShareARide. Mom and Dad will wonder what the hell I'm doing."

"And you care what they think," Reyna says.

I shrug.

"You always care what they think," Cam says gently. "You care what *everyone* thinks. I do the same thing, by the way. It's not just you."

"But sometimes you care too much," Reyna points out.

I throw up my hands. "That's the problem. I want to date him, but when they meet him, they're going to see his tattoos and all the things on the surface, not who he is underneath."

"You could give them a chance," Cam says. "They might see what you do in him."

"Really, Charlie," Reyna says. "It's like you're scared to be yourself and show them who and what you truly like."

"I'm not scared of anything," I say automatically. But Reyna's words cut deep. The truth is, I've always been afraid of being myself. Afraid that I wasn't special enough. I wasn't the only girl. I wasn't the firstborn boy. I was just ... a middle child with nothing particularly noteworthy about me.

So I made myself be noteworthy. Good job, good house, all that.

And it doesn't feel like it was worth it.

I've been having more fun poking around in gutters—literally picking through trash—with Rowan, trying to find his plant, than I have at any fancy law event.

And that's probably telling me something.

"This is Cam's intervention, not mine," I snap.

They both chuckle. "Well, maybe you're next," Reyna says. "You're awfully prickly a lot of the time. And maybe you'd be a little happier if you gave yourself what you wanted every once in a while instead of just accepting what was given to you or chasing after the wrong things."

Oh, Rowan is a very wrong thing. And I wouldn't mind chasing him. Preferably to fuck him.

"So, when are you going to bring him by? You don't have to be ready to propose. We can just have the two of you over for dinner at our place," Cam says. I notice how he says "our" and means him and Shelby.

"When I'm ready." I glare at Cam. "Are you going to do what you need to do to tell Shelby your feelings?"

"Yeah." His voice cracks. "He's too important to mess this up."

That's how I feel about Rowan. He's both not on my plan and too important to fuck things up with. I just have to figure out my feelings first. Then I can talk with him.

CHAPTER 21

Rowan

When Charlie finally gets home, I attack him, because he looks way too yummy, and I missed him all day long. It's time to sex him up.

I try to push him down on the couch. Problem is, he's a brick wall, raising an amused eyebrow at me.

"Come on, man," I grumble. "Let me rub my dick on yours."

My soon-to-be boyfriend (already boyfriend?) bursts out laughing, and seeing him so expressive makes me smile in return. "Is that what the kids say these days?"

"It's what I say. Don't you think it will feel good? I'm dyyyying to come."

"All right, baby boy." He lets himself be pushed, and even if it's not my physical strength that got him to lie down, it still makes me feel powerful. "Where do you want me?"

"On your back, Daddy."

"Not your fucking dad—"

"I know, Charlie. Just get on your back, sexy man."

He complies, and again, he looks so damn sexy lying on his couch. He's got his hands behind his head like he's posing. Letting me look at the fabric-covered planes of his body. His beautiful torso. Those strong arms. His long legs and that hard dick in his pants. It wasn't hard a few moments ago, so this is a positive development. Working outside in the sun with Cam keeps Charlie strong and toned. He likes to move his body, use his hands. He doesn't like pushing paper. He's really in the wrong line of work.

I straddle him, which takes a bit of effort, because these pants are tight. I need to buy ones with more stretch.

But I need money for that, so these'll do.

Leaning down, I kiss him, and it quickly turns hungry. I'm fumbling to undo his pants while he's fumbling to undo mine, and once we get our cocks out with our zippers out of the way, I breathe a massive sigh of relief, taking both of us in my hands. He's a little big for me to handle with one hand, but I make do. I'm leaking precome, which I use as lube. It feels really good to rut against him. To get out this sexual tension.

Charlie seems as desperate as I am, given how he's panting and clutching me to him. His hips are thrusting into mine, and he pulls our pants down lower.

I love this. I love how we can't keep our hands off each other. How we can barely stand to waste the time to take our clothes off. How we just fucking go for it.

But more than getting me all hot and horny, he makes me feel safe. I can show him how much I want him, and he can take me at my most blunt.

"I really want to sit on your cock," I say.

Charlie groans a garbled noise. I take that as assent and climb off him. I race down the hall to get lube, shedding the rest of my clothes as I go, and he follows me to bed, climbing in with his clothes still on. Charlie's grin turns feral when I hover over him, my ass lining up with his cock. He's rucked up his shirt, and his pants are down to his thighs, but otherwise, he's totally dressed and I'm totally naked, and I have no idea why this is my thing, but it is. I like being naked around him. I like the way his clothes feel against my skin.

I like it when his dick violates my hole, too. I make so damn much noise as I push myself onto his cock. Ow. Fuck. This hurts. I should know better.

Charlie's eyes widen and then close. His expression goes blissful. I love that I made him look like that.

My body relaxes faster than it did before. I'm getting used to this.

"You are so goddamned hot and tight and wet," he growls. "Bounce yourself on my cock. Come on, I want to see it. Go fast. Now."

I do what he says, because I'm very much on board, too. I want to fuck and fuck and fuck Charlie. I want to spend my entire life with him inside me. I want to go to sleep with his dick in my ass and wake up with it there—or have him start humping me as soon as humanly possible.

I start babbling.

"I want you to hunt me down and fuck me," I whisper, my thighs burning as I raise myself up and down. "I want you to scratch me. To take me. I want you to claim me as yours."

"You already are fucking mine, and you know it," Charlie says with a possessive edge to his voice.

That makes me smile. I play with his nipples and scratch my nails across his chest. Charlie holds my hips tighter. "But I'm serious. If you wanted to chase me down and fuck me like you have no tether ..." I shiver. "I'd so be into that. I'm picturing a forest where I can hide in the trees and you're my scary stalker. When you capture me, wherever you find me, you rip off my clothes and take me right there."

Charlie gasps and comes.

I almost laugh, but it's *so hot* that my words, my kinky fantasy, made him come. He groans, shoving into me hard, then starts jacking my cock, fast, and I come all over his hand and belly. Some lands on his shirt, too. I collapse onto him, content. And wanting to do it again.

"Will you do it sometime?" I whisper, as his dick slips out of me.

"Fuck you in a forest—against a tree or something? Or with your face in the dirt? Scraping you up? Making you bleed for me?"

"Yes," I whisper, and if I could come again so soon, I would.

"From the moment I met you, you've brought out desires I kept buried so deep I didn't realize I had them," Charlie muses. "I wanted to mess up your face, and not because you mugged me. But because I thought you were such a devil with an angel face."

"And that triggered your feral instinct?"

He chuckles. "Maybe. These dirty fantasies weren't even a possibility before I met you. Everything in my life had to be just right."

"We're so fucking wrong, aren't we?"

Charlie nods.

"But it's right for us."

He nods again.

I note that he doesn't protest that we're not an us. Forward movement.

"We should get cleaned up. Wanna take a bath?" Charlie asks.

I snort. "I haven't done that since I was a kid."

"I'd rather be naked with you in a hot tub, but I don't have one."

"Sold," I say, and hop off him.

Charlie laughs and follows me, discarding his clothes. Once the bath water is warm, we get in, Charlie behind me, my back to his front, and let it fill around us.

Charlie starts tracing the tattoos on my body. "You have so many cartoons. Teddy bears. Anime. Cute things."

"A psychologist might say I'm reparenting myself."

"Do you think that's what you're doing?"

I shrug. "I never got the hugs and the cuddles. Maybe I want them on my skin."

His arms tighten around me. "So that's what your tattoos mean? Loving touches?"

"In part."

"Tell me about them," he says gruffly, running a hand down my arm. He touches one image. Then another. And another.

"If you look closely," I say slowly, "you can see that they all cover up scars. In one house, my foster siblings liked to cut me. With scissors. Knives. Whatever."

He goes ramrod straight, sloshing water over the side of the tub, and holds me tight. "What the fuck?" he mutters.

"Yeah." I swallow. "After I got out of there, I decided to take my body back, so I made them all into art." I hold my hand out, and Charlie trails a finger down my arm, stopping on one of the tiny—and not so tiny—pink scars that I've covered up. "I think I have thirty or so."

"You have no idea how angry that makes me." Charlie's voice is deadly quiet. "No one should get away with hurting you. I'm seeing blood running down the street from what I'd do to them, I swear."

"It was a long time ago. I'm fine now. It's all good."

"No, it's not." He pauses. "Do you mind talking about it?"

I'm feeling warm and safe. Floaty. "I'm good to talk," I say. "Anders would hold me down, and Billy would cut me." I gesture at one of the *Naruto* clouds on my ribs. "They carved their initials here. They were two years older than me and much bigger, although that's nothing new."

"That's absolutely barbaric. Why didn't you tell someone?"

"They said they'd kill me if I did."

"And you believed them."

I nod. A lump forms in my throat.

Charlie's arms wrap me up tighter. "I wish I could fix this," he whispers. "I wish I could fix all of it."

"Some things can't be fixed."

He shakes his head. "I want justice."

"Oh, so do I." I grimace. "You know that line from *The Princess Bride* about how he's in the revenge business?" Charlie nods, so I continue, "I'd love to be in that. To make sure everyone who has ever wronged someone—I'm talking big wrongs, not cut-someone-off-while-driving wrongs—get what's coming to them. Besides the ones I have a personal bone to pick with, I'd love to take out all the rapists and murderers. The child molesters and the abusers. The ones who've gotten away with it." I sigh. "That's a dream of mine. To just ... right the world."

"I'm on board with that," Charlie says. "Although I guess that's part of why I'm a lawyer. It's more complicated than that, but it's why I'm working at the firm I'm at. Because the lawyers there are fighting to do the right thing. To make changes in the world for LGBTQ people."

I grin. "That's what I want to do, too. Just a little bit more violently."

We sit in the warm water, letting it settle around us.

Charlie squeezes me again and murmurs, "Do you know *anything* about your birth parents?"

"No. Nothing. I read my case files. My birth certificate is utter crap, with almost no information. Guess I was a home birth. Off the grid. It says I was abandoned at a police station with a note that said 'my name is Rowan' on it. They did a search for recent births at hospitals, but there was nothing, so they don't know who my parents are. That's why I don't know what day I was actually born on. They just guessed I was three days old when I was dropped off."

"Holy shit," Charlie murmurs.

"So a foster family took me in. It must've been hell for them to have a newborn. I dunno. I don't remember the first families. Foster parents would keep me for six months, a year. Maybe more. But then that was it. I'd be moved to a new place. I had behavioral problems, the counselors told me. I have a few photos from families I was with when I got older, but I don't have that many of me growing up."

I feel almost like I don't exist now. Living in someone else's home, using a prepaid phone. My name isn't on anything but the title to a car.

I swallow. "So, when I was really little, I didn't know any better. But then I started figuring out that my life wasn't the same as everyone else's. There wasn't any stability in it. Most places were okay. I'm not going to paint a picture like foster homes are all houses of horror. They're not. Sure, some people do it for the money, but they get inspected and can at least put on a decent show. They were mostly clean, with enough food and clothes and whatever for me." I scrub my face. "Mostly."

"What about those kids who cut you?"

"Yeah, that was the worst one. I got all these injuries, but no one called Child Protective Services. And I stayed there for three years, because no one else wanted to take me. No one wanted to take me, because I was acting out, because I was getting hurt. At least that's how I interpret it now. Back then, I just thought that was what I deserved. That everyone lived in shitty places, and at least I had meals most of the time."

"That's horrible."

"The physical abuse wasn't all of it, either. I mean, that sucked, but they weren't actually trying to kill me. Mostly it was little cuts and a lot of intimidation. The name-calling was bad, too. Words do hurt." I sigh. "Like I told you when I met you, I learned self-defense and how to use a knife from people on the street."

"I take it you've used a knife on someone other than me?"

At some point, I need to admit my crimes to Charlie.

But not yet. "Don't ask that."

"Better if I don't know?"

"Yeah. And maybe I feel a little guilty. I suppose on some level I think revenge is petty. I'm supposed to turn the other cheek. At least, that's what the foster parents would tell me."

"Sometimes revenge is satisfying, though. Sometimes people deserve what's coming to them, and I get this sick sense of joy in the pit of my stomach knowing that karma got them, even if the law didn't."

I nod. "What would you do if you had all the money in the world?"

"Not sure. Probably just quit my job and fix up my house."

"That's it? You wouldn't create a foundation to educate the masses about the creative problems of using klieg lights in movies?"

"Har-har," Charlie says. "I don't know what I'd do. Guess I've never thought about it. I'd obviously take care of family and friends, but beyond that? I suppose I'd want to fix solvable problems."

"Me, too. I'd start a business helping people so they'd never be in any of the situations I was in—abused, bullied, without food or shelter. And I wouldn't make the victim pay for my services. I'd make the motherfucker who made them the victim pay. That makes more sense to me. The person who needs a bodyguard shouldn't have to pay for it. The payment should be from the people who make it so they need a bodyguard."

"Interesting philosophy," Charlie murmurs. "So you want to be a do-gooder vigilante?"

"I guess. Yeah. Kinda. I have a vengeance list that I'd love to start ticking off."

"You want to kill everyone on that list?" Charlie asks lightly.

I scoff. "No. I'm not that evil. But I do want to get my revenge."

"I wonder if you ever will."

"Probably not. Until I met you, I never got anything I wanted. I still can't have it all. I can't even find a houseplant that matters to literally no one but me."

Charlie doesn't reply.

"What?" I say defensively.

"I don't have a response to that. Because I know it matters to you, and I don't have any way to fix it. I could buy you another philodendron, but it wouldn't be Wilbur. And you don't want anything but Wilbur. So I don't want to spout platitudes that aren't going to make you feel better."

"Talk about brutally honest."

"Kinda feels like we've been brutally honest with each other all along."

When we get out of the tub, we go back to bed—to sleep, this time, and I realize he has my whole heart. He's the first person ever to have that.

What I feel for Charlie doesn't just frighten me. It's so much worse. Take all the fears I had as a child about the monsters under the bed, the bogeyman, clowns. The terrors I felt after I learned the horrible things people do to each other—toothpicks under fingernails and terrorism and rape. Take all of those, and Charlie's worse.

Unlike all those other threats, imaginary and real, I'm *giving* Charlie the power to change me.

I wiggle in his arms and turn over to face him. When he's sleeping, Charlie looks softer than he does during the day. Awake, he's got RBF. Now, he looks content. He snuffles, then draws me closer, and it makes my heart beat faster. I love that he likes sleeping wrapped up together. I'm usually so cold that having his body warm and comfy is soothing.

I look at the stubble on his jaw. Feel his strong arms around me. Listen to his whiffling snore.

He has so much sway over me, and he doesn't even know it.

CHAPTER 22

Charlie

I wake in the middle of the night spooning Rowan, his bare, warm body nestled securely against mine. I've never been good at sleeping—literally sleeping—with anyone before, but with Rowan, it's easy. Rowan makes me want to both protect him and watch him in awe.

It's dark, but I can make out a few of the inked designs on his skin.

Rowan's tattoos cover scars.

He has so many tattoos—lots of little ones everywhere. But when he showed me in the bath ... yep. If I look hard, I can see scars in the middle of some of them.

Fucking hell. How did someone get away with that? I clench my teeth, grinding them so hard my jaw hurts. I want to call CPS, but it was a decade ago, it sounds like.

My movements must wake him up. "Wha?" Rowan mutters.

"Go back to sleep, baby," I say.

"'Kay." He kisses me.

"Sorry to wake you. Night."

"Good night."

Soon, his breathing evens out, but I stay awake for a long time, processing what he told me earlier. I wasn't kidding when I said I envisioned blood pouring down the street. I'm twitchy, edgy, and my throat is dry. I want to hurt every single person who ever hurt him. I don't know if that's the best way to help him, but I will help him however he wants.

Sad sack me at the bonfire wanted someone to be with. Now I've got a man in my arms who excites me and terrifies me. I'm pretty sure that if I'm not all in this relationship with him, I need to tell him now. Before our fifth date that he's insisting on. Or is it our third?

Problem is, I'm already in too deep.

I've already decided that he's mine.

So. Okay. Decision made, then. This prickly pear of a human called Rowan Jones can hang out with my saguaro cactus, and we can poke each other.

I should tell him about my history. But he knows I hate bullies. I'll tell him at some point—just not when it would pivot a conversation about him to my own shit.

I can trust him with my secrets, because he's trusted me with his. With that all set, I sigh, tug him closer, and fall asleep again.

The next morning, Rowan's still in my arms. He wiggles, and I shove my nose into his pink fluff of hair. First thing in the morning, it looks like a dandelion or something.

"Hey," I say, my voice thick with sleep. And then I remember what he told me, and I remind myself not to treat him differently. I don't want to be funny around each other now that he's shared a lot.

"Morning, Daddy," he slurs, and I sigh. Then I grin into his neck and kiss that "baby boy" tattoo.

"I hate you," I say.

"No, you don't. You're just too stubborn to admit it."

"Coffee?" I ask, knowing I won't win this argument.

"Yeah. In a minute, though." And he proceeds to thoroughly wish me a good morning.

Cam shows up at the office and proposes to Shelby all over again. Which confuses half the people in the firm who thought (correctly) that they were already married. After he takes Shelby out and does whatever—I don't want the details—he texts me.

CAM

What do you think about waiting until after the
holidays to do more renovations on my house?
Is that okay?

CHARLIE

It's fine.

CAM

Do we need content sooner than that?

CHARLIE

I can edit old footage and post compilations.
No problem.

How eager I am to tackle another project with Cam makes me think I really should take steps toward being able to quit my job. For now, I just go back to drafting interrogatories.

Oh, and I think about Rowan constantly.

* * *

The next afternoon, Saturday, I'm at my parents' house helping them string lights and put ornaments on the Christmas tree. Cam and Shelby are there, too, along with Reyna. This counts as my weekly call. Rowan begged off to go drive rideshare customers, though I don't think I was imagining that he wanted to come along.

But it's too early to let him meet my mom—she'll start planning the honeymoon.

"CharlieBoo," my sister says, "what's that on your face?"

I frown and wipe my cheeks. "I don't know."

"It was a smile."

Cam gives me an assessing look. "You're trying to remember that you're the cranky grump of the family, aren't you?"

"Whatever," I mutter.

"What's going on?" Mom asks, coming into the room with a tray of cookies and hot cocoa. It's not cold enough outside for cocoa—it's a clear 75-degree day—but it all tastes good and feels seasonal.

"Nothing."

She gives me that mom look, and I relent. "There's a guy I like, but it's complicated."

Mom schools her face into not being too excited, and I love her for it. "What's so complicated about it?"

"I guess I'm nervous to bring him around and have you get attached to him. What if things don't work out?" The words taste like those wooden sticks you get with an ice cream. Like nothing, but I might get splinters if I bite too hard.

"I'd love to meet him. But only when you're comfortable."

"He's not what you would picture for me," I admit, thinking of Rowan's criminal activities, lack of background, and completely irreverent looks and way of talking.

She puts a hand on her hip. "Stop thinking about what we want. Think about what you want."

What would happen if I did just that?

CHAPTER 23

Charlie

So, surprising no one, Rowan talks me into going axe throwing with him on Saturday night.

I have no idea how a business gets insurance to do this. It just seems like a recipe for someone to lose a toe. That could be a good thing in some contexts—it would be a place to start with those fuckers who hurt Rowan—but I have to think most of the customers here deserve to keep all their appendages.

A hot guy in a plaid lumberjack shirt shows us how to throw the axe—and he hits the bull's-eye immediately both times.

Then Rowan and I do it, and Rowan gets a wild gleam in his eye. He's such a damn menace. He follows the rules, to my surprise, and he hits the target, although not as precisely as the worker. I do the same and am just glad to hit the wood.

A group of tiny white-haired ladies has the booth next to us, and they're cackling up a storm. "Go, Mildred!" one of them chirps.

Mildred, wearing a rose-pink tracksuit, lifts the axe and follows the prescribed procedure. She hits the wall but wildly misses the target.

I point a thumb over my shoulder and whisper to Rowan, "I'm digging our neighbors."

"Me, too. I love it that this is what they chose to do today. I've always wanted a grandma."

That makes something ache inside me. How much has he missed out on? There's nothing I can say or do to make it all better, but I wish I could.

He picks up an axe and seems to contemplate its weight. "So I know your pet peeves. What are the things you love?"

His question makes me pause. *Is* there anything I love? A thunk sounds behind us as another party's axe hits the target.

He chuckles. "You don't know?"

"Not off the top of my head, no. I mean, my family, obviously."

Rowan shakes his head. "That's not 'obviously.' Some of us don't have a family, and some people have families that aren't worth loving."

"Yeah. True. Sorry."

He sets up and lets his axe fly. "It's okay. But, apart from your family, what do you love?"

I pick up my axe. "I have no idea. Is that bad?"

"That you could list off things that bug you in two seconds, but you can't think of anything you love?"

"Yeah." I stand at the line and hold the axe behind my head. I glance over at the older ladies. One in a pale aqua sweater and black pants is openly ogling me. I turn my head back to the target and focus. This time, I manage to get the axe almost in the middle. Rowan claps, as does the entire group next to us. I give them an up nod. "Hello, ladies."

"Hello, handsome," a woman in all bright yellow, with a bright yellow turban, says. The rest of them whistle.

Rowan smiles widely. "Figures you'd be popular with the ladies. Should I invite them over so they can flirt with you?"

"I hate you," I mutter. "Your turn."

He walks up to the line and easily hits the target. "Maybe you've been focused on the wrong stuff. The things you don't want instead of the things you want."

"No, I've been keeping track of what I want. I just don't think it's what I love."

"Okay, then what do you *like*?"

"I like hiking, making and editing videos, being snarky with my friends, going to the club, fucking ..."

"Much better," Rowan whispers. "Now I'm getting the real Charlie."

As we go on flinging our axes to the wall, we both get better and better at it. The ladies next to us are now drinking margaritas, and their axes aren't going anywhere near the center.

"What about you?" I ask, ordering us beers from the QR code menu.

"I like manga and anime, the dirtier the better."

"There's dirty anime?" I ask, then shake my head. "Of course there is."

"If you haven't seen it, we can watch *Goblins Cave* together," he says. "It's basically porn, but a cartoon. The plot is 'prince gets assaulted by large and small green goblins.'"

My voice drops, and I step closer. "Why do you like it?"

Rowan tugs at his collar. "I think it's one of those fantasies I'm not supposed to have. Having your choice taken away in real life is truly awful, but the fantasy of 'Oh, no, help'"—he says this part flatly—"'I'm being taken against my will by these really hot green dudes with big peens.'" He fans himself.

"Where can we find the men with big peens?" rose-suited lady asks.

"It's online," Rowan calls.

"Shame," she sniffs, and everyone laughs.

Rowan addresses me more quietly. "I guess the noncon thing hits my lizard brain just right."

"Hmm." Our beers are delivered, and we both take sips.

"It feels really subversive, too," he continues. "Because it bucks what's right. I know what's right: consent and safe sex and all that. But deep down, some part of me wants to be thrown around by a daddy who has his way with me."

"Shit, Rowan, you need to stop." I gesture at my zipper. "We have to change the subject, or we're going to give our neighbors a show."

"I think they'd be into it." He gives me an assessing look. "So you *do* like the idea of taking over. You weren't just saying it before?"

"I've never done anything without consent. But part of me wants to ... find out what it's like. As long as I know the consent is actually there, underneath." My cheeks heat. This feels extremely personal.

"Good." Rowan widens his eyes all innocent and leans against the wall, his body on display for me.

"Knock it off, baby boy. Seriously, change the subject," I hiss. "You said you liked metal and pop music. Why those?"

"My moods are either black or pink. No in-between." He gives me an accusing look. "You just listen to whatever's on the radio, don't you."

"Kinda, yeah." I pause. "I do like picking music out for a video, though." I shiver. "When the music beat drops in time with the video? That's the best. I don't care what the music is. If it works, it works." I heft the axe in my hand. Then I fling it.

"If you could do anything at all, what would you do?" Rowan asks me, sipping his beer. "I mean besides me."

"I told you: not be a lawyer. But I can't."

"Why not?"

"I need to make money to pay my bills." I pause. "I think there's something else, too. I'd feel ashamed giving up my law license. Mom and Dad are so proud of having two lawyers in the family."

"Do they want two lawyers? Or do they want happy kids?"

I don't answer him. He knows he's right. I don't need to confirm it. "At that bonfire where you tried to mug me—"

"I was successful—"

"No, you weren't." I glare. "At any rate, they were doing this funny ritual where they were burning bad decisions or bad memories from the past. And all I could think was that my supremely bad choice was going to law school."

"It doesn't sound like it was that bad. It got you here."

"Yeah." I sigh. "I'm whining. I'll stop."

"You can whine to me," he says.

"Many people would kill for the life I have. I got an excellent education in a prestigious field. I work at a cutting-edge law firm that does things I support."

"But are you happy?"

I stare at him for far too long. "With you, yeah."

He smiles. "What about at work?"

I shake my head.

"I want to help you to be happy."

"I'll be happy if I can make a bull's-eye," I mutter.

"They let us project an image of someone we want to throw axes at," Rowan says.

"How will you possibly choose just one?"

We end up displaying a photo of the dude who stole his car, who hasn't closed his ShareARide account, and Rowan seems happier when he gets the guy in both eyes and the throat. The ladies next to us clap loudly.

I close my eyes and shake my head. "You're so into violence."

"This is a healthy outlet for it. You don't want to know what I'd do if I had the money to fund my vengeance list."

Our time is up, and as we walk through the lobby area to the exit, I hear a gasp.

"OMG, are you Charlie Cooper?" someone says from a group of several young men on a couch, waiting their turn. At my side, Rowan stiffens.

"Um, yes." I give them a smile.

Rowan's hand is in his pocket, and I'd bet he's fingering his knife. I squeeze his arm.

The most eager-looking guy in the group grins widely. "I love your Ad/VICE account. You and your brother."

"Oh. Thanks," I say. While I wanted the social media attention, I'm never quite sure what to do when people approach me in real life. Cam gets stopped more than I do, simply because he's on camera more than I am. But this happens to me from time to time, too.

"Do you mind taking a selfie with me?"

Out of the corner of my eye, I see Rowan open his mouth to say something snarky. I lean down and kiss his neck, and he melts against me. "It doesn't mean anything, babe," I murmur. "You okay with it?"

Rowan shakes his head, then changes his mind and nods.

The guy gets up, and we lean close to take a photo. He squeezes my ass as we part, and Rowan hisses, "I will murder him."

"No, you will not murder my fans," I say.

"Yet."

* * *

When we get home, I go down the hall to my office and pull out a file folder. Rowan snorts at the P-touch label. "'Ten-year plan'?"

I nod. "Open it. I want to show you this."

He slides out the single sheet of paper and reads the things I wanted to accomplish by the time I was thirty. "This has been my guiding principle since I was twenty."

"This is a very ambitious list. Most people would be happy with one or two of those things."

"I've always had a lot of ambition. I wanted to distinguish myself."

"To keep up with your brother and sister?"

"Maybe. I don't know the psychology of it. I just have always had this drive, you know? I wanted to make myself be better. Do better. I needed to show the world that I was someone."

"And did you have to be perfect to do that?"

"Of course. I don't know any other way."

"I've always thought being perfect was a form of fear. Like, fear that other people would judge you to be lacking. I just kind of embraced the fact that other people would find me lacking—I mean, they were going to anyway, so I leaned into it. Too short and small? I wear clothes that emphasize how small I am. An outsider? I make myself look even more of one with all my body art and dye jobs."

"You definitely make an impression," I say.

"I'll note that your husband requirement is very specific."

My cheeks burn. "Yeah, well. That's what I wanted when I was twenty."

"What's a Cartier Love ring?"

"Cartier has these bracelets that you put on someone else with a screwdriver. The rings are the same design—simple. I just like them."

"Do you have to screw on the rings?"

"Nope."

"How do you feel about the social media followers?"

"At some point, it gets to be overwhelming. I'm not in love with having people ask me for selfies, though I guess it doesn't bother me as much as it bothers you. The online part is easier. I don't even read most of the comments anymore. I just like posting the videos. And I don't engage with online bullies." I let out a breath. "I had bullies growing up, too."

Rowan studies my face. "The night we met, you said you hated bullies."

"That's because they did some vile things to me when I was young. I was scared to tell my parents that I was gay and that kids were picking on me because of it. I was smaller than I am now—

obviously—but I was smaller and younger than the other kids, too. When my brother found out what was happening—the teasing, locking me in rooms, making me piss my pants—he beat some of them up. But I didn't like him having to fight my fights for me, so I asked my parents for tae kwon do lessons. I learned self-defense. But I didn't end up having to use it more than once or twice." I scrub my face. "My parents never knew that I had problems, and I wanted to keep it that way."

"It sounds like you were always trying to be perfect. Maybe so they wouldn't be upset that things weren't going well with you."

"Maybe." I grimace, now feeling super awkward. "Just ... you shared things with me, and I wanted to share things with you. Things that suck."

Rowan leans in and kisses me gently. "Thank you."

"Actually, I'm questioning whether I want anything on my list anymore," I admit. "Fuck ten-year plans that are basically me regurgitating every success magazine article I've ever read."

"Definitely. No wedding for us. Got it." His face falls.

"It doesn't mean I don't want a committed relationship. We're exclusive, baby boy," I assure him.

"I'm just never going to be Rowan Cooper. Fine." Rowan mock sighs, but I can hear the hurt behind it.

"If you really want to change your name to that, you can. I can't stop you."

"Hmm." He worries at a nail. "I'll think about it. Jones as a last name has never suited me, I don't think. But you're right. I can change it without marrying anyone."

"You're not marrying anyone else," I growl.

"Sheesh, Daddy. Possessive. I love it." Rowan spins to look at me and pokes me in the chest. "With a husband on your ten-year plan, I figured you'd be a secret romantic." I go to shake my head, but Rowan holds my face. "You don't want the big proposal and the wedding and all that?"

"No, I don't," I say. "I see my friends with their happily ever afters. They've all found their perfect person, and most of them are married or are getting married. But I don't know that I want what they have—although I do want a partner. Club culture was getting a little boring and repetitive for me. I'd like someone to settle down with—but my own version of settling down."

"And that someone isn't me?"

I take both of his hands in mine and stare into his dark blue eyes. "Rowan, it very well may be you. Things are moving super fast with us. I just don't want to get married."

"But we can still be together?"

I don't like how insecure he sounds. Knowing his history, though, I appreciate how vulnerable he's being with me. He's letting me see his fears. It makes my heart expand to fit him all the way inside. "Definitely. It'll just be up to us to say what that means. No more influence from anyone else. We're going to do only what we want to do, and that's it."

"Can I get a ring?"

"You can have one for every finger. Just not your ring finger."

He leans up and kisses me. "Deal. I promise to never marry you."

"And I promise to never marry you," I say.

CHAPTER 24

Rowan

On Sunday night, I'm in the living room playing on my phone when Charlie comes out of his office, where he's been working on a video. "I'm done. Come on. Get your shoes on."

"Where are we going?"

"I think we need to do a few seasonal things," he says.

"I'm intrigued." But honestly, I'm a little moved, too. He's got something planned? What?

Charlie first drives us to a coffee shop, where he gets us both peppermint hot chocolates with whipped cream.

"I'm not four," I say, but I'm not really complaining.

"You definitely aren't. But you need to do some of the holiday things I think you missed."

Then he drives us to a street in the San Fernando Valley. There are a ton of cars backed up. He rolls down the windows as we drive slowly past a house that is so covered in lights I worry about their electric bill.

"These guys sure decorate," I say.

"Yep."

When I see a sign, it dawns on me that we're at one of those

Candy Cane Lane places where all the neighbors decorate their houses to the max.

People are walking around. There's music playing. Even some carolers. We see houses that are complete light shows, with lasers where the music syncs with the lights.

Charlie looks over at me and grins like a little kid.

He loves this. And I love that he's giving it to me.

I also love the soft look in his eyes that makes me believe I matter.

"I've never done this before," I say.

"I figured. I told you we'd do some holiday things," he reminds me. "This is my favorite. I'm not that into movies or music or white elephant gifts, but I love seeing how far people go when they decorate with the intent to go all out."

"It's cool," I whisper, and we keep driving and looking at the holiday lights.

* * *

On Monday, I'm back in my car. The radio is chock full of Christmas songs. Charlie is headed up to Santa Barbara this evening to go to an event with Tristan. That doesn't make me happy, but I trust him.

Since going back to work, I've learned my lesson about a few things. For example, I don't accept rides from new accounts. Not sorry. Even with my new dashboard cam, I still need social proof before I take them on. It's for my safety. And the safety of my plant. Who I don't have.

I've driven from where I was supposed to pick up "Pierce" to where the police found my car more times than I care to admit. Each time I take a different route, driving slower than usual, with no metal music, hoping to see where they chucked Wilbur. I always assumed that they'd get rid of Wilbur fast, so I've even pulled to the side periodically and walked around looking for him, even though Charlie and I already combed the ditches multiple times.

But ... nothing.

I've just dropped someone off in Oxnard and am headed back down the coast when I decide to take one last look on the other side of the road, up maybe a mile or so from where my car was stolen. It's an area that's popular for taking photos, so there's a few cars parked along the highway and some people walking on the beach.

I pull into a parking area on the northbound side and find a spot between a few cars. And, again, having learned things, I turn my car off and lock it, and I make sure I have my phone with me as well as my wallet and knife.

A few cars whiz by, but it's not a super busy area. I hear traffic above me while I'm down in the ditch, looking around, and then I see something behind a group of rocks below the grade of the road.

"No. They wouldn't have," I say, my heart rate increasing as I take off at a run. I spy a little spot of green. I go around, and *yes! There he is!* I pick up the shattered pot of my Wilbur. My heart leaps. He's back! A bit bedraggled, but at least we had some rain over the past few weeks, so he's not dead.

"I can get you a new pot," I coo, picking my way up the ditch and back to my car. I pop the trunk and get out an old plastic bag to put him in, doing my best to keep his soil around his roots.

Shaking with relief, I set him in his macramé cradle and close the passenger door, ready to walk around to the driver's side.

But then the cool metal of a gun touches my temple.

Holy shit.

And also, what the hell? I have nothing to give anyone. Literally *nothing*.

"What the fuck do you want?" I hiss, despite knowing that it's unwise to get mouthy with someone who has a gun. He's not alone, either. Someone else has appeared on my other side. I don't get a good look at either of them, since I don't want to move my head, but they're both taller than me. Practically everyone is, of course. I can hear someone else behind me. There may be more than three, I don't know.

Then I see the sleeve of an Adidas track jacket.

I should've called the cops on the man in the Dodge Charger. I knew something was wrong, and so did Charlie. "We need to talk with you," he says. "Come with us." He's not the one with the gun, that's the guy on my other side. But they're all standing closer to me than is socially acceptable.

"What if I don't want to?" I ask, because I never said I made good, smart decisions.

Tracksuit man tsks. "We've tried to talk with you nicely, but you haven't made it easy, so this is the way we're going to do it."

I feel like I'm in some bad mafia movie, only this is real life. "I'm taking my plant with me." I don't want him to fry in the greenhouse of my car or wilt in the trunk.

"What the fuck? No."

"No. Either we both go or we both stay," I snarl, not clear why I'm willing to die for my plant.

Then Charlie's face comes into my head. I'm not willing to die and never see Charlie again. I'm about to open my mouth to say I'll just stash Wilbur somewhere when they relent. "Fine. Bring the plant."

The kidnappers throw Wilbur into the back of the Charger none too gently and then secure my arms behind my back with duct tape.

"That's gonna hurt," I say.

They put duct tape over my mouth as well.

I mumble some curses at them, but they (obviously) don't hear me. They're shoving me into the back of the car when one of them stabs a syringe into my arm, and the world goes dark.

* * *

I wake up in a bare, windowless room. I don't know what time of day it is. I don't know where I am. How long was I out? Are my organs going to be harvested? Did those assholes take me across the border into another state? Another country?

The walls are painted white, and I'm lying on a couch in a room with a chair and ... that's it, besides a door. There's no bathroom. Good thing I don't have to pee. Someone took the tape off my hands and mouth, at least. I'm glad I wasn't awake for that.

Okay, what the actual hell? Am I being trafficked?

Then I look up, and there's a security camera very high up pointed at me. I flip it off.

Ugh. How do I get out of this one? I check my pockets, but they've confiscated my phone, wallet, and knife. At least this time it's not my fault that I don't have them. I remembered to take them with me. Wilbur, of course, is nowhere in sight. They'd better not have done anything to him.

I hear a key in the lock, and the door opens.

A man comes into the room. A very well-dressed man, but he's not looking too good. Like, his skin is gray, and he's quite thin.

Then his eyes catch mine, and my mouth falls open. I stutter out a bark of laughter.

His navy blue eyes are the exact shade and shape of mine.

His nose is like mine. Long and slender, with a flared end.

His lips are like mine. Thinner on top and thicker on the bottom.

"I'm sorry they were rough with you," he says. "Bringing you here wasn't supposed to go like that. I've fired the one responsible."

"What the fuck is going on? Who are you?" I ask, my skin tingling. I'm breathless, and I'm shaking my head in denial. I know what's coming—what has to be true.

He stares at me. He tilts his head, and I can tell that he's done the same facial analysis I did. "I think you know who I am."

"My father?" I whisper.

Part Two

CHAPTER 25

Charlie

"You ready?" I glance at Tristan, who's sitting in the driver's seat of his late-model Mercedes-Benz. We're parked in his reserved spot in the main faculty parking lot of Albrecht College, which is situated on a bluff in Santa Barbara overlooking the Pacific Ocean. The view must be gorgeous during the day.

Tristan nods, his lips pressed tightly together. He's as handsome and put-together as always, in a dark burgundy velvet jacket, black slacks, and a bow tie. His familiar expensive aftershave is subtle but present. But he's pale, with a bead of sweat visible on his forehead.

"Are any other faculty here LGBTQ?" I ask.

"Based on statistics, yes, but none that I know of." He looks over at me. "It should make me feel better that so many brave people have gone before me and told the world who they are, but it's the opposite. I feel pressured. Like, why haven't I done it yet?"

"I'm sorry if you ever felt like I put pressure on you," I say, now thinking about all the times I wished he was out. Except ... I think, deep down, I was glad he wasn't, because then I didn't have to face some truths about myself. Truths like how Tristan's better as a friend and I don't want to marry someone to check a box on my ten-year plan.

He waves my concern away. "Whatever you did or said doesn't matter, because what I said in my head was a hundred times worse."

He's wringing his hands. He needs a distraction.

"You know," I say, as I look in the lit-up mirror on the back of the sunshade and straighten my tie, "I once attended a speech where a straight dude argued that the concept of 'the closet' is a gift to the world from gay people."

Tris squints at me like I told him he should dye his hair pink and cover his body in cartoon tattoos. "What? Like, he wanted to put all queer people in the closet? What a bigoted idea!"

I snap the mirror shut. "No. The opposite. The speech was gorgeous. His proposition was that there isn't just one kind of closet, and everyone must deal with their own. While the idea originated with sexuality, it's universal."

"Hmm. If we didn't have the concept of 'the closet,' we'd still have people who lived life on their own terms and didn't care what others thought of them," Tristan argues.

His color's returned, and he's not looking so ill. Mission *Distract Tristan* accomplished.

"But the metaphor helps," I say, "because it lets us visualize the idea of embracing who we really are. And also, that it's—hopefully —a *decision* to step out that's available any time, depending on the society we live in."

Not that I've been struggling with figuring out what I truly want or who I am lately or anything. Without my ten-year plan, which I've pretty much tossed out the window like Rowan's Wilbur, who am I? I don't want to think about it at the moment. Easier to focus on Tristan.

I continue, "We all have secret parts of ourselves we hide because we fear we'll be shunned, shamed, and ostracized if we let others know about them. And we see people who *have* stepped out of the closet, who *are* shunned, shamed, and ostracized, so the fear is valid."

Tristan sighs. "What a painful and awful truth. If you're trying to give me a pep talk, it isn't working."

I reach out and touch his velvet-covered forearm, forcing him to look me in the eyes. "All I'm saying is that you're not alone, and this is tough, and you're being brave. Also, I know you feel under a lot of pressure to come out, and I don't want to add to it. If you want to turn around right now and go home, we can. I won't hold it against you. *Ever.* The idea that people are somehow *entitled* to your truth is a bunch of bullshit. In a perfect world, which I'll admit doesn't exist, you come out only on your terms. If that's not tonight, it's absolutely okay."

Tristan's quiet for a long moment as he first stares at me in his passenger seat, then looks out his front window, exhaling so the glass fogs up.

I'm quiet, too. Because I'm serious. I'm never going to push him on this. Just because I work in a very inclusive and accepting environment doesn't mean that the rest of the world is that way. And Tristan is one of my best friends. I haven't previously acknowledged him as such—excluding him from my mental list of confidants like Danny, Cam, and Reyna—but over the years, we've learned a lot about each other and have become close, even if I've realized there's no spark between us.

I now know what a spark really feels like, thanks to Rowan.

But I can help Tris with this.

"Thanks for saying that," Tristan says quietly. "I *do* feel a lot of pressure to tell people my sexual orientation. By not being out, I'm letting down the team. I'm sitting on the bench while others are playing the game."

"If you're a benchwarmer, then so be it. Again, no one's forcing you to do this."

Another long, silent moment where Tristan taps the steering wheel and stares out the window. Finally, he straightens his shoulders. "No. It's worse than benchwarming. I'm hiding in a maintenance supply cabinet behind the locker room. I want to come out. I've had enough of feeling like I have to hide this major part of me from my colleagues. My family. The world. *Enough.*"

"I'm here for you," I murmur. "You got this."

"Thanks."

"How do you want to arrive? Together? Want me to meet you inside?"

"I want to walk in there holding a man's hand," he says, another bead of sweat appearing on his forehead. It makes my heart squeeze.

I give him a confident and hopefully encouraging smile. "Then let's do it."

We exit the car, I extend my hand, and Tristan takes it. I've touched this man hundreds of times. This is the first time his hand has ever been clammy. He's holding my hand tight, like I've fallen down the bluff we're standing on and he's pulling me up.

We walk briskly out of the parking lot and along a well-land-scaped, winding path lined with lights. A few other dressed-up people are walking toward a grouping of several older, smaller structures that must be administration buildings and perhaps the chapel. I think the dorms, classrooms, and library are in the other direction.

"Where is the party being held?" I ask.

He gestures toward a smaller, storybook-style building with a steep roof, uneven shingles that look like thatching, stained glass, and lots of gables and turrets. "The manor house. This property used to be my great-grandparents' estate. They gifted it to the university."

I dig in my heels, which makes Tristan stop. "Wait, your great-grandparents? I thought your last name was Graff, not Albrecht."

Tristan shrugs. "I hadn't told you? My mom's an Albrecht. Veronica Albrecht Graff. I'm sure she'll be here tonight, as will other major donors. My father's now the chair of the school's board of governors."

I raise my eyebrows, and we start walking again. "I wasn't nervous before," I say, trying to joke, but also being serious, "but you just upped the stakes. I have to be on my best behavior, or, what, Albrecht doesn't get its endowment? You get sacked?"

"I have tenure, and the school's endowment is only slightly less than Harvard's, so I'm not concerned about that." He sighs. "It's more ... social standing. Getting shunned, shamed, and ostracized —or whatever it was you said just now."

"Okay." I pause. "I'll do the best I can."

He opens the heavy wooden door to the manor house, and as we step inside, we're hit with the scents of fresh pine, cinnamon, and warm, savory food. The interior is tastefully lit with gold-hued lamps and candles, and guests are dressed in holiday finery or business attire. Lots of people in little black dresses and heels, or suits and ties like me. At least I know we fit in in terms of appearance.

I'm still holding hands with Tristan. No one's even noticed us.

Well, that was anticlimactic.

We go to a table where Tristan picks up his name tag—the faculty apparently have engraved brass ones. There's a preprinted disposable one for me. After we pin them on our jackets, he grips my hand again.

He really is being brave. Okay, let's do this.

"Want to get a drink?" Tristan asks, a slight tremor in his voice.

"Definitely."

We make our way over to the bar. Tristan's holding my hand so tight, I think he might be cutting off my circulation.

But I'm looking around with my head held high. Finally, I notice a few people who've clocked our arrival. We get some curious looks, but as I secretly suspected, being in a same-sex couple on a liberal arts campus—even one with a conservative donor demographic—isn't the end of the world. Me showing up and posing as Tristan's partner is 10 percent about his work environment and 90 percent about Tristan and his demons. But we still have to face his family, so I reserve the right to adjust my percentages.

Tristan orders us each a glass of red wine, and once we receive them, we stop to talk with a slim man in his late thirties or early forties who's standing by himself. The guy looks professorial, and he's rocking a bow tie and a glen plaid jacket. "Hey," Tristan says. "Good to see you. Wolfe, this is my friend Charlie Cooper. Charlie, Wolfe LaBella."

We exchange handshakes and greetings, and Wolfe looks us up and down, his eyes zeroing in on our joined hands. There's an awkward pause.

"Wolfe is a professor here," Tristan says. "Charlie's a lawyer in Century City."

"And what are you doing up here? Are you thinking of working as an adjunct professor?" Wolfe asks.

I glance at Tristan, because it's his moment. He can decide how to describe me to every person we meet tonight. "No, Charlie's here as my ... friend. At least, now we're friends. We used to be ... more. Not partners, but more than friends."

Wolfe heaves a sigh of relief. "I'm so glad to know that. I've been feeling alone in this faculty, but I figured I couldn't be the only gay professor on campus. Or, you know, queer person identifying with whatever letter in the alphabet."

Tris lets his head fall back, closes his eyes, and takes a deep breath.

I knew he wasn't alone.

"You aren't," Tristan assures him. "And this is the first time ... You're the first person I'm coming out to."

Wolfe touches his chest. "Me? Wow. Thanks, Tristan," he says, with awe in his tone. "That really means a lot."

Tris blows out a breath. "Okay. One down, ten thousand to go."

"It's a never-ending process," I say. "Don't get me started on every time you fill out a demographic form."

"Right," Wolfe says. "Ugh, forms." Apparently Rowan isn't the only one who dreads filling out forms.

My chest gets warm. Should I text Rowan and see how he is, or is that being too *daddy*? That baby boy has me overthinking. No, I don't want to be rude and have my phone out constantly. I'll check in on the menace in a little bit.

When I'm back paying attention to the conversation, it seems I missed something, as Wolfe is choking on his drink.

"Sorry?" I say. "I zoned out for a second."

"I was just asking Wolfe if he was seeing someone," Tristan explains.

Wolfe rubs the back of his neck. "Um. Well, that's a hard question to answer. It's complicated."

"Say no more," I chuckle, holding up a hand.

Wolfe's voice drops. "Can I tell you both something in confidence?"

Tristan and I nod, our shoulders brushing as we face him.

"I kind of got together with this guy who's really great. It was a one-night stand, but I wanted to see if there might be something there with him, you know?" We nod. "Before anything more could happen between us, though, he walked into my classroom this fall as a student."

"Holy shit," Tristan says.

Wolfe quickly adds, "He's an older student. I didn't know. But" —he rubs his cheek—"I have no idea what I'm doing now." A group brushes past us, and Wolfe shuts up. Looking at Tristan, he says, "I'll catch up with you later, Tris. Maybe we can go to lunch and talk."

"I'd like that," Tristan says. Wolfe smiles at us and moves to talk with another group.

I squeeze Tristan's hand. "You did well."

"Thanks."

We move toward a few women I presume Tristan knows, given how he greets them all with kisses on the cheek. "This is Bree St. Thomas," he says, introducing me to the first one, and I do a double take. The St. Thomases are one of the richest families in the country. The whole world knows the St. Thomas name—they've been one of the biggest American business titans for the past century or so. "She's the director of donor relations."

Bree is a slim, tall woman, older than me, younger than my parents, wearing a sapphire satin cocktail dress with a large bow on one shoulder and matching high heels. On some people, that could look like the eighties redux, but on her, it looks chic and appropriate. Her matching jewelry probably cost more than my house.

But I've met plenty of rich people. They hire lawyers. While some of the attorneys at Weston & Ramirez do their estate plans and I tend to do litigation, it doesn't change the fact that, most of the time, our fees are paid by people like her.

Bree seems ... calculating. Like she's evaluating my net worth based on my shoes—which are nice—and deciding whether I'm worth her time.

Fuck her and what she stands for.

Regardless, I can still be polite. I shake her hand. "Nice to meet you. Charlie Cooper. I'm a friend of Tristan's."

"I'm sure you are," she says, with a knowing look that's on the judgy side. I see no need to correct her assumption, because one, what I said is true, and two, it's up to Tristan to say what he wants to her. She doesn't seem very accepting, but her thinking we've seen each other naked is accurate.

Thinking about sex makes me think about Rowan. I really should text him.

"Part of Bree's extended family lives up here in Montecito," Tristan is saying.

I do my best to be polite to her when I really just want to text Rowan. Finally, Bree leaves us when someone comes up and tugs her away, and I have a chance to pull out my phone.

Checking in on you. You doing okay tonight?

I get no response, which is weird. He usually responds right away.

Hmm. Maybe he's doing a rideshare pickup and can't talk right now.

I slip my phone back into my pocket, and when I turn around, about to reach for Tristan's hand, I see a pained expression on his face. He's looking at a tall, older woman wearing an impeccable black tweed Chanel suit.

"Hello, Mother," he says.

CHAPTER 26

Rowan

I stand and face this stranger. "Why has it taken you twenty-three years to show up?" My voice is as quiet as a graveyard at midnight.

But that stillness hides the atomic bomb detonating my insides and leaving them a wasteland. I want to beat my fists against his chest. To scream.

I'm used to not showing weakness to anyone, though, so I call on every single wall I've ever erected in my brain and raise them all.

The number of questions I have may be too many to be answered in this lifetime. For starters, besides, *Where am I?* I have:

What's your name?
What's my real name?
Why did you have armed men kidnap me?
Why are they such losers?
Where's my mother?
Why did you abandon me?
How did you find me?
What are you going to do with me now?

There's no good place to start, so I go with, "Where have you been all this time? Didn't you care about your son?" I flap my hands but hold my head high.

My *father* scrubs a hand over his face and sighs heavily. He looks kind of small standing here. Sure, he's well-dressed, and he's got an aura of authority, but something about him makes him seem ... human. *Dammit.*

Part of me wanted my parents to have been killed in an accident, which would explain why they never came to get me. Or that I was taken against their will. That something went wrong with the universal plan, which is why I've been alone for my entire life.

My body's all tensed up in preparation for his answer. I'm waiting for him to say that he didn't give a shit. That he left me to fend for myself like an orphaned kitten. Heat flushes through me, and I draw in a slow, steady breath.

He grimaces and stares down at his feet. Then he starts shaking his head repeatedly. When he looks up at me, his eyes are glassy. "Rowan, I've been looking for you ever since I learned you existed."

Fuck. I can't breathe. My chest seizes up.

Get it together.

Peeking over my internal wall like a meerkat, I blink at him. "You've been ... try-trying to find me?" It seems too good to be true. Nevertheless, my fool heart dares to hope. I try to steady my racing heartbeat, but that's a lost cause.

"I have. For decades." He has a grim twist to his mouth, and everything about his manner oozes sincerity. Still, it's hard for me to believe what he's saying, for obvious reasons—namely, that it took him this long.

"How?" I demand, a hand on my hip.

He pinches the bridge of his nose, his eyes closed, as he paces in front of me. "Every way that was within my power. Besides the private investigators, I even got the FBI involved. You just ... were nowhere to be found."

I chew on that for a moment. "What changed now?"

"When you were fingerprinted recently, the person who processed them cross-checked them against a missing person report and found that your first name and birth date were consistent with what we were looking for. We've never been certain of the last name you were given. I had an investigator put you under surveillance to see if you were who I hoped you were. He thought you were, because you look like me, but we had to be sure. He wanted to get you alone to talk with you, but you were always with someone. And he said you weren't cooperative." He crosses his arms over his chest and taps his fingers on his biceps.

I wave that away and sit down. "If you're talking about the dude in the tracksuit, he was a dick. He could have just said 'I have a question about your father.'"

My father shakes his head. "Not in this situation, but I'm not happy with how he handled it, either."

"Okay, I'll set that aside for now. My question is, I've been fingerprinted before. They didn't need it for foster care, but there were a few times ..." I decide not to tell my father my criminal history. The juvenile stuff got expunged, thanks to a competent public defender. "And they already had my name and birthday."

He throws his hands up. "I don't know why the match only pinged now." He sits down on the couch, an arm's length away from me. I think that's the correct place for him. Any closer would feel weird, but it also seems wrong to shove him away after I've been wanting to find him for so long.

I rub my forehead. "I don't even know who you are. Or who my mother is."

My father reaches out and lightly touches my shoulder. "My name is Remi, and your mother's name is Bianca. I haven't seen her since before you were born. This is all I had to go on to find you." He takes a folded white envelope out of his pocket. "I think you should know the truth." He hands it to me, and I pull a folded sheet of paper from it. The edges are tattered and worn, and the message is in large, cartoonish writing, similar to mine.

Dear Remi,

For months now, I've tried to gather the nerve to tell you that you're going to be a father. Then, when I finally was brave enough to try, your nosy secretaries wanted to know why I was calling. They said you were a very busy man and didn't have time for random calls. I could have gone to see you in person, but I knew the moment I walked into your office, they'd figure out why I was there, and part of me wanted to protect you, I guess.

Well, you now have a son. He was born yesterday, April 16. 7 pounds, 12 ounces. 18 inches.

He's got your blue eyes. His name is Rowan John. I can't keep him. I have my own life to live.

Don't worry, I didn't put your name on any birth certificate.

Bianca

I look up, and before I can begin asking questions, he says, "She was a woman I met at a communications convention in Las Vegas." He clears his throat. "I only saw her that one weekend. I remember her saying she lived in California, but by the time I got this letter, I couldn't remember what company she worked for or any other details about her. Except that she had a very pretty face. I was able to get the name of the company from the event organizers, but when I followed up, she had left that job."

I glance at the envelope. It has no stamp and in the same handwriting says:

Remi St. Thomas
c/o St. Thomas Industries

St. Thomas Building
4314 St. Thomas Blvd.
Los Angeles, California 90012

I look up at him with dawning realization. St. Thomas. St. Thomas Industries. "You're ..."

"Remi St. Thomas." He clears his throat and looks at me expectantly, bracing himself for impact.

Holy shit. "St. Thomas as in ..."

He nods. "As in the family you've likely heard of."

St. Thomas is usually mentioned in the same sentences as Getty, Rockefeller, Vanderbilt, and Carnegie. Industry titans who built America. Generational wealth.

This can't be happening. I stare at the letter, then at this man who very much looks like me.

"And you're my father?" I ask again, scratching my jaw, needing to be sure.

"Yes, Rowan."

I set down the letter and run my hands through my hair, tugging on it. "But that means ... I can't be ..."

"The son of a billionaire?" he asks.

I nod.

"You are."

CHAPTER 27

Charlie

Tristan leans forward to kiss his mother's powdered cheek. Despite the fact that I'm out and this isn't a life-changing event for me, I still have an empty feeling in the pit of my stomach, and my mouth is dry. So I sip my wine.

"Hello, dear," she responds. Then she looks at me.

And now the reason why we're here. Tristan takes a deep breath. "Mother, this is Charlie Cooper. He's a lawyer in Century City. And he's my ..." Tristan fumbles over the word. Friend? Partner? Boyfriend? We should've sorted out what he was going to say to her. Finally, he says, "lover," and his mother blanches. "Charlie, this is my mother, Veronica."

Lover's a pretty bold choice, Tris. But he might as well get the point across plainly.

Recovering, she holds out a cool hand to me. "Pleasure to meet you." She says it in a way that makes it clear that it's not in fact a pleasure to meet me.

Fuck. Great. I still return the pleasantry and shake her hand. "Likewise."

"Is this how you tell us you're ... homosexual?" she hisses to

Tristan, her voice barely audible over the conversations and holiday music.

He starts to redden and shrug and then remembers that he's an adult, and this is what he came here to do. "Yes, Mother. I'm gay."

She glances around, clearly unhappy, but also clearly good at playing the game of putting on a face in public. Watching it snap back into place is amazing. It also makes me never want to pretend to be anyone but who I am ever again.

I've been putting on a face for enough of my life. Caring what society thinks of me. Wanting the right car, right clothes, right job, right look. For what? So I can come to a fancy cocktail party and be looked down upon by someone who'd never recognize that people like me have just as much right to live as she does?

Fuck that.

But I can control my irritation. This isn't about me, it's about Tristan. He seems to be coming to the same conclusion, as he slings an arm around my shoulders and kisses my cheek.

I need to count my blessings. My mother and father have always been there for me. Sure, there were things I kept from them, but when I came to them with my troubles, they listened and did their best to help.

They weren't like Mrs. Albrecht Graff.

Veronica narrows her eyes at Tristan. "Don't bother coming to Christmas dinner," she says, and spins on her heel.

Taking all the oxygen out of the room as she walks away.

Well, fuck.

I'm pretty sure it's better to have no parents at all—poor Rowan—than it is to have ones who don't support you.

Tristan looks like he's been slapped. Which he has, in a way. I grab his hand. "Come on, let's get some fresh air."

He nods, and we hightail it outside into the pretty grounds. The buildings around us are lined with large white bulbs for the holidays, and the distant crash of the Pacific is before us. The air is cold, but California cold.

"Fuck," he says, pacing in front of a park bench. "That did not go the way I wanted it to."

"I'm so damn sorry, dude," I say, and I fold him in my arms.

He holds me tight, his body shaking. Despite the rich fabric of his jacket and the warmth of his solid body, bigger than mine, part of me thinks he's going to evaporate in a puff of smoke. I hold him for a long time. Finally, he mutters into my neck, "I didn't think she'd be that prejudiced."

"She's horrible. Sorry, dude."

Tristan sighs. "Yeah." He steps away from me and looks out into the dark night, wiping at his face.

"How are you feeling? I mean, do you regret doing this tonight?"

"I do not regret it. Even though the worst thing happened—at least as far as her reaction—I still feel like I can breathe for the first time in my life."

I give him a small smile.

"Still sucks that she reacted like that, though."

"Do you think she'll come around?"

"No. Fuck. My dad will be the same way." He throws out his hands. "Can we go home? I did what I wanted to do."

"Yeah," I say quietly. "Tonight kind of sucks all around. I wish I could fix things for you."

"You can't. But you were here for me, and that's what counts. Let's get you back to your boyfriend." While my inner autoresponder says that Rowan isn't my boyfriend, I'm pretty sure that he might be. We need to go back to Tristan's house for me to get my car, though.

While Tristan drives, I text Rowan again.

CHARLIE

Hey, baby. I haven't heard from you in a while.
Is everything okay?

I'm being paranoid and overprotective. I'm sure he's fine.

Just because you're paranoid doesn't mean they aren't after you.

Besides a few texts from Danny and Cam, my phone is flooded with notifications from Ad/VICE, as usual, and—as usual—I pretty much ignore them. In the beginning, I tried to respond to every comment, but these days there are just too many. I guess that's a good problem to have.

Tristan invites me inside, and while I want to go home to Rowan, Tristan's had a hard night.

"How are you doing now?" I ask, once we're sitting in his living room with drinks. Whiskey for him, beer for me.

"I'm ... pissed and hurt." Tristan's sprawled on his armchair, his jacket and tie off and his collar unbuttoned. He's taken off his shoes, and he looks ... diminished.

"I'd be angry, too," I say, loosening my tie.

Tristan takes a long sip of his whiskey. "My anger feels useless, though. What good is it to be pissed off? I can't do anything to change her."

I sit forward. "I saw something that said that anger's important, because it helps us identify injustices. It means we want to make things right."

"Anger can't actually make things right, though. It doesn't fix a damned thing."

"No," I say. "But being angry acknowledges the fact that something's broken. That's valuable."

"Maybe. I don't let myself feel much at all most days." Coming from Tristan—someone with whom I've never had a heart-to-heart —that admission feels huge.

"Maybe you should try feeling what you feel. Let yourself be angry. You have a right to be. I think, as a certified asshole, that it's morally correct for you to be angry that your mother's homophobic."

He studies me. "You know, Charlie, you always refer to yourself as an asshole. But you aren't."

I scoff. "Whatever. I'm not the nicest person on the planet."

"Just because you're not all smiley and friendly doesn't mean you're not nice."

I want to wave him off again. "Maybe," I allow. "But what are you going to do about your mother?"

"Do? Nothing. What is there to do? She *unvited* me to Christmas."

"Think about it, though. Is there something you want to say or do? If anger is a moral act—is vengeance?" I've clearly been spending too much time with Rowan.

Tristan snorts. "I'm not going to get even with my mother for being a closed-minded bigot."

"Don't you want to?"

"Well ... yeah. Kinda. I'm tempted to donate all the money in my trust to an LGBTQ-friendly charity in her name."

"That'd teach her."

"But it's more ... I just want her to accept me. Aren't parents supposed to be there for you and accept you the way you are?"

"In theory, yes. I'm one of the lucky ones, because mine did. My boyfriend—he's an orphan. He has no idea who his parents are, and he grew up in a series of group homes."

"I wonder if it's better to have no parents than to have terrible ones," Tris muses, echoing my earlier thoughts.

CHAPTER 28

Rowan

"What the fuck?" I whisper. My brain's all fuzzy, and I can't think. I slump with my head in my hands. "No. No, this is impossible."

Remi shakes his head sadly. "It's not impossible. I have missed out on so much with you."

"With all those resources, you still couldn't find me?" I snarl, lifting my head high and glaring at him. "If you're *Remi St. Thomas*, don't you have enough money to fund an excursion to the moon with a bus full of investigators to search there or anywhere else in the galaxy? I've been in LA the entire time. How, exactly, have you been trying to find me?" Sweat is starting to gather at my hairline and down my back, and I want to punch something. Kick something. Stab something. Instead, I flatten my lips and crack my knuckles.

Remi—it's hard to think of him as my father—lets out a theatrical groan. "The note didn't give us much to go off of, and it was days before I actually received her letter. We called every police station in the greater LA area, in Las Vegas, San Francisco, but no one had reports of a baby being dropped off."

"And why the kidnapping tactics? Why couldn't you just knock on my door?"

Although I'm the one who chose to mug Charlie instead of asking for help, so maybe it's a weird family thing.

Remi pinches the bridge of his nose, and spots of color infuse his cheeks. "That's the last thing I wanted to have happen."

I frown. "What?"

"I put Lonnie on you, but you were never alone so he could talk with you. We weren't going to announce to any witnesses that you might be my son. Lonnie says when you did talk to him, you pulled a knife on him."

"Lonnie wears an Adidas tracksuit?"

"Yes."

"What kind of PI wears a tracksuit?"

Remi tugs at his collar. "His uncle Albert provided security for my family for decades, and he was excellent. Right before Albert passed, he asked me to give Lonnie a job. We tried Lonnie in several positions, but he seemed more fitted for being out in the field than working in an office or in another capacity. This investigation seemed well aligned with his skill set." Remi swallows hard. "I couldn't go back on a deathbed promise. But then he had his associates pull a gun on you, and that was one step too far. He no longer works for me."

So Remi is loyal. Interesting. "I don't understand why he even thought it was an option."

"While I'm not sure what was going on inside his head, I had impressed upon him the confidentiality of this issue. Imagine if you weren't my son and we approached you saying that you could be a child I had out of wedlock. If we were wrong, there's the risk that you would contact the press or demand payment anyway, even if you weren't entitled to it. We had to be sure." He reaches in his pocket and hands me another piece of paper. After a moment of studying it, I realize that it's results from a paternity test. "We're sure. While you were unconscious, we swabbed your cheek and used a rush lab test." He gives me a wry smile. "It usually takes longer, but money buys speed."

I look at the test results. Fifty percent of me is a match to him. He's absolutely my father.

"I sent in my DNA, looking for a match," I whisper, squinting at it. "There was nothing. Not even a remote relative."

Remi swivels his head as if he's looking for backup, then remembers it's only him and me in here. "I'm not on any ancestry sites, and no family members are, either. We don't want anyone showing up and claiming they're an heir. We have enough headaches as it is."

I open my mouth to criticize him again, then shut it. Then I tug at my shirt. "I'm still fucking pissed you kidnapped me. Like, what the hell?"

"I know, and I apologize. I asked Lonnie to prioritize discretion, but he took it in a way I didn't intend."

"This is ... I don't even know how to describe this." I kick at the floor, feeling younger than I've felt in a long time.

Remi's voice is quiet. "I can imagine it's a lot to take in. And there's more to tell you." He smiles, and it's weird. Not quite warm and friendly. Not quite cutthroat and dishonest. More like he's unused to smiling. "Most of our family's money is held in my grandfather's trust. I'm already taking steps to acknowledge you as my son, so you'll be the beneficiary when I pass. You have a legacy you need to learn about."

It's all too much. I'm starting to shake, and I pull my knees up, not wanting to show any weakness. "Legacy? For the practically homeless kid from the foster system? The kid who drives a Share-ARide even though he's technically too young?"

"I do want to talk with you about every part of your history," he says. "For now, do you have a place to live? You've been staying with your boyfriend, correct?"

"He's letting me stay with him, but I feel like I'm freeloading,"

I admit, not contradicting Remi's description of Charlie, even though it probably exaggerates our relationship status.

Well, not from my perspective. As far as I'm concerned, we're mated for life. Charlie might think we're not that far along in our relationship. I don't care; he can be wrong.

Also, I'm studying my father—ugh, that's such a weird word—for any sign of homophobia. But he seems not to be focused on the boyfriend thing.

What would it be like to not have to depend on Charlie? To not be living from meager paycheck to meager paycheck?

"You don't have to feel like you're freeloading anymore. You're going to have family money."

"Not that I earned that, either," I interrupt. I should shut my mouth.

He sighs. "Don't worry about that. For now, do you want me to put you up in a hotel? Until we can get you a place to stay permanently, of course. I can also give you access to one of the houses."

It's tempting to have my own place. But Charlie's more important.

I shake my head. "No, I want to go back to my boyfriend." If he is my boyfriend. I think he is.

"Very well. But we will be putting a security guard on you before you leave—it won't be any of the people who brought you here today; don't worry. I'm sorry, but that's not negotiable."

"Why do I need security?"

"With your standing comes increased danger." He glances at me, likely taking in that I'm barely holding it together. "We'll have time to talk about that later. Right now, I have a credit card for you so you can get anything you need, and we'll have a bank account for you shortly."

"Holy shit. I'm not asking you to do any of that," I say, even though I should be quiet and let him do what he wishes.

"I think you've gone long enough living without," he says. He passes over a black credit card that says "Rowan J. Jones" on it. "We had this account set up for you. There's no spending limit. Go shopping. Buy whatever you like. New clothes. Fancy food. A television. A video game console. Hell, buy a car. Get yourself the things you never had. Do you want to drive your own car back, or do you want to use one of our until we get you a new one? I'm happy to give you anything you desire. I hope you know that."

"What I want is a family," I blurt. "To belong to someone in this life. To know I'm not all alone. It's all I've ever wanted."

He jerks his head back, his posture suddenly stiff. Then he nods. "Then we'll go out to lunch. Tomorrow."

I can see what kind of man he is. Busy. Willing to pay for what he wants, because money is meaningless to him. I don't know if I should be happy that he suggested going to lunch with me or if that's a way of keeping me from getting too close—anyone can get up and leave a restaurant. But maybe he's simply giving me privacy and time to sort this out, because this is too much of a mindfuck for my poor brain to handle.

"I don't want you to feel like I'm using you," I say. Remi crosses his arms over his chest, but he's listening. "I never had that much as far as stuff, but all I really needed was food and a roof and clothes. Nothing more. It can be hard to get the basics when you're being shunted from foster home to foster home."

Remi winces. "Your days of living like that are over. No more. You will always have proper clothes, enough to eat, a good place to stay, and anything else you desire. I promise you. Do you have any questions I can answer right now? I'm sure you have plenty."

"Were you ever married?"

"Yes. Hilary, my ex-wife, left me and had children with someone else, but I never remarried."

"What happened with my mother?"

"I tried to track her down after I learned of your existence, with no success. One investigator heard a rumor that she took her own life after she gave you up, but I've never been able to confirm it, so for all I know, she could be living somewhere. Maybe she changed her name or is going by a different one. No searches have ever been able to find her, and we've tried, although we gave up when all the trails went cold. Not being there for her is the biggest regret in my life next to my unsuccessful search for you." His face looks a little gray—grayer—and he coughs, pulling out a handkerchief. "Excuse me."

I want to soothe him, but he finishes coughing and gives me a pitying look. Like he's aware of everything I didn't have because he didn't find me sooner.

Something in me splinters.

I need to leave. Now. It's too much. Fuck all this shit. My throat is thickening again, and my face is tingling. I can't meet his eyes.

Eyes that look like mine.

I've spent much of my life trying to find this man, and now I need to get out of here as fast as humanly possible.

"I want to go home," I say to my Vans. "I need to think about all this. And I want my plant."

Taking a chance, I glance up at Remi, who gives me a sad smile. "I can understand this is overwhelming." He reaches inside his jacket and pulls out a brand-new phone, still in the box. "This has my number and the numbers of your drivers, my assistants, and your accountants, among others. Do you want to take one of my cars?"

"Something that runs better than my piece of crap?"

"Yes. It's new. Let me have your items transferred." He pulls out his phone and texts someone, coughing again. "They are moving your personal belongings." Digging in his pocket, he hands me a car key. "Until you pick out a vehicle you like, take this one. It's bulletproof. Just in case."

Wow, he's paranoid.

Just because you're paranoid doesn't mean they aren't after you.

I hold the key in my hand, turning it over. It's for a BMW. It probably has a tracker in it or some such tech. Accepting it means that I'm going to be accepting this new way of life. Eventually.

He looks at me with sincerity in his eyes. "I know it will take some time to sink in, but I'm going to make sure you understand how much power and influence you have now. You don't have to be on the bottom anymore."

What if I want to be? my brain snarks, thinking of Charlie.

"Okay," is all I say, and I kick myself for being so ... passive.

But what else can I do? I'm not foolish enough to say no. This man can afford a hundred of me. More. And apparently he thinks he needs to atone.

"Rowan, I'm so sorry it took this long to find you. You've had to do without. But you don't have to do that anymore. You can have whatever you need."

"Including getting to know you?"

He smiles. "Yes. We can start that tomorrow at lunch, if you like. I'll text you the address of a restaurant." He looks me over one more time. "I can't believe I've finally found you. I'm going to take care of you." A dark look passes over his face. "For as long as I can."

"Thanks." I don't know what else to say. It's too enormous for me to process.

"Come on." I follow him out the door.

I think we're in an office building, judging by the corporate art in the hallways and the closed doors. "Where are we?"

"This is the headquarters of St. Thomas Communications," he says.

"Why did you bring me here, of all places? And why the hell do you have a secret interrogation room?"

"This building has good security and hidden entrances. We can get people in and out without them being noticed." I open my mouth, and he continues, "In case I was wrong about you and the paternity test came back negative, we needed to have control of the situation. Again, I'm sorry that the security team used tactics that frightened you."

"I wasn't frightened. Just annoyed."

He looks at me appraisingly. "You really are a St. Thomas."

He leads me down some halls, then down a flight of stairs and into a parking garage full of fancy cars, all shiny, with tinted windows. He beeps one of them and points me to it. "Use this one to get home."

Wilbur is sitting in the passenger seat. My lip trembles. "What's going to happen to my car?"

"It's over there." He gestures down the row of parked cars, and yep, there's my car sticking out like a rat turd in a jewelry display. "I asked them to put your personal items in the BMW's glove compartment, and you can have your car moved wherever you wish."

What's it like to just say something and know it's been done?

"If you like this car, feel free to keep it. If you want a different one, just let me know, or pick one out yourself if you prefer. You'll also have a driver at your disposal."

"Okay, thanks. I want to go back to my ..." My Charlie. "My boyfriend now."

Remi and I stand there, awkwardly, looking at each other. He coughs harshly into his elbow.

Has he really been trying to find me my whole life?

Wow.

I can't even articulate how this changes my world view. I thought I was all alone.

My throat is starting to feel scratchy, and my eyelids are hot.

Do I give him a hug? He's a total stranger, and I'm not particularly affectionate to anyone but Charlie.

Finally, I shake his hand, feeling ridiculous, and climb into the car.

It's nicer than the nicest place I've ever been. Sparkling clean. Leather seats. Digital displays of everything. It takes me a moment to get the seat adjusted—hey, I'm short, and Remi must have tall drivers—and to put the mirrors in the correct position.

I roll down the window, my chest tight. "See you tomorrow."

"Bye, son."

Son.

The world seems to wobble and slow down. No one's ever called me "son." Not even my kind foster parents, because they knew I wasn't really theirs.

So many years. So much lost time. So many things I'll never have, because of circumstances beyond his control. Beyond our control. I'm not going to hold it against him that he couldn't find me, because it sounds like he tried. But I'm still pissed.

My vision's blurry, and my chest aches.

I never got a birthday party with my father. Or a day spent at a park. I never got to show him my report cards or to go to the same school the whole way through. I didn't get to talk with him about any of the questions I had growing up—about how the world works, my sexuality, how I was going to make it through life. What I was interested in.

Fuck. I missed out on a lot.

I back up, my hands shaking. I'm feeling extremely self-conscious, and I don't want to scrape this expensive car on anything in the underground parking garage. I emerge into the night and find I'm in the middle of Los Angeles. Charlie's address is already programmed into the GPS, which creeps me out a bit, but obviously Remi knows where Charlie lives, if he sent tracksuit guy—Lonnie?—to watch me there. I follow it home on autopilot. Scenery streams by, but I'm zoning out and don't register it.

A keening noise comes from somewhere.

Me. It came from me.

I'm starting to hyperventilate.

I think this is what it feels like to have my heart break.

When I spy Charlie's house, I'm overcome with the urge to get the fuck out of this car. I park it haphazardly across the driveway, grab Wilbur, and race inside. As I do, I notice a black Escalade pulling up across the way, and the driver gives me an up nod.

So now I have a bodyguard. A constant shadow.

I wanted a father for twenty-three years. I was so alone, but now I have … too much.

I can't fucking handle it. I can't fucking breathe.

When I get Charlie's door open, I slam it behind me, set Wilbur in the bathroom sink, and run down the hall to Charlie's bedroom. I pace, throwing my hands in the air, then go over to the door and bang my forehead on it. I clench my hands into fists and shake.

I slide down the wall until I'm sitting with my ass by my heels. For the first time since I was a teenager, I burst into tears.

CHAPTER 29

Charlie

It's late when I pull up to my house, but when I go to turn into the garage, I can't get to it, because a brand-new, black BMW 7 Series sedan is taking up my entire driveway.

I glare at it, my stomach rolling, a sour taste in my mouth.

What the hell? Who's here? Where's Rowan?

I end up blocking the car in, because of course there's no street parking, and sprint to my front door, fumbling with my keys. But then I realize it's unlocked.

When I step inside, Rowan isn't sitting on the couch where he usually is, and he doesn't come running into my arms.

"Rowan?" I call. "Baby?"

Nothing.

Ice pours into my veins. What the hell is going on?

"Rowan?"

I hear a choked sound, which makes my adrenaline spike. I hurry down the hall to our bedroom, where I sag against the door-frame. He's here. I get a better look at him, and my hackles rise again.

Rowan's crumpled on the floor in the corner, his back against the wall and his knees pulled up to his chest. He looks as small as

I've ever seen him. His eyes are red-rimmed, and his face has pink splotches on it—closer to fuchsia than his hair.

Spots flash in my vision, and my throat tightens painfully. Seeing him crying makes me feel all kinds of things: a deep protectiveness—he's my mermaid without a tail, my selkie who's lost his skin, *mine*—but also a simmering *need* to fix whatever hurt him. By whatever means necessary.

"Hey," I say quietly, crouching down next to him and holding up my hands like he's going to bite. "What's wrong?"

"Things," he mutters to his knees.

Panic lances through me. "Did I do something wrong? Nothing happened with me and Tristan at the party. He had kind of a shit night, but that's because of things outside of you, me, or him. Are you pissed at me?"

He shakes his head, his bangs flopping on his forehead, and my chest eases a little. "I just don't want you to see me like this."

I put my hands on his knees and squeeze them. "Baby, I've seen you desperate." I don't want to rub salt in his wounds, but having his car stolen and getting evicted had to be low points in his life. "I'm not going to hold anything you tell me against you. Whatever your feelings are, they're valid. Everything is going to fucking be okay." I don't know that I can promise that last part, but it makes him finally look up at me, so I vow to fix whatever happened to him. Especially when I see that his dark blue eyes are full of pain— so much pain that I can't breathe. "What is it?"

"I found my birth family."

That ... wasn't what I was expecting. "Is that ..." Now I don't know what kind of tears these are. Happy? Sad? Relieved? Angry?

"It's fucked up."

My stomach sinks. "I'm so sorry. Give me one second, and we'll take care of this." I shuck off my dress clothes, letting them fall wherever, and yank on lounge pants and a T-shirt. "Come to bed with me." I remove Rowan's shoes and jeans, then tug him onto the mattress with me, letting him lean on my chest while I sit with my back to the headboard so he doesn't have to look at me as he processes whatever he learned today. His tiny ass is in my lap, and his arms are around my neck. Mine are around him. "Okay, now. How are you? What happened?"

"Ch-Charlie, I'm so …" And he starts sobbing again. His entire body shakes as he howls into me. It makes tears come to my eyes, too.

Because what must he be feeling? To not know anything about his history—even his exact birthday, his parents, none of it. And now that he does, who are they? Please, universe, let them not be homophobic like the Graffs. Let them accept him for who he is.

Rowan starts scratching me, and I allow it. He beats on my sternum and cries and swears, his voice getting louder, then softer, then incomprehensible. He's snotty, wiping his face on my shirt, and I let the storm happen. I don't even try to soothe him, other than holding him, because he needs to get this out. Suppressing this much emotion wouldn't be good.

After quite a while, he hiccups and calms. "I told you I didn't want you to see me like this."

"And I told you I could handle it. I'm here for you, baby. Whatever you need."

He snuffles into me, and I squeeze my arms tight around him like I'm holding him together. I might be doing just that. "You smell good," he says. "It's that lotion, isn't it?"

"You spying on me?" I tease. "Go through my medicine cabinet?"

Rowan wipes his eyes and sticks his nose in the air. "Obviously. You and your fancy products."

"They're not that fancy."

"I looked them up, and I couldn't afford them. I guess I can now, though." He starts sobbing again.

So … I guess his family is well-off? That seems like a good thing, unless they're bigoted creeps after all.

"Hey, baby," I whisper. "It's okay. I'm here."

I hold him through another round of tears. I don't know what else to do, and I don't like being helpless to make him feel better. Finally, his tears ebb, and he clears his throat.

In a low voice, Rowan says, "The most fucked up part is that he says he's been looking for me the whole time."

Rowan has suffered so much, and it was possibly needless? That makes me feel physically ill—a deep, sudden nausea. I swallow hard and try to keep it together. "Really?"

Rowan nods. "He used private investigators and everything. But he paid to keep his DNA off the websites, which is why I could never find him."

"How did he find you?"

Even in his misery, Rowan smirks. "Because someone who has perfectionist tendencies and is a rule-abiding lawyer with a love of plans and lists insisted that I go to the police station when my car was stolen and do everything by the book."

I blink rapidly and then openly stare at him. "*That's* how he found you? Our trip to the police station?"

He snorts. "Kinda. He didn't know what last name my mother put down for me, so he's been looking for a Rowan John my age, born on April 16. When we went to the police station, someone noticed I met his criteria and contacted him, and I guess then he put me under surveillance and when they decided I might be his son, he fucking had me kidnapped so he could do a paternity test."

I have to have heard him wrong. "You wanna say that again?"

"He had to be sure I was really his, so he had some jackasses—his PI or whatever, I guess, though you'd think he could spring for a better one—pick me up. The dude who's been in front of your house? He was one of them. They pulled a gun on me. Then they shot me up with some kind of drug to make me fall asleep, and I woke up in a windowless room. After he'd taken my cheek swab and sent it off to some speedy lab."

I'm apparently stepping on the same emotional roller coaster

Rowan's been on, because anger flashes through me like a chemical fire. "What the hell? Is he some kind of gangster?"

"No." Rowan studies me, clearly waiting to see how I'm going to react. "He's Remi St. Thomas."

I stare at him. "As in ..."

"Yes. It sounds like my rightful name might be Rowan St. Thomas."

There's no other word to describe what happens when he confirms the name: I'm *stunned*. My brain goes haywire, and my body stiffens. For real, this is a bombshell.

I have no idea how much money the St. Thomases have, but I know one thing for certain: I'm in bed with the heir to *billions*.

Rowan's not a guttersnipe—he's a prince.

Get it together, Charlie.

But still, what the actual fuck?

I don't question him. There's no way Rowan is joking. "Wow," is all I can think to say.

Because money like that changes everything. Especially for a man who was in a position like Rowan was—where he had nothing and was one step up from living on the streets.

"Guess I met one of your relatives tonight," I say. "Bree St. Thomas. Not sure where she sits on the family tree. She was kind of a bitch. Gave off homophobic vibes."

"Huh. You know more than I do." He sighs. "Now that I told you who I am," Rowan *St. Thomas* says, picking at the sheets, "I'm scared you're gonna treat me differently."

To be frank, so am I. And I'm afraid he'll leave, now that he won't need me anymore.

"You're still Rowan," I say slowly. "I've been attracted to you since before I knew your name—before *you* knew it. I've wanted you since you pulled a goddamned knife on me and I got you on your back."

"I like it when you put me on my back."

That makes me grin despite everything.

"But now everything is fucked up," he says.

"I'll be honest: I'm shocked, and my first reaction is to agree with you, but my law school training is kicking in here, and I want to question the premise. Yes, assuming your ... father ..." Rowan doesn't react, so I figure it's okay to use that word. "Assuming he wants to help you out, bring you into the family, whatever—right? Is that the idea?" He nods, and I take a breath. "Well, then yes, that'll mean you have access to more money"—a *lot* more—"and you now know a big secret about yourself that you'd wondered about your entire life. Those are big changes, sure. But do they make *you* different?"

"I think they do."

"How so?"

"Because ... I don't know. I'm so confused, Charlie. Don't make me figure everything out right now."

I kiss his cheek. "Fair. I won't. I'm sorry, I'm not cross-examining you. I'll stop. Wait, I lied. One more question for now: Is that BMW in the driveway from your father?"

He nods. "He said he'd give me a car and a house and money for clothes and food. He gave me a credit card and says he's setting up a bank account or something with the lawyers. He says he's been looking for me the entire time I've been alive. He wants to have a relationship with me."

"That's a lot to process," I say, holding him closer, his bony ass sharp on my thighs. He might leave a bruise. I don't care.

"It's just so, so messed up," Rowan whispers. "I feel screwed out of *life*. I could've had a family growing up, and instead, I got ..." He looks pointedly at his tattoos. "And what the fuck? My mom gave me up *intentionally*." He sighs. "I can empathize with her maybe feeling scared that she was pregnant and all alone. Remi showed me a letter she wrote him. But still. I'm pissed at her, too. She fucked me over."

While there's no guarantee his life would've been perfect with the St. Thomases, things certainly would have been different if he'd known his family. I nod. "It's a clusterfuck. I said I'd stop asking questions, but I'm kind of guessing a few things here, and I'd rather hear it from you. You don't have to answer if you don't want to. Wanna tell me how you're feeling?"

Rowan sighs, and even though I've seen him at some pretty low moments, until now I've never heard him sound like the weight of the world is on his shoulders. "I don't know. At first, it was rage. Like I've been cheated. I put up with so much shit, and now I find out that I'm ... I can't even say the word." He squares his shoulders. "Rich. That I might be rich. That I have a family I didn't know about, and they have more money than I can dream of. And then, do I deserve any of this? Shouldn't I be happier? How is my life going to change? It's so damn overwhelming. Most of me doesn't believe it's true. Like, this is someone playing a prank on me."

I run a finger along his jaw. "Pretty elaborate prank, if it is."

"I need to do some research on them."

"Do that. Or you can just ask Mr. St. Thomas. Remi? I assume he gave you a way to get in contact with him."

"Yeah. Oh, by the way, we're going to need to get used to having someone tailing me. I guess now I'm going to have body-guards or security or something."

"Holy shit." I nuzzle his head. "This is going to take you some time to think through."

"Yeah." He breathes in. "I'm sorry I took it out on you."

"It's what I'm here for," I rumble. "I care about you, baby boy. In case you haven't figured that out."

"I care about you, too," he whispers. "A lot."

We fall silent. A car horn blares outside, and then a neighbor must open a window, because rap music starts playing.

I'm worried about Rowan. Something about this does feel too good to be true. Even if it did come with a side of kidnapping.

"Back to him having people pull a gun on you," I say. "What the hell? Why would he do that?"

"Because he didn't want me extorting him for money if I didn't turn out to be his son. Although he says the gun wasn't part of his plan."

I scoff. "Yeah, right. Then what would he have done? Killed you?"

Rowan shrugs and runs a finger down my jawline, his eyes searching mine. "He's a powerful man. I have no idea. I guess he fired the guy who orchestrated my kidnapping."

"You must've been scared."

"Me? Nah."

I give him a raised eyebrow look that says *bullshit*.

Weird that the part that bothers me the most isn't the crime they committed against him today, although that does make me livid.

The part that bothers me the most is the decades that Rowan lived not knowing who he was, when he was Someone with a capital *S*. I think deep down, he sensed it. Maybe he was acting out—dyeing his hair, making his appearance unforgettable—so they could find him.

"I'm supposed to see him tomorrow for lunch," he says. "This time without the kidnapping."

"How do you feel about that? Do you want me to go with you?"

He shakes his head. "I can handle it."

"I know you can. But do you want me to go anyway?"

Rowan blinks. "This is what it's like to have a boyfriend?"

Butterflies bounce around in my stomach, but that term feels very right. I grin at him. "Yep."

We kiss lightly, but I don't take it any farther, because he's pretty wrung out. "What do you need now?" I ask. "Do you have any aftereffects from the kidnapping? Do you need to go midnight bowling?"

"*Now* you're asking me on a date?" Rowan's entire face lights up, even though it's still splotchy from his tears.

"The timing is bad, I'll admit." I hold him tight. "You know I was attracted to you before your hoity-toity family name and money, right?"

"You proved that many times over." He snuggles into me. "Today's too much to handle. I just want to stay here with you."

"As you wish."

"Ugh," Rowan groans. "I'm all up in my feels. I don't know how to put all this aside so I can relax. Part of me wants to just go punch something."

"You can fight me," I offer.

If he needs to beat me up, I'll take it. He scratched me up some during his crying jag earlier, but that wasn't a fight.

He gives me a long once-over. Is he going to say yes?

Finally, he shakes his head. "I need to check out more than I want to fight."

"The main things I do when I want to check out are whiskey, weed, or sex. Do any of those appeal?"

"Of those options, I can't believe I'm picking weed," Rowan mutters. "I'd think I'd always pick sex, especially with you, but I'm just too stressed out and today's been too much and I need chemical help."

"You got it, baby." I scoot him off me and reach over to the bedside table, riffling through it until I find my vape pen. I hand it to him.

He reads the side, then brings it to his mouth and inhales deeply, holding his breath. "I didn't know you vaped," he says when he exhales.

"Not that often. Just sometimes."

"Yeah, me, too."

I tug him back into my lap and kiss the top of his head. He sucks on the pen again, then passes it to me, and I take a hit. Because I might need something to help me check out, too. That or therapy. My boyfriend isn't who I thought he was. He's so much more.

"I found Wilbur," he says, his shoulders relaxing as he melts into me.

I laugh with surprise and smile against his hair. "You did? Where? How is he?"

"He was behind a big rock kind of near the campground. His pot was broken, but I put him in a bag. Right now, he's in the bathroom. I need to get him a new pot."

"I probably have one out in the shed that would work," I say. "Want me to get it now?"

"Not yet. Can I have the vape?"

I nod. We keep passing it between us until we're both lying down, and I'm in that buzzed-out state where I'm separate from real life—where I'm observing things instead of a part of them. It's letting me relax but still be aware.

I'm on my back, and Rowan's sprawled out across me. He's playing with my hair and snuggling his head under my chin. I'm drawing shapes on his ribs. We stopped talking a while ago. What else is there to say?

It's all different now.

Rowan's been the missing boy for so long. And now he's found. No wonder he needed to zone out.

I'm not worried about the money. Or not *just* about the money, if I'm being honest. It's the fact that Rowan is now going to be all into his family, and he's not going to have time for me.

Wow, is that poor little me talking? I have to knock that off immediately. I shouldn't let the drugs loosen my brain too much. Rowan's just found a family he's been searching for for decades, and I'm making it about me. I'm such a tool.

We stay like this a long time. Even when the position gets uncomfortable, I don't move. If he needs to hear me breathing, so be it. I'm here for him.

I can't imagine what all is going through his brain. Going from nothing to, maybe, everything has to be a complete mindfuck.

After a while, staying still does get to be too much, and I

stumble into the bathroom to pee and get a warm washcloth for Rowan's face. We're both kind of a mess.

"Want a midnight snack?" I ask.

"Yeah," he says. "I forgot to eat all day."

"Then let me make you a sandwich, and after that, we'll go to sleep."

"Deal."

CHAPTER 30

Rowan

The cool click of a gun near my head makes my body go rigid.

Shit. They got me.

What about Charlie?

I need to protect him. I can't let them get him.

Bang!

Horror washes over me. I failed. I scream—only to wake up in bed next to Charlie, gasping for air. I claw at my cheeks, squeezing my eyes shut.

I've sweated through the sheets. My heart is racing.

You're okay. It was just a dream. Or rather, a nightmare.

In the darkness, I can make out Charlie blinking next to me. "Hey," he says, his voice raspy. "What's the matter?"

I bite the inside of my cheek so that the pain distracts me and take a few deep breaths.

When my pulse is back to normal, I snuggle into him. I don't answer his question.

But I should've known that Charlie wouldn't let me get away with that. "Rowan. Baby. What's wrong?" He moves us so he's the big spoon. I lie in his arms and breathe for a while. I've never had anyone to just … hold on to. And I like being touched.

"Bad dream," I say at last.

"Sorry, baby." Charlie holds me tighter. It's easier for me to talk when I don't have to see him.

I glance at the bedside clock. It's three in the morning. "Guess it was a flashback from the kidnapping."

Charlie presses a kiss to the back of my neck. "Your fucking family. You must've been terrified."

My default is to say no, but this is Charlie. "Maybe a little." I snuggle closer into him.

"You're safe now. With me."

"Thanks."

Charlie smells so good. It's not just that he smells like hinoki. He smells like comfort. It's a good smell, light and fresh, and I want to burrow into him.

So, of course, I do that as much as I can.

I like the way Charlie's biceps feel around me. I like the way my waist feels against his. I like the way we just slot in next to each other.

"Are we going to get a happy ending?" I ask Charlie sleepily.

"Why wouldn't we?"

Why wouldn't we?

I fucking love Charlie, and that's all there is to it.

I knew I was in love with him when he helped me look for Wilbur, but it might have happened earlier. Like when he gave the money to the unsheltered guy when we walked into the restaurant in Malibu. Or maybe when he called me baby boy the first time.

I don't believe in insta-love, but he had my heart already.

Then he kept looking out for me. Watching over me when no one else would.

Now he's stuck with me, even though I'm not who either of us thought I was.

I wish I could tell past Rowan that he was a secret billionaire and to hang in there.

But I suppose all that crap I went through made me stronger. Or some new age bullshit like that.

It made me who I am now.

Which is someone who's desperately in love with his boyfriend. My grumpy, perfectionist boyfriend, who seems to have thrown out all his rules since he met me. Who seems like he's alive now. I don't know what he used to be like, but the way he is now is nothing short of amazing.

There's no one else I trust like him.

I cuddle into him and eventually fall asleep again. This time with no nightmares.

* * *

In the morning, I wake up in Charlie's arms. We shower and get in some vigorous blow jobs before heading into the kitchen for breakfast. When we walk into the living room, we realize how badly we parked last night and move both our cars into the garage.

"How are you feeling?" Charlie asks as he sets a stack of toast and a mug of coffee in front of me.

"I'm still … raw from yesterday. Raw isn't quite the right word. But I'm both empty and full at the same time. I'm tender and hardened. I'm eager to go meet my father for lunch and kind of dreading it, too. I'm not sure why."

"I get it."

"Do you? How many people do you know who have had what happened to me happen to them?"

"Exactly one. You." Charlie gives me one of his rare smiles, and it fills up the parts of me that were feeling empty and soothes the parts that prickle.

"Hmm." I eat some toast and stare at my phone. "It's Wednesday. Don't you have to go to work?"

"Yeah. But before I go, let's repot Wilbur," Charlie says, taking his coffee mug with him out to the backyard.

Charlie's backyard isn't the smallest, but it's not huge, either. Like he says about his house, it has potential. I follow him out, carrying my own coffee, which is also in one of his homemade-looking mugs.

He's got a large shed in the back corner where, I found when I was snooping, he stores his lawn mower and some tools. He rummages inside and emerges with a gorgeous blue-glazed pot just the right size for Wilbur, along with an open bag of potting soil. "Will this do?"

"Yes!" I chirp. "It's perfect—so pretty! Thank you!" I set down my mug and race into the house to get Wilbur.

Together, we sit on the back stoop and settle Wilbur carefully into his new digs. Patting his leaves affectionately, I coo at him as Charlie waters him from the hose. I know it's my imagination, but I think Wilbur perks up immediately.

"All better?" Charlie asks.

"Definitely." I give him a wide smile. I help him clean up the potting soil that got loose, toss the plastic bag that served as a temporary pot, and then take Wilbur inside and set him in a place of honor in Charlie's kitchen window. "Is it okay if he goes here?"

"Yep." Charlie refills both of our coffees.

"That pot is cool," I say, my voice bubbly and light. Things do seem better in the morning. Especially when I'm with my boyfriend. "It looks handmade."

Charlie gives me a fond smile. "That's because it is."

"Do you know the artist?" I ask.

"Me." He seems to be bracing himself for judgment.

I knew it. How perfect is it that Charlie not only gave me a home, he made one for Wilbur? "Did you make these mugs, too?"

Charlie nods. "Ceramics class in college."

"You're so artistic."

"Yeah? I think they're kind of amateurish."

"Nah, that's what gives them their charm."

Charlie's cheeks glow. "Maybe."

"Definitely. You made them, which makes them special anyway, but they're super cool. I think you've got a real artistic side. I know you like editing videos, but do you enjoy other kinds of art?"

He stares at me for a long moment. "When I was a kid, I used to draw. I haven't done it in a while."

"Maybe you can start up again. Maybe you can let yourself do the things you want to do."

"Yeah," he says, getting up. He puts his coffee mug in the dishwasher. "Maybe."

CHAPTER 31

Rowan

With trembling legs and cold hands, I walk up to the entrance of a fancy restaurant in Beverly Hills to have lunch with my father. Words I never figured would apply to me.

I almost didn't come. Nerves started to get to me, and Charlie was at work. But I called him, and he walked me through my feelings, encouraging me to go to lunch but reminding me I could leave at any point if I wanted to.

I don't quite understand why it's so scary to get what I've wanted all these years. Maybe because now I'm worried it's not going to live up to what I imagined it would be? Regardless, I wish my brain would just let me enjoy something for once rather than make it difficult.

Although I do have a secret weapon: *Daddy*. Not Remi, but my boyfriend. Charlie reminded me that I'm the bravest motherfucker who ever lived, given that I attacked *him*. He made me laugh. Somehow, he always knows what I need to hear.

So I got in the car early enough to make it here on time.

My breath caught for a moment when the valet took the keys to my brand-new BMW. Things being done for me ... still weird.

My old car showed up this morning, washed, gassed up, and parked on the street with the keys in an envelope on the front porch.

Also, did you know that valet parking is free in Beverly Hills? What the hell? How come the rich don't have to pay for things? At least I have a few dollars on me for a tip. Charlie insisted that I take some cash with me, and now I'm glad I did.

I step into the restaurant and almost back straight out. Except, no. I have a right to be here. I'm sure I'm not the first pink-haired person to dine here, and I won't be the last. I'm wearing my favorite black T-shirt and my cleanest skinny jeans. I'm wrapped in Charlie's brown suede jacket that he put on my shoulders when we met—and that I'm never returning. I needed to bring him with me, even if I wanted to do this on my own.

The place is decorated for the holidays in a restrained style, with fresh greenery and silver balls hanging from the ceiling in artful clusters. Classical holiday music plays in the background. The place announces that you must have money to enjoy its offerings. But that doesn't surprise me. In fact, I feared it'd be worse—that I'd be turned away at the door for having too many tattoos or not passing a credit check. Instead of showing me the exit or giving me a snooty attitude because I'm underdressed, the greeter addresses me in a professional manner. "I'm here to meet Remi St. Thomas," I say.

She smiles. "We're expecting you. Right this way."

I follow her through the maze of tables covered in white table-cloths, and she shows me to a discreet table located behind a wall of plants, where my father waits. He's seated, checking his phone, and wearing a sport coat over an oxford shirt, jeans, and shiny loafers, all of which fit his small frame perfectly. When he sees me, his eyes light up, and I get all these wiggly feelings inside me that I don't know what to do with.

He stands and shakes my hand. Which feels weird, but less weird than hugging a stranger who donated half of my DNA and had me kidnapped yesterday. His grip is strong, like he learned to shake hands heartily when he was three. His hand is the same size as mine—which is something else I'm not used to. I sit, and the host puts the napkin in my lap and hands me a menu, then leaves me alone with Remi.

"This is awkward," I say. "I've never been in a place like this."

An expression like regret washes over my father's face.

"Movies always talk about not knowing which fork to use, but it's not even that. I don't know what I'm supposed to do here or order or say," I admit.

Remi gives me an understanding nod. "It's my fault you don't feel comfortable, so maybe we let you pick the next restaurant." He pauses. "From a list of mutually acceptable places."

Despite myself, I smile. He's scared I'm going to make him go to Taco Bell. "I figured you'd be all into ... manners," I say. "I'm not sure mine are up to snuff."

"Nothing you could do here would make me upset. You could swear at me or dance on the table. Yell at me in anger or rage at the world. Turn this place upside down and have them ask us to leave. I don't care. I'm just glad to have found you."

Does he mean that? He cares where we go but not how I act?

"Why are you being so nice to me?"

I suppose he could just buy the restaurant if he wanted to let me run rampant like a toddler. It's an entirely alien way of looking at the world. One where he's in control of life, not the other way around.

He must read the disbelief on my face. His voice lowers. "Rowan, I promise I'm not going to nitpick about your behavior or anything else. I prefer a certain quality of food if I'm going out, but there are much more important things going on."

"Oh, like what?"

The server comes by, and Remi orders a gin and tonic for himself. I get a Coke. I need a clear head. I don't care if it makes me look unsophisticated. I *am* unsophisticated.

Once the server leaves, he sighs. "Now that you're going to be a St. Thomas, you have a lot to learn about the family. And me."

"Isn't that a little presumptuous? I mean, I already have a last name." I scrunch my nose. "What was Bianca's last name?"

"Ackerman. Of course you can keep the name you're used to, if you prefer. Or change it to Ackerman or St. Thomas—or anything else, I suppose. But regardless of the name you use, you'll be part of the St. Thomas family. That's what I meant."

I blink, needing to process. But Jones never felt like a real last name to me. I always figured that the cops just put that down so they could finish filling out the form.

"You don't need to decide now," he says, "but if you wish, the lawyers can prepare a name change petition." He coughs, and it sounds ... not good. Is he okay? "I believe it takes a few months to publish and get a court date."

"Have them do it. Rowan St. Thomas."

Or should I use Rowan Cooper? No, that's a little presumptuous, even for me.

"I met with my lawyers this morning," Remi says. "You are now in line to become the sole beneficiary of the St. Thomas family intergenerational trust, which was created by Grandfather almost a hundred years ago. That's in addition to being the beneficiary of my own trust from my business ventures."

Holy shit. "Um ..." I blink. "I'm not sure I know what to say."

"That's quite all right. I'm sure you're going to need some time to process this."

"Speaking of your grandfather, do I have grandparents who are alive?"

"I don't think so. On my side, you have Nana, who is my aunt, so she's your great-aunt. She's ... a character. I think you'll like her. Certainly more than some of the rest of the family. I told her we found you, and she invited you over, but I said you might need some time."

I shake my head. "No, I want to meet her."

"Then you shall."

"Where does she live?"

"Here, in Los Angeles. Her house used to be Harry Houdini's estate. It's quite interesting—there are secret rooms and underground passageways and even some of his memorabilia. It's a house that befits his legacy."

He's trying to distract me, and I'm okay with that. "She's not old enough to have known him, right?"

Remi chuckles. "No. I believe he died in the mid-1920s, and she may be elderly, but she's not that old."

"Don't tell her I asked that, then."

It's hard to imagine her. Is she an eccentric old lady? Or one who wears sweater sets and drinks tea? Maybe I've seen too many movies, but I'm picturing some grand dame with a cigarette in a long holder, wearing a caftan. Or a grandma wearing a rose leisure suit, wielding an axe.

For the first time in a long time, I'm looking forward to my future. When I met my father yesterday, there was no anticipation —just shock. But meeting my great-aunt ... yeah, this is cool.

"We will renew the efforts to look for Bianca, though."

I gulp. "Yeah, I'd like that."

"Then consider it done." He texts someone. Then his face gets very serious, his mouth downturned. "There's something else I need to tell you, and this isn't good news."

That makes me scowl at him. I uncross and recross my legs under the table, the white tablecloth getting in the way of my movements. "Don't keep me in suspense. I waited long enough to know who my parents are."

Remi scrubs a hand over his face and squeezes his eyes shut. Then he rubs his chest and looks at me, sighing heavily. "There's no easy way to say it: I have pancreatic cancer."

I want to ask him if he's joking, but that's not something you joke about. And I could tell he had health issues when we first met.

But this ... Things just keep coming at me, one after another.

I feel like I'm sinking through the floor. Then anger surges. I want to throw my Coke at him. I want to be that toddler raging around. I close my eyes, trying not to hyperventilate.

Where's Charlie when I need him? I told him he didn't have to come today. That was a bad choice. Not that I can't handle this on my own, but I don't *want* to. And I don't have to. I can rely on Charlie. I trust him. He's seen me at my most desperate, and then even worse, and all he did was hold me. Hence why I love him.

Still, though, finding out you're a long-lost billionaire heir messes with your head. I hoped I'd be getting a family, too, which is what I've always wanted.

But the universe is saying *nope*.

Fuck, everything has been too emotional lately. I swallow hard, gather myself, and say as calmly as I can, "Cancer?"

Remi gives me a solemn nod. "Yes. It's not public yet."

I stare down at my empty palms. "And what's the prognosis?"

"Not good. Maybe six months. Maybe less."

"Dammit, I'm sorry," I say, bringing a shaky hand to my forehead.

He gives me a sad smile. "I'm sorry for both of us. I want more time with you."

I chew on my lip, not knowing what to say. Not sure I could talk, anyway. My throat is constricted, and my chest is tight.

Thankfully, at that moment our salads are placed in front of us. I take a small bite of the most delicate vegetables I've ever eaten. It's like they're perfectly fresh right now, but they were too small yesterday, and tomorrow they'd have been past their prime. I'm astonished. But on another level, they taste like cardboard.

After a few bites, I put down my fork, my voice quaking. "It feels like the universe is cheating me, I gotta say. I know it's selfish, but I'm going to say it anyway, because it's how I feel. Why the hell did I go so long not having a father, only to get one ripped away so fast?"

And I don't even know how I feel about this particular father I manifested. Him not knowing where I was, I can logically forgive, but my emotions still have the same raw edge they had last night. Remi having me kidnapped was overkill, but on some level, I understand it. Showering me with wealth ... I'll accept, because I'm not going to say no. But add this diagnosis to it, and I again want to leave.

At the same time, I want to know everything about him. Will it tell me more about myself? I take a slow, steady breath.

Remi nods sorrowfully. "I agree. It's not fair. To either of us."

I notice that he's not eating much.

"You really don't think you're going to live that long?" I ask.

"I don't know. No one does. But I trust my doctors, and it's not looking good right now." He sighs. "It sucks, to put it bluntly. But I've had time to come to terms with it, to some extent. I've had a full life, and I've done a lot. I've built our business up even beyond what it was when I took over. And now, at last, I found you."

But you didn't find me sooner, I want to say. I clench my fists and keep my mouth shut. I don't want to be a brat. Or a bigger brat than I usually am.

Remi keeps talking. "I have so much to tell you about your family."

"Who are they?" I ask, putting on a smile. Hopefully this is a safer topic than his health.

"My grandfather and your great-grandfather, René St. Thomas, married Ada, and they had three children: Raleigh—my father and your grandfather—Reese, and Rhonda, who is Nana. Neither Reese nor Nana had children of their own, although Reese had stepdaughters and Nana's partner has a son. I was an only child, so you're the only true St. Thomas of your generation." Remi dissolves into a coughing fit. I nudge his water closer to him, and he sips it, then takes a deep breath. "Reese was kidnapped before I was born. Although the family paid the ransom, he had already been killed."

Chills run down my arms. "That's awful!"

Remi nods. "That's why we have many layers of security now. Please work with them. It might take some getting used to having them around, but it's for the best."

I grumble an acceptance.

"I wish I had more time with you. Absent that, I don't know what I can give you, other than the family's money."

I lean forward, looking at him intently. "You can give me a history. Roots. Ancestors."

He tilts his head. "You've always had those, even if you didn't know it."

Something inside me cracks. A wish for things I've never had. Longing for things that will never be. Nothing about my life is ever going to be what is depicted on TV.

Maybe that's its strength: that my life is my own. Maybe I need to lean into its uniqueness.

It still sucks to have a dream die so quickly. I'm getting a tension headache, and my jaw aches.

Servers come and take our salad plates, even though they're barely touched, and refill my Coke. Then we wait for our entrées. My ears are ringing, and I have tunnel vision. Remi doesn't seem much better.

I feel very small, but I have to ask again, "Are you really going to die?"

"We all are. But yes, I've already lived longer than my doctors predicted. Soon, I likely won't feel well enough to go out like this. I'm glad we've met before it was too late."

Part of me is glad the mystery is solved. But part of me wants to tell the universe to fuck off for finally giving me a family only when my dad is apparently not long for this world. "I wish it could be different," I finally say. "Can I see you a lot until ..." I fall silent, not knowing a good way to finish that sentence. Once again, while I'm with him, I want to be alone.

"Yes, absolutely. Are you going to keep living with your

boyfriend? As I said yesterday, if you want a place of your own, we can get you one, and you may stay at the Montecito house until you find something you like."

A place of my own? What would that be like?

I've never had a place that was *mine*. I've never had a *home*.

A fierce longing develops inside my chest. To have a home, one I create with Charlie. And to have a connection with my family.

"Where's the Montecito house?"

"On the beach just down from the Four Seasons. It's my weekend retreat. There's staff there now, but that's it." *Staff*.

I love Charlie and want to live with him. But I also feel like I was bringing nothing to our relationship. It was so unbalanced.

It also might be good to give him a little breathing room. I can be a bit much. I'll ask him.

"I'll be sure to visit you," my father continues.

"Okay," I whisper, and I wrap my arms around my middle. "May I talk about it with Charlie first?"

"Of course. While you're at it, see if you both want to go to the family Christmas party Bree is throwing next week. I'll get you the details. Bree is one of my uncle's stepdaughters. The other one is Anastasia."

"I think my boyfriend met Bree at a party last night."

Remi gets an irritated look. "She's often at those." He pauses to cough. "I'll have the staff ready the house, just in case."

I get the address, and he texts the staff to tell them I may be coming up. We finish lunch, and I thank him and head back to Charlie's house, still feeling all over the place.

The universe took my family away from me for far too long, but it's giving me a lot right now. Too much, in fact. I think I have to take the bad—finally meeting my father, only to find out he's in poor health—with the good: I have a family.

At least, I hope it's good that I have a family. Who knows? Maybe they're all psychopaths.

CHAPTER 32

Rowan

I want to talk to Charlie, but he's at work. There's too much to think about with Remi's illness, so I shove it from my mind and instead think about Charlie.

I fantasize about walking into his office, which I imagine is on a high floor of a skyscraper, and blowing him under the desk while he takes a call.

No, I imagine him *ordering* me to suck him off. God, that would be hot. The command voice? I shiver.

Then I scold myself. I need to focus on things that aren't sex for a while. Because, as much as I want to be naked with Charlie all the time, I have other things to deal with.

When I arrive at Charlie's house this time, I park properly in the driveway. My old car now lives in his garage. Once this newfound wealth and security sinks in—if it ever does—I'll give it to charity. The security guard who followed me to and from lunch takes up a spot on the street. I decide to ignore his presence. I don't know exactly how I'm supposed to handle being accompanied everywhere, but that seems like the simplest option.

What should I do about where I live?

I want to connect with my family and find out who they are.

Maybe going to the Montecito house will give me clues. I could see if Charlie wants to come up with me, but a strong part of me wants to see the place on my own. To find out who I might've been if I hadn't been abandoned as a newborn.

And there's a restless excitement inside me at the idea of finally having something that feels like it might be mine. A real *home*. Though, for it to be home for me, maybe I should bring Charlie up there after all.

Then again, I don't want to force him into living with me if that's not what he actually wants. It's one thing for him to rescue me from eviction, but it's another for me to take over his life indefinitely.

Even if we are mated for life and he'll eventually come around.

To distract myself from my thoughts, I redye my hair. It was getting too pale. Then I wait for Charlie to finish work.

Finally, I hear the garage door, and I stand up from the couch where I've been watching *The Titan's Bride* anime. (The manga is better.)

I feel rather like a dog waiting for its owner to come home. "Hey," I say when he opens the door, shifting my weight on my feet.

Charlie walks straight over to me. "How did lunch go?"

God, I love how interested in me he is. How he cares. I wrap my arms around his slim waist and bury my head in his chest. Then I back off fast. "Shit, I just dyed my hair. I don't want to get pink on your shirt."

He waves me off. "You're more important." He puts his hands on my jaw and kisses me—and this is the typical murderous Charlie kiss, not a sweet, light one. The kind that claims me. My favorite kind.

After he's done and we're both panting, I blink a few times. "First off, lunch was fucked up, because I get a father, only to find out he's got terminal cancer," I blurt, because I've been holding that in.

"Oh, shit," Charlie says, giving me a heavy nod. "I'm so damn sorry."

"Yeah. It's hard to know what to feel. I don't know him, but it's ... it's just wrong for him to be taken from me so fast. Or that he's likely going to be. If things go the way his doctors say. And why wouldn't they, because he's rich and can afford good doctors." I'm breathless from saying all that. And while I'm not retreating behind my mental walls—this is Charlie, and he gets all the parts of me—I'm still on edge.

"I think we might need to get you some therapy," he says quietly.

My first reaction is to nope the idea. But then, I huff, "You think? Maybe."

"You might need to talk to a professional." He grins. "You can afford it now."

"That might be true. I'm still at the start of processing all this. Like, I now have a father, and it's not any normal father, it's a famous rich one—not just rich, but in this entirely different world —and then he's going through health problems, and there's all that. Lunch was ... very weird. I'm not used to things being given to me, period. But this was so far beyond ... I mean, a fancy lunch, okay, that's something you might treat me to. If you wanted. Not that everything you've already done isn't— I'm just saying, that's, like, normal stuff for other people, right? Nice food, maybe clothes ..." He is *not* getting that jacket back. "But with Remi, it's like 'Go out and charge yourself a fancy car. We'll get you a house.' If I said I wanted, I don't know, a plane or a yacht, I bet he'd text someone and it would be done by the end of the week. When I woke up yesterday, I couldn't afford to rent a shitty apartment. What even is this?"

He wraps me in his arms, and I inhale his comforting scent. "I understand that. It must be very disorienting. Tell me what happened."

And so I do. We go to the couch, and I sit down with him, my ass perched on his legs, and I start talking. After I tell him about lunch, I bring up me moving. "I think I want to go up to the Montecito house for a while. I want to find out more about my family, and maybe I'll get some answers there."

His arms tighten around me. "Then do that. I'll miss you, but this isn't about me."

"It is about us, though. It's time for me to stop mooching off of you and start mooching off of my father instead."

"You haven't mooched off of anyone," he says sternly.

"Well, if I'm going to, it makes more sense for me to be spending his money. Especially if he already has the house just sitting there."

"And family is supposed to take care of each other," Charlie says.

"That's what the stories say."

"Then let's just take it one day at a time," Charlie says, kissing my forehead. "What about the car? Do you like the BMW?"

"I'm keeping it for now, but maybe I'll go pick a car I want."

"What do you think you'd pick?"

I snuggle into him. "I have no fucking clue. Do I get something practical?"

He shakes his head. "You know the answer to that. You get something fun that suits your personality. He can afford it. Go wild."

"Sometimes I want to blend in."

Charlie actually laughs. "No, you don't. You wouldn't have this hair and this body art if you wanted to be the same as everyone else." He pauses. "Well, you might have chosen to hide the scars in a less flamboyant way. You know, I've been learning a lot from you. I always wanted to accomplish the same thing as my peers. Now, though, I don't know what I want. Except you." His words make my whole body warm up.

"So I have a place to stay. I'm just ... a little scared, I guess."

"If anything goes wrong up there, or you don't like it, you can come back here," he says immediately. And my heart tugs even more strongly toward him.

I nod.

"So this is what you want?" Charlie asks quietly.

"To live away from you? No. To live in a place where I don't feel like I'm mooching? Yes."

"When are you going to go?"

"I'm not sure. He was readying it for me tonight."

Charlie's hazel eyes bug out. "Seriously?"

"Yeah," I say. "I think my father doesn't like it that his offspring has been living so badly. And now he wants to make up for it."

"Do you think he'll ever be able to do that?"

"Yeah," I say. "I think he will. Though I don't know why I believe that. It's not like anything good has ever happened to me before."

"I'm good," Charlie says.

"Well, yeah, but you came as a result of a kidnapping. Or carjacking. Or mugging." My eyes widen. "That must be why I trust my father: He kidnapped me. Maybe good things only happen to me in connection with crimes."

"Uh, no," Charlie says firmly. "We're not going to have that be part of your personal narrative."

"What if I say ... I trust things more if they come out of adversity?"

"Well, that can certainly be true. Some of us think that if things come too easy, they don't matter."

"This is coming pretty easy," I murmur.

He snorts. "No, it's not. You lived two decades without a family. You suffered through more living situations than you can count, and some of them were pretty bad. No stability whatsoever. Whatever 'easy' is, it's not that."

"Fair enough." I kiss him. "So do you think I should go?"

"Yeah," he says. "I think you're too curious not to. You don't have to stay if you don't like it."

"Do you want to come with me?"

"I do, baby boy, but I think this is one you may want to try without me." This time he kisses me. "How about this? Call me if you need me."

"Deal." I hop off his lap. "Want to help me pack?"

"Sure." I hold out a hand, and Charlie takes it. "Do you want to borrow my luggage?"

"Nah. I'm probably going to end up tossing everything, anyway. Better to use a trash bag and avoid the middleman."

At the end of the packing session, I'm taking very few things. I go to throw the rest of my clothes in the garbage, but Charlie says to keep them here.

Something about that makes me smile.

Maybe I do already have a home: with him.

* * *

The BMW's GPS navigates me through a neighborhood of verdant hedges and winding streets to a tall gate.

This is where I live now?

With a guard following close behind, I pull up and roll down the window to press a call button—my father didn't give me any keys or anything—but it opens automatically. I have no idea if it recognizes the car or if someone's watching. I have an empty feeling in the pit of my stomach, and my breaths are quick.

You can do this, Rowan.

I drive half a block to an immaculate house. It looks more like a hotel than a home. Big, interesting. It's nighttime, but there's landscape lighting, and the front area is all illuminated. The place has white stucco walls draped in bougainvillea. Red tile roof. The front door has a large glass panel. Like it's safe to have someone peep inside, because no one who's not supposed to be here could get past the gate.

I park in the circular driveway in front of the house. Three people come out to meet me, all with smiles on their faces.

"Are you Rowan?" the younger man, probably around my age, asks. He's wearing a white button-down shirt and black slacks. A woman who looks to be in her forties follows him, along with a man about the same age.

"I am."

"I'm Hector Gutiérrez. These are my parents, Matilda and Lionel."

I shake all of their hands.

"I'm your assigned driver," Hector says, waving at the guard who followed me up here. "I'll also be your security when you're in Montecito."

"And I'm the housekeeper," Matilda offers. "My husband, Lionel, is the groundskeeper."

"Nice to meet all of you. This place is incredible."

We step up to the front door, and I can hear the ocean.

"It is nice," Hector agrees. "You get used to it, though."

"I don't think I'll ever get used to this." I feel like a breathless princess in a movie, but right now, I'm entitled to be. Because I'm Cinderella, and this is a goddamn castle.

Matilda ushers us inside, and I gasp at the foyer. It's ... gorgeous. A grand staircase—on two sides—goes up to a second story, but the back wall is all glass. In fact, the entire back wall of the house might be glass. An illuminated pool is right outside the back doors, and I'm pretty sure there's direct access to the ocean beyond.

The floors are shiny wood, and everything seems expensive but comfortable. While my style, if I ever had money to spend—oh wait—is more modern, I can still appreciate the quality and workmanship here.

"I'll show you to your suite." Matilda heads up the stairs, and I follow. "And then you can explore as you wish."

"I'll park your car, and Dad and I will bring in your things," Hector says.

While I want to argue with him, that is his job, I guess. *Get used to having people help you, Rowan.*

"Thank you," I say.

At the top of the grand staircase, Matilda leads me along a hallway that has windows looking out over the front of the house.

She opens a door on the ocean side, and I finally do gasp. I can't help it. It's just so extravagantly beautiful.

The suite is the size of Charlie's entire house. It's comfortably furnished, with a huge bed with downy white sheets that look really fluffy. Tons of pillows. Framed black-and-white photographs of Santa Barbara on the walls. The furniture is modern pale wood, and there are upholstered chairs in a navy material, a TV with a video game system that Matilda shows me (it's concealed in its own custom cabinet), and a bathroom the size of Montana.

Oh, and the room has an entire wall of floor-to-ceiling windows, the curtains currently drawn against the darkness.

"You'll enjoy the view. You can see up to Santa Barbara and down to Ventura." Matilda smiles. "Plus the pool and the beach."

In short, this is amazing.

We find a place for Wilbur in my bedroom, hanging in front of a window. Matilda assures me she'll keep an eye on his water levels, though I'm used to taking care of him and don't plan to stop now.

Next, she shows me my father's suite—in the other wing—before taking me back downstairs to tour the kitchen, living room, other bedrooms, home office, movie projection room, gym, and a bunch of other rooms I can't even keep track of. She tells me that I can ask for whatever food or snacks I want. I open the fridge, and it's already stocked with most everything I can imagine.

* * *

After I've had some homemade potato leek soup and a green salad, as well as a piece of cherry pie, in a kitchen nook that's big enough to be its own dining room, I go up to my room and pace.

The ocean's loud.

Apparently Remi owns acres along the beachfront.

So *no one's* here. I'm all alone. Hector, Matilda, and Lionel live in a coach house on the property.

I flop down on the overstuffed bed, still in my clothes. I should be doing better than this. I should be feeling good. I finally have all the things I could ever dream of.

It's lonely as fuck.

I feel better having Wilbur in my room, at least. Wherever I go, he goes.

Only now, there's someone else I want with me. A someone who talks back.

I realize I have a choice. I could wallow some more, or I could fix this.

Charlie answers immediately, again proving why I'm in love with him.

"Charlie," I whisper, my voice breaking.

His voice is soft and deep. "Baby, what is it?"

"This place ... I've been rootless my whole life, but I've never felt as lonesome as I do right now. There's no one else here."

"What's the address? I'm on my way."

CHAPTER 33

Charlie

I t's nearly midnight by the time I pull up to the gate of Rowan's new home, which is, of course, a mansion. I need to change my world view—from Rowan, knife-wielding demon, to Rowan, rightful occupant of an enormous and very expensive estate.

I push the gate button and am immediately buzzed in. Rowan races out of the house and tackles me the moment I step out of my car, jumping up and wrapping his arms around my shoulders and his legs around my waist.

I hold him tightly to me. "Hey," I say, kissing the top of his head.

What I want to say is *I'm here. It will be okay. We'll figure it out.*

But I suspect Rowan showed more vulnerability than he was comfortable with when he phoned me, and he probably doesn't want me to call him out on it. At least, if I were him, I wouldn't want me doing that. Maybe I'm projecting, but whatever.

He's all in his head, I can tell. That's understandable. The change in his fortune is a lot to process.

Rowan's allowed to not be his badass self around me. I'll keep his secrets.

"You came," he says into my shirt.

"You called. I'll always come when you call."

Lifting his head, he plants a kiss on my lips, and then it seems like he's ready to be put back on his feet, so I set him down and look around.

I don't know how many acres the house is on. Enough that you can't see a neighbor. You can hear the Pacific Ocean, very close. There's a large main house, then a number of smaller buildings off to the side, which I assume are garages, guest houses, caretaker houses. I have no idea what else. The grounds are formal and clipped in a way that indicates staff. I want to explore in the daylight. I mean, I have a thing for home improvement—but I'm not sure this could be improved.

While my parents aren't poor, and I'm starting to make plenty of money at Weston & Ramirez, this is a level of generational wealth and history that I have no access to.

Taking Rowan's hand, I give myself a quick talking-to. I need to get myself together and not be intimidated by all this. I can be his shoulder to cry on and his asshole protective boyfriend. I'm good with that.

"Want to see the house?" Rowan asks shyly. "I've been walking around it all night."

"There's no one up here but you?"

"There's a family that are the main staff, but they're in another building."

"Then show me around, baby. Let me get my overnight bag."

I fetch it, and Rowan takes me in through a side door that opens into the kitchen. I thought I'd be grateful to be spared from some huge entryway as big as my house, but I'm really not. This kitchen could eat my parents' house and still have room for leftovers. It's built to cook for hundreds, if not thousands.

They've probably done that here. There's certainly enough

room to entertain a thousand people. All the surfaces are clean to the point of gleaming, although they do seem used rather than brand-new. The appliances are all top-of-the-line, and I guess that fits: These people buy things that are meant to last.

Beyond the kitchen is a smaller room that appears to do nothing but hold dishes.

"Holy shit," I whisper.

Rowan glances at me.

"Your dad's really fucking rich," I mutter.

A dark look passes over his face, and then he shrugs. "I can't help that."

I squeeze his hand. "I know. And it doesn't mean anything bad. It's just ... maybe you're not the only one reorienting yourself here."

He goes up on his tiptoes to kiss me, and I wrap my arms around his middle. Every time I kiss Rowan, I feel this tug in my belly. Like we're lashed together on a rolling ship, staying afloat while everything around us is in turmoil. I growl and intensify the kiss, and he kisses me back just as hard, giving me his tongue the way I like it. I pull away far enough to suck on his bottom lip, and then we're kissing again, so deeply that it makes me breathless.

A door opens behind us, and while it startles me, I do my best not to react. I slowly stop kissing Rowan, then kiss his nose. Then we both turn around like a creaking lazy Susan.

A shorter, dark-haired woman in her midforties is in the room.

Rowan grins at her. "Charlie, this is Matilda. Matilda, her husband, and her son take care of this place for my father. Matilda, this is my boyfriend, Charlie."

"Nice to meet you," I say, holding out my hand.

She shakes it, giving me a big smile. "It's very nice to meet you. We saw you drive up and wanted to check to see if you needed anything." She seems very content. I think most people would be pretty content living in a place like this. The staff quarters could be miserable, of course, but I doubt it.

Rowan shakes his head. "No, we're good until the morning."

"Then we'll give you privacy. What time would you like me to have breakfast ready?"

He looks at me. "Do you need to get to work early?"

"Nope." The benefits of being in charge of my own schedule. I'm lucky I don't have court tomorrow.

"Then not that early. Maybe seven thirty or eightish?" Rowan says, shifting his weight. He's clearly not comfortable with being waited on.

"I will plan on that," she says. "Any special requests or allergies? Foods you don't like?" He shakes his head. "Then I'll make a few things, and you can choose what you'd like."

"Thank you. I'm just going to show Charlie around before bed. We're sorry to wake you."

"You didn't. Come with me, and I will show you how to set the alarm when you want to close up for the night."

Rowan goes with her. He returns a minute later and proceeds to give me a tour. This place is old, huge, and very, very fancy. And it's been kept up, pristinely maintained in a way that is not usual for a place where people actually live. It's on par with museums like the Getty Villa or Hearst Castle.

But while he's showing me around, he's gazing at me more than at the mansion, and he keeps giving me these flirty touches on my forearms and hips. I'm pretty sure he wants to get fucked. Hell, I spent the entire drive up here fantasizing about what I'd do to him tonight. I figured the least creative plan was I'd take him in his bed, but now I see how vast this place is. How overwhelming. How he needs to make it his own.

So when we get to the end of yet another hall, I grab him and throw him over my shoulder in a firefighter's carry and head upstairs. "I want to bend you over the balcony and fuck you," I murmur.

Is that enough, though? Does he need more? Did this change of fortune scramble his system so much that he needs me to take him down to his basest level—a place where he's scratching and bleeding and I'm the one who makes him feel?

"Yes," he whispers. "God, yes, please. Make me forget all the mess that's running around my brain. Make it go away—family and money and *who am I* and *what am I doing*. Give me what I need."

His desperation makes my dick hard. Rowan sticks his hands in my back pockets.

"So, princeling, what do you need?" I growl.

"You," he gasps. That makes me feral. He needs me as much as I need him.

"Tell you what," I say. "It's dark. No one can see us, right?"

"What do you mean?"

"Are there security cameras?"

He nods. "Outside. Matilda told me the cameras face the street and the entrances to the house."

"That's it?" My heart is racing even more than it did carrying him up the stairs. My entire self is aroused. I need my baby boy. But I'm also in the mood to try something, if he's up for it.

"Yeah."

I lean down and look directly in his face, my nose mere inches from his. "Run. I'm going to fuck you wherever I find you."

Rowan's eyes light up. "Seriously?"

I raise an eyebrow. "Say 'red' if you want me to stop."

A laugh bursts out of him. "A safeword? You're kidding."

"I'm not. I'm going to fuck you hard, but I don't want this to get out of hand."

"Does it have a chance of getting out of hand?"

I nod. "So if you stop me, I'll stop immediately, no questions asked."

His grin is breathtaking. Then he shivers. He must have caught the look in my eyes.

"Do you need a moment in the bathroom?" I ask.

"Nope. I had time to prepare for your hard cock while you were driving up here."

"Good."

Rowan's posture perks up, and he sidesteps me, keeping just out of reach. "So we finally get to play?"

"Ten, nine, eight …"

Rowan sprints away.

I keep counting down. When I get to one, I stop and listen.

I hear a door shut somewhere downstairs. It could be an interior door. But I know, instinctively, that Rowan has gone outside.

Perfect.

Some small part of me knows this is nuts.

But the rest of me knows this is exactly what Rowan needs. He's overwhelmed by all the changes in his life, and this will ground him. Literally. It will make it so he can't do anything but feel me. Feel how much I want him.

He won't be in his head, thinking about his current situation and all the things that could have been different in the past. He's just going to feel what *is*. Now.

It's also what I need—I've been wanting to do this since the moment I met him.

I jog, trying to be light on my feet so he won't hear me coming. I find a door to the outside and step out into the night. The walk is paved, not gravel, and my steps are quiet.

My cock hardens further at the thought of what I'm going to do when I catch him.

I can't hear any leaves crunching or branches breaking. A lone coyote howls a long ways away, following it up with a cacophony of yips.

Then.

Silence.

Something in me relaxes—then paradoxically tenses. Now's the time. It's like when I used to run track in high school, and I'm looking around at the beginning of the race, sizing up my opponents. Wondering if I can beat them.

It's the day of the final exam, when the professor says "You may begin."

It's the moment when the clerk swears in the first witness, but I haven't yet asked any questions.

All possibilities exist in this instant. And I intend to make them mine.

Make *him* mine.

I could be a gentleman and announce that I'm coming, but what's the fun in that? Primal fucking has no rules.

I consider heading in the direction I think Rowan went, but if I know him—and I do—he's doubled back.

In fact, I should probably be expecting Rowan to come up behind me with a knife at my throat. That thought makes my dick even harder. It's going to be tough running with an erection, but I'll manage.

Where are you, baby boy?

I take a step off the path, but my sneaker crunches on dry leaves that must have just fallen tonight, otherwise they'd surely have been raked away. In the silence, the sound is clear.

I'd better stick to the path for now.

A rustle catches my attention. Is it him? Or is he faking me out?

I decide he's faking me out and head toward the area where I think he could have thrown a rock from.

Rosemary is strongly scented, even at night, and in the moonlight, everything takes on a different shape.

I stay away from the lights and move in the shadows. My senses are heightened, and my chest feels light. My pulse is racing. I'm so fucking *alive* right now. Hunting my prey with the cool breeze ruffling my hair. My pretty little violent baby boy who just wants someone to take over so he doesn't have to think about anything.

Who doesn't want to cry about his past anymore. Who wants to *be*.

I don't know the grounds, but neither does he. I'm trying to avoid the other buildings, as I expect he did. We don't need Matilda getting an eyeful of us fucking.

With the intermittent waves crashing down, it's hard but not impossible to hear low noises.

Where are you, princeling? I want to call. I stay quiet, though, searching. Finally, I see him crouching behind a manicured bush. I race toward him, sacrificing silence for speed. He runs, and I grab at him, my fingers catching his waist, but he slips out of my grasp and is off again.

"I'm gonna get you," I whisper. And I start after him.

CHAPTER 34

Rowan

Yes, *fuck* yes.

This is what I want.

I'm trying to be as quiet as I can while moving fast on unfamiliar grounds. For all I know, the bushes around me could be topiaries of dinosaurs or something. I pass by a fountain and a tennis court, but there's also plenty of trees and footpaths.

I stop and listen for Charlie. He already almost caught me once. I don't want this chase to end indoors, so I keep going around the side of the house, toward the ocean, where there's another area full of trees.

This place is incredible. I can't believe I have access to it. Not two full weeks ago, I was living with Floyd in a crappy hellhole.

I follow the sound of the ocean, but I run up against an obstacle—a wrought iron fence with a locked gate, keeping me from getting down to the beach. I suppose it also keeps people from getting onto the property.

Shit.

I need to turn around, but I hear a branch break. Cool ocean air soothes my skin. My pulse is thundering in my ears, and my entire body is on alert. Even though I know Charlie won't really hurt me, I'm getting off on being chased. I want him to take control.

I want his dick inside me. I want him to scrape me up. I want to rip at him. Let this be my *Goblins Cave*. He can claw hash marks into my ass to count how many times he takes me.

But I also want this part to go on longer.

I take off in what I hope is the opposite direction of where he's coming from, but an arm comes out of the dark, and Charlie grabs me around the waist.

I struggle and kick. He bites my shoulder as he wrestles me to the ground, and it makes me even harder than I was.

"You need to be fucked?" Charlie growls. "You need my cock in your ass? Need me to use you?"

He's undoing my pants as I struggle. My elbow's scraped up, and my jeans are torn.

This is what I want. To not be in control. To not have to think about my next move.

The freedom of pain. The freedom of pleasure. To be able to just fucking feel.

Charlie makes me feel. He always makes me feel. Sometimes it's too much, but— I kick at him, hard.

I wouldn't do it if I didn't know he could take it. But I've seen the gleam in his eyes. I know he's all buttoned-up lawyer with his damn ten-year plan, when really he wants to be living a messy, dirty life where he chases his boyfriend down to fuck him.

I adore it.

I grab a handful of leaves and dirt and fling it in Charlie's face. He blinks and swears, and I manage to get free and race away.

My heart beats heavy and fast.

I don't know where to go.

Thump. Tha-thump. Tha-thump.

Shit.

Even though much of the property is manicured, there are still plenty of places to hide. Part of me wants to go through the house so I can run down to the beach. I'm tugging up my pants and trying to fasten them again while still running, but it's not working, and I look around wildly.

Tha-thump. Tha-thump.

I dart toward the garage. Charlie's gaining on me, because I hesitated. That's okay.

This game, I love. *Charlie*, I love.

The air bursts from my lungs as he tackles me again. I fall hard onto the dirt. Pine needles. Grass.

Something pokes my skin. *Ow! Dammit.*

He's tearing my pants open.

I gasp when he spits on my hole, and I wriggle, attempting to get out of his hold.

"Lube or no lube?" Charlie asks, taking me out of the moment, because I know he cares. He doesn't want any actual damage. Nothing more than a few scrapes and bruises.

"Lube," I say. I'm not as much of a badass as all that.

"Get your face in the dirt, then," he orders, and he shoves my pants down, rubbing his hard cock against my ass.

I groan. Warmth radiates through my body.

Charlie is forcing me, except if I said the word, he'd stop immediately.

And having him make all the decisions for me, when I've been making them all my life and now I'm in this new situation where I don't know anything ...

It's magical.

I know I'm going to have bruises on my hips from how hard he's holding me. Through the tear in my jeans, my bare knee is getting more scraped.

The rip of a package.

And his lubed-up cock invades my ass. No prep.

It fucking stings. My dick always softens a bit when he first enters me, because of the pain.

I've now had enough experience with Charlie to know that the burning stretch will subside, but it takes a moment for my body to get used to the intrusion that I want so much.

Usually he gives me time to adjust before he pushes inside all the way, but not tonight. He breathes heavily in my ear, and the fact that he's letting me see how into this he is—that's a gift, too.

"You're so fucking tight," he groans. "Your perfect ass. *Fuck.*"

Tha-thump. Tha-thump.

Charlie might be grumpy and closed off with everyone else, but he's open with me.

I'm starting to see the cracks inside him. I'm starting to see all the ways he cares. Ways he'll never admit to, but that's okay.

He pulls out a little, dribbles more lube on his dick, and forces me up on my knees so the angle's better. Better for both of us. My body gives, until his groin is against my ass.

Charlie fucks me. He starts slowly. He's saying worse things to me than he's doing, muttering how he's going to break me, rip me apart, make me bleed. And that makes it more of a fantasy. I don't actually want him to cause any internal tears or anything. But I do like to pretend. To find that edge where it's just real enough to matter.

He speeds up, his hips pistoning in and out of me, and it's so good. He repositions us so he's pressing down between my shoulders, holding my cheek to the ground.

Fuck, I like that, too.

My dick hardens again.

I'm going to get off.

I'm making noises, like I don't even know what. When he puts a hand over my mouth, I bite it, and it makes him push into me extra hard.

My face is in the dirt, and I'm being fucked in the exact way I would've requested had I put in an order.

Rough.

Dirty.

Dangerous.

I'm his, and he's mine.

"Is that all you've got?" I taunt, my heart beating fast. "Fuck me harder. Fuck me like you mean it."

Charlie growls and surges into me. He slaps my ass—first one cheek, then the other. Then he does it again and again, until my skin is on fire.

My heart drums in my chest, and I'm ultra-awake, like I'm high on adrenaline.

He's holding me up, dragging me toward him, and he's coming. I can feel him pulsing into me, hear his ragged breaths and guttural groan.

Then he's pulling out of me and throwing me onto my back. In a flash, he's between my legs, sucking me off.

His warm, soft, wet mouth is the most decadent thing I ever could've imagined.

I once saw a video with a monk who held his hands in fists for four minutes because letting go was such peace. That's what this is: peace, after being run ragged. I've gone to the end of the world and can now take a break.

My eyes are watery, and I moan. Then my body tenses ... and the lightest sensation washes over me as I spill into his mouth.

When he helps me sit up, I realize I've marked him, too. He has a cut on his face, likely from my nails, and he's just as dirty as I am.

We look at each other and start laughing.

"Guess we broke in your new home," he says.

CHAPTER 35

Charlie

I burst out laughing again once we're back inside the house. Mansion. Palace. "What the fuck did I do to you, baby?" I kiss his dirty nose and hold him to me. My pulse is still racing, but I don't think it's from running around the compound or even from fucking him. It's simply … *him*.

"To quote Morticia Addams, you scared me." He comes up on his tiptoes. "Do it again."

I kiss him on the lips and take his hand, hyperaware of how close he is, even though I just had him naked. "Let me clean you up. I dirtied you too much."

Rowan smirks. "Yes, please."

I sigh in amazement. How did I find this guy who fits me so perfectly? Who lets me enact my darkest fantasies—the ones I'd hardly admit to anyone? How did I find this other half of my soul?

Hand in hand, we go into the bathroom made for a princeling, and Rowan inspects his face and laughs again. "Holy shit."

Swallowing hard, I stiffen. "Was I too rough?"

"Not at all. Fuck, I love this." He lifts his chin and swivels his head, inspecting the scrapes and dirt.

My stomach flutters just looking at him. "Let me clean you up."

"Aftercare?" Rowan says.

"Yeah, baby. Let me take care of you. Don't do a damned thing. I ruined you; now I get to indulge you." Noting that the knees on his jeans are ripped, I decide he needs to soak, not stand in the shower. I start the bath and roll up my sleeves.

Rowan gazes at me, one eyebrow raised.

His doubt makes something soft and gooey form inside me. I want to protect him. Always. "Come on. I'll treat you like the little prince you are."

His smile shorts out my brain.

What is it about this guy that makes me lose awareness of everything around except him?

While the tub fills, I drag his hoodie over his head, then his T-shirt. Touching him makes my body tingle. I kiss along the nape of his neck, across his shoulders, and down his back to his waist.

He moans in pleasure.

Dropping to my knees behind him, I reach around and undo his jeans, then help him kick out of his remaining clothes until he stands before me, pale and naked.

His ass is red where I spanked it. His elbows are bloody. He's going to have bruises on his hips.

A lump forms in my throat. "While I know that was all consensual, I don't want you to suffer."

"Oh, I'm not suffering. I'll just be a little stiff tomorrow."

I vow to take care of him.

I swish my hand in the bathwater, checking the temperature, then dump some bath gel under the faucet and return to Rowan. Before he can say anything, I pick him up. He wraps his legs around my waist and puts his head on my shoulder.

My throat closes even tighter.

"Okay, baby. Let's get you nice and clean." I stand him up in the shin-deep water, his hair mussed, face dirty, skin scraped. "Is this temperature okay?"

"It's perfect, Daddy. Mmmm." He sinks down into the tub, eyes closed. He hisses when the water makes contact with the scrapes on his knees and elbows, but then his expression eases.

"Not your fucking daddy," I mumble, but my heart is going all wiggly.

The bubbles cover his shoulders, and he scoops some up in his hands, then blows them to the side.

I undress, then take a washcloth from the cabinet and dip it in the water. Rowan looks at me with undisguised interest, licking his lips. A lock of his pink hair is sticking to his forehead, and his big, blue eyes are too much for me to bear.

I shake my head. "Don't tempt me, menace."

I wash him, using a light touch—especially on the spots where he's got a scrape or bruise—to methodically clean every single part of him. I make him sit up so I can get all my spend off his ass and spread his legs to reach every nook and cranny.

Mine. This merman ... selkie ... bird in a cage. *Mine.*

He sits back like the little royal he is and watches me work, a contented smile on his face. And his dick is getting hard, so I give him some extra attention there with soapy, slippery hands. He sighs in happiness and whines when I stop.

"Don't worry, I'll take care of you," I say. "Let me finish cleaning you up first."

When I'm done with his body, I ask him to lean back, and I dip his hair in the water. I lather him up with shampoo, then use a cup to wash away the suds.

To finish, I help him stand and then turn the shower on. I get in with him and rinse off all of the soap, then tend to my own cuts and scrapes. My dick is fully hard again, because Rowan always makes me hard.

He also makes me feel safe. Whole. Right.

We get out, and I wrap him in the biggest, fluffiest towel I've ever seen. Pretty sure it could cover a car.

I wipe myself down with another towel, then kneel before him. "Let me bandage you up."

"You don't have to—"

"Yes, I do." I pull out a first aid kit that I find under the sink and rub antibacterial ointment on any scraped skin, place a Band-Aid on one knee, and smooth cream over his bruises. Then, after warming lotion between my hands, I work it into his skin. Back, shoulders, chest. All down his arms and legs, too.

He stands silently, watching me worship him. I love worshipping him.

"Come on, little prince," I say when I'm done, taking his hand. "Time for bed." He nods, and I walk him to the enormous bed, then pull down the sheets and fluff up the already-fluffy pillows. His hand goes to his crotch, but I tsk. "Don't touch that."

"But—"

"No buts. Let me get you something. Hold on."

I rummage in my overnight bag for my sweats, find my way downstairs to the kitchen, pour a glass of ice water, then return.

Of course he's stroking himself. I roll my eyes and decide to ignore it. He likes to be a brat.

I might like him being a brat.

He drinks the water gratefully. I also bring him a dose of pain reliever. Once he's done with the water, he hands me the glass, and I set it down on a coaster. I'm caring for him as if he's a child, but he's special, and I made him super vulnerable. I need him to know I can be safe for him, too. If he'll let me, I will always take care of him.

I shed the sweatpants and climb into bed behind him, arranging us so that my dick is nestled in his ass, both of our heads are on his pillow, and my arms are wrapped around him. Skin to skin. My warmth to his. My body along his. I take hold of his dick, and he groans. "Thank fuck."

I rut into him, his ass being the object of all of my desires. It's heaven inside him. "Are you too sore for me to make love to you again?" I whisper.

"Oh, god, Charlie. Please fuck me again."

"I'll do it, but gently this time, okay?"

He bites his lip and nods. After lubing up and playing with his hole, I ease into him. He shudders when I'm all the way in, and I stay there a moment, gently rocking my hips—not thrusting, but simply enjoying being inside him. Then I reach around and grasp his length, and he moans.

"Good boy," I whisper, and now I'm going exceedingly slowly, making every move count. Every minute angle, every thrust, every pull back. With my hand, I'm focusing on the head of his cock, but every once in a while I'll go down and massage his balls, making him shudder.

"I wanna see how long this can go," I say. "How long can you take my cock. Do you think I should fall asleep with my dick in your ass?" I grimace. "Maybe not. But let me make love to you for a long time. I promise I'll get you off. I just want you to have this … downtime. You know? When you're cradled and loved up."

His voice cracks as he says, "Yeah. Okay." Then, "Thanks, Charlie."

It's not characteristically Rowan. He's usually so brash and bold. Having him be quiet against me—I know he needs this comedown. This time to reconnect. To know that I'm safe for him, even if we play rough sometimes.

I rock into him over and over again, like we're on a rowboat in a quiet lake—little movements. I don't pound his ass. I don't overwhelm him. I just let the feeling build and build and build until he cries out. And this time he's coming first—I'm going to make sure he gets all his pleasure out before I take mine.

When he's done, I thrust one last time and let myself release. Then I collapse against him, tugging him close.

Rowan bursts out crying.

"Baby," I say, leaning around and kissing his cheek. "No, no, no. No tears."

"That's not why I'm"—he sniffles—"crying. I loved that. Fuck, it was so good. You just got me all up in my feels, and that's not a place I usually go."

"I know, baby. I know."

I pull out of him and cuddle with him for a moment. But it gets too messy.

"Be right back."

Leaving him in the warm bed, I get a washcloth and return to clean him up as gently as I did in the shower. I notice a scrape I missed before, so when I go back to the bathroom to hang up the cloth, I get another Band-Aid and put it on him.

Then I get in behind him.

"You good, princeling?" I ask, as we lie in his kingly bed in his palatial room by the magnificent ocean.

"Yeah, Daddy. I'm good."

"Don't fucking call me daddy."

"Okay, Daddy."

This man will kill me one day. I'm sure of it.

Problem is, I'm too in love to care.

CHAPTER 36

Rowan

Charlie snuggles so I'm under his chin. He's bigger than me, obviously, so he kind of engulfs me. He consumes me. I want to be one with him.

"Rowan?"

"Hmm." I'm drifting off to sleep.

"I love you."

I freeze, and my panic button starts flashing wildly. For a moment, I don't know what to say. Because I love him with every cell in my body.

He reads me wrong, because he starts to pull away, but I turn around and grip him by the waist with my legs, not letting him move. "Don't you go anywhere, Charlie Cooper, until I have a chance to tell you what I really think of you."

"I tell you I love you, and you're going to list all my faults?"

"Faults? Okay, we need to unpack that, but no, what I'm going to say is that under that prickly exterior of yours is the fiercest protector I've ever known. I've never felt safer than when I'm with you."

"You don't really need protect—"

"I'm not done. You protect me from myself. From the times I get lost inside my head and don't know a way out. You give me ways to express myself that are safe."

"Anyone would do that."

"Anyone would not do that. No one ever has. You're my person, Charlie. Period. I love you so much I don't know what to do with it."

Charlie looks up at me, his eyes glassy. "Yeah?"

"Fuck yeah, I love you. You belong to me, and I belong to you."

I wrap my arms around him. I'm shaking, and it's starting to get worse.

Charlie cares about me. He makes that clear by everything he does for me, even if he doesn't usually say much about it. Which is why he surprised me just now.

* * *

I sleep better than I have in a long, long time—a deep, contented rest like I've sunk into the mattress in the best way, not a *Nightmare on Elm Street* way. Apparently all I had to do to get proper *zzz*s was have Charlie chase me through the manicured woods of a coastal estate, clean me up, then make love to me again, then confess that he loves me. It's a magic formula, I guess. I don't even mind the bruises or the soreness in my body. They're minor compared to how blissfully blank my mind went. How deeply in the moment I was—*we* were. How completely I could trust Charlie to give both of us what we needed without taking it too far.

Even better, when I wake up, I'm warm in his arms. I move to study him, but he yawns, clearly awake already.

"Morning," I mumble.

"Morning, baby," he says, kissing the top of my head.

No doubt about it: Sleepy morning time in bed with my boyfriend is the ultimate way to start the day. I take in his beautiful face, the stubbly beard growth along his defined jaw and the small gash above his left eyebrow. Oops. I did that last one.

Charlie's hair is getting long. Long for him, that is. His plan had him getting his hair cut every ten days (*what*???), and I know he's gotten it cut once since we've been together. But it does seem like he's loosening up a bit.

I'm about to open my mouth to comment on him being a slacker, when I realize something. I jerk up, the sheets falling to the side. "How late did we sleep? Do you have to go?"

"Told them I'd be late," he mutters, tugging me to him and rubbing his nose through my hair. "I already sent an email."

I sink back into the bed and exhale. "Cool."

I look around the enormous bedroom, with its comfortable sitting area, large-screen television, and ... space. It has space. All this room for me? I don't need it. I've survived in places that were barely bigger than a standard closet.

But I guess I'm not living like that anymore. I've found myself with an embarrassment of riches, but the most important part of that is Charlie. I move to straddle him, and he puts his hands on my waist, gazing up at me with hooded eyes.

"You good this morning?" he asks, raising one hand to trail a finger down my cheek and along my neck, shoulder, and arm until I shiver. "Not too sore?"

"Not too sore," I assure him. "Better than ever, honestly. I don't want to do that every night, but can we do it again sometime?"

"Yep." He gives me a crooked grin. "Always suspected that I had a thing for primal play, but I never had a chance to try it before."

"And your verdict?"

"Guilty as charged. I love it."

Even though we were both into it last night, it's reassuring to hear that from him now that he's had a chance to process.

I lean down and kiss him, and as usual, our kissing turns athletic. A sleepy sort of athleticism, I guess.

Then, without warning, he's down between my legs and sucking my very hard cock. I buckle with pleasure. "Fuck, yes, Daddy."

He grunts and groans, waving off the nickname with his free hand, but I know he likes it when I call him Daddy.

I must say, also: Charlie is *very* good at blow jobs. Not that it's a competition, but I'm pretty sure he's the best ever. Something about the pressure of his suction combined with the cadence of his movements, and I'm tipping over into a blissful orgasm very fast. Spent, I lie panting, my fingers tracing through his hair. "Wow," I whisper. "Good morning to me."

He crawls up my body to kiss me, and I dunno, I like tasting myself on him. Before long, though, I shove him onto his back— he cooperates—and return the favor.

"I could get used to this, I think," I murmur after Charlie has come and he's holding me quietly, my back to his chest, both of us on our sides. "Living in a big mansion on the beach, feeling good with my boyfriend, not worrying about anything. It's hard to process. I need to acknowledge this moment."

"Yep," Charlie says. "Your fortunes have definitely changed."

Then my stomach growls, because even the perfect morning can be improved.

I ask, "Want breakfast? I can get you something."

"Maybe coffee to start." He goes to get up, but I tsk at him.

"Just stay." I pull on sweatpants and a shirt and am about to pad out to the kitchen, having to remind myself where it is, because this place is so huge. But then I glance at the windows and open the curtains. "Holy shit," I breathe. "The ocean is *right there.*"

Charlie comes up behind me, stark naked. "That's gorgeous."

"Yeah," I say, awed. After a moment, I say, "Let me get coffee, and we can enjoy it."

I make my way down to the kitchen, where a fresh pot of coffee is being brewed and Matilda is slicing some fruit. She gives me a broad smile. "Good morning, Rowan. Would you like some fruit juice? And coffee? Tea?"

"I'd love coffee, thanks," I say. "And coffee for Charlie, too. We both take it with cream, please." While I don't usually have the best manners, I want to be sure to treat everyone working for me really well.

"Right away." Almost before I'm done talking, she hands me two mugs of coffee. "Would you like breakfast in your room or somewhere else?"

"We'll come down in a little while and have it here. Thanks, Matilda," I mutter, fiddling with the drawstring to my sweatpants and not at all comfortable being waited on. But she seems happy, so maybe my father pays her properly. I make a mental note to ask her and any other staff members I meet.

Up in my bedroom, Charlie's lying in bed. I survey him, propped up on pillows with his chest bare, an arm behind his dark head of hair, the sheet pooled very low around his toned waist.

Damn, my boyfriend's fine. He's a better view than the coast outside.

"Breakfast is being prepared," I say.

He grins and sits up. "Must be nice."

"I'm just finding out." I hand him the coffee, then carefully make my way back into the bed with him, making sure we don't spill.

We drink our coffee, then shower and go downstairs for breakfast—pancakes, fresh fruit, and sausages. I'm very happy to be able to eat a leisurely breakfast with Charlie on a poolside patio, watching the ocean.

When we're done, I know what I want to do before Charlie goes to work. "Do you need to leave right away? I'd like to look up more about my family," I say.

Charlie smiles. "Sure."

We find a large, comfy armchair in a sitting room with a view of the waves. Charlie sits down, and then I get in his lap, my ass on his legs and my legs hanging over one of the arms of the chair. See? He's a total daddy.

I take a deep breath and find an article on the history of St. Thomas Industries. "Remi St. Thomas," I read aloud, "is the grandson of mogul René St. Thomas. In the 1920s, René, along with a business partner, purchased much of what is now the San Fernando Valley. They also started investing in movies from the inception of motion pictures in California."

"I'd heard of René St. Thomas," Charlie says. "And St. Thomas Communications, of course. I didn't realize they were that deep into land development."

I keep reading. "In the 1950s and 1960s, René's son, Raleigh St. Thomas, along with his siblings, developed the San Fernando Valley and sold off whole tracts of homes. In the 1970s, they began investing in computer technology."

"It feels like your family was ahead of the game in all of the local industries."

"It's so weird to say *my family*," I murmur. I tilt my head. "And, wow. It seems like some of them died in weird ways. My great-uncle was kidnapped and killed—my dad told me about that. And this says my great-aunt's husband was drowned sometime after she divorced him."

"Sounds like all their money hasn't been able to protect them from a lot of shit," Charlie says.

"It hasn't. But they're—we're—everywhere, once you think about it. I've seen St. Thomas movies," I say. "In fact, I think the first movie you and I watched together—that action one, the day you brought me to your house—was a St. Thomas production." I go to say something else, but a call comes in on my phone—the one my father gave me, not the one Charlie gave me—and I accept it, because the screen reads "Remi." A shiver runs through me—the good kind. I've never had a parent, a *real* parent, call me. "Hello?"

"Rowan?" Remi sounds good today. At least, he's not coughing yet.

"Yes. It's me."

His voice warms, and I get an impression of genuine concern. "I wanted to see how you were doing. Do you like the Montecito house? Is everything going all right up there?"

"Yeah." I swallow. "It's great." Then I pause. "Actually, it was a little lonely, so I asked Charlie to come visit."

"That's good. I want you to be comfortable there. And I'd like to meet him," he says, and then the coughing starts.

I wait for the coughing fit to subside, each one racking me almost as much as it's hurting him ... because they're a reminder of how little time I'll have with my father. Once he quiets, I say, "I'd love that." I look over to Charlie. "You okay to meet my father?" That's never going to sound routine. He nods. Cool. I didn't want to commit him to something he didn't want to do.

Remi continues, "Nana wants to meet you. Maybe you can go visit her tomorrow or this weekend. Will that work with your schedule?"

"I think the weekend is better, because Charlie has to work. Hang on." I turn to him. "We're invited to Nana's house. My great-aunt? She's down in LA. Would you want to come with me to meet her?"

"Absolutely. I want to meet everyone who's important to you." Charlie swallows, and his voice drops. "If we're in the meet-the-family mode, I want to reciprocate. I've been scared to introduce you to my mom, because she gets so attached to people my siblings and I bring home with us. You're not temporary, though. Maybe Mom *should* get attached to you."

"When you're ready," I say. Even though I want to know every single thing about Charlie *right now*.

Turning back to the phone, I say, "We can come."

"I'll let her know," Remi says. "How about noon on Saturday?"

I glance over at Charlie, who nods. "Sure."

"What else do you need, Rowan? Have you purchased sufficient clothing?"

"Not yet."

Remi pauses. "I'll tell my accountant to make a house account for you at …" He names a famous high-end department store. "Just have everything delivered to the house." He coughs.

"How much are you expecting me to buy?" I ask, almost coughing myself from his implication that it will be more than I can carry.

"Son, you could buy the entire store. I don't want you to do without ever again. Get every single thing your heart desires … and then get some more." His voice lowers. "You and I don't know each other, and I don't know how much time I will have to get to know you. I will feel better knowing that you're happy." He pauses. "If I could erase those years of hardship, I would, although I do think they've molded you into a very strong person. You'll need to be strong to deal with our family. But that doesn't mean you can't have a little fun, too."

What do I say to that? "Thanks," I choke out.

"I don't know if you're interested in the business. If you are, we can bring you around and see what kind of position suits you. If not, you'll be a shareholder, and we can get you a seat on the board when I, um, retire."

"This is all too much, still," I say.

"I know. It's hard to cram in a lifetime with you in just a few short months."

We talk a little more, and then I hang up.

Charlie's looking at me agape. "Wow," he mouths.

I smile. "I guess I'll go shopping while you're at work, then. Not sure what else I'm supposed to do with all this newfound money." Although I definitely have some ideas that go beyond putting fancy jeans on my ass.

"Sounds like you're just getting started being the richest person I'll ever meet."

CHAPTER 37

Charlie

I t's midmorning by the time I drive away from Rowan's new-to-him but old money Montecito compound, and I have a lot to think about. I'll need to stop by my house to change into work clothes before I go into the office. I darted out the door last night without throwing much more than loungewear into my gym bag. And I'll probably have to work into the evening, because I'm starting so late.

Worth it, though.

Worth it to spend time with Rowan.

Rowan's more than an addiction, like I thought before. He's an essential part of me. We don't say we're addicted to oxygen or water or other natural needs.

The Pacific Ocean is on my right as I head down the coast toward Ventura. It's a pretty stretch of coastline with a few islands offshore. World-class views for my now world-class boyfriend. A thought hits me out of nowhere: Since Rowan's now a little prince in his castle, what if he doesn't want me anymore? My throat constricts, and I chew on a knuckle.

Do I have some kind of caregiver complex? I liked the way Rowan looked in my jacket the first night I met him. I liked feeding him and making sure he was clean and warm. I liked buying him a phone and rescuing him from his crappy apartment.

Am I really a fucking daddy?

God, I hope not. I'm only twenty-nine. How can I be a daddy? They're ... older than me. Different.

But if Rowan no longer sees me as a daddy, will he still want me? Is he going on a new adventure and leaving me behind? Just like everyone else, riding off into the sunset with their perfect partners.

Then I remind myself: Ten years ago, I designed the exact life I have right now—or that I had before I met Rowan—and I managed to achieve most of it. But it didn't make me happy.

What *has* made me happy was chasing Rowan around the manicured grounds of his estate, going bowling with him, and scowling at him while he ate all the Thai food I ordered. I'm happy taking care of him.

So what happens, now that he doesn't need to be taken care of? When his real father swoops in and gives him everything he's ever needed and so many things it would never have occurred to him to dream were possible? Now I feel ... unnecessary.

Fuck this shit. I call him from my hands-free, not even caring that I'm being the needy one.

"Rowan?" I ask.

Rowan seems surprised to hear from me but reacts fast. "Hey, Daddy," he coos. And something inside me rearranges itself, just like that.

"Hey," I say, my voice husky.

"What's wrong?" Rowan asks.

"How could you tell that something was wrong from one or two words?"

"Because I know you."

The thing is, he does. I signal to get out of the fast lane. "I was driving away, and I was feeling bad, and rather than sulk, I figured I'd call you."

"Why are you sulking?" he asks.

I tug at my hair. "In part because I miss you."

He's quiet for so long that I look at the display to see if the call dropped. "You do?" he finally asks in an awed voice.

"Definitely."

"I miss you, too."

I remind myself of all the vulnerability he's shown me and try to follow his example. "And I guess I'm feeling rather irrelevant."

"Why?" Rowan's tone is one of genuine astonishment, which makes me feel better.

I tap my steering wheel. "Because you won't need me anymore. Now that you have ... everything."

More silence, which I'm not sure how to interpret. Then Rowan says fiercely, "You listen, Charlie, and you listen well. I found you, and I'm not giving you up. I wouldn't trade you for all this stuff from my new family."

"I'm new, too," I argue. Then I wince, because why am I arguing against what I want? Other than because that's what I always do.

"But I chose you," Rowan says. "I want you."

"Okay," I say.

"No, Charlie," Rowan says more urgently. "I *want* you. It has nothing to do with need. It has to do with me wanting you in my life. You're the only person I've ever clicked with like this. Don't you feel it?"

My pulse pounds in my throat, and my nerve endings tingle. "Yeah, baby. I feel it, too." I exhale. I needed him to say that.

I want to keep talking to him for the rest of my drive—the rest of the day, really—but I know that's not a good idea. "I'm getting down into Ventura, and there's more traffic," I tell him.

"Then I'll let you go, but know that even if this stuff changes me, it's not going to change how I feel about you. It's not going to change the fact that I want to be with you, and I want you to be happy."

I snort. "Tough for me to be happy when I'm headed to the office."

"How would you make work better?"

"Make it more of what I want and less of what's expected of me."

"Right. Do that. Give it a try, at least. Think of it as a Christmas present to yourself."

"Speaking of which ... is there something you want? Something I can get you?" I ask, wondering what to give the man who can now have literally anything.

"I don't know," he says slowly. "I'll think about it. What about you? You still have a cat on your list. Do you want one? Or is that going to go the way of your precise haircuts?"

I shrug. "I like cats. They seem to require the exact amount of attention that I'm willing to give. But don't get me one yet. I want to be sure I'm going to be around to take proper care of it, and I have a feeling I'm going to be spending a lot of time on the road between Venice and Montecito."

"I hope you do. And I hope I'm with you most of that time."

"Me, too, baby."

* * *

What Rowan said is cycling through my brain as I race into my house, tear off my jeans, and put on a suit, then turn around and head for work. I park in the garage and take the elevator to the fourteenth (thirteenth) floor.

I know who I need to talk to.

The Weston & Ramirez office is sleek, with a nice reception desk where Shelby is perched. The art on the wall behind him and down the halls celebrates LGBTQ+ milestones and events. Before I can talk myself out of it, I pause at his desk rather than waving and proceeding on my usual way to my office.

"Hey," I say, shuffling my feet.

"Hi, Charlie," Shelby says. He's looking festive in a pair of candy cane suspenders over his white polo.

I roll my neck. "Is Noah here today?"

Shelby gives me a wide smile. "Yep. And he doesn't have any appointments until later."

"Cool, thanks." I head down to Noah's office, rap on the doorjamb, and take a seat when he invites me to do so.

"I want to talk to you about something," I say, biting the inside of my cheek.

Noah gives me a sincere, worried look. "Sure. Of course. How can I help?"

I tap my knees with my fingertips, stare at the floor, and grimace. Then I look him in the eye. "I hate being a lawyer."

Oddly, he doesn't seem surprised. "I'm sorry you aren't happy here."

"It's not anything to do with the firm." I fidget. "You guys are amazing. This is the best law firm on the planet. But I don't like the work. I don't like dealing with clients who are rude or unreasonable or don't pay their bills, and I don't want to do this anymore."

Noah's expression is kind. "Charlie, we'd never want you to stay and keep doing work you hate. You know we'll support you in whatever is right for you. Are you planning to transition to something else? What is it you'd like to do?"

"That's the thing. I don't know. The only thing I know I like doing are the videos with my brother."

"Then do more of them and see where that goes. If you want to take some time off, do it. If you leave, we'll miss you, but you need to do what you need to do. I never want anyone to be unhappy here. And even if you leave the firm, we're still friends. You'll still be friends with everyone here."

I don't know why I thought it would be so hard to tell him the truth. Now that I've done it, it's a relief—this weight off not only my shoulders, but possibly his, too. This unspoken thing that was keeping me from being my authentic self. It's true what they say: the truth shall set me free.

Kinda. It's not that easy, though. "Still, I feel like I'd be making a mistake, throwing away all that schooling. All that money. The sunk costs are huge."

Noah waves a hand. "There's a reason they call it the sunk cost *fallacy*. Trying to keep doing what you've always done, just so you don't lose your investment, is a bad idea. If it's never going to make you happy, is it the right investment?"

"True."

"And you're never going to lose your investment in yourself. You can do what you like."

"Yeah," I say slowly. "I don't have to do what I've been doing. Just because everyone expects me to be a lawyer doesn't mean I have to stay one."

Noah looks at me expectantly.

I can do anything.

"I don't want to leave," I say. "At least not yet. Not until I have a better idea what I want to do."

"Take the time you need to figure it out. You can keep working, or you can take a sabbatical. What we want is for you to be happy, Charlie," Noah says.

I can't believe that tears are stinging my eyes. I never fucking cry. But something about his sincere concern makes me realize that I underestimated him. I thought he wanted more billable hours from me when he really cares about me as a person.

"I do know one thing: I want to stop working for jerks like Cormac Esmond."

Noah grimaces. "I've never understood why we've kept him as a client. He's more trouble than he's worth. Drop him, dude. Let him find an attorney who's better suited."

Later in the day, when Cormac calls, I interrupt his rant right off the bat. "It sounds like Weston & Ramirez isn't the right firm for you. I'll send over a substitution of attorney."

"What?" Cormac blurts. He starts sputtering, but I remain calm, even though I really want to tell him what a miserable excuse for a human being he is.

"This business relationship isn't working out," I say. "We need mutual trust. If you're going to scream at me for protecting your interests in the best way I know how, then I can't do my job properly. Either you sign the substitution, or I'll file a motion to be relieved as counsel. Check your email in an hour."

And then I hang up.

I think this is the first time I've ever hung up on a client.

I smile.

It might be the first time I've smiled at work in weeks.

Merry Christmas to me.

CHAPTER 38

Rowan

After Charlie leaves, I gather my wallet with its new, shiny credit card and my phone and step outside to find out where Hector parked my car. Remi's car. Whatever. The car I drove here. I was too distracted yesterday to worry about where he stored it, but I think I figured out which building is the garage: the one with six doors. But I think the cars may be stacked on lifts, so maybe it's a twelve-car garage? I tug at my bottom lip.

Hector sees me immediately through the open door and comes out of the garage with a smile. "Good morning, Rowan. What can I do for you?"

I crack my knuckles. "I need my—a—car. To go shopping. I didn't bring much in the way of clothes up here—mostly because I don't have any. My father wants me to go buy some nicer ones."

"Then let me take you. That way you can relax, not worry about traffic or parking. I can assist with your bags, too."

"Thanks, that'd be great," I say, rocking on my feet.

"Let me get the car. I'll only be a moment."

He pulls a large Mercedes-Benz out of the I-don't-know-how-many-car garage, and I reach out to open the front passenger door, then second-guess myself. This former ShareARide driver doesn't know how to be a passenger.

Or how to behave, in general.

"Hector," I say, then clear my throat. "Do you want me to sit in the front or the back?"

"That's up to you, but Mr. St. Thomas likes to sit in the back so he can focus on things other than the road."

"Okay." I fidget a bit more.

I get another kind smile from Hector. "Sit in the back. Let me take you where you need to go."

So I do. Hector asks what kind of music I want to listen to, and when I tell him my favorite bands, he grins. "I like those, too." He starts one of their albums on the sound system.

I sink back in the leather seat and watch the tall hedges of Montecito go by.

Okay, I could get used to this.

Hector pulls up in front of the department store, throwing on his blinkers so others have to go around us. "I'll be nearby when you're ready to leave," he says. "Just message me, and I'll come."

I'm about to ask for his phone number, but I check the phone my father gave me, and of course Hector is programmed in there. As are a bunch of other names, including Matilda and Lionel. I rub my chin. "Okay, thanks." I open the door and get out of the car, noticing a man lying against the side of the building, just around the corner from the entrance. I have no cash to give him. I need to be like Charlie and carry a little cash for situations like this.

Hector waits as I stand outside, my stomach tense and breath catching in my chest. The doormen monitoring the shiny entrance have surely noticed me by now.

Should I just get back in the car? I don't belong here except as some kind of novelty. I'm the discount burger wrapped in paper served on fine china. This is going to be a *Pretty Woman* situation where the sales clerks are too snooty to help me.

I feel the same as I did walking into the restaurant to meet my father. Plus, I'm sore and bruised from last night.

A small voice in my head argues that maybe they're used to rock stars or whatever who walk in wearing clothes like mine—jeans and a T-shirt from a thrift store.

One of the uniformed attendants smiles at me and opens the door. "Right this way."

With a fluttery feeling in my chest, I give him a curt nod and push my shoulders back. Inside, the place is utterly pristine. So much white, so many shiny things. Fresh wreaths with satin ribbons provide a tasteful wintertime display, and everyone in here looks like they're straight out of a magazine.

I stare at my shoes. Fuck what those people think. I could buy this store. Or my father could, at least.

Which means I'm never going to wear the same outfit again for the rest of my life, if I can help it. Where the hell is the most expensive pair of jeans in the store?

Something pricks my conscience, because I know that's wasteful.

I assuage my conscience. I'm making massive plans to help people with my funds, if I ever get them. I'm allowed to splurge.

A well-dressed woman glides over to me. "Hello, I'm Norinne. Do you mind me asking if you're Rowan Jones?"

My legal last name is starting to sound weird now. I furrow my brows. "I am. Why?"

"Your father called and said you'd be coming in. His office opened up a house account for you. He said you were in the process of changing your name to St. Thomas."

"I am."

"What would you prefer me to call you?"

"How about Rowan?"

She smiles. "Do you mind showing me some ID, just for confirmation? Mr. St. Thomas described you as having pink hair, so I figured it was you." I pull out my wallet and hand it to her. She reads it and gives it back to me with another warm smile. "Welcome. Then, Rowan, let's see what will suit you."

The next few hours can only be described as rage-buying.

With Norinne standing by approvingly, I select Dior T-shirts and Saint Laurent varsity jackets. White Christian Louboutin sneakers with silver studs and red soles. Alexander McQueen hoodies. Balenciaga jeans. Paul Smith underwear. Other brands I've never heard of but that sell clothing I want to wear. Basically, I get a version of all the clothes I already have, but at a hundred times the price. Or more.

Everything. I get *everything*. I buy every single thing I've never imagined being able to own.

Then I decide to upgrade even more and pick up slim velvet blazers, metallic silver pants, pointed shoes in shiny leather. I touch fabrics and figure out what I want next to my body—soft, comfortable, sleek.

I go into the couture department and get measured for a few custom-made suits. I'm gonna sparkle like a Christmas tree.

It takes four people to package up all of the things I buy. Hector may have to make two trips. Then I remember I can have this all delivered.

So, yep. I know I went from Donald Duck (no pants) to Scrooge McDuck (still no pants) in a very short period of time, but can you blame me? I've gone far too long with too little. If someone says I'm swinging too far over to the indulgent side ... well. They can deal with it.

I finish shopping for myself and start looking for things for Charlie. I pick out dark brown and gray cashmere sweaters that will look delicious on him and sunglasses that are his style. I'd buy him more, but I'm not sure what he'd like. I find his hinoki scent and buy one of every formulation it comes in. I pick up fancy hand lotion for Matilda and a T-shirt for Hector. When I've spent more time with Lionel, I'll get him something, too.

Money might be running through my fingers like water, but I

know I'll calm down after this orgasmic shopping trip. After all those purchases get rung up and my father's accountant approves them, I get a glimpse of the total damage I've done. It's more than many rich people make in a year. In several years.

Damn.

But I'm the son of a fucking billionaire. He's spoiling me, and I'm going to show it off. I'll look the part even if I don't feel like it yet.

Fake it until I make it.

I leave the store in stretchy, black skinny jeans and a mint green mohair sweater, along with the lightest, most comfortable sneakers I've ever worn. I dumped the clothes I had been wearing in the dressing room trash. I never want to see that old life ever again.

New life, here I come.

* * *

My father joins me for dinner in the Montecito house. "This is one of your new outfits?" he asks, once we're drinking coffee on a back patio while waiting for dinner.

"Yep. I bought out the store, I think," I admit.

He chuckles, which turns into a cough. A nurse named Bettina wraps a plaid blanket around him. "I'm glad. I hope you got some pleasure out of it."

I nod. "Thanks. I got some of the coolest and nicest clothes I've ever seen."

"You seem to have a very distinct style." He pointedly looks at my pink hair.

"What's wrong? You don't want a son with tattoos?"

Remi's eyes warm. "I *definitely* want a son with tattoos. And whatever color hair, whatever personality. I like that you're yourself. That's going to help you."

"I tried to have my own style before, but I had no money, so I had to get creative. With money?" I shrug. "It's easier. So thank you."

"You're welcome. And where is Charlie?" Remi asks, looking around as if Charlie's going to pop up from behind a potted plant.

"He had to go to work today. In LA."

"Okay, well, I look forward to meeting him." He looks sheepish. "Not because I have any right as your father to say who you date. But because I want to know more about you." He sighs. "I'm sorry. I want to be sure I know you as much as I can before the cancer claims me. Though getting to know each other might cause you pain when I'm gone, and for that I'm sorry. But I prefer it to the alternative of not getting to know you."

I straighten my legs under the table. "Me, too. I appreciate that you're making an effort. It shows." It's true. He's taken time to see me, in person, when I'm sure he has other things on his mind. And he could use the rest.

It's not his fault I've been so angry and bitter my entire life. I'm just going to accept that he found me as soon as he was able.

"Ever since I got that letter telling me you existed, I have wanted to know you and everything about you. It took a long time to find you, and the timing is terrible, but," he shrugs, "maybe I'm selfish in my old age."

"If you're selfish, I am, too."

Remi laughs, and the sound is so genuine. Now I have two people I want to make laugh.

We sit down for dinner. Matilda has made us a deceptively simple dinner of steak and french fries with a tossed salad, but every single thing is so perfect that I suspect it cost more than my food budget for the past year. Or at least a month. The label on the wine we're drinking says it's local, but that doesn't mean it isn't expensive. As we eat, Remi asks me about my history and listens intently as I talk. I wish I could fix the sad expression on his face, but I can't. After a while, we switch to other topics.

Remi sips his wine. "So, Rowan. You should know a few

things before you go see Nana or meet other members of the family. To begin with, you need to be careful. Now that you have money, people are going to come out of the woodwork and try to be friends with you. Try to convince you to spend it in ways that aren't good for you."

"Like buying out a department store?"

"That's different. I encouraged you to do it. And it's natural to go a bit wild at first when you receive this kind of fortune."

"Okay, true."

He smiles. "But you do need to stay vigilant."

"I'm pretty good at figuring out if I'm being used."

"What about Charlie?"

I snort. "Charlie's the exact opposite of someone who would use me. He took care of me when I had nothing. Charlie literally picked me up off the street, fed me, replaced my phone, gave me a place to stay overnight, drove me home, and picked me up a week later when I was getting evicted ... then gave me a home indefinitely. He's done so much—he even went on a wild-goose chase for my favorite plant."

"You have a favorite plant?"

"I'll bring him down to meet you," I say. "He's upstairs. He went with me to every foster and group home and crappy apartment for the past fifteen years."

He takes a bite of his tender steak. "I'm heartened to hear that you can rely on Charlie. You're going to need someone to stand with you. You are the only direct descendant in your generation, but my uncle married a woman who already had children, and her children and grandchildren are very much interested in the family wealth. Be careful when you meet them." He looks at me intently. "Since you're unmarried, you won't have control of the money until you turn twenty-five, which means—assuming my doctors' predictions are correct—other members of the family will have a considerable length of time to put roadblocks in your path."

My fork pauses on the way to my mouth. "Where would the, um, inheritance go if I didn't exist?"

"Those children and grandchildren I just mentioned. Your appearance is going to affect the rest of the family very significantly. We need to protect you from their … machinations." He starts coughing, and Bettina appears from nowhere. "When you have as much money as we do, you're always a target. Sometimes from within."

"Oh, shit." I look down at my plate and decide I'm full.

He nods. "I don't want you to be overly concerned, but you do need to be careful." He dissolves into more coughing and pushes aside his own plate. "I think I need to go lie down."

"Is there anything I can do to help?" I ask.

"No. Please have a good time at Nana's on Saturday. Send her my regards."

Remi stands up, but he's unsteady. I stand, too, intending to walk around the table and assist him to wherever he wants to go, but Bettina gives me a tight smile and says, "Let me help you, Mr. St. Thomas."

Shit, my father really is ill.

"Are you going to spend the night here?" I ask.

Remi shakes his head. "I'm going to rest for a moment and then return to LA."

After I've established for myself that I can't do much more for him, I head up to my rooms.

I open the bank of windows to let in the cold ocean air and start pacing.

I'm going to enjoy my father as long as I have him. But I need to face the fact that, before long, I'm set to inherit some money. A fuckton is the exact amount, I believe.

Today's orgy notwithstanding, I don't really like shopping, nor do I need a lot of things. I don't need to buy more clothes than I already did. Hell, I didn't need to buy half that many. I just needed to get the newfound freedom out of my system.

If I have that much money, I'm not selfish enough to keep it.

So ... what would I want to do with it?

An idea that's been percolating—besides my vengeance list—is to make it so kids like me, who grew up in the foster system without a safety net, have better access to the things they need. Help LGBTQ+ kids feel more comfortable in their own skin. Help people experiencing homelessness and hunger receive housing and food.

But after I set up those plans—perhaps some foundations—I'm going to seriously get to work on my vengeance plan. I never said I'm a saint.

For that, I need some muscle. People I can trust, who will keep their mouths shut. I remember a few from my teens I could probably find again. And I need to get dialed into computer shit, but Xavier can do that.

I call him, and when I get him caught up on the past week or so of my life, I can feel his jaw drop from hundreds of miles away. I don't blame him. It's hard for me to believe, and I'm living it.

Then I look around this enormous, lavish, empty room. I don't want to be up here without Charlie. It's nice to have the view, the luxury of being waited on, the pool, the grounds, but it's more important to be where my boyfriend is. Period. I pick up the phone and hit his number.

"Daddy?" I say.

"Not your daddy. But what's up, baby boy?" Charlie says, his voice warmer with me than it is with other people.

"I miss you."

"Then get your ass down here, or I'm driving up." His tone shifts to the commanding one I love.

"I'm on my way."

Having already heard my father leave, I say goodbye to Matilda. Hector offers to drive me, but I like driving. I gather Charlie's presents and a few of my new things, settle Wilbur carefully in the BMW's passenger seat, and take off down the coast. A guard is already waiting outside when I get to Charlie's street. I roll my eyes, but I guess I'm grateful he's watching over things.

I race into Charlie's house, not bothering to knock. But he's waiting for me at the front door, and he kisses me like I've come home from the war. We kiss and kiss and kiss. My hands are all over him, and his are all over me.

When we finally take a breath, I still won't leave him alone, doing my best to climb him. He helps me out by hoisting me up and putting my back to the wall so he can brace me there while my legs are wrapped around his waist. And he kisses me again.

"I don't like us living apart," I say, my body shaking and my eyes closed. "I'm clingy."

"I like you clingy," Charlie says into my neck.

I love this man.

"What are you wearing?" Charlie asks, once he gets a chance to look at me.

"Remi told me to go shopping, so I bought one of everything." I hold out my sleeve. "This is some up-and-coming brand. And the jeans are YSL."

Charlie whistles. "You're all fancy now."

"I want to make you fancy, too. If you want." I grin. "Actually, I bought you a present. Or ten."

He shakes his head. "You don't have to do that."

"I know. But I wanted to. I'm not going to receive all this largesse and not share it."

"I'll accept whatever you give me, baby boy," he growls, "but you know what I really want is your ass."

"Yes, Daddy," I whisper.

"Not your daddy." Charlie hoists me over his shoulder like a sack of potatoes, and I laugh. Then he carries me to his bedroom, where he proceeds to make me come. Twice.

Being the son of a billionaire is going to change a lot of things about my life. But I'm not going to let it take Charlie away from me.

CHAPTER 39

Charlie

I lie next to Rowan, catching my breath after our reunion-after-a-whole-twelve-hours-apart sex, sneaking looks at him when I hope he's not paying attention.

He's changed in the past few days. While he's naked now, he walked in transformed into some kind of couture-wearing twink. He'd hate it if I called him a twink. But he looks great in his new clothes. He's always looked otherworldly, with that shiny, messy pink hair and those big, navy blue eyes. He's got a little bit of Marilyn Monroe to his look—that sexy innocence with a mole on his cheek under his eye. He should be sitting on a throne with a gold crown while everyone falls at his tiny, imperious feet. Princeling indeed.

He hops out of bed, absolutely perky after being fucked within an inch of his life. "I want to give you presents."

"Are these early Christmas presents or to make up for the fact that you still haven't returned my suede jacket?"

Rowan blinks up at me all faux innocent. "What suede jacket?"

"You know exactly which one."

"No, they're not to make up for it, nor are they Christmas presents," he says. "If you want your jacket back, I can return it." His grin is too quick, and he doesn't meet my eyes.

"I like that you have it," I admit.

Rowan smiles a sweet, sad smile. His voice gets very small, his most vulnerable voice. It's my favorite. I've seen him bluff and bluster and puff his chest out. But this voice means he's exposing his true heart's desire. "Can I stay here with you, even now that I have another house to go to?"

"Yep."

"Cool," he says quietly. I tug him closer. Even if having a family—and what a family!—has changed him, he still wants me.

I want him, too.

We get up, and he hands me several wrapped boxes. I undo the ribbon that's embossed with the name of the upscale department store and open the lid. Inside, nestled in thick black tissue paper, is a dark brown crewneck cashmere sweater from a very expensive brand. Rowan's eyes are full of excitement as he watches me pull it out and hold it up. The fine yarn is soft, and when I put it on, it fits perfectly.

"Thank you so much. This is awesome. You have really good taste, baby boy," I say.

"I know, Daddy."

I laugh and open the next present.

Late Saturday morning, I drive us to Rowan's great-aunt's house, which is in Laurel Canyon, a hilly, tree-filled, secluded part of LA full of artists. I'm dressed in a soft sweater Rowan bought me that feels like wearing a cloud. Rowan's bodyguard from some security service follows us. Rowan explained why he was necessary, but it still feels like a waste. I have a feeling that a lot of the St. Thomas wealth is used wastefully, and he's still figuring out how to change that.

Rowan asks me whether I've made any progress toward trying different types of art or doing other things that I enjoy. "I edited some old footage before you came back down from Montecito," I volunteer, "of Cam's painting projects. He's got a plan for the next things he wants to do to his house. Once we finish his place, we'll get going more on mine."

"Can I help you sometime?" Rowan's voice is both eager and tentative.

"With editing?"

"No, with a DIY project."

I look at him. "You're welcome to come and watch. You don't have to do anything."

"What if I want to? You don't think I can wield a sledgehammer?"

I'm imagining tiny Rowan building up a sweat while he demos Cam's house, and while part of me thinks it's cute, the rest of me thinks I should save his energy for something else. Something more important. Like being chased through the woods.

Seeing him bend over to demo something with a large tool, though ... that would be enjoyable.

Rowan catches the look on my face. "What are you thinking about?" he asks, with a wide grin. "It seems like it might be me doing something without my clothes on."

"Pretty much," I admit.

"Ohhh, you mean you want to shoot *that* kind of video."

I signal to turn up Crescent Heights. "Sure. When we get home, strip naked and I'll film you. But that's just for me."

While I expect Rowan to laugh, he doesn't. Instead, when I glance over at him, he licks his lips. "You can film me," he murmurs, "any time you want. What would you like? Me to use a toy? Or two? Or three? I could have one in my ass and another on my cock, and I could wear a cock ring—"

I cut him off. "Oh my god, you are so sexy. If you were anyone else, I'd say I can't believe you're up for this, but it's you. As far as I can tell, you're up for anything." Then I glare at him. "Don't turn me on when we're going to go meet your elderly relative. I don't want to, like, offend her."

"I wonder what she's like. From what Remi's said, I get the idea that she's a character. And seriously, while you can film me however you like, I meant I could help you with actually doing the work or holding the camera or whatever."

"I'll keep that in mind."

He pauses while we go around a curve, then says, "Remi asked if I want to change my last name to St. Thomas."

"It does seem like you old money types are very much into tradition and your name."

He huffs. "I've been an old money type for less than a week. Give me a little time to adjust. I said yes, though." He reaches over and squeezes my hand. "I told him to have the lawyers get started on it. Unless you want me to change it to Cooper, Daddy." He flutters his eyelashes and wiggles in his seat.

Rowan Cooper. While part of me thinks it seems wrong for Rowan, another part of me likes the sound of it. "You belong to me no matter what your name is. We don't have to formalize it that way. You're mine."

"I'm definitely yours no matter what," Rowan says. His words make my heart tingle with something. I think it might be happiness.

The gates of Rowan's great-aunt's estate open for us, and we continue up a long, winding driveway that's super lush. Red velvet bows decorate the handrails of patio stairs leading up to a concrete gazebo, and white twinkle lights are neatly wrapped around the trunks of small trees. We pass a huge, gilded mirror posed under a tree, surrounded by plants, and I see the slow-moving reflection of our car going by. I whistle, noting how green everything is. While December is what passes for the rainy season in LA, this is an oasis.

"What even is this?" Rowan asks, his voice in a tone of wonder. "I'm totally out of my element."

"That makes two of us."

"I felt out of place at the Montecito house, but I'm just starting to get the scope of how much the St. Thomas family has." He pulls out his phone and googles the address. "Remi told me this was once Harry Houdini's home, and there's a whole article on it. It says there are natural springs, which is why this area is so full of plants. She must need fifteen gardeners just to take care of it all." He pauses. "She probably has thirty, huh? God, this is a different world."

We pull up to a main house that's late Edwardian style, per Rowan's continued reading. There are palm trees and fountains and an inordinate number of plants, and the grounds are terraced, with all kinds of pathways. In addition to the plants, funny little statues are situated here and there. And mosaics. Mirrors. Glass balls. All kinds of whimsical things. It makes you want to stop and look. I hope we get the chance to wander around some.

Rowan does his usual squaring of his shoulders when he's bracing himself to do something he's nervous about. I lean over and kiss him. "You got this. And I'll be right next to you."

"Yeah." He swallows hard. Then his perky grin resurfaces. "Oh my god, I kind of have a grandma. Let's meet her."

I turn off the car, and hand in hand, we walk up to the front door, which opens immediately. A sturdy woman with very short, spiky white-gray hair, wearing a yellow pantsuit, stands there, smiling. The first thing that catches my eye are the tattoos on her forearms. They're faded, and they seem of an era when women didn't get tattoos. Rowan's Nana gives no fucks, that's for sure. I can tell that before she even says a word.

"Rowan?" she says in an excited whisper.

"That's me!"

"Rowan, baby, come give me a hug." She opens her arms, and

he steps forward so she can wrap him in them. She closes her eyes tight, clearly overwhelmed by emotion.

Something happens to my throat. Rowan needed a solid person to be his family. Someone besides me or one of his old friends from a group home. Someone from a different generation. Someone who can connect him to the bigger picture of who he is.

All his life, Rowan thought he was alone. He wasn't, though. He just didn't know where they were hiding. Which was—among other places—apparently at Houdini's estate.

Rowan's Nana steps back and does the stiff upper lip thing, although she sniffles once. "It's so good to finally meet you, Rowan. We've been looking for you for a very long time."

He nods, and now he's trying to be all tough. Damn, he's cute. He glances up at me. "I've brought my boyfriend, Charlie Cooper."

We shake hands. "I'm Rhonda," she says. "But you can be like everyone else in the family and call me Nana, which is what I prefer. And Charlie, I can't thank you enough for taking care of Rowan. Remi told me that you let him stay with you when he was having issues with his last place. I can't believe all that's happened. But come in, come in. Let's get you drinks, and we can sit down and chat."

Nana is a combination of old-world manners and *fuck it, I can do what I want* attitude. I love her immediately, and I can see Rowan feeling safe here. We go into a parlor where one of the old leather chairs has "Conquer Fear" painted on its back. A woman who isn't as old as Nana but isn't young, either, comes in carrying a tray laden with mugs, a few carafes, and a plate of cookies. She's trailed by a blond man who looks to be maybe five or ten years older than me.

Nana kisses the woman on the cheek. "This is my partner, Barbara. Barbara, this is the long-lost Rowan John and his boyfriend, Charlie."

Barbara sets down her tray and shakes first Rowan's hand and then mine. "Nice to meet you," I say.

"Likewise," she replies. "This is my son, Gideon."

I offer him my hand, and he squeezes it in an immediate challenge. What the fuck? I don't have a weak grip—old-school lawyer training teaches you to not show weakness anywhere. But aren't we just having tea?

Oblivious to the weirdness, Barbara beams.

Pointing to the tray, Nana says, "I may never have had children of my own, nor did I want them, but I'm completely comfortable being everyone's grandma now." She grins. "Especially when it involves cookies."

Rowan and I each take a cookie, and when I bite into mine, I barely stifle a moan. It's the perfect shortbread, melt-in-your-mouth good. We pour ourselves cups of coffee and tea and settle in.

"Remi has told me a bit about your upbringing," Nana says gently to Rowan. "I'm very sorry we were unable to find you until now."

"That makes two of us."

"More than two." Nana leans in closer to him. "You will find, however, that some of the family are less easy to get along with than Barbara and I are. C'est la vie."

"Well, when you're talking about that much money," Barbara says, "you can understand why people are vying for it."

Gideon crosses his arms over his chest but doesn't say anything.

"It all goes to you, though," Nana says, her voice breezy, though I can't tell whether her tone indicates true acceptance or is an attempt to cover something else: hurt or frustration, perhaps. "Or it will. The rest of us live off the interest."

"What do you mean?" Rowan asks.

"The money goes to the oldest child in each generation. That's Remi, because he's my older brother's son, and soon it will be you.

Nowadays, people tend to do things differently—split the money among all the children—but that's not how my father set things up."

"No, what do you mean about you living on the interest?"

"Oh!" Nana laughs without humor. "For tax reasons, interest from my father's fortune goes into a number of subsidiary trusts, and the family members, except Remi, live off that. It's not insignificant. While Father certainly provided for me and the rest of the family as far as basic needs, most of this," she sweeps her hand out, indicating the estate, I think, "is from my late ex-husband." I'm sure her idea of basic needs and mine differ. She sniffs. "He had enough to rival Father anyway. Did Remi tell you about the parameters of the St. Thomas family trust?"

"He said I would inherit when I turn twenty-five."

Gideon shifts in his seat.

"That's true, but it's only one of the ways to satisfy the requirements. The other is to get married. If you did that, the trust funds would transfer immediately," Nana says.

"Why would your father have structured the trust that way?" Rowan asks.

"I think in part because he had a happy marriage with my mother. And in part because he could be very controlling and he wanted to make sure that his legacy—his bloodline, that is— continued on. Undivided money can be more powerful, and having wealth long enough to raise a child to marriage age should enable the parents to set up their own assets before the seed money was passed on to the next generation. My father started investing young and believed that was the right way to do it. If people made mistakes, so be it. For my part, I married at eighteen because, back then, that was what women were supposed to do. I was never going to be in line for the bulk of the St. Thomas fortune, so I could make my own choices... which included divorcing in my mid-twenties. My ex-husband later died without remarrying or changing his trust."

Rowan opens his mouth to ask another question but shuts it again.

Nana reads him, though. "Yes, I knew I was lesbian when I was young. I had no interest in boys. I grew up at a time when people like us had 'roommates.' Ever since my twenties, I've done whatever the hell I wanted, and I'm fully aware that the ability to do so was a privilege. And a scandal. But Barbara was worth any scandal." She looks fondly at her partner. "We've been together almost fifty years."

"Much to our respective families' displeasure," Barbara says, and I wonder about her story. Is she independently wealthy, too? Or does she rely on Nana's ex-husband's money?

"Because of some legal rules, the trust will end with you," Nana tells Rowan.

She must be talking about the rule against perpetuities—that control over an estate can last no longer than the lifespans of a certain group of people living at the time the trust was created, plus twenty-one years. At some point there has to be a final beneficiary; the estate can't just go on forever. I haven't thought about that since law school.

Which means, once the money is Rowan's, he can do whatever the hell he wants with it.

"You will receive the funds without any further strings attached," she continues, echoing my thoughts.

I can read the look in·Rowan's eyes. He doesn't want to make a wrong step here. And he's overwhelmed by possibilities.

"I say don't rock the boat," Gideon says. "Leave things as they are."

Nana studies Rowan. "How old are you? Twenty-two?"

Rowan sets down his mug. "Twenty-three. I'll be twenty-five in less than a year and a half."

If Remi dies before Rowan turns twenty-five, the money will stay in trust for Rowan until then. That should be no problem, especially given how Remi has taken care of so many of his material needs already.

"Or you could get married and the trust would end now," Nana says. She looks at me. "Any interest? If you married Rowan —and yes, I know this is presumptuous when I've just met you, but still—if you married him, he could become a billionaire right away."

CHAPTER 40

Rowan

Charlie's eyes bug out. "I'm sorry, what?" he sputters.

"It's a lot of money. You can take control of the family trust from Remi," Nana tells me. "Just get married."

Is this the kind of bullshit I'm now a part of? I thought that kind of crap only happened on TV shows.

"No," I say. "We're not doing that."

"I ... I can't," Charlie says to Nana. He reaches out to me, and I take his hand. He squeezes. "I don't want to hurt your feelings, and I appreciate the proposal—"

"From my great-aunt, who I just met," I say, laughing. "The idea is absurd. There's no way I'm taking away my father's money."

"You don't even know how much it is," Barbara says.

Charlie curls his arms over his head. "But his father's still alive."

"Precisely," I say.

Nana inhales sharply. "I'm pretty sure he will be in hospice soon, and he knows it. He's been getting his affairs in order."

"This is nuts," I say, dizzy and nauseated. "I can wait."

Nana clucks her tongue. "Just think about it. It's twenty billion dollars."

My stomach drops, even though I'd guessed something like that. "That's a fuckton." I glance at Nana. "Sorry."

"That's quite all right," she says, waving a hand. "Swear away."

Charlie drags his nails down his cheeks and slumps back in his seat. "Even if it would only be for a short time, it's wrong to take the money from his father."

"Agreed," I say firmly.

Nana nods. "I wouldn't pressure you, but I'm concerned about what might happen after Remi is no longer able—or around —to run things. It would calm things down if the estate went to Rowan right away."

Charlie shakes his head over and over again. I press a fist to my lips.

"What do you mean, 'calm'?" Charlie asks.

"There are always people who want a chance at the money," Nana says.

"Yeah, okay. Any time a beneficiary isn't vested, it can lead to a dispute." Charlie looks thoughtful. "Litigation."

"Hell no. I'm not getting involved in any of that lawyer shit," I say.

Charlie raises an eyebrow. "Lawyer shit? That's what I do."

"You know what I mean." I throw up my hands. "I don't want to cause problems with my new family."

"You might not have a choice," he says.

Barbara looks at Nana. "I think we may want to let them have a little discussion."

"Oh, but it's getting interesting," Nana says before relenting. "Okay, fine. We'll be out in the garden."

They stand and leave, taking Gideon with them. I don't like that guy. He hasn't said much since we arrived, but I don't like him. Or maybe I don't like him *because* he hasn't said anything.

"Hey," Charlie says, taking my face in his big hands. "Are you okay?"

I shake my head, my mouth dry and my eyes darting around. "Not really. How can my life have so many amazingly wonderful things in it now—like you and this insta-family—and still be so fucked up?" I hang my head. "While, yeah, access to the money would be wild, what does waiting a year matter? Plus, I can't do that to my father, end of discussion."

"Agreed."

"I'd be a great husband, though," I tease. I have no intention of swooping in and taking away Remi's money. But I can't help but poke Daddy.

"What? No. You'd drive me bananas."

I widen my eyes. "Bananas? Me? How so?"

"Oh, I don't know, menace. Maybe because you keep calling me Daddy."

"Admit that you love it when I call you daddy." I wrap my arms loosely around his neck.

Charlie gets in my face. "*Never.*"

My forehead touches his. "Admit that you love that I ignore you and still do it."

He pauses. And with that pause, he loses. I grin like I've won, because I have.

"Admit that you'll never admit it."

"Yeah. Okay. But don't fucking call me daddy."

"Deal." I kiss him. "Daddy."

"Such a fucking brat," he mutters against my lips.

"Yeah, I guess. And your point is?"

"Is it okay with you if I take a look at what we're dealing with? Do you have a copy of the trust instrument?" Charlie asks.

"No, but I'll ask my father for it." I pull out my phone and text him. He replies immediately, which warms my heart. "He says he'll email it to me."

"Okay, forward it to me. Let me see if what Nana said is accurate."

"Good idea. Maybe you can sort out what's going on." I want to change the subject. "Should we go find our way to the garden?"

"Yeah."

We get up, and I notice a bookcase that's tilted slightly away from the wall. "I think that's one of the secret passageways the article mentioned," I say, gesturing.

"Should we snoop at your great-aunt's house?" Charlie asks.

"A quick look won't be a big deal." I pull on the side of the bookcase, and as I suspected, it's a door. Behind it lies a bedroom with flocked gold damask wallpaper. From the ceiling, a black chandelier with clear crystals hangs over a bed sporting a platinum metallic bedspread and tiger-print pillows. A burgundy rug covers the floor.

"This place is wild," Charlie says, peering over my shoulder.

"Totally."

We close the room up again and head toward what I think is the garden. On the way, we pass a number of devices created by Houdini. "At least he knew how to get out of a tight spot," I grumble, amazed at a metallic contraption that looks like the Tin Man from *The Wizard of Oz*. Framed posters advertising Houdini are next to shackles he used in his escape acts.

I open a door that leads out to a pool. A large jacaranda tree stands nearby, its trunk and larger branches adorned with twinkle lights as well as several huge metal lanterns.

"Cool pool," Charlie says.

"Notice its shape? The article mentioned it, too."

He squints. "Is it a ..."

"Coffin? Yes."

"Wow."

"Nana's ex-husband died from drowning. If it happened here in a coffin-shaped pool, that'd be particularly macabre."

"If it was her *ex*-husband, he probably wasn't here," Charlie says."

"True." I glance around. "I can't decide if I love this place or if it's just too weird."

"Sounds like everything that's happened in connection with your family hits you that way."

"Yep. I just don't know what to think." I take his hand. "Let's go find Nana."

CHAPTER 41

Charlie

When we get home, I do laundry and get organized for the upcoming week while Rowan fiddles with his phone. He receives a copy of the trust from his father, and I read it over. It's as Nana said. My scalp prickles. I'm all too aware how money makes people file lawsuits. Do I need to marry him to avoid the estate ending up stuck in litigation for years?

I come up behind Rowan where he's curled like a kitten on the armchair in the living room and bend down to kiss his neck. He shivers, then half-heartedly pushes me away. "Don't do that," he mutters.

"Why not?"

"Because I'm thinking."

I move to the front of the armchair, tug him up so he's standing, then spin and fall back into the seat with him in my lap. I trace his face with my fingers, and he closes his eyes under my touch. "What are you thinking? That it's a lot of fucking money?"

"That's part of it. But it's all twisted up with me not wanting to hurt my father and wishing he weren't dying. Also, what the fuck is up with my family wanting people to get married?"

I nuzzle his face, the hair lifting on the back of my neck. "Are you tempted?"

"No, and I feel like I'm a fool for *not* being tempted. Who turns down access to that much money? What if it all goes away before I'm twenty-five?"

"You do have access to some funds. The trust your father set up for you."

"This is true. And, even if I wanted to be a dick and take the family fortune away from my father, you and I agreed we're not getting married." He pauses. "I suppose the trust wouldn't care who I married. I could marry Xavier or Gideon or—"

Hot flames travel through my body. "You're such a brat. Rowan, you're mine. You know that, don't you?"

"Yeah." He grins, then sighs. "Besides, it feels wrong to marry for money, not love."

"Exactly."

Rowan sets his head under my chin, and I play with his hair. "Who'd've thought I have a conscience?"

"You have a conscience and a moral code," I say. "I do, too. I want you to have no doubts as to my reasons for being with you." I tilt his head up and kiss him. "It's not for your money—whether you have it or not. It's because *you're the one I'm choosing*. I don't want you to get mixed up, thinking that I'm with you for any other reason."

"I understand," Rowan says quietly. "I promised you I wouldn't marry you."

"I know. But apart from that promise or the trust or anything else, what do you really want? Our relationship shouldn't be all about my issues. Part of being together is, you know, we compromise."

He finally looks me in the eye. "I've teased you about tuxedos for our weddings and going on dates and having a daddy, but with my background, do you blame me if there's some underlying truth to it? I want stability."

"I can see that." I hug him, and he wraps his arms around me tight. "The only way I know how to give you that is to just keep showing up for you every day."

"That's enough," he says into my chest.

I vow to prove it to him. To be there so he knows he's loved and wanted—forever.

"I do want my rings, though."

"One for every finger but your ring finger. I will keep that promise." I pull back so we can see each other's faces, hoping my sincerity is evident. "And I suppose your ring finger is open, in case we both change our minds. Since I've been changing my mind so much in the last few weeks."

He bites his lip and nods, looking at his hands.

"So, are you sure you're good with waiting for the money?" I press.

"Yeah, especially since my father seems happy to give me everything I need."

"Then tell me if that changes, baby. And we'll revisit it." I kiss him on the forehead, and he closes his eyes. So I kiss those, too. Then move down to his lips. "I'm willing to compromise if we have to. But maybe we won't have to."

CHAPTER 42

Charlie

On Thursday night, we're seated in the back seat of a large Mercedes-Benz.

"I'm so fucking nervous, I think I'm going to throw up," Rowan mutters. His driver Hector is taking us to Bel Air for a holiday party at Bree St. Thomas's house.

Rowan looks fabulous. He's wearing some kind of trashed, skinny pants with a shiny button-down shirt, and he looks like a model. I like him in anything (or nothing), but the fancy designer clothing does suit him. Plus, in a way, it's armor. He's meeting the rest of his family all at once—ones who grew up together and have history he doesn't share.

"They're gonna kick me out," he whispers.

"No, they're not. You belong there just as much as they do."

"As what? The long-lost bastard child?"

I squeeze his clammy hand. "You're the only child of your dying father, who looked for you for years. You're the rightful heir to the St. Thomas estate. I read through all the trust documents."

"Hmm."

He stares out the window at the holiday lights and increasingly nice houses we're passing.

How can I help him not panic?

Be his daddy.

"You walk in there like the badass you are," I order. "Back straight, head held high. You fucking belong, baby boy."

Rowan gives me a grateful look I catch in the streetlights. He lifts his chin. *Good.*

"Are you going to own that party?" I ask.

"Yeah," he says, and his voice is stronger than it was a few moments ago.

"Well, then. This should be fun."

Hector pulls through a gate and up a private road, following a line of cars to a circular drive, where he stops at the entrance to what appears to be a transplanted Tuscan villa. The place is as big as a city block and has to be on a couple of acres, which in this neighborhood ... I can't imagine the cost. I'm guessing the house is fifteen thousand square feet. Maybe more.

Holiday lights illuminate the architectural features. A series of arches invite you to stroll across a manicured lawn and terraced gardens overlooking, I believe, a golf course.

We step out of the car, and ... holy shit.

I thought old money types were supposed to be understated— the whole quiet luxury thing where they don't announce their wealth.

This party is the opposite of that. But then, I suppose Bree St. Thomas isn't old money, if I understand her history correctly.

We're serenaded by violinists playing Christmas music as we walk up the stairs. A quartet bundled up like they're from merry olde England sings carols. Candles are everywhere, in quantities like they're trying to burn the place down. Every spot that could be decked in garland, is. An enormous wreath hangs over the front doors.

And that's before we get inside.

The doors open, and we step into a grand entrance hall with staircases going up three floors. We don't have time to goggle as we follow the flow of people into a ballroom. Yeah, there's a ballroom in the house, like we're in the 1800s or something. More than just family is invited to the party—I'd say there are at least a hundred people here. Waiters circle with trays of drinks, caviar on toast, and tiny appetizers like lobster cakes and wild mushroom tarts.

When Rowan and I enter, first one person, then the next, then the next turns to look at us.

Soon, the room is silent, apart from a string quartet over in one corner.

I want to yell *This is the new St. Thomas heir, jackasses*. But I can keep my mouth shut.

Maybe.

I look over at Rowan, who is holding up his chin, his back straight, thousand-mile stare on his face. Oh, yeah. The pink hair. The small stature. He stands out.

And he's a threat to their entire way of life. Because he will control the purse strings in a little over a year.

Thankfully, Nana comes over and hugs him tight. "Rowan and Charlie! I'm so glad you've come."

I give her a hug, too. She smells nice.

The guests start to chatter again, and I'm sure they're talking about Rowan.

"You know how to make an entrance," Nana says, winking at him.

Before Rowan says anything, a short, older man approaches. He's a dapper twin to Rowan, with the same eyes and nose. But his pallor and slow movements, not to mention the nurse moving discreetly behind him, make it clear that he's ill. This has to be Remi.

My heart aches for Rowan.

"Remi," Rowan says, shaking his hand formally. "This is my boyfriend, Charlie Cooper. Charlie, this is my father, Remi St. Thomas."

"It's very nice to meet you, Charlie." Remi shakes my hand

with surprising strength before coughing into a linen handkerchief.

Remi shouldn't be here. He should be resting at home. But if this is his last Christmas, it makes sense that he would want to spend it with his family.

"I'm glad Rowan is with someone who is supporting him," Remi continues. "He told me a bit about his upbringing, and I don't know how I can ever forgive myself for not finding him sooner."

"You tried," Rowan says.

"At least I've found you now."

A movement behind Remi, and a tall, older woman comes up and wraps her arms around his neck. It's Bree St. Thomas, who I met last week at the Albrecht College party. "Uncle Remi, nice to see you."

"Hello, Bree." He nods, gently extricating himself. "Anastasia," he says to a slightly younger version of Bree. "Bree and Anastasia, this is Rowan. I've finally found my son."

"Nice to meet you both." Rowan shakes each of their hands in turn, his movements slow and cautious and his head cocked. His narrowed eyes cut to me.

"Pleasure," Bree says flatly. Her eyes flit to me and widen in recognition.

"Likewise," Anastasia says, echoing Bree's lack of enthusiasm.

A server comes by with champagne, and everyone takes a glass. I'm not sure what I was expecting tonight, but it was not this huge event. I think of family holiday parties as everyone in the kitchen, getting in the way, while football is on in the living room.

I wrap an arm around Rowan's waist and hold him to me. He relaxes against my chest, which tells me I did the right thing.

"Nana told us," Bree says to Remi in a conversational tone, "that you changed the trust beneficiaries because you found Rowan. Is that true?"

Remi makes a teeter-totter motion with his hand. "You know

Grandfather's trust can't be changed. I just clarified that Rowan is my child, in accordance with René's wish to ensure the St. Thomas family funds go to the oldest child of the oldest child. With my own trust, yes, I changed the beneficiary."

"What will happen to us?" Anastasia asks. "When someone new and outside the family is in charge?"

"Rowan *is* family," Remi says sharply. "As for the two of you, stop throwing parties like this and invest what you already have. It's more than enough for you to live on, if you make intelligent choices."

Anastasia pinches her lips together, while Bree's face is stony.

"Are you doing okay?" Anastasia asks Remi, her kind-ish words belied by her uninterested expression.

Remi shakes his head. "Not really."

"So sorry to hear that," Bree says, pasting on a sympathetic tilt to her eyebrows. "Do you have a prognosis?"

"Probably a few months," he says.

Rowan rubs the heel of his palm against his chest.

"That's too bad," Anastasia says. "We hope you aren't in a lot of pain." Her tone suggests otherwise.

I can see Rowan reaching for his back pocket, likely to pull out his blade and show them what actual pain is. And while that would be amusing, I step in and suggest, "If you two don't have anything nice to say, why don't you move along."

After looking Rowan and me up and down, Bree and Anastasia excuse themselves, and Remi turns to us. "Those two have been gold diggers their entire lives. I'm glad that they're not getting the St. Thomas fortune. They'd just waste it."

Rowan swallows a few times. I need to think of something to say that will make this all better, but what could achieve that?

His father's dying.

His extended family is a motley crew, some of whom clearly resent him.

And he doesn't yet feel comfortable with any of this.

A bell rings, and everyone moves into another room for dinner. Long tables like I've seen in photos of palaces are set with fine china.

Rowan and I are seated far away from the main action. I'm on the end, likely intentionally, but I'm good with that, because I don't want to talk with any of these people anyway. Rowan talks with the woman next to him, who is some incredibly distant relative.

The food is pretty great—a chateaubriand en croûte, which is a beef tenderloin with mushroom duxelles covered in puff pastry. At least that's what they tell me. It's served with green beans amandine and hasselback potatoes, and for dessert, a sticky toffee pudding.

Rowan whispers, "I think the beef needed more Frank's hot sauce."

I snort.

Later in the evening, Rowan and I are standing off to the side of the ballroom, talking with Nana, when Bree sweeps over to us. She's clearly had more wine than when we were talking earlier.

Rowan's distracted with Nana, and Bree leans close to whisper in my ear. "I remember you from the Albrecht College party last week. Weren't you there with Tristan Graff? Wow, you get around. Is Rowan your flavor of the week?"

"Tristan's just a friend. Rowan's my boyfriend."

"Oh? Is that so? How long has that been going on?"

"We met last month," I say, feeling foolish that I've fallen so hard so fast. But then I remember that … I've fallen hard and fast. Fuck anyone who thinks that's a problem. Anastasia, who seems to be joined to Bree at the hip, comes up next to us.

Bree sips her wine. "If you don't think Rowan's bought himself a legal fight, you're wrong. Remi's not in his right mind. He's not well. He can't change the trust."

My lawyer training kicks in. "He didn't change the St. Thomas family trust; it was created generations ago. He simply clarified

Rowan's relationship to the current beneficiary. With his own trust, he can do as he wishes. And he doesn't have to be perfectly healthy to prepare an estate plan; the standard for testamentary capacity is very low. He has to know the names and understand what he's doing, which he clearly does."

Bree sniffs. "I'll talk to my lawyer."

I roll my eyes. "No one's stopping you, but I am a lawyer, and I know what I'm talking about. What do you need the money for, anyway? What's the interest on his billions? I'm sure you have enough squirreled away for the rest of your life. Or you could sell this place. It has to be nine figures."

Anastasia gets up in my face. "We want to fund Albrecht's endowment, for starters."

I huff. "What does Albrecht need more money for?"

Bree shrugs. "Then we'll funnel it toward other causes we care about."

Don't ask. Don't ask. "And what are those?"

She gives me an evil smile. "Supporting traditional American values."

Oh, shit. So if we don't make sure Rowan gets his billions, some asshole's probably going to get into power and fuck over the whole United States. Which could filter to the whole world.

My brain goes dark fast.

Anastasia nods. "We want to make sure that all those liberal social causes don't take over." She looks me up and down. "We want to bring America back to the way it used to be."

Okay, that's enough. I know it's Rowan's family's holiday party, but if these jerks want to take away my rights, I'm going to give them a piece of my mind.

Only, before I let loose, they both turn on their heels, fake smiles in place, and descend on their next victim.

"What's wrong?" Rowan asks, wrapping an arm around my waist.

"Bree just threatened to fight you for the money so she can fund despicable causes."

"Ugh. Let her try. I know a lawyer," he says, grinning.

328

CHAPTER 43

Rowan

I t's late when we get home from the party, and we go straight to bed. I pat my tummy, groaning in the dark. "I can't believe this is my life," I whisper.

"What, that you had a good dinner? I feed you," Charlie mutters, tugging me close and kissing the nape of my neck.

"You do," I whisper. "But that mansion was like visiting another planet. All those people with tenuous connections to my father or the St. Thomas family."

"I've been to some fancy dinners with work clients, but ... agreed. That place is a palace."

"Agreed." Charlie runs a hand down my chest, and I cuddle into him even more. "I think this is my favorite place to be."

"My house?" Charlie asks.

"Your bed, with you in it," I say. "A month ago, I was sleeping on an air mattress with a jackass for a roommate."

"You've had quite the month." Now his hand is teasing over my zebra print briefs, and I let him play with me, my dick starting to harden.

"I have. But hands down, you're the best part." I groan as he strokes me. "That and finding out about my family."

"You don't care about the money?" Charlie teases, his hardening dick nestling against my ass.

I talk into the pillow. "If Remi had no money but treated me as nicely as he has been, I would still appreciate him. I just like knowing that I come from *somewhere*, you know?"

"Tell me more," he says.

This is another thing I love about Charlie. He listens to me.

"After bouncing from house to house my entire life, thinking I didn't have any relatives at all, it's amazing to know who I share DNA with."

"So, not Bree and Anastasia?" Charlie's now reaching inside my underwear. So I kick it off. He seems fascinated by my foreskin and spends time gently moving it.

"Not them. They can ... go do what they want," I pant.

Charlie protests. "No way. We have to stop their plans. They're evil."

"I have my own evil plans."

He chuckles. "Oh yeah? What are they?"

I moan, now fully hard. "If I get a lot of money, I don't want to spend my life binge shopping. Don't get me wrong—I'm going to own every yaoi manga that ever existed, and I'm going to wear amazing clothes. But I want to fund projects. Make the world better for people who have it the way I did: kids who don't have food or homes, LGBTQ+ people, you know."

"Those plans don't sound evil," Charlie points out, and I laugh, then gasp as he moves me onto my back and settles between my legs under the sheets.

"That's not the evil part."

He licks my cock. "Tell me, but you should know that the founders of my firm have a charity, Weston & Ramirez House, that helps LGBTQ kids."

"Then it will be fully funded when I get the money," I say, tugging at his hair as he blows me. "*Fuuuuck*," I moan. "Keep going. But I ... I want to use some ... of the money ... for a side project. The revenge business I told you about."

Charlie nods his head and slurps up some of my precome, then starts really going to town on my cock.

"God, you're good at that." And now my brain is spinning into possibilities while my body's being pleasured by my boyfriend. "I'm not saying I'm going to go around murdering everyone. Oh god, right there. Yes, Daddy, you're so good at that. Though I do get off on violence. But oh, fuck, please, uh, god, that's good, I wanna be creative. I just may want to, you know, oh, Daddy, make me come, *encourage* people to think deeply about what they've done in the past and to do better."

He keeps up a steady rhythm, one of his hands rolling my balls while the other helps him stroke my cock.

"I'm gonna come," I warn, and Charlie sucks harder.

Well, then.

A few more seconds and I'm coming down his throat with a shout, trembling through the release. Charlie keeps licking me until I'm oversensitive and push him off. He crawls up my body and kisses me, then says, "You get off on violence."

I grab him and kiss him hard. The kisses I adore from him that taste so salty from my come. With my hands and feet, I shove his underwear down and off. He rubs his cock against my thigh, and I sigh in happiness. "I do get off on violence, but my vengeance is gonna fit the crime."

Now I reach down and, using his precome, start jacking him while he straddles my hips. "When I called you a little criminal before," he says, "I meant that you were mugging me. But you've done more than that, haven't you? Oh, damn, that feels good."

I keep going. "I got revenge against the guys who used to carve me up. Some friends—I think of them as my muscle—I told them what happened, and they wanted to help. So we very carefully made sure Anders and Billy would never be heard from again."

"I thought you said you weren't a murderer," he whispers back.

"I said I wasn't going to murder you," I counter. "Or anyone else who doesn't deserve it."

Charlie groans. "Fuck, we're messed up. I know you feel that you had good reasons for doing what you did."

"I definitely did. I have no remorse." I groan. "You sure you want me to tell you this? It's safer for you not to know."

But I want to let Charlie in.

"I want to know everything about you. Call it attorney-client privilege. I'll sign you up as a client."

I snort. "Deal. So, okay. They were registered sex offenders by the time they were nineteen. I didn't catch up with them until they were in their twenties and I was nineteen myself. But we don't have to worry about them anymore. It was almost easy to have them taken care of."

"This coming from the man who was bored when he was mugging me."

"I was not bored," I say, keeping the stroking going.

"Stay on topic. How else were you a little criminal? Or am I wrong?"

"You're right. I had a juvenile record. Thefts, assault, and all sorts of petty crimes. Generally related to trying to put together enough money and supplies to go out on my own and repeatedly getting caught and dragged back. Then as an adult ... I guess some of the same. It mostly had to do with not having money."

"And then there's the murder you just confessed to."

"I didn't confess shit," I say, smiling in the dark. "Especially if you're my attorney. But going forward, I want to use some of my resources to start ..."

"A vigilante business," Charlie murmurs, his dick getting even harder and his balls pulling up. He's going to come.

"Yeah. Like the A-Team. I saw that movie. I wanna help people who have no one else to turn to."

"I'm not supposed to want to get into a life of crime," Charlie complains, panting. "And yet ... Oh, fuck, I'm gonna come."

"Come on me, Daddy," I whisper, and a few strokes later, he does, his hot release landing on my skin.

I drag a hand through it and bring my fingers up to my mouth.

"Shit, you're gorgeous," he says, panting. "Let me go get something to clean us up."

Charlie returns with a warm washcloth from the bathroom and wipes me down, then dries me off with a clean towel. He fishes both of our underwear off the floor, and we put them back on. Then he puts away the towels and gets back in bed, continuing our conversation like we didn't both orgasm in the middle of it. "I understand where you're coming from, princeling. I think I've understood you on some level from the moment I met you."

"Yeah," I say, nestling back into our original position where he's the big spoon. As usual.

"So ... what do you need, besides money, to make these dreams come true?"

"To track down some people I knew before. And get X involved. He knows tech."

"And you aren't going to charge people for this?"

"Fuck no. This is charity."

Charlie bursts out laughing. "Only you would create a charity that has violence as its aim."

"My aim is to make the world better. Just because I happen to enjoy inflicting pain on bad guys does not mean that the two are incompatible. I'm a St. Thomas. We're all civic-minded. I think. I mean, I'm new to the family, but I bet that's what the official party line is. And that's just one part of my plan. The other parts are above-board nonprofits."

"Maybe you could talk with Sam in my office," Charlie says. "He sets those up."

"Sounds good."

We kiss and say good night.

For the first time in my life, all I can see on the horizon—with the exception of my father's health—are good things to come.

* * *

On Christmas morning, I wake up, as I have all month, in Charlie's arms. It still feels like a present to be with him. I know that sounds cheesy, but whatever. I was waiting for him my entire life.

"Morning, baby boy," Charlie says in his sleepiest voice.

"Morning, Daddy."

"Not your fucking daddy," he mutters, and I laugh.

"Not even on Christmas morning?"

"Nope." He flips me to my stomach, kisses my rim, and proceeds to wish me a very happy holiday.

Earlier, we decided we would split up for Christmas Day and then get back together in the evening to be with his friends. I'm going to go to my father's house in Pasadena. Charlie's going to his parents' house. He offered to have me come along, but this will probably be my only chance to spend Christmas with my father, and he doesn't want to miss his family traditions. I'm good with our compromise.

While we're eating breakfast, I look over at the little tree I put up and see that the floor under it is littered with presents.

"What the hell?" I ask in wonder.

Charlie gives me his best innocent expression—which is funny, since he has such a resting bitch face. "Maybe Santa came."

I snort and go over to the tree. The packages are all about the same size and look like books.

"Can I open them?" I ask excitedly.

"Absolutely."

I rip open the first one, and it's *Ten Count*, a BL manga I love but have only read online. "You bought me manga?" I whisper reverently.

"Yup." He grins.

I look around. "What did you do, buy me a hundred of them?"

"Guess you'll just have to find out."

He did exactly that. I spend the rest of the morning opening *On or Off*, *The Dangerous Convenience Store*, *Finder*, and *Platinum Blood*. I squeal with each one.

"I could not be more happy with this!" I shout as I open *Yagi the Bookshop Goat*. "Charlie, you didn't have to give me anything, but I fucking love you."

"I love you, too," he says, surveying the massive pile of wrapping paper all around us.

In the middle of my package-opening frenzy, I give him his gift: better video equipment. A top-of-the-line monitor and headphones, codes for the best software, a graphics card, and a new camera.

"Holy shit," he says, a gleam in his eyes that I love to see. "Thank you."

* * *

At noon, I drive to my father's historic mansion in Pasadena. It's a pretty incredible place—old, venerable, gleaming. Gorgeous wood trim lines the architectural features without making the house seem dark. There are lovely stained-glass lamps and high ceilings. Remi tells me the home was built more than a hundred years ago by Greene and Greene, who were some famous Arts and Crafts architects, whatever that means. The custom furniture matches the building and was designed to go where it's been placed, which makes everything feel very cohesive. A tall Christmas tree covered with silver ornaments stands in the large living room, and candles and greenery line the fireplace. Remi gives me a tour upstairs, where bedrooms with sleeping porches look out over a large property shaded with oak trees. It smells like lemon polish.

He's moving slowly and tells me he mostly lives downstairs,

where a comfortable room is set up for him with a large bed and a window with a view of a garden.

If my mother had made different choices, would I have grown up here? Played outside? Slept in one of those airy bedrooms with an attached bathroom and a view of treetops?

Best to stop thinking of what could've been.

Once Nana and Barbara arrive, we sit down to a lunch served by Remi's cook. There's a simple soup for him, but the rest of us have a crown roast—I guess that's what it's called; it looks like it's from a cartoon—with vegetables and crusty bread. I love every bite.

Nana and Remi are talking about some new tax laws.

Remi nods. "I have an appointment with my new lawyer to work through them. Roger, my old attorney, recommended him."

"Are you going to miss Roger?" I ask.

"Probably. I could insist he not retire until I'm gone, but he deserves to be able to spend time with his family."

I wonder if I'll ever understand my father fully. He's old money conservative, but he's okay with my tattoos, piercings, and style. He kidnapped me but then gave me everything.

I guess I'm just going to have to live with him being *himself.*

"Don't you think Bree and Anastasia are going to act badly after being pushed out of their inheritance by my existence?" I ask.

Nana leans forward. "They've had plenty of opportunity to use what they already have to make sure they never need more. They've been living off the interest of billions of dollars. Do you know how much that is?"

"A lot?" I hedge.

"Yes, a lot." She smiles.

"Plus, it's a windfall to them," Remi says. "They're not part of the family by blood."

"It's a windfall to me, too," I point out, chewing on my lip. "It's not like I deserve any of this."

Nana says, "Here's the thing about money: No one says you must be a good person to have it."

"You don't have to be a bad person, either," Barbara says. "Money is neutral."

"Just some have access to it, and some don't," Remi says.

These people. It's so obvious they've never had to do without. Am I ever going to feel like I fit in with my own family?

I suppose the more important question is, do I need to fit in?

Maybe I already do, to those that matter. Remi doesn't seem to be fazed by any part of me.

"I'll probably want to start a nonprofit with a lot of it," I admit.

"Then do so," Remi says. "If you fund projects that are close to your heart, that would make me happy."

"What if I give it to LGBTQ+ causes?" I ask, needing to test him.

"Good." He grins. "I have a gay son. I want to be sure he doesn't get screwed over by anyone." Nana clucks and reaches over to hold Barbara's hand. "And my aunt as well."

Remi passes all my tests. He previously scored well on the do-I-accept-my-son-for-who-he-is scale, but some part of me thought it might be a fluke. I like how he keeps pleasantly surprising me. The fact that his kindness is surprising—well, maybe I do need that therapy Charlie brought up.

"I've taught you well," Nana says to Remi.

We finish lunch and sit by the Christmas tree. There's a fire roaring in the fireplace, even though the weather is clement. I'm comfortably full of good food. Another first for me: Christmas with my family. I hadn't known what to expect or what to give people who can buy and sell countries, so I brought jigsaw puzzles for everyone, because maybe they'd enjoy something to do. Judging by the delight in Nana's eyes, I chose well.

Remi passes me a medium-sized wrapped box, kind of like a book. I doubt he bought me manga, like Charlie did.

"What is this?" I ask, holding it tightly to my chest and glancing around to see what the others think. No one gives me a clue except for some kind smiles.

Remi's forehead wrinkles, and he rubs his jaw. "I found a photograph of your mother that someone took at the conference I attended."

My entire body seizes. I'm about to be ripped to shreds, aren't I?

With trembling fingers, I open the package and stare at the photo in a silver frame.

Bianca looks a bit like me. Her hair is light, and she seems little. She's wearing a black cocktail dress, and she's shoulder to shoulder with a much-younger Remi wearing a black suit in what looks like a Las Vegas casino. My eyes sting.

"You like it?" Remi asks.

"Yeah. If I had any more tears, I'd be shedding them right now," I say. "I'm not crying anymore, though. I'm all cried out."

With my heart in my throat, I open my arms and hug my father for the first time.

* * *

It's a dark, quiet night, though holiday displays on the houses we're passing provide plenty of light. I met Charlie at home a little while ago, and we're now driving over to his friend Danny's place.

"So, it's a good sign that you want me to meet your friends?" I ask, scraping a hand through my hair. My knee bounces.

"Yep." Charlie navigates us smoothly to the curb in front of a cute house not that far from his. Blue lights line the eaves, and fake candles glow in the center of each window.

I snort. Charlie's being his usual stoic self. But he's wearing another sweater I got him, and he looks and smells delicious. His dark hair's gotten longer, and it flops in his eyes when he wakes up.

This morning, he styled it back, and I pretty much want to stare at him for the rest of my life.

We go up to the front door, presents in hand.

Danny Villaseñor's a tall, dark, handsome man who has an adorable nerdy partner named Alden Meyer. We're welcomed into their warm home, where a few others from Charlie's firm are gathered.

There's a moment where they all stare at me. I suppose I'm a mythical being: Charlie's boyfriend, when he's never brought one around before. And I don't exactly look like I fit with him, either. I've got on a gray sweater that says "Gucci" in script and shiny black pants, and I feel like a million bucks.

Charlie wraps his arms around my waist as soon as we deposit the gifts under the tree, and my heart goes haywire at him claiming me so readily in front of his friends. I know he's my boyfriend, but old feelings of being rejected by, oh, everyone, don't go away fast.

"It smells so good in here," I say.

Danny grins. "My mom made tamales."

"I'm not sure how I could be hungry again after the lunch I ate, but there you have it."

After introductions, Danny's first question is, "So, have you figured out how to make this guy less grumpy?"

"Yep," I chirp. "But it's a secret."

"I'm sure it involves sex," Danny says.

Charlie shrugs. "Can we change the subject?"

Another of the attorneys, August, laughs. "Absolutely not. You've given everyone in the office so much crap about so many things over the years. We're happy for you, but we're not going to take it easy on you, either. Bringing around a date."

"Oh, he's not my date," I say. "We're mated for life."

Everyone laughs, and Charlie shrugs. "He's right."

"Wow," Danny says. "When Charlie falls, he falls hard."

"And are you really leaving the firm?" Alden asks.

Noah, yet another attorney, looks a little guilty. "I told the partners you might be looking for something else," he explains to Charlie, who's been sitting there all classic Charlie Cooper RBF.

Then Charlie smiles, and any tension in the room goes away. "It's fine. Yeah, I don't know. I might go part time, or … I'm not sure. I just want more variety in my daily life and more choice in the cases I take."

"You want it, you got it," August says. And since he and Noah cofounded the firm, I guess he can make the rules.

We chat some more, then sit down to enjoy Danny's mom's amazing food until I'm officially so full I'm pretty sure I don't want to ever eat again.

Danny's cat, Mamacita, comes over and rubs against Charlie's legs. Charlie leans down and pets her. Every time she enters the room, she seeks him out, and he seems fascinated by her. He absolutely has to get a cat.

When we're done with dinner, we all gather by the Christmas tree in Danny's living room. Danny picks up a small, flat package wrapped in snowman paper and hands it to Charlie.

"What is this?" Charlie asks.

"Open it."

Charlie does and bursts out laughing.

"When Noah said you were thinking of doing something different with your life, we didn't want you to forget us," August says. "So we made sure you wouldn't. Shelby helped."

"What is it?" I ask.

Charlie shakes his head and shows me. "It's a calendar of everyone I work with." He starts flipping through it. January has a huge picture of Danny. "This is Demi, our office manager. And Alden. And August. Owen. Noah. My sister. Shelby." He cracks up.

"Every month, you'll have our smiling faces to remind you of the office," Danny says.

Charlie's grin is infectious. "Thanks, guys."

All in all, it's the best Christmas of my life.

CHAPTER 44

Charlie

It's that dead zone between Christmas and New Year's when a lot of people take time off, but I have a ten thirty video hearing on Tuesday, so I'm dutifully wearing a suit and in the office. I could attend from home, but the court doesn't allow virtual backgrounds, and I prefer to be professional and have the camera show my office rather than my empty extra bedroom. Plus I have plenty of work to do.

I close the window shades so I'm not backlit and slide on my jacket. Even though I'm just sitting at my desk, it's supposed to be exactly the same formalities as being in court. I need to show respect for the process. I have something to look forward to after the hearing, too. Rowan said he'd come by for lunch and we could go down to one of the restaurants in the basement mall.

I've logged into the court's website, and the clerk has checked me in. I mute myself when there's a knock at the door.

"I'm in court," I call.

The door opens, and Rowan walks in. Now that he has multiple closets full of designer clothes, every day is an event: What's Rowan going to wear? I should start an Ad/VICE account for that. Today, he's got on a sharp blazer over a pair of oversized jeans.

"You're early, baby," I say, unable to tear my eyes away from him. "I have a hearing right now."

"I know." He gives me a cocky grin, slinking toward me like he's on a catwalk.

I furrow my brows, while my pulse quickens. "What-what are you doing?"

"Indulging in a fantasy," he says. He slides in between me and the desk.

"Get the fuck out of here," I hiss, pointing at the door. I'm pretty sure I'm not the first person to get a blow job—or the possibility of one—in this office. Maybe not even the only one today, given how Nogust were looking at each other this morning. But ... *court*.

Rowan ignores me and curls up under my desk, settling on his knees between my legs and pulling me in close.

"I have to be on a Zoom appearance in five minutes," I say urgently.

"I'd better hurry, then." Rowan runs his hands up my thighs, which makes my dick chub up in anticipation.

We can't do this. Even though it's a fantasy of mine, in reality it's a bad idea. "No, you'd better *leave*, then."

Pushing my chair so it rolls away from the desk, Rowan crawls out and goes to stand up. "Your loss." He gives me the sexiest smile, and my dick gets harder.

He bites a lip and gives me doe eyes.

"Fuck," I mutter, relenting. "I can't believe I'm doing this."

He grins. "I can. If you tell me to, Daddy."

I undo my pants and draw out my dick. I'm not fully hard yet, although I'm getting there. "Suck my cock," I order.

Rowan gives me a wicked grin. "Now? While you're about to be in court?"

I really, really can't believe I'm doing this. It's such a bad idea.

It's utterly unprofessional. "Yes. Do it. But don't make me come until after my hearing is over."

Rowan's head is in my lap, his hot breath hitting my exposed dick. It feels very wrong to be exposed in the office. Very *strange*, when I'm still wearing a tie and dress shirt on top.

But he runs his nose up the cloth covering my inner thigh, and my cock goes fully erect. Then he snuffles into my balls, taking one, then the other, into his mouth.

I suppress a groan.

Fuck, I need to get my game face on if I'm going to do this.

I scoot so I'm slouching slightly under the desk, and Rowan moves back. He looks up at me wickedly, and then he starts blowing me for real. If I were on my feet, I'd be falling down right now.

Thankfully, I can turn the microphone and the video off until it's my turn. Also thankfully, this hearing is only a procedural one about the status of the case. Not, like, a trial. I'd like to think I really would have sent Rowan away if this were a trial, but ... lord, who knows?

As Rowan sucks my cock, I click the video on and check how I look. My expression is strained, but maybe I'm the only one who'll notice. I answer the clerk's questions, then turn the mic and video back off.

"Fuck," I hiss.

"Keep still."

I spread my legs wider, and he's licking my cock like it's an ice cream cone. Little licks like a kitten. Only I know he's so much more dangerous than a kitten.

Then he just holds my cock in his mouth, keeping it warm. Fuck, his mouth. It's so good. So, so good.

I adjust my legs, trying to accommodate him and still be professional on camera, and tell him, "Suck my cock, but don't make me come. Got it?"

Rowan nods, his pink hair flopping in his face. Having

someone as mouthy as him play along is heady. He knows that this is hot as fuck. That it's naughty as fuck. That if I got caught, I could be sanctioned by the court. I don't think I'd lose my law license, but it wouldn't look good.

I angle my hips slightly forward to give Rowan a better angle so he's not pulling my dick down. I don't want to drop my chair too much. That would be noticeable.

The door opens, and I freeze. Shelby walks in. "Oh, sorry. Is this a bad time?"

"I'm in court," I grit out. "Can you hang the Do Not Disturb tag on the door?"

He gives me a funny look and smirks. "Sure." He pulls the tag off the inside door handle.

Oh, shit. He can probably see Rowan's shoes under the desk.

Fuck. A below-desk BJ is the stuff of my dreams.

The door closes, and Rowan chuckles. "That was close," he whispers.

"Pretty sure Shelby saw your feet. And keep sucking my dick," I growl.

"Yes, Daddy."

I focus on how good the blow job feels—and how much I want to come—but Rowan's playing with me, edging me, so I never quite tip over. Just when I'm about to tell him to focus, the court calls my case.

Shit. "I'm on," I whisper.

I turn on the video and notice my cheeks are flushed and my hair is messy. I quickly straighten it.

Rowan slurps loudly on my dick.

Fuck.

I clear my throat and unmute the call. "Good morning, Your Honor," I say. "This is Charles Cooper for the plaintiffs." Then I mute it again.

This is going to be tough to pull off.

Opposing counsel makes their appearance.

"Thank you, counsel," the judge says. "Please tell me the status."

Opposing counsel starts talking, and I do my best to keep a straight face. Except now, Rowan's decided to double down and is going to make me come.

While I'm on video.

In open court.

Fuckkkk.

"Is that true, Mr. Cooper?" the judge asks.

I unmute my video long enough to say, "Yes, Your Honor. That's accurate."

"Is there a reason why you keep muting yourself?" he asks.

"There's a lot of background noise. I apologize."

He nods but gives me a funny look. "Fair enough."

The court sets another hearing date in six months, and I take notes and get out of the hearing as fast as I can, shutting down the app, exiting all programs, and turning off my computer.

Then I growl at Rowan, "You little menace."

Rowan smiles around my dick, but before he can say anything, he sucks hard and I come, throwing back my head and spurting into his waiting mouth.

Once I'm done, breathless, flustered, my chest heaving, I yank him out from under my desk and kiss the daylights out of him. Then I stand, pull my pants up as best I can, and drop to my knees so I can return the favor.

"Let's see how fast you can have anticipatory early jizz," I rumble.

"Charlie," Rowan whines, as I get his jeans unzipped and pull out his cock. "Oh, fuck, Daddy, make me come."

My little princeling criminal grabs my hair like he's going to rip it out, and now I'm groaning again, because I love the bite of pain. I open my mouth, and he slides his cock in, the salty taste of precome strong. I love it when he gets turned on.

I hear voices approaching in the hall. I'd better be fast. I focus my efforts, my tongue worshipping his cock, my throat taking some abuse.

I love this.

He gets impossibly hard and comes, gasping. My eyes are watering, and some of his spunk dribbles down my chin.

Crap. Well, at least I'm done with court for the day.

After we've caught our breath and wiped off with tissues, something occurs to me. "Do you want to meet Sam before we go to lunch? He's the one I said might be able to help you with your nonprofit projects."

"I'd love to. Just tell me where the bathrooms are, so I can clean up a little better?"

"I'll come with."

Five minutes later, we walk into Sam's office together, both more presentable.

I rub my hand over my face and try to hide my grin. "Um, Sam? This is my boyfriend, Rowan."

Sam sticks out his hand, and Rowan shakes it. I'm grateful we washed up, because otherwise that would be really gross. Rowan's lips are still swollen, although if you didn't know him, I'm not sure it would be noticeable. And I wasn't able to get my hair entirely back under control, but it's usually mussed by the end of the day anyway from me pulling it in frustration.

"Nice to meet you," Sam says.

Rowan gives him an innocent smile, one I've never seen on him. It almost fools me.

Almost.

"Same." He lets go of Sam's hand and tilts his head. "Charlie says you do nonprofit organization?"

"I do." Sam smiles. "I love doing that kind of work."

"Transactional attorneys are happier than litigators like me," I grumble.

Sam pats me on the back. "Charlie's our resident grump. Though he has a heart of gold."

"I know," Rowan says, and this smile is genuine. "So I had this idea," he begins. "I want to start a few nonprofits with some funds I'm going to be getting. And then I want to do this other thing. This is all confidential, right?"

"Right. There's attorney-client privilege."

"Then can you help me start up the A-Team?"

"I'm not sure what that is, but it sounds interesting." Sam grins.

CHAPTER 45

Charlie

Cam texts me after New Year's to tell me he's free and to ask if Rowan and I want to come over and have lunch. I've caught him up on Rowan's situation with his family. It's definitely time for them to meet in person.

"So this is our twenty-first date," Rowan announces as we pull into Cam and Shelby's driveway. They live in a remodeled home on a nice street in the Valley. Rowan gets out of the car and waits, not so patiently—his eyebrows raised and hands on his hips—for me to join him at the front door. I had to grab a drill I'm returning to Cam out of the back.

It's one thing to introduce Rowan to people I work with, even those who are close friends, like Danny. It's another for him to start meeting my family, because no matter how much work I've done on myself, a big part of me still cares what my family thinks. Not enough that I'd break up with Rowan if they didn't like him, mind you, but it would cause some tension.

And I won't be able to hide my feelings about him from my brother. Good thing I don't want to.

I knock and give them a moment before I walk in. Cam and Shelby want to have family just walk inside, but after I caught them in compromising positions more than once, I decided that the best tactic was to give them a warning. Even if they knew I was coming over at a certain time, that didn't stop them from doing things I don't want to see my own brother doing.

I hear a cheerful "Come in!" from Shelby, and we enter.

A general contractor, Cam had been living in a construction zone for a long time before he met Shelby, always putting his customers before himself. But now that Shelby's been helping him, it's a warm, comfortable, livable space.

Also, it's weird how both my brother and I got serious boyfriends—okay, he has a husband—in the past six months or so. They're both smaller and younger than us, too.

Do I like the same kind of guy as my brother?

"Hey!" Shelby chirps. He's a bit taller than Rowan, and he's got dark tan skin, brown eyes, and bleached platinum hair that's been cut recently, so it's not its usual overgrown mess. He's wearing a T-shirt that says GALACTIC OSHA INSPECTOR. I guess there's some inside joke there.

Apart from their size and propensity for hair dye, Shelby and Rowan are nothing alike. Shelby's all sweet; he's a scrapbook of love.

Rowan's a switchblade.

I set down the drill case in the foyer, give Shelby a hug, and say, "This is my boyfriend, Rowan."

Rowan smirks and shakes Shelby's hand. "I saw you in the office." I shove my hands into my pockets, hoping Rowan's referring to passing by the reception desk rather than Shelby catching him giving me a BJ. "But it's good to officially meet you."

"Likewise," Shelby says. "Nice to meet you formally this time."

My brother comes down the hall and stops short. I don't think he was expecting to see me with such a tiny dude, and one with pink hair and tats—even though I told him—but he recovers fast.

"Pretty sure we just activated some force in the universe with these two meeting," I mutter.

Cam gives me a weird look, then holds out his hand to Rowan. "Hey, I'm Charlie's older brother, Camden."

"I can see the resemblance," Rowan says saucily, taking Cam's hand, and I glare at him. He studies me, his eyes wide. "Oh my god," he whispers. "Are you jealous? That's so hot."

I want to throttle him. Or claim him. So I do the latter, wrapping my arms around him and giving Cam an up nod. Cam looks like he wants to comment, but he holds his tongue. "Barbecue okay?" he asks instead.

"Perfect," Rowan crows. "Need any help?"

"Nope, we got it," Shelby says. "But come out and join us."

We follow my brother and his husband out to the pool, where Cam hands us beers, and we all—except Rowan, who's inspecting the landscaping—take seats. "This is why we live in LA," I say. "It's winter, and it's still shorts weather."

"Not at night," Rowan murmurs, likely thinking of his trek down the coast.

"True. Not at night," I say.

Instead of sitting in one of the open chairs, Rowan sits on my lap, his hand snaking behind my head to run through my hair. For fuck's sake, he's going to end me. I swear it.

I'm looking forward to expiring, though, if it's with his soft weight perched on me like a bony little bird. His cute butt is somehow soft and hard at the same time. Before I know what I'm doing, I wrap an arm around him and draw him even closer to me.

Mine.

Rowan is mine.

I don't want anyone else to even look at him.

"So, Charlie's always been my grumpy Gus of a brother," Cam says, a wicked grin on his face.

"Great, here we go with the embarrassing stories," I mutter.

"Yes, please," Rowan says, clapping his hands. "I want to know all of them."

"Cam will keep his mouth shut if he knows what's good for him," I growl, tugging Rowan to my chest and kissing his neck.

Both Cam and Rowan laugh. Shelby, on the other hand, is watching me with undisguised fascination, his lips parted and his eyes wide.

"What?" I mouth.

Shelby raises his eyebrows and shakes his head. "Nothing."

Shelby's never seen me like this—in love, into a guy, not afraid to show it. I've never been like this before, either, so it's new for all of us.

Oh, sure, I've dated a few guys, and I've gone to bed with plenty. Danny, the recently reformed playboy, beat me in numbers, although not by that much. But I've never been this openly affectionate with anyone in front of my family. I've never wanted to bite someone on the back of his pretty little neck, right on that fucking script tattoo. I've never had anyone wiggling his ass in my lap, just tempting me to excuse myself from my own brother and go fuck him.

"Behave," I warn. "Or you'll get it tonight."

"Promises, promises," Rowan whispers.

I'd be embarrassed about all this flirting if I hadn't witnessed Cam and Shelby falling in love. If I weren't one of the first people, if not *the* first person (other than Shelby) Cam told he was bisexual. If I hadn't seen them love each other openly.

I hadn't realized how much I wanted that kind of affection. I kept everything so close to the vest. I didn't let people in unless they were my family, and I rarely showed my true self.

Now that I have this relationship with Rowan—where we can do horseplay in a bowling alley and flirt at an axe-throwing place and make out in front of my friends and family—I'm *happy*.

Yeah. I'm happy.

Wow.

"So you're bringing Rowan around," Cam says quietly, when

we're eating tri-tip sandwiches. "Does that mean you're ready to introduce him to Mom?"

"Yeah." I clear my throat. "I'm pretty much completely head over heels for him." I smile at Rowan.

"Maybe with Cam married," Shelby says, "you won't feel so much pressure when he meets your mom."

Rowan bites his lip. "Charlie and I aren't ever getting married. Though if we did, I'd inherit some family money faster."

Cam looks at me as if I'm nuts. "What are you waiting for? Marry him and get the money. You want a sugar daddy, don't you?"

"Oh, no, Charlie's the daddy," Rowan says. "Not me."

"If we got married, we'd be taking the money away from his father," I explain to Cam. "The St. Thomas family trust is clear: The oldest child of the oldest child receives the funds when they marry or turn twenty-five. So we're not doing it."

"He can't be that far from twenty-five anyway," Cam says. "What difference does it make if he gets the money now or a few years from now?"

Rowan and I look at each other. "Rowan's father's suffering from a terminal illness. We don't want to do anything that would hurt him."

"Doesn't he have so much money that it doesn't matter?" Cam asks. I stare at him, and he throws up his hands. "What? If he's a St. Thomas, I'm assuming as much. Is he really going to miss it?"

"I guess it's the principle of it," Rowan says. "I do have some semblance of morality."

"I'm sure you'll sort it out," Cam says. "In any case, it's nice to see you both so happy."

In the car on the way home, Rowan says, "I like your brother a whole lot. While you're all growls and spines—which I love—he seems solid and dependable. And Shelby's adorable. Too cute for words. Not my type, but he's super sweet. He's like a windup doll or something, except he's got way more personality than that."

"You pretty much have that right," I say.

* * *

Saturday night, Rowan and I walk into a midnight showing of *The Rocky Horror Picture Show*. It's been playing at the same theater in West LA for decades, and the place is, frankly, intimidating. All these people line up in costume, when I'm just wearing jeans and a hoodie. Rowan's in something similar, although his displays a designer name.

"Have you seen the movie before?" a girl wearing a sparkly hat along with a shiny vest over a white button-down shirt asks us as she checks our tickets.

"No," I say, pursing my lips and rubbing the back of my neck. What am I getting myself into? I swallow hard.

"Nope," Rowan says cheerfully, looking around at the commotion with glee. More than half of the people here are in costume—at least, I presume they're costumes from the movie. Who knows?

"Ohhh, virgins!" She pulls a lipstick out from between her boobs and reaches toward me with it, the end blunt and very, very red.

"What the hell?" I ask, taking a step back.

"If you're a 'virgin,'" Rowan whispers, "they paint a red *V* on your forehead."

"How do you know?" I ask.

"I read about it."

"Well, I'm not a fucking virgin," I mutter.

"Just go with it, Daddy," he says.

"What am I getting myself into?"

Rowan giggles. "A fun night with me?"

"Yeah, okay, baby," I say, and let her do it. She paints one on Rowan, too, and we both look ridiculous.

We enter the theater and grab popcorn, then find seats.

"If we're in the front, I think we might get squirted with water," Rowan says.

"Another thing you read about?" I study the rapidly growing crowd.

"Yep. They spray people during some scene when it's raining."

I raise an eyebrow. "Okay."

"When there's a scene where someone makes a toast, everyone in the audience throws bread."

"I knew there was a thing about *Rocky Horror*," I say, "but I didn't know any specifics."

"Guess we're about to find out." Rowan is clearly ready for anything.

The place is painted black, and the floors are sticky. It seems that there's a live show that goes on at the same time the movie plays—in addition to the audience being dressed up. So it's not my usual experience at the movies by a long shot. I just hope I don't get more messed up than this damn lipstick on my forehead.

"Please silence your phones," an announcement sounds over the speakers. I'd been frantically searching "what to expect at Rocky Horror," but I turn it off and slip it into my pocket.

Rowan pulls his phone out—the one from his father; he made me return the one I got him—tinkers with it to turn the sound off, then studies the screen and frowns.

"What's the matter?" I ask, a prickling sensation skittering across my body.

"I just got this weird text." He holds his phone up, and I read *Watch your back*.

My breath catches. "What the actual fuck? Do you know who it's from?"

He shakes his head. "Blocked number, of course." He studies the screen a bit longer. "I'll have Xavier look at it. See if he can figure out who it's from."

"Do you think it's a prank? Someone from your past?"

"Or someone related to my family?" He sighs. "I've got no

fucking clue. It's probably a joke. I'll look into it tomorrow. For now, let's just enjoy the movie, okay?"

"Yeah, baby," I say, squeezing his hand.

But no one gets to threaten Rowan, even if it is a joke.

A man dressed in black lingerie with a long black robe and high heels, his lips painted fire-engine red and his hair long and dark, saunters over to us. He puts a finger under Rowan's chin. "Aren't you the most precious thing ever," he coos.

"Take your hand off my boyfriend before I chop it off," I growl.

"Sheesh, sensitive," the man says, and saunters away, swinging his ass.

"Someone's possessive," Rowan says gleefully.

"I can appreciate the confidence it takes to wear that outfit," I admit. "But no one touches you."

"That's correct, Daddy," Rowan says, holding my hand.

Then the lights go down, and the movie starts.

When it's over and we're walking out, Rowan asks, "So, what did you think?"

I raise an eyebrow. "That was quite an experience."

"You loved it, didn't you?"

I grin. "Maybe."

Since we don't get home until three a.m., Rowan says he's going to wait until morning to text Xavier.

"I wonder if you need more security," I say. The security service is still watching us, as usual.

"Maybe," Rowan says, hooking his arms around my waist and tugging me down the hall. "For now, I need *you*."

CHAPTER 46

Rowan

The following weekend, I finally get to meet Charlie's parents.

X said the text was from a website service that provides anonymous texting, and the username associated with the account was a fake. Figures. I deleted it and moved on to more important things in life like learning where my boyfriend comes from.

We pull up to a larger, older family house in the San Fernando Valley, one that looks like it has enough room for lots of kids and their friends to come over and play. I press my lips flat and try to shut down the burning sensation in my stomach. Charlie grew up so normally. It's no wonder I'm jealous.

Before we get out of the car, I run my palms down my pant legs and scrape my fingers through my hair. Then I clear my throat. "Should I have colored my hair something normal?"

Charlie scrunches up his nose, shaking his head slightly. "Why would you do that?"

"So I could look more respectable. We could go do it really fast. And I could put on long sleeves—"

He looks like he wants to scoff but thinks better of it when he sees my face and how serious and nervous I am. I've never met a boyfriend's parents. Mostly because I've never had a boyfriend. "Rowan, one, they're going to like you just the way you are. And if they don't, I choose you."

My cheeks burn in a good way, and I feel all warm inside. He's the first person to ever say that to me.

"Second, they've met Shelby. So don't think that you're the first person to join the family with hair that isn't in its natural state."

Join the family. In the past few weeks, I didn't just get one family; I got two. How is this my life?

"What about—"

Charlie holds up a hand. "Have a little faith. My parents are cool. They have three queer kids. They know we all go our own way." He pauses. "I have my own shit to deal with, but it mostly didn't come from them. They're good people."

I pick at my mint green nail polish. "I'm still worried."

"That just means you care, which I'm going to take as a good thing. Come on."

We get out of the car and head up the concrete walkway. Charlie wraps his arms around me and hugs me before he reaches for the door. "You're going to be okay. It's all going to be great."

While I appreciate him trying to be reassuring, I still feel faint.

I'm starting to understand why it's such a big deal to meet your partner's family and friends. I'm seeing where he comes from and what his life is like when he's not with me. I got the idea that he's different with me from things Danny and Cam said, and I'm starting to see it, too.

Charlie knocks once, then opens the door. "Hey, anyone here?"

"Come on in!" a woman calls, and we do. The living room is full of framed family photos and cozy couches. It's the kind of place that invites you to stay for a long time.

I tug at my sparkly black Balenciaga tank top.

Am I always going to feel wrong wherever I am? Too small, too loud, too weird, too feral, and now too rich? (Old me would've given anything for that last problem.)

Charlie's mom is tall, like him, with the same dark hair and hazel eyes. She's wearing a cream turtleneck sweater and jeans.

"Mom, this is my boyfriend, Rowan. Rowan, this is my mom, Holly Cooper," Charlie says.

I hold out a hand, but his mom takes one look at me and pulls me into her arms. She smells lovely, and her arms are soft. Everything about her is soft, and her hair smells nice, and oh my god, I'm going to cry, because I've never had a mom and I'm not soft and I can't do this.

"Rowan," she murmurs. "It's so nice to meet you. Welcome to the family."

I have never received a welcome like this.

"And this is my dad, Keith."

Charlie's dad comes over and shakes my hand. If Charlie ends up looking like his dad when he's older, I bagged myself a babe. Not that I'm that shallow—and I don't need to window-shop, now that I have the best man ever. Keith's hand is firm and calloused. "Nice to meet you, Rowan. We're glad you're with our Charlie."

Again, a sob almost bursts out of me, and I have to chew on the inside of my cheek to stop it. My legs feel weak. I need to sit down.

I think I may be more overwhelmed than when I met my father. Because I'd always been looking for him. I hadn't been looking for this kind bonus family.

Shelby comes over and gives me a hug. I've pretty much decided that he's my second-best friend, after Xavier. (Charlie doesn't count; he's the love of my life.) Cam hugs me, too, more briefly, and then I turn and meet a tall woman who looks like a female version of Charlie. She's wearing slim jeans and a short-sleeved green sweater, with dangly earrings.

"Hi, I'm Reyna," she says, extending a confident hand. I shake it.

"Are you all just genetically blessed?" I blurt, then touch my fingertip to my lips.

She laughs. "Come on, Rowan. Let's get you something to drink. Want a beer? Or prosecco?"

"Beer is good," I say.

Charlie tags along as Reyna and I go into the kitchen. Keith and Holly are messing around with the oven.

"Something smells great," I say, and Charlie nods. Reyna opens the fridge door and hands me a bottle of beer, then passes another to Charlie. She pours sparkling wine for herself and Holly. We clink bottles and glasses.

"We made Cam's favorite casserole," Keith says. "It's got rice, chicken, cheese, broccoli."

"Yum," I say.

"How come I don't get my favorite?" Charlie asks. I know him well enough to know that he's mostly joking, but there's an element of truth in there.

"Because it took you this long to bring your boyfriend by," Holly says, moving to the kitchen table. Plates are already on the table, along with a green salad and bread. Everyone goes to take their seat.

Before I sit down, Charlie puts his arm around my shoulders and tugs me to him. He kisses the top of my head. "I'm sorry, Mom. I wanted to be confident we were solid before I brought him over, because you get so hung up on our dates."

Reyna nods. "You do."

Holly pouts. "Hmm." She starts passing the salad while Keith dishes up the casserole. Everyone fills their plates.

"But me introducing Rowan to you means that I'm sure about us," Charlie says. "He's the one for me."

This makes Holly brighten. "Then tell me how you two met."

"He tried to mug me," Charlie says, and I burst out laughing.

"Ha ha, very funny," Holly says. "Really, how?"

"That's how," Cam says. "Charlie told me."

I nod. "My life was in a bad place when I met him. Things are going much better now."

"Oh, and why is that?" Reyna sips her prosecco.

"Because meeting Charlie changed my life. And—also because of him, come to think of it—I found my father."

"Had he been missing?" Keith asks.

"Oof, it's a long story," I say. "Are you sure you want to hear it?"

Everyone nods. While my instinct is to pull back and not share myself with strangers, these aren't strangers—they're people the love of my life loves. So I tell them the whole story. Well, the highlights, at least. Of being orphaned and in foster care and group homes until Charlie made me get fingerprinted. And then how my father found me.

"Oh, and my father is Remi St. Thomas," I say, sipping my beer.

Three sets of eyes bug out: Keith's, Holly's, and Reyna's.

"So you're a long-lost ... billionaire?" Reyna says carefully.

"Kinda, yeah."

"Well, shit," Holly says. She gives Charlie an amused look. "Here you are jealous that Cam got a special casserole, but you're dating a *St. Thomas*."

"His family doesn't matter to me, Mom," Charlie says. "Only Rowan."

I nod. "The only thing I've ever wanted was a family. To belong. Charlie makes me feel like I belong."

"He's mine," Charlie says, as if on cue.

Everyone laughs. But Charlie's possessiveness makes me feel safe.

Charlie makes me feel safe.

"You're good for him," Reyna tells me when we're washing the dishes after dinner.

"Sorry?"

"You're good for CharlieBoo. He's been unhappy for so long. But around you, he's all smiles. It's like you help him be the person that he never let himself be."

"Apparently he lets you call him CharlieBoo," I say.

She smirks. "I'm his little sister. I can do what I want."

I spend the rest of the evening hanging out with Charlie's family and marveling at the fact that I finally belong somewhere.

* * *

Over the next few weeks, I live at Charlie's house and visit my father in Pasadena when Charlie's at work. I don't go up to Montecito. Why would I want to be there without Charlie?

Day by day, I watch Remi decline. Not being able to ease his suffering hurts. And it's going to hurt more when he passes, which is going to be soon.

But what choice do I have? Not knowing my father was a huge void in my life. Having answers to my questions and some time to spend with him is more than I ever imagined I'd have. So I'm doing my best to stop bracing against future sorrow and just be with him now. Sometimes we talk, and I amuse him with things I say. Other times he asks me about my past, and it seems to make him feel worse when I give him honest answers. Often we sit in silence. He knows I'm there, and I stay as long as I can.

It matters to both of us that I show up.

Today, we're in his bedroom. I sit in a chair with my hands folded in my lap. He lies in a hospital bed with an IV drip. I'm staring at the rug, something undoubtably priceless. I notice my own slow, even breathing, because his is labored. Bettina comes in and out periodically, checking his vitals.

"I should have everything taken care of for you, as far as I can do so," Remi says.

I give him a weak smile. "I don't know what to say, other than that I wish you weren't sick. And thank you."

What was Remi like when he was healthy? It seems like he would've been vigorous, vital, engaging.

"The biggest regret of my life was not finding you—and the biggest accomplishment was that we finally did. I'm just so glad to have you in my life even for these few short months," he says. "And I found something else." He grimaces. "It's not good news, but it is closure."

"My mother?" I ask.

"She passed away twenty-two years ago. The rumor I'd heard was true."

My eyes are hot. "Some part of me always hoped she'd magically appear."

"For you, I wish that were true. But no, she overdosed on medications." He sighs. "She had moved out of state, which was why I didn't find her sooner. But the private investigator found information about her in Arizona."

"Why there?"

"I think she had connections there."

I sit up straight. "Does that mean I have an aunt or uncle somewhere?"

"No," Remi says. "She was an only child." His phone buzzes with a call, and he glances at it. "That's odd. It's Matilda." He answers. "Hello?"

The volume on his phone is up high enough that I can hear her. "Someone was caught on the security cameras earlier today, and we called the police," she says.

Ice goes through my veins, and I tug at my hair. Remi and I exchange worried looks. He puts her on speaker and lets her know I'm in the room. "Did the police catch them?" Remi asks.

"No, and we didn't get a good image," she says.

"Who do you think it was? Just some random person?" I ask.

"It's never random with the St. Thomas family," Remi says. "We're constantly making sure no one gets into our properties."

"Hmm." I rub my face. "What do you think it's about?"

Remi's voice lowers. "A number of months ago, Bree and Anastasia wanted me to give them more money than they were entitled to from the trust. I said no, and they brought a lawsuit against me ... and as part of that, we ended up needing to increase security, because they hired some unsavory people to surveil me—though I'm not sure what they hoped to discover."

I take a deep breath. "I guess that explains why you've been so insistent on security for me," I tell Remi. "Although I would hope that family members wouldn't be the reason for an attempted break-in."

"When this much money is at stake," Remi says, "you'd be surprised what family will do."

Matilda hums. "Things seem under control here now, but I wanted you to be aware." They exchange a few more words, and she hangs up.

Remi gives me one of his small smiles. "In case you don't know, I love you," he says, and my throat gets scratchy. "I loved you from the moment I knew you existed, but the real you is so much more than I'd imagined. You're lively and fierce and loyal and fun. You somehow made it through your nomadic upbringing with a sense of humor and smarts. You're a marvelous young man, Rowan. I'm overwhelmingly grateful that I found you."

My vision blurs, and my heart hammers. I take a deep breath. "I love you, too, Dad."

Remi missed most of my life, but it wasn't his fault, and he's more than made up for it now, both with all the time we've spent together and how accepting he's been of me. Like Charlie, my father's never asked me to change. He's only asked me to spend time with him.

I'm going to miss him when he's gone.

At home that night, I tell Charlie about Bree and Anastasia

while he and I are cuddled on the couch, my back to his front. I'm drained from the long day, and my chest aches from keeping myself together.

"He told me he loves me," I whisper.

"Of course he loves you," Charlie says.

I shake my head. "There's no 'of course' about it. Meeting him feels so fragile. Like he's this ephemeral being who came into my life and answered questions I never could have gotten answers to otherwise. He sprinkled the fairy dust of wealth on me." I kiss Charlie. "You came into my life when I needed you, too. But you're solid. He's a wisp in the wind."

"I wish your past were different." Charlie runs a finger along my arm. "And that you had more time with your dad."

"I guess there really are some things that money can't buy." I sigh. "At least I told him I loved him."

Charlie beams. "Yeah?"

I nod.

"Good."

I look around Charlie's living room, which is still pretty bare. "You should get that cat. Something to give us a little more chaos in our lives."

A raised eyebrow. "You think we need more chaos?"

I shrug. "You've wanted a cat for ten years."

"I don't have time for a cat."

I give him a mock glare. "You told me you were going to take time off to create videos. In between you hauling around heavy bags of concrete, shirtless, and painting, also shirtless, you'll have time to feed a cat."

Charlie huffs in amusement. "I have to do construction work shirtless?"

I hold up my hands. "I don't make the rules. Besides, cats aren't like dogs. They don't require as much attention. We had some in a few foster care homes, and they were mostly fuzzy slugs who lay in the sunshine. With a little chaos."

"I'm not sure I want more chaos. And it sounds like you might be walking into even more family drama," Charlie says slowly, shifting our position on the couch. "It seems like Bree and Anastasia are no strangers to litigation, and what your father said about being targeted worries me."

I tug at my earlobe. "Bree and Anastasia are spiteful hags, but they weren't raised the way I was. They grew up in this spoiled, glittering bubble. I can't see them hiring unsavory people. How would they even find one?"

"We shouldn't underestimate them. I don't like them at all, and I don't trust them."

"I trust that my father has it covered."

"We still need to watch out for you," Charlie says, kissing the back of my neck. He loves the tattoo there.

"You always watch out for me, Daddy. But you know I have my own resources, too. First, X. I need to get him dialed in on the computer stuff I want to do, anyway. And then I think I need to call some old friends—Chet and Fabian."

Charlie tilts his head to the side. "Who are they?"

"Muscle I can trust. They helped me get revenge on the bullies who cut me."

"Ah." His touch lingers on my belly.

"Wanna know how I first met them?"

"Of course."

"We were in a group home together. I helped them with their English homework. We were studying *Catch-22*, actually."

"Is that why you remember it so well?"

"Likely so. When I have to explain something to someone else, I find I learn it better. Anyhow, I want to get them caught up on my life these days and see if they want a future job working for me."

"On the A-Team? Or whatever you're calling it?"

"Precisely. I might as well get it going." I look at him. "There's nothing like someone who's gone through hell and back with you when you're talking about trusting someone with your life."

Charlie rubs one of his eyebrows. "I've never really trusted your security. Or, at least, I have a bone to pick with the people Remi hires, ever since that Charger-driving jerk kidnapped you."

"I'll be fine."

He doesn't look convinced.

* * *

I call my old friends at the gym where they work, and they agree to meet me on the Santa Monica Pier for hot dogs and fresh-squeezed lemonade. I could take them somewhere fancy, but they wouldn't like it, and I want to be outside where the sound of the waves will cover our voices. I tell today's security guy to stay back and give us space to talk.

"Rowan!" Chet says, picking me up in a hug like I'm a small child.

I hug him back. Fabian gives me a high five. "Hi, guys!" I say, once Chet finally puts me down.

Chet and Fabian are even bigger than they were when I last saw them, which was maybe two years ago. Before, they were the size of boulders. Now they're small mountains. We've kept in touch, but we haven't seen each other because I was in Lancaster.

"You're looking good," Fabian says. "Is that a real Versace sweater?"

"Yep." I grin. "We have a lot to talk about. You first?"

We stand in line to order food, and they catch me up on their lives. They're my age but are in the process of buying their own gym, and they teach all sorts of fitness and self-defense classes. When we turn away from the window, balancing cardboard trays and drinks in our hands, I spot a perfect bench to sit on that's away from most of the foot traffic. It's also plenty noisy, with the ocean thundering below us, the breeze ruffling our hair, and the music and other distractions on the pier.

While they each eat three corn dogs, I give them the rundown of what's happened to me since Black Friday, watching their eyes get bigger and bigger as I talk.

"So you're a billionaire?" Chet says when I finish, his tone incredulous.

I shake my head. "Not yet. But I will be. And I want to do something good with that money. I was wondering if you two want in."

They look at each other. "What are you talking about?" Fabian asks.

I suck the last of my lemonade out of the cup and rattle the ice that remains. "I've got a lawyer creating a nonprofit for me to help LGBTQ causes and kids without homes or adequate resources."

"That's noble of you." Chet glances at the people walking down the pier.

"I also want to do something that isn't so noble. It's more ... personal. Although maybe it will end up being noble, too, in a twisted Robin Hood kind of way. Do you two remember my vengeance list?"

Fabian smirks. "Yeah. We didn't get that far down it. Just the bastards who cut you." He cracks his knuckles.

"I'm thinking about something like that, only sophisticated. Planned. I want to clear the world of monsters who hurt people who can't fight back. I wondered if you two would want to help. I'd obviously make it worth your while." I'm thinking, no matter what happens, they're getting the money for the gym of their dreams.

They don't even hesitate. "We're in."

We shake hands.

It's good to have friends in your corner.

CHAPTER 47

Rowan

In early March, my phone buzzes in the middle of the night. I startle and fumble for it, then rub my eyes and read the name on the screen.

A chill passes through my body. Now fully awake, and with a sense of foreboding, I answer. There's one main reason why my father's nurse would be calling me at two in the morning. "Hullo?" My voice wakes up Charlie, who stirs, pulling me closer.

"Is this Rowan?" Bettina asks.

"Yes." I burrow further into Charlie's embrace, a sudden heaviness on my chest that has nothing to do with his burly arm holding me like he's attached with a rubber band.

"I'm sorry to wake you, but I thought you would want to know that your father passed away about ten minutes ago. He was in no pain."

The world seems to slow down, and my eyelids are hot. I nod, even though she can't see it. I bite my lip. Charlie squeezes me hard. My phone's loud enough that he can hear both sides of the conversation.

"Okay. Do you need help with anything right now?" I ask.

"No. The funeral arrangements are already taken care of. We'll notify everyone for you. We just wanted you to be the first to know, since he listed you as next of kin."

"Should I come by anyway?" I stare out into the dim room.

"No, there's nothing for you to do. His body is being removed by the mortuary."

"Okay. Thanks," I say, my voice quiet and my throat dry.

What else is there to say?

"I'm sorry, Rowan," Bettina says quietly. "You were very special to him, and he loved you. I'm available if you need to talk."

"Yeah, sure."

We say goodbye, I hang up, and Charlie nuzzles into my neck. "I'm sorry, baby boy."

A tear drips down my face onto the pillow, and I press my palms into my eyes. My nose starts to run.

"Even though I've been expecting this since the moment he told me, it still hurts. Bad. I didn't know him very long," I whisper into the dark. "But I wanted him my entire life."

"I know, baby. You loved him, even for a short while."

"I did."

And I start telling Charlie all kinds of things he already knows, just because I need to say them out loud. How my father spent years trying to find me, and when he did, he went out to lunch with me, came to see me in Montecito, and invited me to his home in Pasadena, even though he was too sick to be comfortable, even though he surely had other important things to do, even though his time must have been more precious than ever, given how little he had left. How he was kind. How he accepted me for who I was and never told me that I should be different or more like him. How in the short time we knew each other, I felt he cared.

How I'm going to miss him. But even more, I miss what we weren't able to have.

* * *

A week later, Charlie and I step out of a St. Thomas limo driven by a driver I've never met before—Hector and his family are attending the funeral as guests—close to my father's gravesite in the grassy, private, expensive cemetery. Both of us are wearing black suits and sunglasses. My suit is Gucci. Charlie's is something he already had, probably from Brooks Brothers or somewhere equally traditional. We look like we're in *Reservoir Dogs* or something.

I'm numb, weighted down. Not sure how Charlie's feeling.

For a man with such a famous last name, Remi's funeral is small and intimate, because it's private as per his request. It's only an interment, and everyone will be going back to his Pasadena house later for a memorial.

Going up on my tiptoes, I whisper to Charlie, "This is the first funeral I've ever been to, which is perhaps not that surprising, given that I've never had the continuity of hanging around people long enough for them to die." I bite my lip and admit, "Die in a way I didn't have a part in."

Charlie kisses the top of my head. "Don't say that in public again. Even if we are alone."

We walk, holding hands, over to a group of chairs under a sunshade. The grave is open, the casket gleaming off to the side, a huge flower arrangement on top. The place smells like cut grass and fresh dirt. It looks out over a freeway to houses and hills in the distance.

I hope Remi likes this as his final resting place. He chose it, after all.

In the seats are Bree, Anastasia, Nana, Barbara, and Gideon, as well as a few nurses and close helpers or staff. Bree and Anastasia give me sidelong glances, but whatever. I'm never going to be friends with them.

Nana stands up first and turns to address the small group with a microphone handed to her by a cemetery employee. "My nephew Remi left his mark on the world. Most people will remember him as a powerful businessman who invested in tech communications but also loved the finer things in life." After mentioning more of his legacy, she smiles at me. "While all of that is important, his greatest accomplishment, I think he'd say, was finding his son."

When Nana is finished, Bree stands up and gives some sicky-sweet speech about how "Uncle Remi" was her favorite uncle and how sad she is that he's gone. I don't believe a word of it.

While most of me wants to remain silent, I stand up in my place and say, "I'm just glad we were able to spend a little while together and get to know each other before the end."

Nana's eyes are shining, and she nods and smiles, but Bree and Anastasia scowl.

I finger the knife in my pocket. I can handle them.

I think.

* * *

Remi's Pasadena mansion is packed wall-to-wall with people wearing black for my father's memorial. This is more like what I was expecting, given his stature in life. Despite the crowd, when I enter a room, people turn and stare. I recently redyed my hair, so it's bright pink. Charlie and I are still in our suits, although I've loosened my tie.

"Want something to eat?" Charlie asks, nodding toward the spread of food off to the side. Although the vibe here is subdued, the mood is certainly less somber than at the cemetery.

"Nah, I'm not hungry. And I bet nothing's spicy enough, anyway."

He touches my nose. "Do you know anyone here?" he asks. "Besides the family and employees I've already met."

"Just a few of the nurses. I invited Xavier, but I don't see him yet. Where did all these people come from, anyway? It's more than were at the St. Thomas Christmas party."

"Society types who want to be seen." Charlie swivels his head, then perks up. "Speaking of society types, I see someone I know. Want to meet Tristan?"

I scratch my jaw. "He's here?"

"His family must be close to yours."

Yet another reminder of all the history I don't know, because I didn't grow up with the St. Thomases.

Do I want to meet Tristan? Knowing he's fucked Charlie a hundred times or more doesn't make me happy. My lips press together in a slight grimace. "Should I put him on my vengeance list?" I mutter, and Charlie barks out a laugh. Everyone looks at us, since the sound is much louder than the rest of the conversations, and a tall, very handsome man who's about ten years older than me smiles and strides over.

"Hey, I thought I might see you here," he says warmly to Charlie, shaking his hand.

My hand goes into my suit pocket again. Charlie sees me and rolls his eyes. "Tristan, this is my boyfriend, Rowan St. Thomas."

That's my legal name now. The lawyers got the name change published and the court order approved fast.

"Hi," I say, wary. Charlie is twice my size, and this guy's even bigger. And perfect and beautiful. He matches Charlie, unlike me: No visible tattoos, hair-colored hair, and he seems to have the polished mannerisms that I most definitely do not have.

"Nice to meet you," Tristan says, sounding sincere, which makes me want to scratch his eyes out. "I can see why Charlie's so fascinated by you."

I scowl. "What's that supposed to mean?"

He holds up his hands. "Don't worry, I'm not stepping on your toes. I just wanted to meet the man who captured the heart of this perpetual grump."

I want to say *Charlie's mine* and push Tristan away with the point of my knife, but he seems ... nice. Ugh. I'd hoped to hate him.

Charlie shoves Tristan's bicep. "Whatever, Tris. Don't you have some relatives to go antagonize?"

"Oh, me hanging out with you will do that, never fear."

There's a tap on my shoulder, and my heart does flips when I see who it is. "X!" I leap into his arms, and he catches me easily.

"Hey, Ro-Ro. How are you, man?"

"Oh my god, you made it! I haven't seen you in so long."

He sets me down. "I needed to come and pay my respects, even if I never met the man."

I remember that I should have some semblance of manners. "Charlie, this is my best friend, Xavier Martinez. X, this is Charlie and his ... friend, Tristan."

Charlie shakes X's hand, and then I notice that Tristan's staring at X like he just got hit by a truck. Like Charlie, X is tall and dark-haired, though his tan skin is much darker than Charlie's. Does Tristan have a type? X seems equally affected.

That's interesting.

They shake hands. "Nice to meet you," Tristan says.

Could there be a spark between Tristan and Xavier? X could do worse than Charlie's nice, rich ex.

Rowan

The cold muzzle of a gun presses against my skin.

Not this again. *Fuck*.

"Keep your mouth shut," a harsh voice snaps.

My body's frozen solid. I can't move or do anything. I'm in a white room, and there's nothing below me. Nothing above. All there is, is the gun at my temple.

But I look, and there's another gun pointed at the back of Charlie's head. He stands with his hands up.

I start hyperventilating, my heartbeat thrashing in my ears. My blood boils, and I fucking lose it.

They can hurt me, but not Charlie. *Never* Charlie.

Jerkily, my entire body sweating, I throw myself at the gun.

I scream.

With a gasp, I wake up.

Another nightmare.

Again, it's the middle of the night.

Again, I wake Charlie with my movement. Though apparently I only screamed in my nightmare.

"What's the matter," he mumbles, turning toward me and throwing an arm across my back.

I mutter into the mattress, "Charlie, I'm not twenty-five yet."

He tugs me to him. Like always, his embrace calms me, but my heart is still racing. "I know, baby."

"I'm not even twenty-four." I play with his hand, intertwining our fingers. He's so warm and solid.

"That's true." He says it without sarcasm or amusement.

"I just had a dream that someone came after us."

Charlie nuzzles his nose into my neck and strokes my hair with his free hand. "I'm sorry, baby. That's scary."

I nod a few times, but I realize: I have some security with the trust my father set up, for which I'm grateful, of course. But if I want to save the world, I need to hurry up and be thirteen months older.

"Charlie, you protect me, but who's going to protect you?"

He huffs into my hair. "Me? I'm fine."

I snuffle into him. "I don't know that the protection we have is enough."

"It's scaring you?" Charlie whispers.

"Yes. What's going to happen? Remi had me all concerned about security—having a bodyguard, a bulletproof car. How can we be safe?"

"Those things will help. But there's never going to be complete safety."

"Charlie," I whisper. "I love you, and I want to honor your preference not to get married. But it feels more important to do everything we can to keep us both safe. Will you marry me? Please?"

He shudders and holds me close. He takes a few breaths. "Yeah, baby. Of course. I love you, too. If this will help, I'm in."

If he'll do it to keep me safe, and I'll do it to keep him safe, maybe we both win.

"I wish I didn't have to do this," I say. "I know how much you don't like the idea. But marrying anyone else is just not acceptable."

"Fuck no." Charlie actually growls. "And, Rowan, marriage may not be something I wanted in my new plan, but I can think of a lot worse fates than being your husband."

"Even that may not be enough to keep us safe," I say.

"But if those harpies know there's no way they can get the money, that should calm things down."

"Yeah," I say. "Getting the full inheritance isn't going to solve all my problems. But it will solve the problem of how to keep my creepy new relatives from getting it."

"We'll do it first thing tomorrow," he says. "I think we can get an emergency license. Cam figured out how to do it, so it can't be that hard. Is that okay? If we're going to do this, we shouldn't wait."

"Okay."

I'm getting married to Charlie.

I flop around in bed. "Now I'm too excited to sleep."

He chuckles, then pushes me to my back, climbing between my legs. "Sorry, baby." He leans down and kisses me.

"We need to get you more security, too," I whisper between kisses.

"We'll figure it out."

Charlie's hand is snaking down, distracting me. "Deal."

* * *

At ten thirty the following morning, I'm pacing on the steps of a same-day wedding chapel in Valley Village with Xavier. We're fresh from the jewelry store, having gotten there when it opened. I have two rings in my pocket—a surprise for Charlie—and a boutonniere pinned to the lapel of my Prada suit. I'm holding a clear plastic box with another boutonniere for my fiancé.

I'm nervous AF.

I'm getting married.

It's a cool spring day. People file into the dollar store next door.

A woman passes by with a baby in a stroller. Xavier steps in gum and goes over to the curb to wipe it off his foot.

I check my watch. Charlie's running a little late, but traffic can be terrible, and he was going to do some work he couldn't put off before leaving the house.

Camden walks up hand in hand with Shelby, all smiles. "Hey!" He shakes my hand, introduces himself to X, then looks around. "Where's Charlie?"

I check my phone. "Not here yet. The security service is picking him up, so we'll only have one car here." The driver will then take Xavier back to the friend's house he's staying at.

Just then my phone buzzes, and it's Charlie. "Hey, husband-to-be," I answer.

Silence.

My stomach drops. Why isn't he saying anything?

Is the connection bad?

Is something the matter?

Charlie clears his throat, and when he speaks, his voice sounds strained. "Rowan, I need to talk with you. We can't get married. I can't do this."

"What?" My brain is fuzzy. He *just* agreed last night. I thought he loved me. *Loves* me. "Why?"

"Because," he says in that same weird voice, "I thought love was the answer. That I could go back in time and fix things. Ride a bicycle built for two with you while listening to free-form jazz."

I scratch my head. Um, what the fuck? Charlie hates all those things.

Freezing ice solidifies in my gut.

Charlie hates all those things.

"But I can't. I can't marry you. I'm sorry, Rowan." He hangs up.

I look up at Camden. "Something's wrong."

Think, Rowan. Do something. Act.

Save Charlie.

Cam is grinning, but his smile fades when he sees I'm serious. "Charlie's not getting cold feet, is he?" He shares a long look with Shelby, who has a frown on his cute face.

What would Charlie do?

I shake my head. Something happened to him after I left this morning. I think maybe he's been kidnapped. He was definitely trying to tell me something, because what he said made no sense.

Charlie would call the police.

"He called off the wedding?" Cam asks.

I'm not Charlie, and I hate the police.

"Yeah." I start pacing.

"Oh no!" Shelby says.

Still, Charlie's rule-abiding ways did enable my father to find me.

Xavier curses under his breath. "I'm sorry," he says, reaching toward me for a hug, but I dodge him.

Cam looks thoughtful. "Part of me isn't surprised. While Charlie always had it on his list that he wanted to get married, deep down, I don't think he actually did. I'm sorry, Rowan."

I shake my head. "No, that's not it. I trust Charlie. I think one of my relatives got to him. The St. Thomas family is seriously messed up. They wanted to stop the wedding so I wouldn't inherit yet. I just can't figure out how they found out what we were doing. We just told security because Charlie needed a ride."

"What do you mean that they got to him?" Cam says, concern starting to show on his face.

"Not sure." I blow out a breath, pull my phone out, then pause.

Am I going to be wasting time if I call the police? I can picture their reaction: *So, Mr. St. Thomas, how do you know he's been kidnapped if Mr. Cooper simply said he doesn't want to marry you? Did he actually say he'd been taken?*

Fuck. I need to do this right, or it could backfire. And we have to be fast.

They will not harm him. I won't let them. Whoever they are.

I turn to X. "Do you have your laptop?"

He nods. "Sure, it's in my car."

"Can you find Charlie based on his cell phone?"

Xavier's already taking off in the direction of the parking lot. "Let me see what I can do," he calls over his shoulder as the rest of us follow.

Don't *you dare fucking panic, Charlie.*

Adrenaline courses through me like white water, and I'm scanning for anything I can use to get out of here.

I'm sitting in a hard chair in a room with no windows, bare walls, and a closed door, likely locked. A camera is mounted high in one corner. My hands and feet are bound with duct tape, otherwise I'd be flipping the camera off. They've taped my legs to the chair, too.

I'm in a suit, but unlike James Bond, I don't have some fancy gadget in my cuff links.

This is less than ideal.

Problem is, I've seen too many movies. What are these people going to do? Torture me? Leave me without food or water for days, and then no one will find my body? Kill me now?

So, okay. My brain goes dark fast.

Think.

I have no idea how long it's been since I was knocked out, and there are no clues inside this room.

Rowan must be panicking.

Shit.

Rowan must be panicking.

I don't want him to come and save me. I want to get out of this myself. I don't want to put him in any danger.

I'm assuming that this is real danger and not some St. Thomas hazing trick.

When the black limo pulled up in front of my house, I had butterflies in my stomach, because I was about to get married. Rowan and I had decided to have a driver pick me up, because we didn't want two cars at the wedding chapel. Rowan said he wanted to surprise me with something—I'm guessing rings; he's not that sneaky—so he and Xavier would take his car, and I'd meet up with them after I did some urgent work from home.

"Might as well take advantage of some of the perks of being a St. Thomas," Rowan had said as he texted about the transportation arrangements. The wedding chapel was very responsive as well, letting us know we could get married the same morning and they'd take care of the documentation.

At the scheduled time, a driver arrived, got out of the limo—leaving it in the middle of the street—and walked up to the front door as I was locking it.

"So, you're getting married to Rowan today?" he asked.

I followed him back to the car, straightening my tie. "Yes." My muscles were twitchy with nerves, and I had an empty feeling in the pit of my stomach, but I still hurried, wanting to get moving before we backed up traffic on my narrow block. *I love Rowan*, I repeated to myself as the driver opened the back door for me. *This will keep him safe. His security is the most important thing.*

"You're meeting him at the wedding chapel on Laurel Canyon, correct?" the guy asked.

"Yeah. Well. I'll have to google it again. I think the cross street is Magnolia."

"You got it."

I settled in the back seat of the limo, and he closed the door.

I was getting married. I hadn't told my mom. She wouldn't like how I was going about this, since now both of her sons would have deprived her of proper weddings by eloping. Old-fashioned term, I know, but it applied.

In truth, marrying him didn't sit entirely right with me. It had nothing to do with loving him. I love Rowan, and I want to spend my life with him. Being forced to get a piece of paper to prove that to someone else just feels ... unnecessary.

I also don't like that, to keep Rowan safe, we're literally getting married for money.

Early this morning, I drafted a prenuptial agreement that basically said I agreed to not ask him for any money whatsoever. Rowan ripped it up without reading it. "None of that bullshit," he said.

"I'm just trying to protect you," I protested, shaking my head.

"From whom?" Rowan asked, a hand on his hip.

"Me." I printed the prenup out again, and he took it from the printer and ripped it up again.

"You're never going to hurt me," he'd said, his chin lifting and his fierce eyes flashing. "Not unless I want you to."

"That's true."

So I gave up. The lawyer in me doesn't like not having things documented, though. Rowan will be receiving too much money to fathom. I want to protect him from everyone on the planet. Including me.

Though, I suppose, if I don't get out of here, that concern will be moot.

As we drove from my house to the wedding chapel, I wondered what Rowan was wearing. How he was feeling.

Mostly, though, I thought *I'm getting married, holy fuck.*

The limo glided up the 405, past the Getty, and then pulled into the right lane.

Wait a minute.

We exited at Mulholland, and I rolled down the screen

between the driver and me. "Is there an accident on the freeway? I think we took the wrong exit."

Suddenly, there was a gun pointed at my face.

What the fuck? Was this how Rowan felt when his dad had him kidnapped?

"No, Charlie. We're going exactly where we need to," a different man said. He must've been hiding in the passenger seat when they picked me up. "Now, hand your phone to me and do exactly what we say."

They pulled over and made me call Rowan and tell him I wasn't coming. They looked at me weirdly when I started talking about jazz and bicycles built for two, but that was the only way I could think of to say *Rowan, I'm sorry, I'm not doing this on purpose*.

Then they duct-taped my hands and injected something into my neck.

Now I'm here in this dank room—wherever *here* is. I don't know who told the driver to take me, although the list of suspects isn't that long. The limo driver must've tipped off whoever he's working for when we arranged for the ride. The question is, which one of Rowan's jackass greedy family members got desperate enough to stop our wedding?

* * *

The door opens, and two men walk in, the limo driver and his sidekick. Does that mean I was wrong about a wannabe St. Thomas heir orchestrating my kidnapping? If it's not one of those assholes, though—Bree, Anastasia, even Gideon—who is it? My mind starts racing.

Well, shit. I thought I had this figured out and was reviewing my tae kwon do skills, picturing dispatching Gideon with a strong kick.

Apparently not.

One of the men is built solid, like a defensive tackle. The limo driver is tall and lean. I'm more worried about him, and I'm not sure why. Maybe Rowan has taught me not to underestimate people based on their appearance.

The slim one stares at me like he's expecting me to say something. I don't know what. Bargain or try to talk my way out of this, maybe. Yell at him. Cry.

I do none of those things. I just keep quiet.

Think, Charlie. You're the king of the assholes. Leverage that.

After what could have been one minute or ten, he sighs and clucks his tongue. "You're a disappointment."

Of all the things I guessed he'd say, that wasn't on the list.

I have no response, so I glare.

"Aren't you going to argue with me? Fight me?" he asks. "Threaten me?"

I sigh. "Fight you? While I'm tied up like this?" I know I'm sounding like I'm giving up. I hope he thinks I am. That could give me an advantage. Maybe he'll underestimate me.

"Why are you here?" I ask.

The stocky one shrugs. "We take various jobs."

That makes my heart pound. Maybe they're just petty criminals, and this has nothing to do with the St. Thomas fortune.

If these guys are some kind of contract criminals, then ... well, shit. What am I going to do?

The door opens, and Gideon walks in with tracksuit dude.

Gideon looks stressed out, and the other guy looks smug. He looks down his nose at me. Literally, since I'm sitting and he's standing just inside the doorway.

"You bastards," I hiss.

"I wanted to chat with you on your own," Gideon says. "Lonnie mentioned that you might be headed to a wedding chapel."

"How did you find that out?" I blurt.

Lonnie—of course his name is Lonnie—rolls his eyes. "Remi

fired me, but I still have friends who work for him. When you called for a driver for your wedding, they tipped me off."

"Who did that?" I ask.

"Not saying." But with how he exchanges a nod with the limo driver, it's clear who it was.

Gideon crosses his arms over his chest. "It doesn't matter who told us. Your little fiancé—that goddamned interloper's not getting twenty billion dollars. He's ... *nothing*."

"Rowan is very much something," I argue. "It has nothing to do with who his father was, either. It has to do with his inner strength. I'd like to see you get through the things he did and come out as chipper and enthusiastic as he is."

Gideon waves a hand. "I don't care about shit like that. I care about the money."

"If you wanted to talk to me, you know you could have just ... asked. What the fuck is up with you St. Thomases and kidnapping?"

"Sometimes it's the only way to get people's attention. So they know you're serious," he says.

"I know you're serious. Just let me go, and I'll talk with Rowan about sending you some money." I have no intention of giving these assholes any money, of course, and every intention of calling the cops the first chance I get.

"No. We're going to keep you here a little longer. Until we get rid of your fiancé."

That makes my spine go rigid. They can do whatever they want to me. Put needles under my fingernails or whatever.

But they will not hurt Rowan.

Then the football-player type punches me in the face.

Ow.

Fuck. That hurt.

"Big man, hitting someone who can't hit back," I jeer.

What are you doing, Charlie? Don't antagonize the giant.

"I can do worse," he says.

If I could get my legs free, I could do some of the kicks I learned in tae kwon do. But being restrained is a problem. I'm not Black Widow or another one of those Marvel heroes.

"Don't you dare fucking touch Rowan," I snarl, spitting blood.

"You talk him into signing over the trust," Gideon says, "and we'll let you go."

"No."

The big guy hits me again, and this time, I pass out.

CHAPTER 50

Rowan

"Would they bring him to the St. Thomas headquarters? That's where they brought me." I squint at the digital map on my phone. "Probably unlikely."

I don't know that I've ever been more frantic. Racing heartbeat, dry mouth, sore throat. I've been sitting in my car in the parking lot at the wedding chapel with Xavier while he does every hacking trick in the book, obsessing about where Charlie is and who took him.

Cam and Shelby took off to see if they could find Charlie in any of his usual spots and promised they'd be available by phone. They've already called to say that Charlie left the house locked, his car was there, and his keys and wallet were gone (Cam used his key to check). Whoever got him intercepted him on the way to the wedding.

It also makes me very suspicious that some of the St. Thomas non-heirs are responsible. Although how did they know we were getting married? The only people who were in on it were our friends and the driver picking Charlie up. So it must be someone within security or the driving staff. I suppose it could be Hector, too, from when we called security to order a driver. But I trust him. I take a chance and call him.

"Oh, shit," he says when I explain what's happened. "I bet it's someone on the inside. Or maybe Lonnie, the bastard. He's a slimeball, and he knows everyone on staff. Let me pull up security footage," he says. "See if I can find something."

"What do you have access to?"

"All of the St. Thomas properties," Hector says. "I have GPS data on the cars, too. Give me a little bit, and I'll find out where they all are."

"Do you think it was Lonnie?" I ask. "I've never liked him. When my dad wanted to meet me the first time, that jackass kidnapped me at gunpoint."

"I don't know," Hector says. "I haven't seen him around since Remi fired him. But I wouldn't put it past him, either."

"I think I got something," X interrupts, studying his laptop. "The GPS data is showing Charlie in Laurel Canyon."

I glance around. The wedding chapel's on Laurel Canyon Boulevard. "Do you think they threw the phone out the window?" How close did Charlie get to us?

"It's possible," X says.

"If Charlie's in Laurel Canyon," I start, "maybe they went to Nana's house. It's the opposite way, but ..." I bite my lip.

"Maybe she's in on it," X says. "Maybe her partner or her kid you told me about wants the money. So maybe they're behind this whole thing."

"No," I say. "Why would Nana have Charlie kidnapped? That makes no sense. She's the one who wanted Charlie to marry me in the first place."

Hector interrupts. "The limo's there, at the Laurel Canyon residence. I can see the dot on the screen."

"Then we know where to go. Thanks," I say.

"I'm also on my way. I came down in case you needed

assistance after the wedding," Hector says. "I'm not far from there." He hangs up.

"Nana's house is supposed to have underground passages and secret tunnels. Maybe that's why they took Charlie there."

"Are we all going to go in, guns blazing?" X asks.

I swivel my head toward him. "Do you have a gun?"

"No. I meant it more as a figure of speech."

"Then maybe we should pick up our old friends," I say. "Chet and Fabian." I find Chet's contact on my phone.

Xavier grins. "Those guys are awesome."

"I think the gym where they work isn't far. Let's go."

* * *

I zoom up the twisty road to Nana's house with Chet and Fabian in the back seat, X frantically looking up floor plans to the historic house. Before I can worry about the gate, it opens. Good thing I'm driving a St. Thomas BMW, which must be recognized by the security system.

Who the hell took Charlie?

I'm assuming it was Lonnie, but who is he working for? Gideon? Bree? Anastasia?

I wonder for a moment if I should just give whoever it is the money. Yes, it would be giving up, but I didn't deserve to inherit it. I didn't earn it. Neither did they, but what makes me different from them? Absolutely nothing except the accident of birth that my father was the oldest and I'm the only son he had. And Charlie's worth more than money.

Fuck that. I will get Charlie back safe, no matter what, and I'll make anyone who threatened or hurt him wish they'd never been born a St. Thomas or anyone else.

There are a few cars parked in front of the house, including a St. Thomas limousine I've taken before, I think. We all get out, and

I pound on the front door. Chimes clang in the trees, and the wind whistles through the leaves.

No one answers.

I listen for voices but hear none. I try the door, and it's open.

"What are you doing?" X asks, coming up behind me.

"Rescuing Charlie." I glance at my friends. "Get back in the car." It has tinted windows, and Remi told me it's bulletproof. Here's hoping it will keep them safe and hidden.

The grimness of their expressions as I explain what I'm planning to do gives me second thoughts.

"Should I just call the police?" I ask. "Am I going to get Charlie hurt?"

"Let's call them after we know Charlie's safe," Xavier says. "Because if they come in here, they might not believe you." He winces. "I mean, you are the new guy."

"Yeah. Agreed," I say.

I race inside, aiming for where I think a secret passageway begins, from what I remember in the article. Then a throat clears behind me, and I turn around.

Gideon is standing in the doorway to the secret room that Charlie and I looked at the first time we came here, the bookcase pushed aside. He looks terrible.

"Of course," I mutter.

"Rowan. How nice of you to come," he says.

"How fucked up of you to kidnap my fiancé," I hiss.

"This isn't kidnapping. I just fetched him so we can chat. So you can drop this bid to get the family money. And let it go to me."

"Fuck the money. Give me Charlie."

"I hoped you'd say that. I have some paperwork here that says you promise to transfer everything you receive from the St. Thomas family to me."

"I'm not signing a fucking thing until I get to see Charlie," I snap.

"Fine," Gideon says. From behind him, a man emerges who I never wanted to see again. I should've stabbed him the first time I saw his smarmy face and that Adidas tracksuit.

I hope I'll have a chance to later.

For now, though, I do my best to fight him off but am unsuccessful. And I let them take me away down under the house.

CHAPTER 51

Charlie

I regain consciousness to realize Lonnie is carrying in a struggling, squirming Rowan, his mouth duct-taped and his hands tied behind his back. He's in a tailored suit and looks like a million dollars. A billion dollars.

My heart does this thing it's never done before, where it threatens to shatter because he's hurt.

He looks at me with those wide blue eyes, pink hair falling into them. He's clearly trying to convey something without words, but I'm not in tune enough to understand.

Fuck.

The asshole leaves, locking the door, and I start trying to hop the chair over to him, hoping I can get his duct tape off so we can talk to each other.

But before I move more than a few inches, Rowan's gotten his arms released and is ripping off the duct tape himself. Then he bounds over to me.

"How the fuck did you do that?" I hiss. "Are you actually James Bond?"

"They didn't check me for my knife," Rowan says. "Amateurs."

"What the fuck?" I whisper.

"Daddy, no time. Let me get you out of here."

He uses the knife to cut the tape on my hands, and then we both work on my legs.

"How are we going to get out of here?"

"That's where Chet and Fabian come in."

I hear a commotion outside the room.

"I don't want to sit here and wait for them. I feel like that's a bad idea. I've been so fucking worried," I admit.

He holds me in his arms and kisses me. "I've never been more scared in my life than when I figured out that they had you."

"You didn't believe I'd ditch out on our wedding?"

He kisses me again. "I may have worried for a second. But I figured out pretty fast that something was wrong."

"You St. Thomases have a deep-seated tendency toward conspiracies and machinations, don't you," I say.

Rowan giggles. "True. I fit in better than I ever imagined."

"What are you going to do now? Enact a vengeance plan?"

"Perhaps." He grins. "Or maybe I'll take a lesson from you and call the police."

I raise an eyebrow. "You?"

Sirens sound outside. "Xavier already did. Are you disappointed in me?" Rowan asks. "That I'm not actually going to kill my relatives?"

I smile. "I just wanted the chance to use a roundhouse kick."

* * *

"I can't believe there are stars from the Hollywood Walk of Fame in the concrete outside the station," Danny says as he walks into the room Rowan and I are hanging out in in the LAPD Hollywood Station.

Despite everything, I chuckle. "It's LA, man."

"Yeah, I know. Still."

"The Walk of Fame is everywhere," Rowan says. He's been sitting in my lap the entire time we've been at the police station, refusing to move even when the officer pointed out a perfectly good chair right next to him. I wrap my arms around his middle and hold him tighter to me. We're calmer now that we've updated Cam, Shelby, and everyone else and assured them that we're all okay.

We're in a meeting room in a midcentury modern brick building with terrazzo floors and tired furniture. I'm perfectly capable of giving a statement to the cops without legal representation, but I know I shouldn't. Maybe there is room for the law in my life after all.

Danny came over right away when I called. Rowan won't get off of me so I can give Danny a bro hug, so I settle for clasping his hand in a kind of high five that morphs into a handshake.

"So, what happened?" Danny asks, settling down at the table and pulling out a legal pad.

Over the course of the next few minutes, Rowan and I each tell our pieces of the story. "I'm so glad you figured out what I was saying," I tell him.

"The moment you said love is the answer, I knew something was wrong," he says.

Danny laughs. "Wait, Charlie said that love is the answer? He hates it when that's the conclusion in movies or whatever."

Rowan nods. "Exactly. So that clued me in."

"Smart. Okay, continue," Danny says.

When we're done talking with Danny, he invites in the officers, who take our statements.

"What's going to happen to Gideon and Lonnie?" Rowan asks.

"They're being processed," the officer says. "I'm not sure what the judge will set for bail."

"At least we got to see them get handcuffed," Rowan says.

"That was satisfying. What happened to the other guys? The muscle?"

"Rodney Smith and Chester Brown, the limo driver and his associate, have also been booked on multiple charges," Danny says. "Right?"

The officer nods.

It wasn't a surprise that Lonnie held a grudge against Rowan. What we hadn't known was that he'd developed a sort of bond with Gideon while he'd been working for the St. Thomases—birds of a feather—and they'd kept in touch after Lonnie was fired.

If Rowan hadn't been found, the money in the trust would eventually have gone to Nana. Gideon must have been hoping that Nana would share it with Barbara, and he'd eventually get his hands on it. All of that is assuming that Anastasia and Bree didn't litigate, which they assuredly would have, hoping for a chunk of the money in a settlement. But as it is, they all will get nothing. Gideon confessed that, after hearing Nana's suggestion about marriage, he had hired Lonnie, as well as Rodney and Chester, who were monitoring calls as part of the security team, to bring Rowan and me to him before the wedding could take place. So far, there's nothing tying Anastasia and Bree to Gideon's actions, but I hope the police bring them in for questioning anyway.

When we're finally free to go, we say goodbye to Danny and return to Nana's house. Apparently she and Barbara had been away for the day at a garden called Lotusland in Montecito. When she found out what had happened, Nana called Rowan and asked him to come up immediately.

So now we're back in Nana's funky living room, eating her shortbread and looking between her and Barbara. It feels particularly surreal after being imprisoned in one of the secret rooms in the same house.

"I really don't understand," Nana is saying, her face drained of its usual color. "Explain it to me again."

Barbara has her head in her hands. "The police are talking to Gideon."

"Actually, ma'am, they took him into custody," I correct.

"He had some belief that since Remi had no children, he'd get some of the money?" Nana asks. Her chin trembles.

Rowan nods.

"This feels like a betrayal," Nana says, her eyes wide and brows furrowed.

"That's because it is," Barbara says.

They give each other a significant look. Nana reaches over and squeezes Barbara's hand.

"And Lonnie was in on it, too?" Nana asks. I nod. She sighs. "We all have weak spots that we can't see. Lonnie's uncle was a very good man who helped Remi for years. I imagine Remi felt indebted to him."

"That's what he told me," Rowan says. "I wasn't particularly pleased when Lonnie kidnapped me."

Nana gasps, and she spreads her fingers out in a fan against her breastbone. "He what?"

"That's how this whole thing started," Rowan says. "My father wanted to find out whether I was really his son, and Lonnie's answer to that was to stick a gun in my face and drug me." He shrugs. "Okay, I wasn't particularly receptive when Lonnie first approached me without the gun. But still, escalate much?"

"I had no idea. All I knew is that the long-lost heir was finally found." Nana rubs her cheeks. "So what do we do now?"

"I'm utterly torn," Barbara says, her eyes shiny with tears. "What Gideon did was inexcusable, but he is my son. He shouldn't be rewarded for his actions, and I don't want to pay for his legal defense. But ..." She wrings her hands and repeats, "He's my son. I don't know what to do."

"You don't want to pay for his defense," Nana says, "because you know he did it. Maybe he can enter into a plea deal."

"I don't think I'll feel safe when he and Lonnie get out on bail," Rowan admits. "What if they come after me again?"

"Well, maybe in the short term, you and Charlie can be sure to be far away when he's released. And in the long term, Nana and I will have a discussion with him about what he can and cannot reasonably expect from this family." Barbara shakes her head.

Nana looks harried. "I feel like so many problems could be resolved with just a little more communication."

"And a little less greed," I say. Although I feel like a jackass saying it, since my boyfriend is going to be one of the richest people on the planet in a year or so.

"Make no mistake: When Gideon is released, he is not receiving any of my money, either," Nana says. Barbara nods. She turns to Rowan. "I'll talk with my lawyers and make sure of that. Is that satisfactory? Or do you want more retribution?"

"It's not really okay, but it's probably the best we can do," he says. "I don't want Barbara to have her son rot in jail. I just want him to change and not be the way he is."

"And that's probably not possible," Nana says.

Rowan looks up at the ceiling. "Maybe he won't care as much if Charlie and I get a little distance from him and don't see him often."

"Leave him to us," Barbara says. She turns to both of us, her face serious. "I want to apologize to both of you. I'm sorry for what Gideon did to you. You didn't need to go through that. I don't know where he went wrong, but clearly he did, and I'm so sorry I didn't see it sooner."

"It's not your fault," Rowan says, and I nod. As Rowan said, it's not really a satisfactory outcome, but I don't see a better alternative. Still, Barbara's regret seems sincere, and it feels good to have our fear and discomfort acknowledged.

* * *

A week later, Rowan and I are in our swim trunks, lounging on the deck of a superyacht he chartered in the south of France.

The sun is setting, and we're wet from a dive in the Med. The breeze is warm on our faces, the scent of flowers wafting over us.

A uniformed crew member brings us each a crystal flute of champagne with a strawberry in it. Rowan and I take them and clink our glasses to each other.

Then we sip. The champagne is dry, but the sweetness of the fruit balances it out. It's pretty perfect, actually.

"Is this a honeymoon without the wedding?" I ask Rowan.

He shrugs. "Eh, sure. Or it's just time to enjoy being with you in a swimsuit." He leers at me, and I laugh.

He sets down his drink, gets off his deck chair, and prances over to mine. Straddling me, he produces his switchblade from thin air, opening it and holding it to my neck. He grins. "For old time's sake."

"Quit it and kiss me, baby boy," I growl.

He does as Daddy asks.

CHAPTER 52

Rowan

I t's Charlie's thirtieth birthday, and I wake him up with a blow job.

"Happy birthday to me," he pants when I'm done. "I fucking love you so much."

"I love you, too," I whisper, crawling up to kiss him.

Over the past few months, things have calmed down. Charlie's been only taking cases he likes and has started drawing again. I've helped him and Cam on some DIY projects, and he's spent time editing his videos. He gets lost in the creativity, and I love finding him.

I smile and snuggle into him. "Congratulations. Your ten-year plan is complete. Or do you want to go get a cat?"

"I like cats, but I'm okay with waiting until we find the right one. I like Danny's cat, Mamacita, a lot, but he's never agreed to part with her. Asshole."

"You could kidnap her. St. Thomas tradition."

He rolls his eyes. "Um. No. That's not part of your narrative anymore."

I giggle. "And you're sure you don't want to be married."

"For now," Charlie says, and my heart flutters, because I know

Charlie will always give me everything I want. I just want to make sure it's right for him, too. "Is that okay with you?"

"Absolutely. We're mated for life. We don't need a legal ceremony to prove it."

"Yep," Charlie agrees. I swoon. "I'm not disparaging the idea in general." He gets a glint in his eye. "Come to think of it, we need to go shopping."

An hour later, we're walking into Cartier Beverly Hills.

"Um, Charlie? It's your birthday, not mine."

He fingers the ring I gave him, which he wears around his neck, on a chain that matches mine. "I get to decide how I want to celebrate."

"That's true."

Charlie takes my hands in his and brings them up to look at my fingers. He kisses my knuckles. "We'll leave space for whatever the future holds." He marches up to the counter. "My partner needs nine rings, please. Nine Love rings."

I blink. "That's a fuckton of money, Charlie." Not that I can't afford it. But can he?

I'm already in love with Charlie. He doesn't need to give me presents.

But this may be the sexiest thing he's ever done. Making me his nine times over. Maybe it's Charlie's middle finger to the way the world works—a little rebellion against the mainstream. But it feels like us.

When we walk out an hour and a half later, I'm wearing a Love ring on every finger *except* the ring finger on my left hand.

I spread my hands in front of me like I'm some kind of hand model. "I really like them," I whisper. I get a lump in my throat.

He leans down and kisses me. I of course kiss him back just as hard.

"Come on, let's go to your parents' house for your birthday dinner."

* * *

After a celebratory meal with Charlie's entire family, we're spending the night up in Montecito, because he wanted to wake up by the beach.

As we step out of the Mercedes that Hector drove us in, I pause. It's a clear night, full of stars, and I can hear the ocean beyond the house. The air smells of salt. This place is starting to feel like home.

Actually, home is anywhere Charlie is.

I'm walking up to the kitchen door when I hear a soft, high-pitched noise. I pause and squint, tilting my head.

"What is it?" Charlie asks.

"I'm not sure. I think I hear something. There it is again. It sounds like a bird chirping."

He stills, listening. After a moment, he whispers, "Yeah, there's something all right." He starts off in the direction of the noise, and when he gets around the corner of the house, stops by a little enclosure where the gardeners store hoses.

Charlie gets down on a knee and peers at the ground, holding up his cell phone flashlight. "There you are," he says, his voice a low rumble.

I stand beside him and see what he's looking at.

A tiny baby kitten, his eyes still closed, is crying piteously. He has gray fur except for a white stripe across his eyes like a reverse raccoon and a dark stripe along his nose.

"Where's the mama?" Charlie asks, looking around.

Hector comes up behind us. "What did you find?"

"A kitten," I say.

"Have you seen its mom?" Charlie asks.

Hector shakes his head. "There have been a few feral cats along the beach, but I haven't seen one in days."

We all stand there looking at the kitten.

"What are we supposed to do with it? Do we call animal control?" Charlie asks.

"We could," I say. "But ... Charlie, you always wanted a cat. Do you think we can keep it?"

He scoffs. "It's barely a cat. It looks like a mole rat."

"But ... his mama left him." Charlie looks at me, and I don't need to point out the obvious parallel.

He kneels down and gently picks up the shivering little creature. He's dirty, and I think I see fleas. He squeaks at Charlie's touch, and he fits in the palm of Charlie's hand.

"I don't know how to take care of a cat-rat," Charlie says, moving toward the kitchen.

"Then let's find out," I say.

Inside, we quickly google and learn that we need to bottle-feed the kitten and clean him up and keep him warm. Hector heads off to the store for kitten formula, bottles, a heating pad, and a carrying case for him to sleep in tonight. Tomorrow, we can check in with a veterinarian.

"Guess we're going to be cat parents," I say, smiling.

Matilda brings Charlie some towels, and we gently bathe the kitten in warm water, then dry him off. By the time we finish, Hector is back with supplies, and we manage, with Matilda's help, to make a warm bottle of kitten formula.

Charlie wraps the tiny cat in a soft blanket, which he cradles to his chest, and holds up the bottle until the kitten fumblingly starts nursing.

I was already in love with Charlie, but watching my soft-hearted man baby this feline baby? Heart eyes for days.

He cradles the kitten after the bottle is empty and murmurs, "Hey, Junior. You're going to be okay. We got ya."

When we're ready for bed, we place the kitten in the warmed nest in our room, under Wilbur, and the kitten, after mewing a bit, curls up and falls asleep, safe, satisfied, and comfy.

We both sigh in relief.

#PlantDads. #CatDads.

"What do you want to name him?" I ask.

"Maybe Remi. After your dad. The one who gave you roots."

"If you keep the kitten," I note, "then you've basically got everything on your list. Except being married."

"We don't need my list," he growls, stepping toward me and kissing me. "You know that."

"Yeah," I say. "I do. We're mated for life. I really did manifest the daddy of my dreams."

"I'm not your daddy," Daddy says.

I kiss him. "Yes, you are."

ROWAN

I take Charlie on a little drive. "I want you to see what I've been working on while you've been editing videos."

He's still at Weston & Ramirez, but only four days a week. The other day he works on construction projects with his brother, outside, creating things with his hands. While Charlie is never going to be an effusive person, he's happy now. I know it.

I drive him to an industrial warehouse located in an area that's sleepy on weekends. Charlie helped me find this place, but he hasn't been here recently.

I use my thumbprint to open the door, and we walk in. I've bought a few unmarked vans, and X has got the computing power going. I keep my old car here, though we've repainted it and changed the plates and the VIN so it's not traceable to me. I show Charlie Chet and Fabian's workout room.

"Things are all coming together," I say.

"Are you actually going to do anything with your vengeance list?" Charlie asks. "And if so, are you planning to kill them all? Because I might be okay with you being a villain, but I don't think you should become a serial killer."

"No, I don't think I need to have them all leave the face of the planet in order to right some wrongs. Most of them, I think, just need to see some serious consequences for their actions."

"That makes sense. But it seems to me you're too softhearted —at least when it comes to the people who didn't physically hurt you. I mean, even though you found Pierce, you haven't done anything to him. And I'm sure you could figure out a way to get to him in jail."

I grin. "That's because I took him off the list."

Charlie's jaw drops open. "What? Why? I thought he'd be right at the top, after what he did to Wilbur."

"Because he led me to meeting you."

The look Charlie gives me tells me crossing Pierce off the list was an excellent idea.

"You could still mess with him," he says. "Like, I bet X could fix things so every time he books a ShareARide, his account gets debited twice—once for the ride and once for charity."

I grin. "Sounds good."

"What about other people who hurt you in the past?"

"Don't you worry. I'll be coming for them when they least expect it."

"Well, if you're ready, I think I might have a client for you," Charlie says. "An old friend of Sam's called me, and he could use some help. Revenge for some horrible shit that happened to his boyfriend."

I nod. "Okay. Set up a meeting."

* * *

On my twenty-fifth birthday, I get a call from the lawyers. "The money is now yours."

I smile and ask them to send some of it to Weston & Ramirez House. We're going to help all the LGBTQ+ kids we can, here and everywhere.

And now I'm firmly going to start my revenge business.

* * *

Thank you so much for reading *Ferocious*! Don't forget to leave a review. There's a bonus scene for newsletter subscribers that has more CNC. Plus knife play. If you aren't subscribed to my newsletter, here's the link to join the fun: http://eepurl.com/hD9a4r

In case you were wondering, here are some of the Easter eggs and cameos:

Where do I read about ...

Cam and Shelby? *Curious.* (Which has the opening bonfire scene, as well as some others, from their perspectives.)

Danny and Alden? *Studious.*

Noah and August? *Oblivious.*

Jules and Sam? *Ambiguous.*

Rowan and Charlie also show up in *Notorious.*

Reyna's bestie Max and his two firefighter boyfriends are in *TMI.*

Wolfe is in *Mixed Motives.* I have plans for a story for him, as well as Xavier and Tristan. Stay tuned!

Acknowledgments

Thank you to Tracy Dalton for helping me with the theme of *Ferocious*. For each of my books, there's usually an overarching question I'm interested in that I want to explore underneath whatever plot I write. For example:

Undone: What is sexuality?

Unmanageable: What is romance?

Ambiguous: What are labels?

Studious: What is virginity?

Oblivious: What is friendship?

Curious: What is marriage?

Notorious: What is shame (and its opposite, pride)?

And so on. But I was having trouble with the theme for *Ferocious*. I was talking with Tracy about my ideas (that perhaps the question in *Ferocious* is: What is attraction?), and later in our conversation, she asked, "What is a happily ever after?"

I blinked, thinking *She's read a ton of romance books, so that's an odd question,* and responded something along the lines of, well, usually in romance books, a happily ever after is when the couple ends up together and all is well.

She laughed and said, "No, what if that's the theme for *Ferocious*?"

I got chills, because I knew she was right. Especially since in a queer relationship a happily ever after might not necessarily be the same as in a hetero relationship. Or maybe it is. I certainly don't have all the answers, but I like exploring the questions. Thanks, Tracy.

Thanks to Alix for calling Rowan an "unhinged twink in couture" on Instagram.

Thank you to Mary Carr, Kristy Lin Billuni, Lex Martin, J.E. Birk, Rachel Ember, Katy Cuthbertson, and Megan Dischinger for plot help and beta reading. Thank you to Virginia Tesi Carey, Jerica MacMillan, and Katy Cuthbertson for proofreading.

Thanks to Alicia Z. Ramos for thoughtful editing.

Thanks to Tracy and my street team for all of your support. Thanks to Heather Roberts for PR.

Thanks to Cory Stierley and Chris H. for the cover photograph. Thanks to Garrett Leigh for the cover design. Thanks to RJ Creatives for the alternative paperback cover.

Thanks to my sister-in-law Katie for the idea of Blackest Friday. I forgot that in addition to death metal and a bonfire to burn cursed objects and protest capitalist society, she also said we should paint things black, so if you have your own Blackest Friday celebration, be sure to include that.

Thanks to all the things I see IRL that inspire my stories: the person driving around Ventura with a plant hanging in their passenger seat, the dude getting his nails done who had "baby boy" tattooed on the back of his neck, the newborn kitten my children found next to our barn, my husband for his pet peeves. So many details in my books—especially what seem to be the most unbelievable parts—are inspired by real life that I'm always amused by the comments challenging those bits. I'm like, uh, that really happened. But I digress. Thanks so much for reading, and Rowan will be hanging around in future books.

Also by Leslie McAdam

IOU Series (lower angst m/m)

*Ambiguous** (audio narrated by Hamish Long and Kirt Graves)

*Studious** (audio narrated by Declan Winters)

*Delicious** (short story)

*Oblivious**

*Curious**

*Notorious**

Ferocious

* Also available in German

Creepin U: A Monster Romance Series (shared-world m/m)

The Nøkk and the Jock (audio coming soon)

Pretty Fly for a Vampire Guy (with C.D. Rachels)

With J.E. Birk and Rachel Ember (holiday m/m/m)

ILYBSM

TMI

FASTER series (shared-world sports m/m) (also available in Spanish)

Off Track

Sarina Bowen's World of True North (shared-world m/m)

Undone (audio narrated by Iggy Toma and Tim Paige) (also available in Italian)

Unmanageable (audio narrated by Jacob Morgan and Teddy Hamilton)

Albrecht College Series (college m/m)

Mixed Motives (short story)

Look for more in this series coming soon!

All American Boy Series (shared-world m/f)

Boy on a Train (audio narrated by Desiree Ketchum and James Cavenaugh)

Romantic comedies with Lex Martin (m/f)

All About the D (audio narrated by Stephen Dexter and Ava Erickson)

Surprise, Baby! (audio narrated by Jacob Morgan and Muffy Newton)

The Giving You ... series (m/f)

The Sun and the Moon (audio narrated by Tor Thom and Charley Ongel)

The Stars in the Sky

All the Waters of the Earth

The Ground Beneath Our Feet (audio narrated by Tor Thom and Charley Ongel)

Love in Translation series (m/f) (also available in Hebrew)

Sol

Sombra

Stand-alone novella (m/f)

Lumbersexual (audio narrated by Tor Thom and Charley Ongel)

www.ingramcontent.com/pod-product-compliance
Lightning Source LLC
Chambersburg PA
CBHW062109290726
48975CB00001B/171